THEY WERE CAUGHT IN A DANCE
ONLY ONE WOULD FINISH

Horag shortened his sword for a death thrust—and Jase came up inside the shield and swordguard of the bigger man and thrust Horag through the shoulder. Horag dropped the sword and threw his good arm around his smaller opponent to break his back. Jase, letting go his sword hilt now that there was no longer room to use the weapon, reached up and clawed the throat of his opponent.

They fell together.

"Dickson is among the best storytellers we have ever had . . . one of the finest makers that our field has ever known."

—Poul Anderson

Other Tor books by Gordon R. Dickson

Alien Art
Arcturus Landing
Beyond the Dar Al-Harb
The Dragon Knight
The Far Call
The Final Encyclopedia
Gremlins Go Home (with Ben Bova)
Guided Tour
Hoka! (with Poul Anderson)
Home from the Shore
The Last Master
Love Not Human
The Man From Earth
The Man the Worlds Rejected
Mission to Universe
On the Run
The Outposter
Planet Run (with Keith Laumer)
The Pritcher Mass
Pro
Secrets of the Deep
Sleepwalkers' World
The Space Swimmers
Space Winners
Spacepaw
Spacial Delivery
Steel Brother
The Stranger
Wolf and Iron
Young Bleys

GORDON R. DICKSON

NAKED
TO THE
STARS/
THE
ALIEN
WAY

A TOM DOHERTY ASSOCIATES BOOK
NEW YORK

Tor SF Double No. 31

NAKED TO THE STARS

THE ALIEN WAY

A Tor Book
Published by Tom Doherty Associates, Inc.
49 West 24th Street
New York, N.Y. 10010

Cover art by Brian Waugh

ISBN: 0-812-50396-1

First Edition: April 1990

Printed in the United States of America

0 9 8 7 6 5 4 3 2 1

CHAPTER ONE

The voice, speaking out of the ancient blackness of the night on the third planet of Arcturus—under an alien tree, bent and crippled by the remorseless wind—paused, and cleared its throat.

". . . ahem," it said. "Gentlemen . . ."

It seemed to lose its way for a second. It faltered and fell silent. Then it appeared to find strength and speak again:

". . . it's this way with the soldier. What makes the soldier different from the common, garden-variety murderer is the cause for which the soldier kills—" the voice broke off to clear its throat, which had become impeded by something soft and liquid.

"Bull!" said another voice, out of the wind-dry darkness.

"In a war," continued the first voice, unheeding, "to defend his hearth and family, for a crusade, during a definite limited time—the shield of high purpose and the feeling that his cause is just may be kept clean and bright. But soldiers become veterans—"

The voice broke off once more, on a liquid cough. It cleared its throat with effort.

"Some do. Yeah," said the second voice.

"—become veterans. And veterans become professional military men. So much so, that while it may remain a fine thing to let the enemy attack before the soldier goes to war, it becomes the practical thing to go to war first. When this happens, the aforementioned shield of high purpose, the heretofore unsullied escutcheon . . . ah . . .'' the voice hesitated in its tone of impersonal dictation and muttered off into nonsense.

"Throw another nerve block into him, Joby," said Section Leader Calvin Truant, of the 4th Assault Wing, 91st Combat Engineers, Human Expedition against the Lehaunan.

"If I do," replied the voice that had been answering to the lecturing one, "I'll shove both thumbs through his spine. It's had it."

"Do it now," said Cal. There was a rustle, and the muttering broke off with a light gasp. There followed a moment's unnatural-seeming silence, then the voice resumed confidently.

". . . become veterans. And veterans become profess—with regard to the present situation of the Expedition, I can only report it as bogged down from the viewpoint of a Contacts Service Officer. Normally, at a time of truce we would expect to make considerable contact on the level of cultural understanding. However, it is by no means clear that the Lehaunan understand exactly what we mean by 'truce'—"

"You tell 'em!" said another, younger voice. "They were real trucy to you, weren't they, Runyon?"

"That's enough of that, Tack," said Cal. "Get back to the cable phone. See if Division hasn't got any orders for us yet."

"Right," said the younger voice. Cal heard feet moving off among the gravel and stones of the dark hillside along the side of the little hollow where they all lay, toward the eighty-three other men of what still called itself the 4th Assault Wing. In the nearly opposite direction, up the slope of the hollow, there was a faint glow in the night sky; a reflection of lights in the valley beyond where the small local community around the Lehaunan area Power Center was. The glow would have been invisible to any but men who had had no illumination but this for the past hours since the great orange orb of Arcturus had set.

". . . nor do they think of war in the same sense as we do, apparently. Although evidently capable of defending themselves, with great skill and effect against any powered attack, the Lehaunan appear largely ignorant of the idea of individual angers and hatreds. It appears almost as if they look on the weapon that kills them as somehow unconnected with the soldier who fires it. Under conditions other than these of war, possibly they would be a kindly and naive people. . . ."

"Yeah, you put that down, Gutless Won—" the exhaustion-hoarse voice of Joby broke off in a slight note of embarrassment, similar to that of a person who finds himself talking out of turn and too loudly at a funeral. "—Contacts Officer," he amended.

From behind, along the slope, there was the rattle of displaced gravel.

"Section?" It was the young voice of the soldier Cal had called Tack.

"Well?" said Cal.

"No orders."

There was a moment of total silence. Even Contacts Officer Lieutenant Harry Runyon paused in the dictation of his delirium-born reports to his superiors.

"How about the other thing?" said Cal. "They get the word passed on to Medics we've got a basket case here?"

"Sure, Sec. But they said no beamed-power equipment to be used for fear of the Lehaunan blowing it up. Period. Including ambulances."

The rest of them could hear Joby spit, in the darkness.

"Thought you didn't like Contacts Officers, Joby?" jeered Tack.

"And your sister," said Joby. "He's attached to our outfit."

"Cut it," said Cal.

His own words came to his ears sounding unreally quiet and distant. He was a little surprised to hear them. It was like somebody else talking. The feeling was part of the general sensation he had of being somehow without a body; a feeling he knew was essentially lightheadedness from lack of sleep. He had not slept for one—two days now. Not since Lieutenant James, the last combat commissioned officer, had been taken off by ambulance, leaving Cal, a Section Leader only, in command of the Wing. (Runyon, of course, being a Contacts Officer and forbidden to take any part in the fighting, did not count.)

"Tack," said Cal. "Up top and take a look."

The sound of a quiet slither went away up the slope from them.

"Truce was up at sunset," said Joby. The Contacts Officer had fallen silent again. Perhaps he was mercifully dead. Neither Cal nor Joby moved to find out.

"Get Walk over here," said Cal. Joby went off, back toward

the eighty-three men and the cable phone. Left for a moment with no one to know what he did, Cal felt a sudden, almost drunken desire to lie down. He fought it away from him. He heard Joby's return; and Joby spoke.

"Here we are."

"What's up, Cal?"

The second voice, that of Section Leader Walker Lee Blye, had a quality and tone something like Cal's, the latter's exhaustion-tricked and unreal sense of hearing noted. It was not the same voice in an ordinary sense, being deeper, harsher, and more clipped. But there was something in the phrasing, in the breathing, that made it seem like his own voice speaking back to him out of the pain and darkness of the night. It was as if that part of Cal himself which, suffering, struck out in blind retaliation at the universe, had answered back. Cal pushed the light-headed fancy from himself.

"Tell you as soon as Tack gets back down here," he said. They rested together in the darkness, the three of them, able-bodied soldiers. Harry Runyon had taken up his muttering once more, but now in too low a tone to be understood. Joby spoke.

"You ever get the urge?"

They thought about it for a moment in the dark.

"You mean Earth?" said Walk's voice. "Stay back there? Go civilian?"

"Yeah," said Joby.

"I thought of it," said Walk. "I thought of it. At the end of every expedition I think of it. But I'm not built for it. When I get rich and they shovel me under there'll be the slow drums and the trumpets. Not some damn civilian organ in a mortuary."

Cal listened without saying anything.

"Lanson went back," said Joby. "No new coat of varnish for him this trip, he said."

"I know."

"He's a Congressman from South McMurdo now."

"Kerr went into business back there. Deep-sea farming off Brazil someplace. Guess he did all right."

"Nah," said Joby. "He got himself another coat. Hundred twenty-seventh Armor Assault Group. Section in Ballistics told me."

"Well. And he likes it. I got a letter . . ."

"After a while, I guess—"

"—we must," said Runyon, strongly and suddenly out of his

muttering, "distinguish. The one from the other. The innocent from the guilty. The defenders from the attackers. The—dear sir, if you will refer to my previous reports . . ." he trailed off back into mumbling.

"Lots like him back home now," said Walk. Cal woke a little out of his lightheadedness at the statement, and looked at Walk's direction. He could not see the other man, but he could imagine the sudden flash of the white teeth in Walk's lean face as he said it, and the sudden glittering glance thrown through the obscurity at Cal.

"You mean, Runyon?" said Joby.

"Him."

"Don't know why the ex-Service people in Government don't put a stop to that," said Joby. "All the good men and women we lost against the Griella. Now against the Lehaunan. And now they start letting these Societics, these Equal-Vote, Non-Violence people put on uniforms right beside us and turn right around after peace is signed and do their best to give back everything we took. Who'n hell has to make friends with Aliens, anyway? We can lick'm, can't we?"

"Civilians!" said Walk.

"We've got ex-mulebrains in Government," said Joby. "What's wrong with them?"

"Well, I tell you," said Walk, and again Cal imagined the flash of teeth, the glitter of eyes in his direction. "They marry civilians; they've got civilian relatives. It affects their point of view."

"No," Cal made himself say with a heavy effort. "The ones who crack their varnish and quit always were half-civilian anyway. That's what it is."

"Someday," said Walk, "a bunch of us'll go back. Up ship, a full Expedition and go back armed."

"And fight Headquarters," said Joby.

"Headquarters'd be on our side."

"Then why don't they order us back?" asked Joby. "What the hell—you, me, any of us—we go back there and what happens?"

". . . only young men should fight wars," said the voice of Runyon, suddenly and clearly out of the blackness, "to reduce the tax burden and . . ."

"I mean," said Joby, raising his voice above the sound of Runyon's, "I go back. All right, I've got my own vote plus one extra for being a veteran. I got veteran's bonus points for government job tests. I got land option and combat pension. Why fight? I ought just be able to take over.''

There was another moment of silence during which Runyon muttered about nothing being more certain than a soldier's Death Benefits.

''No,'' said Joby heavily, after a moment. ''I guess not. Not worth it. We can sweat these holier-than-thou gutless wonders out, I guess.''

''No,'' said Walk. ''You were closer to right to start with. You and I know what the answer is—the same answer that always works. Clean them out. Get rid of them.''

A sound of slithering descent approached them down the slope, invisibly.

''Sec?''

''Here,'' said Cal.

''Well,'' said Tack's voice, now in their midst, ''it's still going on. I sat up there with Djarali and watched one myself. Something like a truck, and one comes out of that hole in the hill into that walled compound, up at the far end of town. One about every twelve minutes. Djar says he's counted nine more since he went on sentry; and he hasn't seen any go back into the hill.''

''And the truce quit at sunset,'' said Joby.

Cal stood up. He looked back through the darkness to where the eighty-three men waited. In his mind's eye he saw the heavy equipment and weapons back there all parked and idle with the protection of a little rise in ground between the men and them.

''Walk,'' he said, ''go back and get on that cable phone. Tell them I'm asking for orders—from the General if necessary. And tell them if they can't get an ambulance up here, they can at least get a runner in here with some drugs for Runyon. Joby can't keep on gigging him with a nerve pinch forever. Tacky!''

''Right, here, Cal.''

''Got your sketch pad and junk with you?''

''I got a pocket kit.''

''All right. Keep that.'' Cal began to unclip his weapons harness. ''Get out of your other gear. You and I are going for a stroll, down into that town.''

''Down among those Lehaunan?'' said Walk.

''That's right. You're in charge until I get back. I'm going to try and find out what those trucks, or whatever they are, are bringing in. Ready, Tack?''

There were a few final clinks from Tack's direction, and then the sound of a dropped harness.

"All ready. But, oh Section Leader, sir"—Tack's voice scaled up in bad mimicry of a high-voiced recruit—"isn't this one of those volunteer missions?"

"Shut up," said Cal. "You're to stick close and not play any games. Walk, give us three hours to get back. After that, it's all yours."

"Right. *Have fun!*"

"Oh, we'll have a ball."

Cal led the way off the slope, hearing Tack close behind him.

CHAPTER TWO

In the Lehaunan town, once Cal and Tack got into it, there was plenty of light. It came from tall glowing, barber pole affairs that were the local equivalent, evidently, of street lights. They cast a dim but, to human eyes, garish glare over the rounded buildings and small protuberances that looked like half-barrels sticking up out of the pavement between the buildings. Cal took his way from sight-to-sight.

There were no true streets, but simply spaces between the buildings and he had not dared to bring even so simple a mechanical device as a compass, after the way the Lehaunan had reacted to Runyon's voice recorder, some hours previously. Cal was fairly sure he was proceeding as directly as was possible through the town to the walled compound against the hillside beyond, but it was slow going and after fifteen minutes or so of threading his way between the buildings, he sat down on one of the half-barrels and waited for Tack to catch up.

There were two barber pole street lights in this particular open space. One was about fifteen feet high and three feet in diameter, the other about eight feet high and two feet wide. Both glowed with the crackling, hard, amber illumination. It hurt the eyes to look directly at them, but for all their size, the light they threw on the curved walls of the buildings thirty and fifty feet away from them was little more than a campfire in the center of the same area would have provided. A couple of the adult, sooty-furred Lehaunans passed in opposite directions through the space while Cal sat resting. But neither gave him more than a casual glance that seemed to at once recognize his lack of a weapon harness.

What was delaying Tack was a young Lehaunan, looking like a black-furred raccoon about three feet high, who had apparently become fascinated by Tack's sketch book and pencil and was tagging inquisitively after the soldier. In the weird glare from the barber poles, they made a humorous-looking pair: the young Lehaunan like a human child encased in animal Halloween costume and shoving close to the fresh-faced young man in the dirty coveralls. Tack had let himself be worked upon to the point where he was actually drawing pictures for his small pursuer.

"Hurry it up," said Cal numbly.

"Be right with you, Sec," said Tack. He made a few steps toward where Cal was sitting, then paused to add several more lines to the sketch he was making at a rough distance of six inches under the curious orange nose of his companion. "He's cute. Y'know?"

"I know," said Cal under his breath. He had started thinking again, however, about Walk Blye, and his mind swung off at a tangent. There was a danger in Walk.

The man had a streak in him. Walk was like a wolf the Wing had once raised from a cub and tried to keep for a mascot, until it went berserk in its fifth year and had to be hunted down with fire rifles, out in the boondocks back of camp. The wolf had been perfectly like a dog in all respects but one. He would press against your knees, shoving his head forward as you petted him. And then, suddenly, there would be something like a light touch against the back of your hand. All at once, blood would bead up along a thin line where he had slashed you. But when you looked from the hand back to him, there he was, still pressing against your knees and begging to be petted.

At the end he had gone wild, slashing and butchering at all things about him for no reason. And when he had been knocked off his feet with fire rifles and Cal, who was closest, had come up to do the unhappy job of finishing him off, he had whined and raised his head and licked out his tongue at Cal's hand, not as if supplicating or in shame, but almost as if feverishly seeking petting for what he had done. And a hand to slash.

With Walk, the slash was always in words.

"Right," he had said, as Cal and Tack were leaving. *"Have fun."*

Cal had been twenty feet up the slope before it registered on him that the last two words had not been said in the usual tone of rough and friendly irony, but on a driving note of bitter, sneering contempt. As if Cal, instead of taking on a risky mission required by duty, had been dodging out to avoid some unpleasant task where he was. Like the wolf, Walk had slashed without warning; and Cal knew this to be a sign that something was eating at the man. The bitter part was that he was also Cal's oldest friend. They had entered the Service together. They had saved each other's lives before this, and might well again.

Cal looked up impatiently. Tack and the young Lehaunan were still twenty feet from him, still immersed in their drawing. Cal got heavily to his feet and stalked over to them.

". . . a bunny rabbit. See?" Tack was pointing at a sketch he had drawn and put in the young Lehaunan's hand. "See the ears? Bunny rabbit. Say *bunny rabbit.*"

"Burr . . ." said the young Lehaunan. "Burra . . . brrran—"

"All right," said Cal. "That's enough." He cast a quick glance around, but there were no adult Lehaunan in sight. "Out!" He took two more steps forward and cuffed the young Lehaunan sharply. "Get out of here!"

The youngster cried out, and fell back a few steps, still clutching the sheet of paper with the drawing. He whimpered and looked at Tack.

"Sec!" said Tack.

"Shut up!" Cal said. He took another step toward the young Lehaunan, who hesitated, then held out the paper shyly toward him.

"Burraba . . ." said the little Lehaunan, uncertainly.

"Get!" barked Cal, striding forward. The young Lehaunan cried out and scuttled away into the further dimness beyond two of the houses.

Cal looked around, sweating. But there were still no adults in view. He let out a relieved breath. He had been dull-witted with exhaustion a moment before, but now he felt as if he had just taken some powerful stimulant. He was once more conscious that he was a soldier, with authority and responsibility. He was wide awake. He turned around and led off once more.

Tack followed. Cal could feel the younger soldier's resentment like a hand laid against Cal's back.

"Listen to me," Cal said, without slowing down or turning his head. "You're carrying that sketch book to put down military information about this town. Not to play games with. And just because the Lehaunan let us walk around here as long as we aren't carrying any power equipment doesn't mean they're harmless. You saw what happened to Runyon when he went up to one of the adults just wearing a recorder—and the truce was still on then, too." Cal paused. There was no answer from behind him. "Do you hear me?"

"I hear you," said Tack, behind him.

"All right." They walked on. "And if you're wound up because I had to slap that kid back there, just remember that good military practice—the *smart* thing to do—would have been to chop him over the ear and hide his body some place safe so he couldn't go tell the wrong parties about what we're doing here."

Tack said something Cal could not catch.

"What's that?"

"I said," muttered Tack, "I could have chased him off without hitting him, if you'd told me."

"I shouldn't have had to tell you."

They went on. After about five more minutes, they came to a wall of the compound where the trucks had been spotted. They walked along the outside of the wall from end to end. But there was no way to get over, or even see over it, without equipment they had not dared bring. And there was no way visible through it but a pair of blank, high, locked gates. Tack made a number of sketches, but in the end they were forced to turn away without learning anything that explained the trucks.

"We could try up around the hill from behind," said Tack.

"No time," said Cal. He looked at the timepiece set in his wrist scope. "Five hours to dawn. Come on back to camp."

On their way once more through the town, they did not see the little Lehaunan again.

"Sec?" said Joby's voice as Cal and Tack came down the slope near the cable phone and the waiting men.

"Joby?" said Cal. "How come you're still here? Runyon get rich?"

"No, he's still alive. A tech-nurse made it in from Division on her own two feet. You know that Lieutenant Anita Warroad that came out with the replacements last month? That little brunette?"

"No," said Cal. "She bring drugs?"

"Yeah. She's got him back knowing where he is."

"Any news from Division?"

"That's what I've been going to tell you," said Joby. "There was a directive to all units from General Harmon, over the cable phone. All unit commanders, pending further orders, are to take whatever independent action they consider individually necessary to hold their present positions."

"Yeah," said Cal softly, under his breath.

He stood for a second.

"All right," he said, raising his voice. "Everybody in here where I can talk to them. Get them in, Joby. Where's Walk?"

"Here," answered Walk's voice, so close at hand it was startling.

"Want to talk to you."

Cal led off into the darkness. He could hear Walk following. After a dozen steps he turned and stopped. Walk's steps stopped.

"That order," said Cal in a low voice. "It leaves it up to me."

"It does that," said Walk, without expression in his voice.

Cal waited a moment, but there was silence.

"Have *you* got something in mind?" said Cal.

"It's your show."

"Yes," said Cal. "That's right, I guess. It's my show. All right." He stepped around where Walk would be and headed back. He heard Walk's footsteps start and followed behind him again like a mockery. Cal counted off the dozen steps back and stopped.

"Joby?" he said.

"They're all here," said Joby.

"All right. Section units," said Cal. "Sound off. One?"

"Here," said a voice out of the night, "all present and accounted for."

"Two?"

"Here."

"Three?"

"All here."

He went on down the list of Sections. All six from A to F were there. Eighty-three sound men, plus Tack, Joby and Walk waiting on his words in the darkness.

"Morituri te salutant!" he heard his dead father's voice say suddenly and clearly upon the waiting air. *"Ave, Caesar."* With a sudden superstitious horror he clamped his jaw shut and discovered it had been himself that was speaking with the exact pure accent and intonation of the older man. For a moment he stood numb and shaken, expecting anything in the way of response and questions from the armed and waiting men before him. But no sound came back; no voice queried. The exhaustion-hazed world settled back toward sanity around him. Perhaps, he thought, there was no one among them who had recognized the ancient salute of the Roman gladiators in its original Latin. *"Those who are about to die. . . . ."* He shoved the thought from him with almost a physical use of muscle. He cleared his throat.

"Right, then," he said, clearing his throat again. He spoke a little louder. "You all know how we stand. The truce was up at sunset, according to Division. At dawn, the Lehaunan in that town down there will probably be hitting us, especially since they seem to be getting reinforcements or supplies from somewhere underground into that walled power center compound back of town. If we wait until dawn, they've got us. If we hit them now, considering that they don't like to fight at night, maybe it'll be the other way around."

He paused. There was no sound from them.

"So that's what we're going to do," he went on. "Hit them now. Harness up with hand weapons, fire rifles, only. In five minutes we're moving out in skirmish order of Sections. We'll move in skirmish order right to the edge of the town and when I signal, we go in shooting and fight our way through town and into that compound. That's all. Section Leaders here to me."

The leaders of the Sections—in some cases they were not even Squadmen, so reduced was the Wing's rank and strength—gathered about Cal for their individual orders. As soon as he had disposed of them, Cal went in search of the tech-nurse who had walked in to take care of Runyon. He found her with Runyon in the same anonymous patch of darkness where he had left the wounded Contacts Officer earlier.

"Nurse?" he said, peering into the obscurity. "Lieutenant?"

"We're over here, Section Leader," said a young woman's voice that had some ring of familiarity to Cal's ears.

"You know me? Have I met you before, Lieutenant?" said Cal.

"You came into Medical HQ about your ambulance liaison

last week," was the answer. Cal nodded to himself. He remembered her now. An almost tiny little girl with penetrating brown eyes. There had been a shift in ambulance assignments in the field units and she had seen to it that he was put in touch with his new driver.

"I remember," he said. "Lieutenant, we're moving up. All of us. You'll be left here alone with the Contacts Officer. I can't even spare you a man for the cable phone. But if you sit tight right here, you'll be okay. Division'll have an ambulance out at dawn."

"Cal . . ." it was Runyon's voice, weak, but no longer irrational. "You aren't going to attack that town."

"If you'd like, Nurse, we can move you and Lieutenant Runyon back to the cable phone."

"Cal," said Runyon. "Cal, listen. They don't think the way we do, these Lehaunan. Not like us. I'm positive they think the truce is good until tomorrow, dawn. Don't you see what that means, then, if you hit them tonight? It'll be proof to them that we make truces and—"

"Sorry," said Cal. "But the outfit is a sitting duck for any sort of morning attack from that town, Lieutenant. Now, Nurse—"

"You can't do this!" cried Runyon feebly. "It's murder."

"What do you know about it, Gutless Wonder!" exploded Cal suddenly, as a white flare seemed to burst suddenly in his brain. "You got a theory for the situation? Well, stuff your theory! Stuff your ethics! Chew on them and use them instead of a backbone, you—"

"*Section Leader!*" Cal found himself literally being wrestled back by the small invisible figure of the tech-nurse. "This man is badly wounded! And he's officer rank. And you can't—"

"And I'm in command here!" Cal jerked roughly back out of her grasp. "Remember that. Both of you. It's a combat area, my Wing, and my responsibility. So do what I tell you and save your breath for the brass back at Headquarters!"

He turned and stalked off.

"Cal!" It was Runyon's voice behind him, calling. "Cal!"

"Walk?" said Cal, halting where he judged the men to be lined up. "Section Leaders?"

"Here," answered Walk. And the Section Leaders also answered. Over their close, low-pitched voices, he could hear the distant calling of Runyon, struggling against the nurse's attempts to quiet him.

"All right. Moving out." Cal led off up the slope into the darkness and toward the distant, sky-reflected glow of the town.

And it was then that his later memory began to fail him.

What happened came back to him afterwards as a series of disconnected incidents, like a badly edited film:

They were spread out in a skirmish line and going down the slope on the far side of the hill. The nighttime city was distant, small and amber-colored before them. The slope was steep and he could hear men losing their footing with the weight of their equipment and the fact that they could not see where their feet were stepping. He could hear them sliding on down through the gravel and weeds for some distance before they could dig in their heels and elbows to stop.

"Keep close! Keep them together, Sections!" Cal kept calling.

And one desperate voice finally snarled back, "How can I keep the sonsabitching sonsabitches close when I can't even keep my own sonsabitching self in line?"

A near-hysterical howl of laughter burst out suddenly at this, off to Cal's right. And then it was cut off again, as suddenly as if the laugher had without warning felt cold hands close about his throat.

They were spread out still in a skirmish line, moving up through the level ground of cultivated fields to the town's outer ring of illumination, and waiting for Cal to blow the whistle that would signal their attack.

"Cal?" It was Walk's voice, suddenly and eerily out of the night almost beside Cal's ear.

"What? What're you doing up here? You've got the rear to take care of!" hissed Cal.

"Yeah. And I'm going back there in just a minute," said Walk. "I just wondered if we still had you ahead of us up here, that's all."

Cal felt a sick, hot rage rising in his throat. He took a slow breath and spoke carefully.

"Get back to your position."

Walk laughed, and his laugh faded away, going away, behind Cal. Cal walked on at a normal pace. When he was a dozen feet from the outer ring of town lights, he put the whistle to his lips, and blew.

Yelling and running, the human soldiers, looking clumsy and unnatural in their harnesses and equipment, burst forward into the glare, black against the hard amber illumination, dodging between the dome-roofed buildings, the fire rifles spitting little pale ghosts of flames from the pinholes of their muzzles, making small, dry noises like the breaking of sticks.

Cal found himself yelling, too . . . running, and his rifle was spitting in his hand.

It had all taken on the air of a carnival, of a pigeon shoot. There was hardly a sputter of opposition. The humans were running between the buildings, calling out to each other. Keeping score. Making bets.

Black-furred bodies lay between the buildings. Half in and half out of triangular doorways. The barber pole lights had holes shot in them, but continued to shed their usual glow over the scene. The buildings had holes in them.

They were at the gates, the high, solid, locked gates of the compound. They had shot the locking mechanism to ribbons but the gates themselves refused to open. Some of the men were cheering and rocking one of the taller, thinner barber poles. It teetered. It leaned farther, and then fell. Men scattered, cheering.

It bounced as it hit, like a great rubber toy. It came down again, knocking over a soldier who had not dodged fast enough. It rolled off one of his legs, leaving it oddly angled below his knee.

The men howled with laughter. Joby, who was standing over the fallen man, went into a fit of rage.

"Why don't you look where you're standing?" he raved at the soldier with the broken leg. The man, who had been laughing with the rest, stopped suddenly and burst into shamefaced tears. Walk yelled at the others to pick up the pole. Twenty of them grabbed it.

It was light. Cal found himself holding it nearest the front. Holding it like a battering ram, they ran at the gates. The gates shivered and sagged; and the barber pole rebounded so springily they almost dropped it.

"Again!" yelled Cal. They ran at the gates again. They burst them open and spilled into the interior of the compound. Inside

there were Lehaunan with hand weapons who immediately began firing at them.

They were past the Lehaunan with the guns. There had only
been a handful of them. The humans were swarming over one
of the truck-like devices, halted just outside the hole in the hillside. By main strength a cover was torn off the vehicle, revealing
inside it a load of jagged rock.

"Ore!" shouted somebody. "Ore cars!"

The men howled like disappointed madmen.

Cal stared.

Under his feet there was a feeling suddenly as if the ground
there, and all the universe attached to it, slipped without
warning and rocked, and he . . .

. . . He was sitting on one of the protuberances like half-
barrels, on one of the open spaces between the rounded, dome-
like buildings. Dawn was washing a pale yellow-pink light over
his surroundings, and a small, cool wind moved about between
the buildings and ruffled the black fur of a Lehaunan adult male,
fallen about twenty feet off. It moved on to blow through the
sooty body hair of an adult female, dimly seen fallen just inside
the triangular entrance to one of the buildings beyond.

A young Lehaunan identical with the one he had cuffed yesterday was tugging and murmuring over the still body just inside
the entrance. He caught sight of Cal and for a moment his orange nose projected inquisitively beyond the doorway in Cal's
direction. Then it was pulled back inside.

Cal sat looking at the wind playing in the fur of the dead one
closest to him. He thought of the youngster he had just seen and
his fingers twitched about the fire rifle lying across his knees.
But that was all. He had the vague notion that he was about to
make some important decision, but there was no hurry. He went
back to watching the movements caused by the breeze in the fur.

There was a noise close by him. A voice.

He looked slowly around. It was the young Lehaunan from
the doorway. Close up, he seemed even more familiar. He was
holding a grimy piece of paper out to Cal.

"Burraba. . . ." said the young Lehaunan diffidently.

Cal stared at the scarcely recognizable sketch of a long-eared
rabbit on the paper.

"Burr . . . abbut?" said the young Lehaunan.

There was a coolness on Cal's face in the blowing wind. He put his fingers to chin and cheek and they came away wet. He was crying.

"Bunnnrra . . . abbut?" said the young Lehaunan hopefully.

CHAPTER THREE

The next thing was that Cal woke to find himself strapped down in a bed in free fall. Above him was the frame and springs of the bed overhead. Through a maze of such tiers of beds with men in them, he saw a white metal ceiling. He was bandaged high on the left leg and there was a bandage also around his body low on the chest. He lay still for some time in this white world, hearing the little sounds of men heavily but not ideally drugged against pain. An orderly came by with a hypo gun.

"Where'm I going?" Cal managed to say huskily, to the orderly.

"HQ Hospital, back on Earth," said the orderly. He had a clean-shaven, uninvolved face. He found Cal's arm under the sheet of the bed and lifted it out into the open.

"How'm I hit?"

"You'll be all right. Leg burn," said the orderly, putting the hypo against Cal's upper arm. "Small scorch on your side." His eyes met Cal's unreadably for a moment. "From a fire rifle, the report says." He pressed the trigger of the hypo gun and Cal, straining to sort out the meaning behind these last words and opening his mouth to ask another question, swam off into unconsciousness.

After this there was a hazy period in which the leg began to hurt seriously. In between shots from hypo guns, Cal was vaguely conscious of arriving back in Headquarters Hospital outside Denver, Earth, and of some kind of an operation on the leg.

There was a short period in which he seemed to be out of his head. Suddenly, with no transition from the hospital, he found himself back in his father's bookstore. They were in the semi-private collectors' room, enclosed by shelves full of not microtapes but bound volumes. Cal stood facing his father, seated behind his father's desk. Above the head of the older man was the regency mirror with the gilt frame giving back an image of Cal's seventeen-year-old face. And on the small shelf below it, between the shelves on either side (holding to the left, Spengler; to the right, Churchill) was a small carving of Bellerophon capturing the winged horse Pegasus. The powerfully muscled arm of the young Greek mythological hero was around the proudly arched neck of a great winged creature, forcing it to the earth. The sweeping pinions were spread wide in resistance, the delicately carved head rearing itself to look the conqueror squarely in the face. The strong equine shoulders hunched in unabandoned resistance. Only one front leg, buckling under the strength of the hero, presented its hoof directly toward the viewer in what Cal had always thought was an ugly, crippled fashion.

"Of course you can stop me," Cal heard himself saying, as he had said eight years before. "I'm not eighteen. You can phone down and say I don't have your permission to enlist."

He looked down at his father, seated in the desk chair with the carved armrest, his father's wide shoulders and upper body showing above the surface of the desk, his sinewy forearms laid out upon the desk's slick top. His father's quiet, long-boned face looked back up at him.

"Do you want me to phone them?" his father said.

"You know what I want," said Cal.

"Yes," said Leland Truant, "you want to go out with a club and beat the universe into submission—" He checked himself. "No," he said, "that's unfair. You want to go slaying dragons, that's all." He sighed. "It's not surprising."

"And you—" Cal looked at himself again in the mirror; his face was white—"want me to stay here and go to tea parties with your Societic, don't-hurt-anyone friends!"

"Now you're being unfair," said his father. 'I've never tried to convert you to my way of thinking, deliberately."

"No, that wouldn't be right, would it?" Cal said, talking quickly to keep his voice from cracking. "That wouldn't be the non-violent way. It'd be violence of the intellectual kind."

"Not exactly," said his father.

"What do you mean, not exactly?" Cal's voice cracked after all.

"I mean it simply wouldn't be fair. That's why I've always tried to avoid it with you. A man has too many opportunities to brainwash his own son, unconsciously, without adding a conscious effort to the business." Leland looked up at Cal for a moment. "If you stop to think, you know that's true. All I ever did was try to set you an example. With your mother dead, I didn't trust myself to do anything else."

"But you wanted me to be just like you, didn't you? Didn't you?"

"Of course," said his father. "Anyone with a son hopes—"

"You admit it. You see? You planned—"

"No," said his father. "I only hoped. I still hope—that when you reach a mature level of judgment you'll find a greater purpose to life than that which involves killing. No matter how justified." He sighed and rubbed his eyes with the inescapable gesture of middle age. "I'll admit I also hoped you'd stay out of the Armed Services and improve your chances of living until you reached that point of mature judgment. But I imagine I was wrong in that. If you believe something, you should follow it."

"You," said Cal savagely, "talk like it was murder. It isn't murder when a soldier kills."

"Isn't it?" said his father. "Never? The killing of a soldier is always justified?"

"Yes!"

"How can you be so sure?" said his father. Cal felt his chin lifting defiantly.

"Because that's what soldiering teaches—responsibility. A responsible being doesn't engage in unjustified killing, in murder. An irresponsible being under our system soon gets weeded out."

Leland Truant shook his head slowly.

"Yes," he said, "I can see how iron-clad and complete that all sounds to you." He rubbed his eyes again. "But I think you'll learn that the human being is more complex than you think now. We're all potential murderers, Cal. Pushed, pulled, stampeded, or maneuvered to the proper point, we can all be brought to where murder is possible to us. And not just accidental murder, but cruel, vicious, even wanton, reasonless murder."

"Words!" cried Cal. "Words, words, words! That's all you ever give me! What would you have done when mom was alive if some scaly lizard of an Alien had come breaking in here trying to kill her?"

"I would have fought, of course," said his father. "I would have grabbed any kind of a weapon I could lay my hands on and done my level best to stop him, to kill him. And if I'd succeeded"—his voice grew a trifle sardonic—"I was a good deal younger when your mother was alive—I would have felt first savagely triumphant, then a little awed at what I'd been able to do against an armed intruder, graduating as time went on to a pleasant sense of superiority and a sneaking desire that other people should recognize it."

"Then what's wrong with what I want to do? What?"

"Nothing," said his father. "You're just young." He sighed. "Besides the fault is mainly mine."

Cal stared at the older man.

"Yours?"

"Yes." Leland nodded at the books around them. "I thought the best way to bring up a boy was to expose him to as much information as possible. I crammed you full of the books that had brought me understanding and tolerance. I forgot that it's natural for a son to seek an opposite point of view from his father. Where I saw the dark tragedy of Malory's *Morte d'Arthur*, you saw the bright clash and bang of Round Table knights unhorsing evil opponents. You swallowed Kipling by the yard. You knew verse after verse of 'The Ballad of the Clampherdown,' and 'The Ballad of East and West.' You missed entirely the deeper messages that he sounded in the music of Piet Lichtenberg, and 'The Half-Ballad of Waterval' slid in one ear and out the other with you."

His father leaned forward in his chair, both hands spread out on the surface of the desk. Cal saw the cords stand out on the backs of those hands.

"I know," said his father. "I know. *Because I did exactly the same thing, when I was your age!* I needed a faith, too. And I went galloping out looking for a banner under which to enlist myself. And that was good. That was the way it ought to be. But then, having committed myself, I made the mistake of setting my conscience aside. I thought that, having committed myself to a good cause, everything I must do would automatically also be good." He gave his son a long look. "There's nothing wrong with soldiering, Cal, as long as you can keep your ideals about it alive. But God help you, my son, the day you murder them."

Cal opened his mouth to speak, but his throat felt choked.

"I don't blame you for being ashamed of me," said his father. "At your age it must be doubly hard to have a parent who not only was convicted and disgraced in his youth for opposing the present veteran-dominated government, but one who is still unrepentant enough to believe in equal voting rights and mankind's duty to search for a better way of getting along with other intelligent races than outkilling them.'' His father's hands relaxed suddenly. Suddenly they were the hands of an older and tired man. "No, I can't tell you what to do. I wouldn't if I could. We have to each follow what we believe in, even if our beliefs take us different ways."

The room seemed to waver and fog about Cal.

He felt as if he were exploding inwardly. All the pressure of the years swelled up inside him and burst out of his throat in the cruelest words he could find.

"You always hated them, because they wouldn't have you!" he cried. "That's why she was killed. Because of you!"

He looked furiously, pointedly, down at his father's clubbed left foot—projecting from underneath the desk at one side toward Cal—in its special boot, hooflike and ugly. He looked back up to his father's face and saw the older man still sitting looking at him. His father's face had not changed. It looked sadly at him. Cal felt his inner fury break and crumble into pain and despair. He had done his worst. He had cut his deepest. And his father still sat, refusing to admit the wrong he had done.

"Alexander of Macedon," said his father, "and Jesus of Nazareth both founded empires, Cal. Where are the hosts of the Alexandrians today?"

Cal turned and plunged out of the room, unseeing.

The mists cleared. He was once more in a hospital bed; in a long ward now with a row of beds down each side of the room. Wires reached out from the robot nurse by his bedside and held him with metallic lack of doubt.

"How are you feeling, Section Leader?" asked the canned voice of the device confidentially.

"A'right," muttered Cal.

A white, translucent plastic tube emerged from the body of the device and nudged his lips.

"You're doing just fine, Section Leader," said the voice. "Just fine. Drink this, now."

He lifted his heavy lips apart, fumbling at the tube, and a cool mint-tasting fluid flowed between them and eased his dry throat. He closed his eyes, exhausted by that small effort. Consciousness of the hospital dissolved from around him once more.

. . . Walk had been waiting for him that day he had the argument with his father, outside the Recruitment Office. Cal saw him pacing impatiently as Cal came slowly up. At seventeen, Walk was thin as a honed-down butcher's knife. And under his straight black hair and startlingly black brows his eyes had a glint of wildness that was close to something berserk. He was like a hungry man who does not care for consequences.

"You talk to him?" Walk said as Cal came up. "What'd he say?"

"It's all right," said Cal emptily.

"You're all set then?"

Cal nodded. He made an effort. "How about you?"

Walk laughed.

"I've been set for months, now. The old man's glad to get rid of me. Almost as glad as *she* is." He was referring to his stepmother, who was ten years older than his father and dominated him as she had failed to dominate Walk himself. "I'm not even going back home again. You going back?"

Cal shook his head.

"Then come on," said Walk. "You want to live forever?" And he turned and led the way into the Recruitment Office. . . .

CHAPTER FOUR

Cal began to recover and was transferred to a convalescent section. In charge of the convalescent section was Anita Warroad, the small nurse who had come with medication for Runyon, the Contact Officer. Cal asked after Runyon, and she told him that the other man had died back at base hospital. He was surprised to find that she blamed herself for it, that she thought if she had come faster or arrived sooner, she might have been able to save Runyon. They found themselves talking like old friends. As the days went by, and Cal grew stronger, he found himself being attracted by her as a woman. They could not fraternize in the hospital, since she was an officer, but then, before he was discharged, a field commission came through, making Cal a lieutenant.

Walk—also a lieutenant, now—and Joby came visiting the

convalescent section. To celebrate both new commissions, they smuggled in a bottle. They had several surreptitious drinks and left the three-quarters full bottle with Cal. That night, after lights out, he started drinking from it by himself. Almost before he knew it, he had finished it. It had been a one-liter bottle of hundred-and-ten-proof whisky. He was very drunk. He lay on his back, holding on to the nightstand beside the bed to stop the room from turning like a shadowy, seasick merry-go-round. After a while the room slowed down and he passed out or went to sleep.

He woke up in the later darkness of four in the morning, dry-mouthed and sweating. He drank all the water in the dispenser on his nightstand, and then lay back. He felt dizzy, sick, and hollow with fear and a sense of his own worthlessness. He lay still, wishing for sleep, but all he could do was lie there, reliving the past. Scene after scene came back into unnaturally sharp focus. He relived the final argument with his father. He went through basic training all over again. He remembered the first flogging he had seen. . . .

The soldier flogged had been a trainee from his own company. The trainee had been seventeen, just as Cal was. The trainee had gotten drunk, for the first time in his life, on his first weekend pass. He had stolen a copter and smashed it up. The military police had got to the scene of the wreck first, and brought him back to the stockade. But the Armed Services refused to surrender him to the civilian authorities. The Combat outfits looked after their own, the trainees were told. The Armed Services made financial reparation, paying for all the damage done. The company was paraded, the trainee given twenty lashes and a dishonorable discharge. The trainee returned to his own home town and another trainee from the same town was able to tell the rest of the company how the discharged boy made out, having the news in letters from home.

The ex-trainee's father was a veteran of the Combat Services, himself. When the boy got there, he found the door of his home locked against him. An aunt and uncle finally took him in. He got a fairly good job in the repair department of his uncle's general store. The other employees, because his uncle was the owner, did not needle him much about what had happened to him. Nevertheless, some three months later, he hanged himself in the basement of his uncle's home. He would have been eighteen in exactly one week.

Cal did not get sick or pass out at the flogging, itself, as some of the other trainees did. Afterwards, however, he lay face down on his cot, staring dry-eyed into the darkness of his pillow. Now that it was over, some of the tougher trainees were beginning to recover and be rather loud-voiced about it. Cal heard them talking, and after a while he heard a voice beside his right ear:

"Hey, Truant! You going to lie there all day?"

"So?" answered the voice of Walk from the cot on the side of Cal's left ear. "There's some regulation against it, Sturm?"

"Well, hell!" said the voice of Sturm uneasily. After seven weeks all the trainees knew Walk, and none of them wanted trouble with him. He was recognized as a wild man. "It's not as if it was his brother got the twenty, or anything."

"No," said Walk. "But he saw his dad get it, when he was only six years old."

"His dad?" said the voice of Sturm. "*He* saw? When'd they let kids—"

"It wasn't on an Armed Services post," said Walk. In the pillow, Cal squeezed his eyes shut desperately. *Don't tell it,* he willed at Walk, passionately. *Let it go!* But Sturm was already asking.

"It wasn't? How come?"

"It was back during the Equal Vote riots. They sent an Armored Wing into our town to put down the rioting. The Reserve Captain in command had dreams of glory or something. He rounded up a batch of the rioters and worked them over to find out who the ringleader in the town was. There wasn't any ringleader, but he finally got the name of the most respected Equal Vote advocate in town. It was Cal's dad."

"Well, hell, if he was one of those—"

"One of those!" sneered Walk. "Old man Truant hadn't stuck his nose out of doors. His wife was expecting and he was standing by to take her to the hospital at any minute. The captain sent a squad of men to arrest Cal's father. He told his wife it wasn't anything, he'd be right back. But from her upstairs window she could see out into the town park. Fifteen minutes later she saw a crowd with the soldiers tying Cal's old man to a whipping post. She sent Cal ahead to tell them to wait, and she tried to get over there herself. But she fell downstairs, had a miscarriage and bled to death. Now, you got something cute to say to Cal?"

There was an uneasy silence.

"Well, cripes!" said the voice of Sturm, finally. "How come the captain had authority to do that to a civilian?"

"He didn't," said Walk's voice. "Seems he got kind of carried away. Old man Truant got a letter of apology from the government and an offer of reparations later on, but by that time his wife was planted and the fifty scars on his back were all healed. Besides, he's got the Societic point of view: make yourself a good example unto all men."

There was a moment of silence that stretched out longer and longer; then the sound of Sturm's bootsteps going away. The talk took up again in the far parts of the room, and after a while mess call sounded and the voices and a clatter of boots moved out, leaving silence behind them. In that silence. Walk's voice spoke, close to Cal's ear.

"You're not the only one that had it not so good. Just remember that."

Then the cot creaked and his boots, too, moved out.

Six weeks later, when they graduated from basic and got their first ten-day leave, Cal and Walk went to a hotel room in New Orleans and lived it up. Cal did not go home then or later. A year and a half after that, just after he shipped out at the beginning of the campaign against the Griella, he got word from a cousin that his father was dead. Cal had never answered any of his father's messages since entering the Services. He messaged back, now, that the family lawyer could take care of everything.

The dawn came finally. After breakfast Cal was told to report to the Examinations Section for his final checkover before being okayed for discharge. He had not expected this until next week, and he expected that his hangover would be noted and questions asked. But he passed through the physical without comment by the examining physicians. He found himself finally in the office of the psychiatrics officer.

"Have a seat, Lieutenant," said the psychiatrics officer, a major who was a short, pleasant-faced man with a brown mustache, not much older than Cal. Cal sat down on the chair facing the officer and at one side of the desk. The chair was cold.

"Let's see now . . ." The officer ran through some papers and wave charts from various testing machines. "How're you feeling, Lieutenant?"

"Fine," said Cal. "My leg isn't even stiff, and you can hardly see where the skin graft goes."

"You had a burn on your side, too?" The officer frowned at the charts.

"Sort of a small scorch. That was healed up long ago."

"Yes. Pretty obviously a fire rifle burn. You don't have any idea how it happened?"

"No, sir," said Cal. "I was pretty much out on my feet from lack of sleep toward the end, there. Things are pretty hazy after we hit the town."

"So I see," said the major, examining one of the wave charts. "There's a good sixteen-hour hold there in your conscious recall up to the time you came to on the hospital ship. And evidently you got burned somewhere during that period. Hmm—" he frowned at the chart. "It wouldn't be a bad idea, Lieutenant, if we went in there with a full exploratory and made sure of the facts for that period. In fact, I'd strongly recommend it."

Cal felt the coolness of the room like a winding sheet about him. Slowly his stomach began to gather itself up in a tight knot, and he felt an empty fear.

"Sir," he said slowly, "do I have to agree to that?"

"No," said the major, looking at him. "Of course not. You're perfectly free to accept or not, just as you wish. But I'd think you'd want the security of knowing you didn't have anything hidden in that period that might cause trouble later." He paused. "We needn't delay your discharge for it. You can go ahead with that and come back for a three-day psych at your convenience."

"I don't think it's worth the trouble, Major."

"Whatever you think, Lieutenant." The psychiatrics officer made some marks on the papers before him, wrote a line or two, and signed the papers. "That's all."

Cal stood up.

"Thank you, sir."

"Don't thank me. My job. Good luck, and enjoy yourself."

"I will, sir." Cal left.

He came back to the convalescent section to find Annie Warroad on duty. She looked at him oddly, and walked away into the section office. He went after her.

"What's the matter?" he said.

She was standing behind her desk. For answer she opened a drawer and showed him the empty, flat, liter bottle of whisky.

"Well, you know the drill," he said. "Report me."

"You know I won't do that," she said, shutting the drawer. "I'll get it out of here. It's just—" She broke off suddenly, biting her underlip angrily. He was surprised to see that she looked close to tears.

"It's that Walk!" she burst out. "He's the weak one. But when you're with him, you—"

She bit her lip again and turned and went out quickly from the office.

"Weak!" he echoed. "Walk weak?" He opened his mouth to laugh at the ridiculousness of it, but found suddenly that there was no laughter in him. The hollow fear and worthless feeling of the night came back on him. He walked out of the office, looking for Annie. She was energetically banging equipment together in the Section laboratory; she turned away from him when she saw him staring in at her.

He went back to his bed and lay down on his back, staring at the white ceiling.

CHAPTER FIVE

It was a three-day business getting discharged. In the process Annie's upset and his hangover got left behind together. That weekend Annie took a three-day leave and they flew down to Mexico City to paint the town red. But they ended up in the little mountain city of Taxco where the silver and obsidian jewelry comes from, sitting in the mountain sunlight on an open-air terrace through the long mornings with a bottle of wine as an excuse on the table between them, and happily, no great pressure to talk. For the first time that he could remember, a sense of peace seeped into Cal. And he found himself talking more freely to Annie than he had to anyone in his life. Now and then, even, things came to his tongue that surprised even himself. One morning when Annie had voiced the same thought of peace that lay in his own thoughts, he quoted without thinking, and before he could stop himself:

"So all the ways—" He checked abruptly. "Nothing," he said to Annie's look of inquiry. "Just some poetry you made me

think of.'' He shook his head. ''I don't know why. It doesn't even fit.''

But she wanted to hear it, and so, feeling a little foolish, he repeated two lines of ''The Last Tournament,'' from Tennyson's *Idylls of the King:*

> *''So all the ways were safe from shore to shore,*
> *But in the heart of Arthur pain was Lord.''*

Repeating them, he frowned, trying to think why these, of all poetry, should intrude on him here, between Expeditions, in the healing morning sunlight of Taxco. Looking up again, he caught Annie looking at him oddly.

''Something the matter?'' he asked.

''It's just that I've never seen you do much reading,'' she said. ''Particularly of things like poetry.''

He laughed. ''That's for people who can't do anything else,'' he said. ''What say we run down to Acapulco later this afternoon for a swim?''

So suddenly the three days were over. Annie went back to Headquarters Hospital, near Denver, and Cal began a four-month period in which he did little but kill time and use up his accumulated back pay. He received a Star Cluster to add to his list of decorations. But rumors of a new Expedition brought him back to Expedition Base Headquarters, outside Denver, in March. He went directly to the Recruitment Office there.

A chinook—a warm, dry wind off the slopes of the surrounding mountains—was blowing down the company street on which he stood and melting the last evidences of a late spring snowfall. The moving air felt cool on hands and face, but the sudden rise in windy temperature was making him uncomfortably warm inside his uniform jacket. The jacket felt strange after all these months of civilian clothing.

Isolated in the western sector of the brilliantly blue sky, the clouds had piled high into a great, toppling, white castle shape. But, as Cal glanced at it, the harrying wind ripped among it and tore it to fragments fleeing over the ramparts of the mountain tops. Cal's head was dull with a slight hangover. He touched his fingertips to the row of medal ribbons on his lapel, and went inside.

The section leader who took his application punched for Cal's records. When they appeared imaged in the filmholder on his side of the counter, he looked them over carefully.

"I'm sorry, Lieutenant," he said, at last. "But I can't sign you yet."

"Yet?" said Cal.

Looking across the counter, then, he suddenly identified the look he saw in the man's eyes. It was the same look he had noticed on the face of the psychiatrics officer, and before that on the face of the orderly of the hospital ship. He had seen it, he remembered now, on Annie, when he had quoted those two lines of Tennyson to her in Taxco.

Now it looked at him from the polite, strange face of this administrative non-com.

"Can't sign me yet?" said Cal again.

Across the room behind the barrier of the counter, a desk printer began to turn out copies of some manual with a faintly thumping noise, as of something being softly hammered together. The sound echoed in Cal's lightly aching skull.

"I'm sorry, sir. You haven't been through Psychiatric Exploratory."

"That's not required."

"Yes, I know, sir. But in your case here, the releasing Medical Officer seems to have recommended it as a condition for reservice."

"I was discharged on a leg burn," said Cal. "On a leg burn, that's all."

"Yes, sir. I see that. But the MO has discretion about conditions of reservice."

"Look," said Cal—there was a moment of polite, desperate silence between them—"there must have been some mistake made on the original records back at the hospital. Could I see your commanding officer here, for a moment, do you suppose?"

"I'll see, Lieutenant."

The Section Leader left. A few minutes later he came back and led Cal through the barrier to an office and a seat across the desk from a Colonel Haga Alt, whom Cal remembered as General Harmon's aide in the Lehaunan Expedition.

"Sorry to bother you, sir," said Cal.

"I was just waiting for General Harmon to finish some business. We're updating equipment. I've got a few minutes, Lieutenant." Alt was a dark-haired, wiry man in his early forties, a little shorter than Cal. "You were Combat Engineers on Lehaunan?"

"Yes, sir." Cal found his back sensitive to the back of the chair he was sitting in, all the way up. He made an effort to relax. "Fourth Assault Wing."

"I remember. You got a Star Cluster for taking that power center town in the hills. That was a good job."

"Thank you, Colonel. Not really necessary, taking—"

" 'Not necessaries' are usually our main job, Lieutenant. An ex-mulebrain like you ought to know that. Cigaret?"

"No thank you, sir." Cal watched Alt light up. "The Section Leader outside there . . ."

"Yes?" Alt took the cigaret out of his mouth, fanned the smoke aside and leaned forward over the filmholder set in his desk. He studied its screen a second. "Yes." He sat back in his chair, which tilted comfortably and creaked in the momentary stillness of the office. "There's no point in pussyfooting around with you, Lieutenant. Your psychiatrics officer in the Discharge Unit evidently thought you had some possible psychological damage that would rule you out for reservice. It's only a guess on his part, of course. Why don't you run over to Medical Headquarters and have them test you and write you a release on this hold?"

"Well," said Cal carefully. Alt leaned back in his chair, watching. His eyes were neither warm nor cold. Cal was suddenly conscious of the fact that one of his feet, in a heavy uniform boot, was projecting out to one side of the desk where Alt could see it if he looked down. It must look awkward and unnatural out there. Cal pulled it back hastily. His heart began to thump. Alt was still waiting for his answer. The room seemed steamy and blurred.

"Alexander of Macedon—" said Cal.

"What?" said Alt, frowning.

"I'm sorry, sir." Cal got a firm grip on the arms of his chair, down out of sight-level below Alt's desk top. The room cleared to his vision. "I guess I'm not too good at explaining something like this. What I mean is . . . I understand the digging around in a psych exploratory sometimes triggers off a difficulty that might never have come to life."

"One chance in several hundred," said Alt dryly.

"But if such a thing happened, I'd be permanently unfit for service."

"True enough," said Alt. "But if it doesn't—and the odds are all in your favor. The exploratory will either show there's nothing wrong in this blank period of yours on Lehaunan world, or it'll show something the medics can grab while it's fresh and get out. So you end up qualified for reservice either way."

"Yes, sir." Cal took a deep breath. "But would you like to bet your career, Colonel, even at those odds, when you knew yourself it wasn't really necessary?"

"Lieutenant," replied Alt, "I would not. And what's that got to do with the situation."

Cal let out the breath he had taken.

"Nothing, I guess, sir," he said numbly. He waited for Alt to dismiss him. But the other man sat instead for a moment, staring across the desk top at him.

"Hell!" he said at last, and shoved his half-smoked cigaret down the disposal in his desk. "Would you like to tell me your version of why you think that psych-hold is on your record?"

"Yes, sir." Cal looked out the window for a moment and saw the unmoving mountains there. The words came easily from him, as if he had rehearsed them. "I've got an area of amnesia during and following that attack on the town when I was wounded. But by that time I'd been in sole command of the Wing for nearly sixty hours and I hadn't had any sleep for that length of time. The outfit was in an untenable position and under combat pressures. The truth is, I was just out on my feet most of the time. That's why I can't remember."

"I see." Alt looked at him for a short additional moment, then got to his feet. "Wait here a moment, Lieutenant." He went out.

Cal was left alone in the neat, white-lighted office for some ten minutes. At the end of that time, Alt returned, followed by a tall, spare man of Alt's own age, who strode in on Alt's heels as if to the measure of silent drums. Three small gold stars shone on his jacket collar. Cal got to his feet.

"Here he is," said Alt to the tall man. "Lieutenant"—he turned to Cal—"General Harmon wants to talk to you."

"Thank you, sir." Cal found himself shaking hands. Deep-set gray eyes looked down into Cal's face as they shook.

"You earned that Star Cluster of yours, Lieutenant—Truant, isn't it? The Colonel here tells me you want to get back on with your Wing."

"Yes, General."

Harmon turned and paced across to the nearest wall of the office. He struck a button there and the surface went transparent to reveal a black background on which a design in white appeared.

"Recognize that, Lieutenant?"

"Yes, sir. A space schema. Our territory out towards Orion."

"That's right. You've had some command school."

"Not officer yet, sir. N.C.O."

Harmon raised his eyebrows.

"We give Space-and-Tactics now in N.C.O. school, do we?"

"No, sir, I . . . looked it up on my own once."

"Very good. Well now, look here." Harmon moved a button and a red line leaped from a center point out through the diagram. "What do you make of that?"

Cal studied it for a second.

"The pattern of our advance, sir, in that quadrant. Since the beginning; since World Unification, at the end of the Twentieth Century. And as far as we've gotten with the Lehaunan, now."

"And to within forty light years of the nearest star systems in the Orion Group." Harmon glanced aside and a little down at Cal. "Lieutenant, why do you think we might be interested, say"—his finger indicated one of the Orion stars—"in Bellatrix, here?"

"Well," said Cal, "it's just about next on the list."

"List?"

"Sir?"

"I said," repeated Harmon calmly, "what list? What list are you referring to?"

Cal straightened slightly inside his uniform. A charge of electricity seemed to have gone through the room. He felt keyed-up, almost feverishly alive.

"No list, sir," he said. "I meant, Bellatrix would be the next system we'd encounter in our normal expansion into space."

"And if we didn't go on with our normal expansion?"

Cal looked up in sharp surprise. But Harmon merely stood, patiently waiting

"We couldn't afford not to, sir," said Cal slowly. "Population pressures, plus natural instincts—We'd be committing racial suicide if we didn't keep on expanding."

"Really, Lieutenant? Why?"

"Why . . ." Cal fumbled for words and phrases he had not needed for a long time. "Halting our natural expansion would leave us . . . with the sort of self-emasculation that ends in racial suicide. We'd outgrow our resources; we'd be sitting ducks for the first more practical minded race that grew in our direction.''

"True enough," said Harmon. "But I wasn't asking you for what everybody learns in school nowadays." He turned square on to Cal. "What I'm interested in is your own feelings. You've been a mulebrain. You've seen the Griella and the Lehaunan from the wrong end of their guns. What do *you* think?''

"We've got to keep moving," said Cal. He looked up at Harmon and said it again. "We've got to keep moving." He felt suddenly that he was saying too much, but the words came out anyway. "We have to keep winning and being the strongest. Every time somebody tries to appeal to somebody else's better nature, somebody gets hurt. We had a Contacts Officer with our Wing against the Lehaunan. The truce was on, and he went into their lines to talk to them—just talk to them. He carried a recorder . . . and they cut him—they cut him—" Cal's voice suddenly began to thin and hoarsen. He broke it off sharply. "The only safe way is to be on top. Always on top. Then you can make sure nobody gets hurt. You've got to win!''

He stopped. There was a strange small silence for a second in the office and then Alt, glancing aside at the space schema on the wall, whistled two odd little sharp notes and raised his eyebrows.

But Harmon put his hand on Cal's arm.

"You're a good man, Lieutenant," he said. "I wish half as many men again in Government thought the way you do." He let go of Cal's arm. "Let me show you something," he said, turning back to the schema. His fingers stabbed out beyond the furthest point of the red line's advance, at a small and brilliant white dot.

"Bellatrix," he said.

He looked back at Cal.

"That's the star where we're going next, Lieutenant. She's got a system with two worlds that we could use. One of them's pretty much available, but the other one's got a race on it called the Paumons. A red-skinned, hairless bunch of bipedal humanoids that're the closest thing to us we've yet run across. They'll be giving us a run for our money and our lives that'll make the Griella and the Lehaunan and all the rest look like members of an old ladies' Sunday sewing circle. We're setting up the Expedition for there, now. I'm going, the Colonel here is going, and your old Wing will be there when we go in." Harmon paused and looked Cal directly in the eyes. "But I'm sorry, Lieutenant—I'm afraid you won't be listed in the table of organization."

He paused. Beyond the open door of the office where the three of them stood, somewhere down the corridor outside, Cal heard a door slam and a man's voice call out to someone on a note of brisk and businesslike urgency.

"I'm sorry," said Harmon.

"Yes, sir," said Cal automatically.

"You see," said Harmon, speaking a little more slowly, "I've no right to risk the men who'd be serving with and under you, by asking the Medical Service to make an exception in your case."

"Yes . . . I see, sir."

"On the other hand . . ." said Harmon. He hit the button below the schema with his fist. The pattern winked out into blank wall once more. Harmon turned back to Cal. "There's that suggestion of mine the Colonel mentioned to you just now."

"Sir?" Cal was hardly listening.

"General Walt Scoby, who heads the Contacts Service, as I imagine you know, is coming along in person on this Paumons expedition. He was asking me the other day if I knew of any ex-mulebrains who might be interested in the Contacts Service." Harmon smiled a little. "He's having a mite of trouble getting men of that sort of experience himself. Of course, your psych-hold applies only to the Combat outfits. If you signed with General Scoby, you'd be coming along to the Paumons with the rest of us, even if only in a non-combatant slot."

"Contacts Service?" Cal lifted his head.

"I know how you feel, Lieutenant. On the other hand, there's a need for men like you, no matter in what capacity." Harmon smiled. "I don't mind telling you, I myself wouldn't mind seeing someone with your experience and attitude high on General Scoby's staff. You might look at it that way: after a fashion you'd still be working for the good of the Combat Units in bridging the gap between the Contacts Service and them." He paused. "Well, it's entirely up to you, Lieutenant. I wouldn't want to talk you into anything you might regret later."

He extended his hand and Cal found himself shaking it.

"And good luck, Lieutenant Truant. Calvin Truant, isn't it?"

"Yes, sir."

"Good luck, Cal."

And then he was striding away from Cal, out of the office.

* * *

It was another day that Cal came across the wide, grassy, parklike mall that separated the Recruitment Office and other Combat Services from the converted hospital buildings that housed the ten-year-old Contacts Service.

He had taken two weeks to face the fact that any kind of Service, for him, was better than none at all. And now, as he came across the mall, the grass underfoot was beginning to turn richly green from its brown tint of winter, and the shadow of the flag before the Contacts Office flashed in his eye like the shadow of a stooping hawk as it whipped in the light spring breeze.

He went up the stone steps and inside. Behind the front door, the offices were cluttered and overcrowded, with a fair sprinkling of civilian workers among the uniformed personnel at the desks. Cal found the Information and Directory desk and gave his name to the middle-aged civilian woman working behind it. He had sent in his application in routine fashion the day before, and surprisingly, that same evening, had come word that General Scoby himself would like to talk to him if he had no objection to an appointment at 1400 hours the following day.

Cal had no objection. In fact, it seemed to him to make little difference. He came now to keep the appointment with about the same emotion a man might bring to having his hair cut.

The woman behind the desk kept him waiting only a minute or two and then took him in herself to see General Scoby.

Stepping through the indicated doorway—at the entrance of which she left him—into a sudden glare of sunlight from two tall windows, Cal caught sight simultaneously of an older man at the desk and of a leopard-sized, long-legged feline of a pale, fulvous color. It was black-spotted and wore a light leather harness from which a hoop-shaped leather handle projected stiffly upward at the shoulders. The large cat lay resting in a corner of the room beyond the desk. It raised its head at Cal's entrance, which brought the eyes momentarily in line with Cal's. The yellow, guarding, animal stare caught Cal between one footfall and the next, and in that fraction of a second Cal tensed, then relaxed, and moved on into the office.

"Good reactions," said the man at the desk, lifting his own untidily gray-haired head. "Sit down, Lieutenant."

Seating himself by the desk as the big cat in the corner dropped with boneless gracefulness back into its half-doze against the wall, Cal turned his glance on the man. He saw an aging, slightly overweight three-star general with bushy eyebrows and hair, a pipe in his mouth, and a uniform shirt tieless and open at the throat. Incongruously, the black and white piping of the Ranger Commandos—the Combat Services' crack behind-enemy-lines units—ran along the edge of his shirt epaulets. His voice rasped on what seemed a deliberate and chronic note of exasperation.

He took the pipe from his mouth and pointed with it at the cat in the corner.

"Cheetah," he said. "Named Limpari. My seeing-eye friend."

Cal looked without thinking at the man's eyes, for they were knowing and full of sight.

"Oh, just periodic blackouts." Scoby jerked the pipestem to-ward his bushy head of hair. "I'm a silver-skull. Plate on most of this side. What's your particular purple heart, Lieutenant"—he frowned at the screen of the filmholder on his desk—"Truant. Cal. What kind of disability have you got, Cal?"

"Sir," said Cal, and stopped. He took a careful breath. "Psych-hold," he said shortly.

"Yeah. That's right," muttered Scoby, glancing once more at the filmholder. "I remember—so many things popping at once here." He looked up at Cal. "In fact, I picked up quite a dossier on you. How come you waited for a battlefield commission?"

"Sir?" said Cal woodenly.

"Don't give me the treatment. I've been there and back, too, Lieutenant. You know what I'm asking." He jabbed the pipe-stem at the film in the filmholder. "You've had seven years. You got a general aptitude rating way to hell and gone up there. You got a top record and two or three of your medals actually mean something. How come you never tried for a commission before the Lehaunan Expedition?"

Cal looked squarely at the other man.

"I guess I didn't want the responsibility, General."

"A mulebrain isn't supposed to think. All he's got to do is obey orders. Is that it?"

"That's right, sir."

"Commissioned officer might sooner or later have to give or-ders he didn't like. Might be required to do things he didn't agree with?"

"Something like that, General," said Cal. "Maybe."

"But a mulebrain's got no choice, so his conscience doesn't have to bother him? That so? Then how come," said Scoby, tilting far back in his chair, swinging it around to face Cal and putting the pipe back between his teeth, "how come you took the battlefield commission when it came through for you? What changed your mind after all these years?"

Cal shrugged. "I don't know, sir," he said.

"No," said Scoby, his teeth chewing on the bit of his pipe and watching Cal. "No, I guess you don't. Well, I looked up your civilian past, too, here." He shuffled about and found some papers on his desk. "I'd heard of your father, matter of fact. In fact, I was on the review board that checked over the court-martial of that Reserve Captain that fouled up in your home town during the Riots. Later on I read some of your father's writings on the matter of Equal Representation and other things. Interesting."

"We didn't agree," said Cal monotonously, between lips that were, in spite of himself, stiff.

"I gather that. Well," said Scoby, leaning back in his chair once more, "we might as well get down to cases. I need you. I need a man with Combat Service experience. But more than that, I need one man in particular who's been in the ranks as well as up in officer country. I need a man who can get along with mulebrains as well as regular officers, and double the usual job and take what's handed out to him as well as I can myself." He stopped and leaned forward toward Cal. "He'll need faith and brains and guts—not necessarily in that order. You got at least two of them. Want the job?"

"Sir," said Cal, and he kept his face as still as water on a windless day. His gaze went impersonally past Scoby's shoulder. "Would the General advise me to take the job?"

"Hell, yes!" exploded Scoby. "I invented it, and it saved my soul. It might save yours. That's a hell of a favor I'm doing you, Cal!"

"Yes, sir," said Cal. He hesitated a moment. "I'll be glad to take the job, General."

"Fine," said Scoby. "Fine. You can start out by ripping off those." He pointed.

Cal's hands made a little instinctive move in spite of himself protectively up towards his lieutenant's insignia on his epaulets.

"My tabs, sir?"

"That's right," said Scoby sardonically. "One of the little

monkey wrenches thrown in my machinery from time to time happens to be a Government ruling that I can't use rank as an inducement to sign men up. All Contacts Officers, regardless of their qualifications, must be run through the regular training cycle. Guess what that means? You climb back into issue coveralls and go back through Basic all over again.''

Cal stared at the older man.

"Basic?'' he said.

"Kind of a kick, isn't it, Lieutenant?'' said Scoby. "Get you out on the firing range and the obstacle course with all the other wet-eared recruits and teach you how to be a man and a soldier before you go goofing off as a Gutless Wonder. Don't look at me like that. I know there's no sense to it. The Combat Units' General Staff knows there's no sense to it, with a man like yourself. It wasn't shoved into the Regulations to make sense, but to make me trouble. Well, how about it, Cal? You figure you can still square-corner the covers on a bunk? Or do you want to back out?''

There was a faint, sharp glitter in Scoby's eyes.

"No, sir,'' said Cal.

"Little slow answering there, weren't you?''

"No, sir,'' said Cal. "I was merely trying to reconcile this regulation with General Harmon telling me he wouldn't mind seeing someone like me on your staff.''

"General Harmon,'' said Scoby. "Well, you're just a little two-bit Lieutenant, Cal; yours not to question why the ways of generals. Or ask generals questions. But next time you're in the library, you might read up on the siege of Troy.'' He turned back to his desk. "That's all. You can go, Lieutenant. Come see me after you've been through Contacts School.''

Cal stood up. Scoby was pulling papers toward himself.

"Troy, General?'' he asked.

"All about a horse,'' grunted Scoby, without looking up. "Good day, Lieutenant.''

Cal stared for a second longer, but Scoby seemed to have forgotten the very existence of any visitor. He was wrist-deep in forms and papers, looking like a seedy bookkeeper, behind in his entries. Over in the corner, the cheetah had fallen asleep and slid down the slope of the wall to lie on its side on the floor, legs stiffly outstretched. It looked like some large, stuffed, toy animal. To Cal, suddenly, the very air in the room seemed stale and artificial.

He turned around and went back to the outer office. The middle-aged woman who had taken him in to Scoby had his papers ready to sign. He signed, and was told to report in five days to be sent out for Basic Training, as a trainee private.

He left the building. As he came down the steps outside, the sun still shone and the wind was still blowing. Only now, under the hawklike shadow of the flag, a pot-bellied Colonel in office pinks was scattering crumbs to a small horde of clamoring sparrows that fought and squabbled, shrieking, over the larger crusts.

CHAPTER SIX

Four days later Cal lay once more on the slight slope of the sand of Hornos Beach at Acapulco, Mexico, watching Annie swimming out beyond the first crest of breakers. It was late in the morning and they had the beach almost to themselves. Also it was shark season, but the dolphin patrol was guarding the shore waters and Annie was packing a stingaree.

Nevertheless, Cal kept his eye out for fins, keeping the dolphin whistle handy. Otherwise, he simply lay and watched Annie. She swam strongly, in a straight line, her white arms flashing against the sun-brilliant blue of the sea, parallel to the beach. *She's got guts,* thought Cal unexpectedly. *Too much guts for her own good, if trouble comes.* And then he felt that clumsy expression of his feelings about her followed immediately by a sudden terrible stomach-shrinking sense of pain and helplessness and loss. He reached for the dolphin whistle without looking for it, put it to his lips, and blew one long and two short.

One of the dolphins on patrol curved aside and slid out of sight under the water to rise a second later beside Annie and nudge her toward the beach. Her arms broke their rhythm; she stopped and looked shoreward. He stood up, waved "no sharks" and beckoned her in. She turned toward him and her arms began to flash again.

He lay down once more, the sudden emotion he had felt dying within him. After a few moments she came ashore in a flurry of foam, sliding up on the sand. She got to her feet, splashed herself clean of the sand, and then, shaking her short dark hair clear of the bathing cap, came up the slope toward him, smiling. A loneliness so deep as to be almost anger moved in him. *To hell with it,* he thought, *I love you.* He opened his mouth to say it out loud. But she came up to him, and he closed it again without saying anything.

He stood up. Standing, he could see how small she was.

"What?" she said, shaking her hair back, looking up at him.

"Let's go get a drink" he said.

Two mornings later, after tests and outfitting, Cal took a Services transport with four hundred and sixty-eight other recruit-rated enlistees. The transport was an atmosphere rocket with the same sort of body shell that in a commercial flight would have been rated at a maximum of a hundred and fifty passengers. This one, however, locked on an extra motor and filled its interior with two double-rows of gimbal-hung seats on each side of a narrow aisle. Cal managed a seat by one of the small windows and sat there with his view of Stapleton Field, trying to think of Annie and ignore his surroundings. It would be no trouble going through Basic again, he had told himself. Just a matter of keeping his head down and going through the motions. It made no difference one way or another. He was completely neutral, between the Combat and Contact Services. If everyone left him alone, he would leave them alone. If anyone started to step on his toes, he would know how to take care of it.

He had told Annie, frankly, of his own contempt for the Contact Service and its personnel, the night before. "Maybe you'll change your mind?" she said. "It won't be easy working with people if you think that way about them."

"You don't know the Service," he had answered. "It's a job to do and so many different bodies and faces to do it with you."

For a moment she had looked as if she would say something more. But she had not.

And now Cal sat in his narrow seat, staring out the window waiting for lift-time, surrounded by men in new forest-green uniforms. The sound of their conversation and the heat of their bodies enclosed him in a shell of unfamiliarity within which he was content. What did he have to do with graduations, girls, relatives, sports. . . .

"Hey, Dad! *Dad!*"

For a moment Cal did not connect the name with himself. "Dad" was what they had called older men in their middle twenties when he had been in Basic. Then he looked up. A grinning, young, sharp-chinned face was peering down at him from between the two seats ahead and in the tier above him.

"What?" said Cal.

"Got a light?"

The transport was still on the ground. The no-smoking sign was lit in the ceiling overhead. But Cal saw no point in wasting his breath after the decision he had made to remain neutral. His lighter was in a side pocket jammed against the wall. He reached into a breast pocket, extracted a self-striking cigaret, and passed it up.

"Hey, one of the field smokes!" said the sharp-chinned face. "Many thanks, Dad." Face and cigaret withdrew. A few seconds later smoke filtered down between the seats.

A minute after that there were steps approaching down the aisle. They stopped at the tier of the sharp-chinned recruit.

"Got a cigaret, soldier?" said an older voice.

"Sure, Sec," said the voice that had called Cal. "Not field smokes. But here, help yourself."

"I will. That all you got?"

"Well—*hey!* What're you doing? That's all I got to last me to the Fort. I thought you only wanted one."

"Don't let it worry you, soldier. As far as you're concerned, you're through smoking for the next three months, until you get out of Basic. And if I were you I wouldn't try bumming from your friends after you get to camp. I'll pass the word along the cadre wires when we get there—maybe your Section Leader can find a little extra something to remind you to believe in signs."

The footsteps went off. Cal tried to go back to his thoughts of Annie.

"That's kind of extreme, isn't it?" said a voice in Cal's right ear. Cal turned to look into the face of the trainee beside him; a good-looking if rather pale-faced, serious, tall young man in his early twenties. "On commercial ships most of those no-smoking signs have been disconnected long ago."

"It's regulations," said Cal, shortly. But the other went on talking.

"You're Contacts Service, like me, aren't you?" he said. "I noticed the color code on the A3 file you're carrying. I'm Harvey Washun."

"Cal Truant," grunted Cal.

"That's one of the things we'll have to watch out for after we become officers, isn't it? Unreal enforcement of regulations like that, just now? There's a responsibility to the fellow man as well as to the alien—to all living things, in fact.''

"That's what I heard," said Cal. He pulled his dodgecap down over his eyes, slouched down in his seat and pretended to go to sleep. He heard a creak from the seat belt (also abandoned on commercial ships of the present day) as his seatmate shifted position embarrassedly. But there was no more talk.

Forty-eight minutes later they took off, and eighty-three minutes after that they sat down at the field attached to Fort Norman Cota, Missouri. There cadre Section Leaders and Squadmen were waiting for them and ran the whole contingent the full distance back to the Combat Engineers Training Center on the Fort's west side, some four miles away.

It was a soft May day in the Ozarks. A puff of cloud here and there in the sky showed above the straight shafts of the poplar and pine and reflected in the puddles they splashed through; puddles scattered here and there in the reddish mud and suddenly blue and pure as fragments of tinted glass. The air smelled warm and heavy and sweet. About him, Cal could hear the grunts and gasps of his fellow-trainees, as they puffed against the prolonged heavy work of the run. Cal was breathing deeply and steadily himself, and it occurred to him suddenly that after these past months of hospital and bumming around he was in no better shape than a lot of them. What made the run more bearable to him was his attitude. He saved his breath for running; his emotions for things over which he had no control. The thought of this made him feel a sudden satisfaction with his decision to stay isolated, neutral and apart.

"Close up! *Close up!*" yelled the cadremen, running alongside the stumbling, winded column of men laden with folderfiles and dufflebags. "Keep it in line, butterbellies! Shag it!"

Their voices struck off a faint echo in Cal's memory of his own first days in the Service. The wild sweats and alarms mixed with the tremendous excitement of being caught up in something big and vital. It had been hell—but he had been alive. Or so he had told himself all these years. He pushed the tag-end of uncertainty away from him, telling himself that now, for a while, he could be alive again. For a moment, he achieved what he sought: the slow, sweet twinge of a nostalgia lingered for a second in him.

They were passing the barracks area of some trainees already in the second half of Basic. Tanned a full shade darker than the men of this contingent, they were having a scrub-up of their barracks area. Shouts of "You'll be sorreee!" and "Tell'm where to send the body!" floated after them. For some reason, this touched off a slight uncomfortableness in Cal; a touch of shame which punctured his nostalgic mood. He settled down to his running and not thinking.

About a third of the contingent finally pulled up—having made the complete run without falling behind—gasping and heaving like broken-winded horses in front of the white-painted two-story barrack buildings of the training area.

A sharp-faced man of Cal's age, with the diamond of a Wing Section showing on the tabs of his sharply creased and tailored fatigues, came out of a small Unit Office building and stood on the top of its three steps, looking down at them.

"You shouldn't ought to bring them in before lunch," he told the Cadre Section in charge. "These muck-faces always make me sick to my stomach." Suddenly he roared. "Atten-SHUN! What's the matter with you? Can't you stand at attention?"

"Of course not!" said the Charge Section. "They're a bunch from that Denver Recruitment Center."

"Well, keep the suck-apples out of my way," said the Wing Section. "Or I'll send them all off on a run around the mountain. Show them their barracks. And see they don't get them dirty."

Silent, detached, Cal saw the men around him introduced to the white-painted buildings, and felt the wave of their exhausted relief at the sight of the mathematically perfect twin rows of bunks on each floor. He watched their feelings change to exasperation as they were put to making up their assigned bunks, storing their bag and files in foot lockers and bunk hooks. And then exasperation turned to silent fury as they were directed to remove their shoes and outer clothing and carefully scrub and wipe every trace of dirt, dust or disarray their incoming had produced. Finally, he saw it all give way to numb shock as they were told to take their ponchos and mess kits out into the open between the buildings, and there were assigned a six-by-three-foot rectangle of earth apiece for their actual living. Because, as their Section's Section Leader (Section Ortman) put it:

"Those barracks were built for soldiers, not pigs. We leave'm there so you can have the fun of standing official inspection every Saturday morning."

Then he drew a line in the air with the swagger stick he carried under his arm and informed them that this was the magic line, ten feet out from the building, and he didn't want to see any of them crossing it, except on a direct order.

Ortman was small and broad and dark. He wore the ribbons of the Lehaunan campaign on his parade jacket, and did not smile as he talked.

Cal was thinking of Annie. Consciously thinking of Annie.

Six weeks later—by the time the contingent was ready for Advanced, the second half of Basic Training—the image of Annie had worn thin. So had Cal's memory of his first Basic, seven years before. A new bitterness had taken its place.

For the first time in his years with the Service, that curious alchemy that draws a soldier close to other men in his own outfit—Wing, Section and Squad—had failed him. He was a man apart. To the rest of the trainees (the facts were in his file; they had not taken long to leak out) he was a veteran. To the cadremen over the trainees and himself, he was a freak—neither true recruit, nor true soldier—walled off from them by the wall of military discipline. To the other Contacts Cadets putting in their stint, he was an enigma lacking in the proper ideals and theories.

Washun, his seatmate on the ride to the Fort from Denver, had tried to bridge the gap.

"I've been talking to some of the other cadets in the outfit," he said to Cal one day after chow. "And we'd appreciate it if you'd give us a little talk, sometime, and help us out."

"A talk?" Cal looked up from polishing his mess kit.

"On how to be a soldier," said Washun. Cal gave him a long stare; but the boy was serious.

"Go get shot at," said Cal, and went back to polishing his mess kit. He heard Washun rise and leave him.

Washun was one of those in Cal's squad who did not fit. Unlike Tommy Maleweski, the sharp-faced nineteen-year-old who had bummed the cigaret from Cal on the transport and was now, after six weeks, practically and effectively broken of the habit, Washun was having it harder rather than easier. Maleweski had threatened to arise from his poncho swinging the first time one of the cadremen woke him with a swagger stick. He had not, and was now a trainee corporal. Washun had worked hard and conscientiously at everything while obviously hating it with a fastidious hatred. But he talked too much about abstract matters like ethics and responsibility and was too thin-skinned for his own happiness. The cracks about "gutless wonders" he and other Contacts Cadets—except Cal—were already beginning to get from the other trainees, wounded him deeply. Unlike any of the others, he had already had one fight with a trainee named Liechen from Section A over the term. He had gone into the fight swinging hard and conscientiously, and obviously hating it, and emerged a sort of inconclusive winner. (This, because Ortman and another Section Leader had discovered the fighters and made them keep at it until Liechen dropped, at last, from exhaustion, and could not be made to stand under his own power any longer.)

As a result of this, however, Washun, after his company punishment with Liechen, had returned to be a sort of minor hero and leader to the Contacts Cadet outcasts. Though he refused all responsibility, they sought him out with their troubles. And this did not make him popular with Ortman, who thought the situation unhealthy.

"Been holding court again?" he would ask, as they stood in line for informal inspection—inspection that is, of their outdoor, or actual barracks area, which was required to be as tidy as any indoors. Cal, standing next to Washun, would see out of the corner of his eye the other man go white, as he invariably did when attacked.

"Yes, Section!" Washun would reply, staring straight ahead, suffering, scorning to take refuge in a lie.

"Washun," said Ortman wearily one day, "do you think you're doing these men a favor? Do you think it's going to *help* them, letting them go on with the habit of having somebody around to kiss the spot and make it well? Well, answer me—no, don't." Ortman sighed wearily. "I'm not up to listening to Societics philosophy this early in the morning. You men!" he shouted, looking up and down the four squad rows of the Section. "Listen to me. This is one damn Section that's going to pretend it's made up of men, even if it's not. From now on if I catch any one of you milk-babies crying on anyone else's shoulder, they both carry double packs on the next night march. And if I see it again, it's triple packs. Get that!"

He turned back to Washun.

"Shine that mess kit!" he snapped. "Can't you get a better fit to your fatigues than that? If you've got too much time on your hands that you've got to listen to belly-achers, let me know.

You've got a long ways to go to be a soldier, Washun. And that goes for the rest of you.''

He stepped on down the line and found himself in front of Cal. For a moment their eyes met. Cal stared as if at a stone wall, his face unmoving.

Ortman stepped on.

"You, Sterreir, tear up that kit layout and lay it back down right. Jacks, wash those fatigues and re-press them. Maleweski . . .''

That evening, after chow, a delegation of the Contacts Cadets, lacking Washun, cornered Cal as he was leaving the mess hall and drew him aside.

"You've got to do something about it,'' they told him.

"Me?'' Cal stared at them. "What am I supposed to do?''

"Talk to Ortman. He's picking on Washun,'' said a tall boy with a southern accent and a faint mustache. "And Washun's doing as well as anybody. That's not right.''

"So!'' said Cal. "Tell Ortman yourself.''

"He won't listen to us. But he likes you.''

"Likes me?''

"He never eats you out like the rest. You don't draw the extra duties. He's all right with you because he knows you've been through it before.''

"Yeah,'' said Cal. "And the fact I do things right's got a little bit to do with it, too. For my money, Ortman's doing just fine with Washun and the rest of you.''

"Sure,'' said a small cadet with black hair, bitterly. "You don't want to do anything for us. You like to think you're one of them, buddy-buddy with the cadre.''

Cal looked around the group. They stirred uneasily.

"Don't get tough with us, Truant,'' said the tall boy nervously. "We're not afraid of you.''

Cal snorted disgustedly and walked off.

The first half of Basic had been films, lectures, classes, drill and company small weapons training. With the start of the second half they moved into field and survival training; forced marches, night movements, infiltrations, tactics problems that turned out to be endurance or escape tests. The Section was melted down from its bloated oversize of nearly three hundred men to merely double the size of a regular seventy-five man Section. The drop-outs went not back to civilian life but to the "housekeeping" services, such as Supply and Maintenance. Among them went all the Contacts Cadets in Cal's section except Cal, the tall southern-accented boy with the mustache, and Washun. And with the going of these other Cadets, came a problem.

Now that the complainers had gone, Cal was forced to acknowledge that Ortman was, indeed, bearing down unfairly on Washun. Though it had not started out that way, Ortman was only human. But if he had the weapon of legal authority in his possession, Washun had the weapon of martyred superiority. It had come down to a contest between them.

It was a war of spirit, with each man trying to force the other to admit his way was wrong. And Washun, it now dawned on Cal with gradually increasing shock, was winning. Already he had bent the minds of the other trainees—the other trainees of his own Section, who did not particularly like him—to a feeling that right was on his side. Now he was bending Cal. And one day he would break, if he did not bend, Ortman.

This was all wrong, Cal told himself. Justice lay with Ortman—it *had* to lie with Ortman. Ortman was doing his best every day to instill in his Section the knowledge and attitudes that would enable them to survive and conquer in combat. And Washun, with no more authority than that provided to him by a handful of half-baked, wildly impractical theories, was setting himself up to treat that knowledge and those attitudes as something slightly unclean.

Cal found himself hating Washun. Washun had broken down Cal's protective isolation. Washun was, as Cal's father had been, one of those who, by an irrational insistence on doing good, caused only tragedy and harm. Cal could almost hear Washun quoting, as Cal's father had quoted:

"Societics: a philosophy which states that mankind can continue to exist only by evolution into a condition in which the individual's first responsibility is to a universal code of ethics and only secondarily to the needs of himself as an individual."

Cal found himself impatient for the day when Ortman would finally lose his temper and rack Washun back for good.

It was not long before that happened. They had been run through the infiltration course several times before, crawling on their bellies over the rocky ground under full pack and with solid shell and fire rifle jets screaming by a few feet overhead. But the day came on which they were sent through during an afternoon thunderstorm. The trainees, who had started out griping at the weather conditions, discovered that the suddenly greasy mud produced a skating-rink surface on which it was almost a pleasure to wiggle along. Spirits rose. They started larking about and a trainee named Wackell either raised himself incautiously or a bullet dropped, as sometimes happened. He took a wad of steel from a high-powered explosive rifle through his shoulder and thigh. He began to yell and Washun, who was nearby, went to him.

"All right," said Ortman, when they all stood dripping water and mud once more in Section formation in front of their barracks. "You all heard it; you heard it fifty times. In combat a soldier doesn't stop to pick people up. He keeps going. Have you got anything to say to that, Washun?"

"No, Section," said Washun, staring straight ahead. Ortman had at least broken him of arguing in ranks.

"No, come on," said Ortman. "I'm sure you've got something to say. Let's hear it."

"Simply," said Washun, whitely, staring at the mess hall opposite, "that that is to be my duty—Wing Aidman to some unit during the initial stages of an assault. Everyone knows that. I won't be carrying weapons, I'll be picking men like Wackell up."

"Fine," said Ortman. "You pick them up. You pick them up when the time comes. But right now you're training to be a soldier, not a Contacts Cutie. And you're going to learn a soldier doesn't stop to pick anyone up! Maleweski! Jones! Northwest and southwest corners of the barracks to shag this man! Full equipment and all, Washun. Get going. I'm going to run you around the mountain!"

Washun took one step forward out of ranks, rightfaced and began to trot around the barracks. Maleweski took a cut at him with the peeled wand that served the trainee non-coms for swagger sticks, as Washun lumbered past.

"Fall out! Shower, chow—and clean equipment!" barked Ortman at the rest of the section. "And watch that mud in the barracks!"

The orderly ranks disintegrated, as Washun came running heavily around the near side of the barracks. Without looking at him, they poured into the barracks.

Twenty minutes later, cleaned, dressed and chowed, Cal stepped once more out of the mess hall with his fresh-rinsed mess kit in one hand, smoking in the cool sunset air. Across a little space from him, he saw Washun still running around the barracks, although Maleweski and Jones had been relieved by two other trainee non-coms so that they could dress and eat. Washun ran, not fast, weaving only a little; but his eyes were already glazed.

It was not unusual for a man in good condition to run an hour or more around the mountain before he gave out. There was no compulsion upon him to make speed, but merely to keep going. The punishment was not a physical one, but mental. The barracks were large enough around so that the running man could not become dizzy. But after about a dozen circuits the mind began to lose count of the number of times the same corner had come up. The turning, rocking world out beyond the barracks took on an unreal quality, as if the running man was on a treadmill. It seemed he had run forever and that there was no end ever coming to the running. It was a small, circular hell in which the mind waited for the superbly conditioned body to give up, to quit, to collapse; and the animal-stupid body, sweating under the heavy harness of equipment, gasping for breath, ran on, struggling to prolong its own sufferings in limbo.

Ortman, of course, could stop it at any time. But he probably would not.

Cal watched the running man. He still felt no kindness for Washun and from his point of view there was nothing wrong with running a man around the mountain. What was bothering him, he discovered, was a tricky point rooted in the sense of right and wrong of a professional soldier.

What bothered him was the fact that the punishment was misapplied. Running a man around the mountain was a last resort; and it was like a scrub brush shower for a trainee that refused to stay clean. It was used for a man who was a consistent goof-off and whom nothing else, probably, could save.

But Washun was not a consistent goof-off. Within certain limits he was as good as any other trainee in the Section. And he was not savable, because he was lost already, to the Contacts Service. Nor could his punishment serve the purpose of a good example to the rest of the Section, who did not walk in Washun's ways, in any case.

Ortman, in Cal's eyes, was the Service. In letting himself be forced into going the limit with Washun, without adequate reason, Ortman had acknowledged his inability to conquer the Contact Cadet. He had lost. And Washun, weaving blindly now as he ran around the unending white walls of the barracks, had won.

"Truant!"

Cal turned sharply. It was Ortman, coming up to him from the direction of the orderly room.

"Get down to the orderly room, on the double," said Ortman. "It's not exactly according to regulations for one of you trainees. But you've got some visitors."

CHAPTER SEVEN

The visitors Cal discovered in the orderly room turned out to be young Tack, Joby Loyt, and Walk Blye from his old outfit. Joby and Tack were wearing Section's tabs, and Walk was now in an officer's gray uniform with the cloth insignia of a Warrant. They had all been drinking and Walk was well on his way to being drunk, although only someone familiar with him would have recognized the fact. The alcohol in him showed only in the fact that he moved a little more swiftly, and there was an added glitter to his eyes which a stranger might have put down to sheer liveliness, but which those who knew him took for a danger signal.

"How about it, Sec?" said Walk to the Wing Section in charge of Cal's training unit. The same Wing Section who the first day had threatened them all with what Washun was now enduring on Ortman's order. "Can we take him off for a little?"

Walk, as Warrant, was only about a rank and a half above the Wing Section, an officer in privilege rather than authority. It allowed him to be more familiar with the Wing than a fully commissioned officer might. The Wing reciprocated. He thought for a second.

"He's not supposed to leave the Wing area," he answered. "But there's a gully in those woods across the road there, if you'll have him back before bed check and in good shape."

"Word on it," said Walk. And the four of them left the orderly room and strolled across into the woods.

About fifty yards back, they found the gully behind a screen of yellow poplar. They made themselves comfortable in it. Thin, flat bottles of bourbon appeared; and Cal learned that his old Wing, along with the original Assault Team were moved in over on the other side of the camp for retraining and shakedown.

"Drink up!" said Walk. And Cal drank thirstily, almost angrily. But there was an awkwardness between them that the drink could not burn away; and he could see that Tack and Joby were affected by it as he was. Walk was an enigma. It was impossible to tell how he felt. He sat in the fading twilight of the woods with them, drinking half again as much as anyone else, as they talked about previous Expeditions. He seemed bored.

When he ran out of liquor and went off to get another bottle he had stashed nearby rather than carry into the Wing area, Cal commented on him, a little bitterly.

"You have to talk very hard to get Walk along?" he asked the other two.

"Hey, no," said Tack. "It was Walk's idea. I mean, the rest of us never thought they'd let you loose to talk to us. He set up the whole thing."

Cal shook his head in puzzlement. Walk came back with the other bottle and the light faded swiftly. The sudden-death drinking they were doing straight from the bottle was beginning to take effect on them all. For a moment time faded and it seemed like the old days. Sitting half in shadow in a stony slope of the gully, Walk drank, lowered the bottle, and crooned to himself in a husky voice.

"*—I—ain't—got—no—ma—ma.*" His slightly hoarse tenor floated low upon their ears. "*No woman, no baby—*"

They all joined in automatically. It was the Mourn, the Assault Soldier's Mourn, and they had sung it on a hundred drunks before. Half buried among the encroaching shadows they keened their total atonal lament:

> "*—no love.*
> *I ain't got no no one.*
> *Nothing but—the Damnservice!*
>
> *Left my home and I wandered.*
> *Never thought I'd end up like this.*
> *Name on a T.O.[1] listing—*
> *Number in—the Damnservice!*

[1] Table of Organization.

> *I get goofed and lonely,*
> *Thinking of those things that I missed.*
> *Nothing but a Goddam Mulebrain,*
> *Mucked up in—the Damnservice!*
>
> *Gonna get rich[2] next Tuesday.*
> *Wednesday, if the first Drops[3] miss.*
> *Bury me where they don't find me,*
> *To plant me in—the Damnservice!*

The last of the twilight was almost gone as they finished singing. They had all become to each other indistinct darknesses in the deeper darkness. Cal felt the fog of the alcohol thickening in his brain; and remembered his kit, uncleaned back at the barracks. He got heavily and a little unsteadily to his feet.

"Got to go," he said, with a slightly unmanageable tongue. "Thanks for everything. See you mules."

"Yeah." It was Tack's voice. "We'll get together, you get done with this Basic junk. You come looking for us, Sec. So long."

"So long, Sec," said Joby's voice.

"Sure," this was Walk's voice, coming low and clear and hard out of blackness. "We'll see you, Gutless Wonder!"

A jarring, icy shock racked suddenly through Cal, checking him as he stood half-turned. He froze, looking back. Above their heads the first pale sky of night was showing dimly through the inky branches of the overhanging trees. But down in the gully where they were, all was steeped in black. Far off, a bird twittered sleepily.

For a moment stark silence hung between them. And then, awkwardly, in a forced manner, Tack began to laugh. And a second later, just as artificially, Joby joined in. A moment later Walk was laughing, too. And then Cal.

But the laughter was not quite genuine, for all that. Cal found his fingers shaking as he fumbled out a cigaret. Ignoring its self-striking end, he scrabbled a chemical lighter from his pocket. Holding cigaret and match, he took a step toward where he knew Walk must be. He stuck the cigaret in his mouth and snapped the lighter.

[2] Combat Soldier's Death Benefits, paid to the next of kin.
[3] Glider and Shoulder Jet Assaults—Personnel.

The flame, springing suddenly into existence, caught Walk's face hanging apparently in midair, his mouth open, his features contorted with laughter. Then the flame winked out.

"Got to go," said Cal. He turned and stumbled up the wall of the gully and back toward the Wing area. He heard the laughter dwindle and die behind him.

He made his way back into his own barracks building. The lights were already out, except in the squadroom where Ortman slept. The door was open, and as he passed Cal saw the Section Leader working on reports at his desk. Ortman raised his head as Cal passed and for a second the two men looked at each other in silence. Then Cal moved on into the dim forest of double-decker bunks in the big room beyond.

Washun's bunk was empty. In the lower bunk beside it, the tall Cadet with the mustache was reading in the dim light escaping from Ortman's open doorway. His eyes came up from his book to fasten balefully upon Cal, as Cal passed to his own lower bunk, farther down the row. The kit still hung uncleaned on the end of the bunk. Cal ignored it. He stripped to his Service shorts and T-shirt and crawled drunkenly under the covers. He closed his eyes and Walk's face, as he had seen it in that moment's illumination of the lighter, came rushing at him.

He had had to see Walk's face in that moment. And he had seen what he had expected. The whatever it was in Walk that must always cause him to try to push things just one step further, had been at operation upon him. Walk had known that if he kept it up, one day he must push too far, must say the unforgivable to Cal. But, like an addict, he had been not able to help himself.

They had been as close as men and soldiers get in service. But they were now openly friends no more. They would have to avoid each other as much as possible, or someday they would be trapped into a situation in which they would have to try to kill each other. Walk had done it. He had done it all on his own, brought it about himself—not because he was drunk, but because of that inner devil of his which drove him to always dare the precipice one inch further.

He had done so, knowing what he was doing. But in the sudden flare of the lighter when Cal had looked, above the wild and laughing mouth, under the officer's cap canted drunkenly over the wide, tanned brow, Walk's darkly glittering eyes had been crazy with loneliness and grief.

CHAPTER EIGHT

Three weeks later, Cal graduated from Basic. With Washun and the Contacts Service trainee with the mustache, and some forty others from other training contingents, they were shipped to Contacts School, back in Denver. At Contacts School, they drew officer's gray uniforms with Warrant tabs such as Walk had worn when Cal had last seen him, and were addressed as "Mister" by enlisted men and officers alike. The first day of Contacts School found them seated in the half-moon of seats of a steeply sloped classroom-amphitheater, facing, across a low section of floor, a raised lecture platform that would place their instructor standing behind a high desk and about on a level with the middle row of classroom seats.

A door behind the platform opened, and a small man wearing an officer's uniform with the insignia of a Colonel limped out with some papers in his hand and laid the papers on the desk.

"Ten-SHUN!" yelled someone. The class rose. The Colonel looked out at them, nodded, and went back to his papers. They stood. Apparently he had forgotten to tell them to sit. When his papers were in order he leaned both elbows on the desk and looked out at them. It was then that they became aware that the look on his face was not that of the weary, little, old, retired officer they had imagined him to be.

"I hope," he said, with a sort of quiet relish, "that none of you considered Basic was tough. Because, you see, we're really tough here."

He ran his eye over their ranks.

"Some of you perhaps discovered that the body responds by adapting to the kind of physical training you received in Basic Training," he said. "It becomes harder and more fit to endure. Our job here is going to be to make harder and more enduring a different part of you than your bodies. During the next ten weeks, we will attempt to do our best, while staying mostly within the letter of the military regulations applying to officer ranks, to break your spirits." He paused, slowly opened a slot in the desk, took out a glass of water and sipped from it. He put it back and closed the slot. "From past experience I may tell you that we will succeed with nine out of ten of you. And most of those nine will be made up of those who make the initial mistake of believing we aren't serious about this."

He paused and looked them over again.

"And of course," he said, "while this is going on, you will be studying simultaneously the three training courses required to fit a Contacts Officer for his triple duties. These are"—he held up three fingers as he spoke, one after the other—"Wing and Company aidman during initial assaults and landings; interpreter, translator, and prisoner-of-war administrator, during and immediately following the campaign; and Contacts Administrator with the responsibility of making friends with the beings whose relatives we have just killed, and whose homes we have just destroyed, and whose pride we have just humbled."

He stopped. He beamed at them in satanically gentle fashion.

"And if you achieve these things and graduate, you will be put to work doing them in actual practice. *And,* if you do them responsibly in actual practice, you will find that those of the conquered who do not despise and hate you will distrust you; that the enlisted man in general will resent you as someone who appears to try to curry favor with non-humans by bribing them with what the enlisted man has just bought from them at the heavy price of his own blood; and the officer ranks in general will regard you as a spy system and hindrance upon them."

He straightened up.

"Under these conditions, it is taken for granted that you will carry on your duties with a high degree of efficiency, ignore all insults and intrigues against you, and while remaining calm, controlled and pleasant at all times, never allow yourself to lose an argument, or close your eyes to a situation that needs your attention. If you do all this successfully—I say, if"—the Colonel paused to beam again at them—"why, we will no doubt find more for you to do the next time."

He shuffled his papers together and picked them up. They had evidently been some sort of prop, for he had not referred to them once.

"That's all, then," he said gently. "That concludes the lecture for this hour. You might all stand there for the rest of the hour and think it over. Those who wish to drop out will find the School Orderly Room open at all hours. For the ten percent of you who will make it through the course"—he stepped back from the desk so that his small figure with the stiff leg stood in view of them all, and raised his handful of papers with a small flourish—"I salute you, Gutless Wonders!"

He turned and went out by the same door, leaving them standing.

It was, Cal discovered, known as hazing. And it had been practiced by many organizations and cultures since time immemorial, and always with the same purpose: to find out if the individual had an inherent resiliency, an ability to take it, which might be required later on. The only difference here was that it was completely nonphysical. But that, Cal began to recognize, was because it took up where Basic had left off. It was, Cal discovered, as the small Colonel with the game leg had said the first day. They were really tough here.

They were tough in all the unfair ways. There was the matter of the ringers.

The second day's lecture in the classroom-amphitheater (they were allowed to sit, this time) the small Colonel informed them, not without some apparent relish, that there were an unstated number of fake Cadets among them. The function of each of these fake Cadets was to pick out one or more of the true Cadets and try every possible means to make him wash out of the course.

"Their job," said the Colonel, "will be to muck you up—" He broke off suddenly, cocking his eye like an interested sparrow at a Cadet in the front row. "Does my language bother you?" the Colonel inquired, and he immediately began to swear at the Cadet in a calm, penetrating voice with every air of enjoyment. The rest of the Class, craning to look at the Cadet, saw him stiffen, and go pale, then red-faced. The Colonel ran down after a minute or so.

"Nor a word from him, either," said the Colonel, turning to the class and beaming. "But then, I didn't expect it. I've just been looking at his personal file. His family, when he was just about seven years old . . ." He commenced reciting in a pleasantly gossiping tone, a catalogue of perversions, cruelties and disgraces dealing with the Cadet's immediate family, whom the Colonel referred to by their first name. ". . . now his older sister Myra—"

Suddenly the Cadet was on his feet and screaming back at the Colonel. The Colonel stopped and leaned his elbow on the desk in front of him and listened interestedly until the Cadet, suddenly breaking off, turned and bolted from the room.

"Well, well," said the Colonel briskly, "there's at least one gotten rid of for today." He made a mark on the papers in front of him. As he did so, his eye caught Cal's, whose seat was in the front row. "Thin-skinned, wasn't he?" he said confidentially to Cal.

"Sir?" said Cal, keeping his expression perfectly blank.

"Ah," said the Colonel, winking at the class. "Here's one of those stone-wall characters. Pays no attention. Words-can-never-hurt-me type." He smiled slowly. "Of course he's had practice ignoring the opinions of others. I've been through his files, too, just as I have with the rest of you. This man's father was once given fifty lashes in his town park for getting some young men of his town in trouble. Isn't that true?" he said to Cal. And then his voice lashed out suddenly. "Answer yes or no!"

"Sir—" said Cal.

"Answer yes or no!"

A whiteness, like interior lightning, washed Cal's mind blind for a second. Then a molten inner anger came to sustain him.

"Yes, sir," he said, with no change of tone.

"You see?" said the Colonel to the class. "He admits it. And you can see it doesn't bother him much. If I were the rest of you, I'd keep a fairly respectable distance from him. He looks to me as if he might have picked up his father's—ah—tastes." Someone else in the audience seemed to catch the Colonel's eyes. "You don't approve of my instruction methods?" he asked someone over Cal's head. Cal turned to look as a voice answered.

"No, sir."

It was Washun, Cal saw. Washun was as pale as Cal had ever seen him when facing Ortman. But the sound of his voice was as determined.

"Please, suggest an alternative," said the Colonel.

"I haven't an alternative immediately in mind, sir." Washun went even paler. "But someday something better should be worked out."

"That's enough," interrupted the Colonel. "Your objection is what we call an empty protest and has no practical value whatsoever." He picked up a pencil and poised it over one of his sheets of paper on the desk before him. "I'll give you one chance, and one chance only, to withdraw it. Do you withdraw it?''

Washun hesitated for a fractionary moment.

"No, sir," he said with effort. "You asked me, and—"

"That's enough. Stand up," said the Colonel. He made a mark on the paper as Washun rose to his feet. "You have the distinction of having gained the first credit point I've given out in this class. All of you remember that. You are *supposed* to speak out and stick by our guns, whether it does any immediate good or not. However, Mr. Washun, since the exercise of virtue in actual existence usually leads not to an immediate reward, but to additional punishment, you will remain standing for the rest of the hour, as an example to yourself as well as others."

With that he turned his attention away from Washun and began to torture a Cadet in the second row who had a particularly youthful face. By the time the hour was over he had reduced the class roster by two more candidates.

"Not a good day," he informed the class as they rose to march out. "And not bad. So-so."

When he reached the next class, Cal discovered someone had stolen his notes from the classes of the day before.

There was the matter of living conditions. The candidates were bunked four to a room, with study facilities, and ate in a central mess hall. The food and beds were apparently good. But things went wrong with them; first one thing, and then another. The bedding they drew from the Supply Room turned out to be too short for the bunks. The Section Leader in charge of the Supply Room claimed he had no authority to exchange it for bedding of the proper size. Sometimes a meal would be unaccountably delayed, or badly served. Solid foods were undercooked, liquid ones, which should have been hot, were ice cold.

There was the matter of uncooperative enlisted personnel. The enlisted men connected with the school were studiedly insulting to the candidates. This was bad enough. What was worse was that whenever they could get away with being unhelpful or outright harmful to a Cadet's requirements or record, they did so. Gradually, the candidates came to understand that there was no single right way of getting through the Contacts School. There was only the least possible wrong way.

There was the matter of individual antagonism from the commissioned instructors. It appeared almost as if the moment a candidate began to acquire credit points as Washun had the first day, a competition was instituted among the instructors to see who would be the first to push him to the breaking point. Verbal abuse and mis-scored tests were among the milder weapons employed by the instructors. Cal, with Washun and a half dozen others, was singled out early for this sort of competition.

But Cal, if he did not have the philosophical armor that he saw in Washun, found a deep and native stubbornness in himself that refused to give ground. As he had told himself, sitting in the rocket that had been about to carry him off to Basic Training all over again, he told himself now that it was simply a matter of putting his head down, pushing ahead, and letting them do their damnedest.

So he did. But as the weeks piled up, the pressure got worse and worse, until he began to feel that he would explode after all; that the moment would come when the upper, sensible, directing part of his mind would no longer be able to hold back the emotion boiling beneath. And the night came finally when he knew that the next day would be his last.

Lying on his back in the darkness, staring at the underside of the mattress of the bunk overhead, a grim solution came to him. Quietly, in the dark, he got up, slipped out of the room barefooted, in his shorts and undershirt, and slipped down the hall of their barracks and out onto the small balcony, to the outside metal fire-escape. Six floors below, invisible in the night, was the concrete surface of the area where the Cadets stood their parade formations.

If the worst comes to the worst, he thought, a quiet tumble off the railing here while smoking a cigaret after light-out would leave them forever lacking a positive knowledge that they had broken him. A savage, angry joy rose in him at the thought. He would not yield. No matter what happened, he could always wait until the end of the day, until night. And the night he could not face another day he would bring his cigarets here after lights-out. . . .

And suddenly, without warning, sanity came washing over him. He woke suddenly to the irrationality of his thoughts. It was as if a stained and distorted window through which he looked out on the world had suddenly been wiped clean so that he saw everything clearly, without distortion and in its proper perspective. The wild thought of suicide as an alternative to submission thinned away and vanished like a mist on the window glass that had made it perfectly opaque before. The pressures the School had been putting on him shrank into the common crowd of pressures that any living would make upon him. Suddenly he saw how helpless such methods were.

Why, he thought with something like wonder, there's nothing they can do to me; there's nothing anyone can do to me. Death was the brittle final ultimate of any weapon; and death shattered pointlessly upon the spirit of anyone who paid out his life in honest coin up to the moment of death. For the first time Cal felt a little of the great strength that moves men of faith, no matter what that faith may be. And for the first time he thought of the millions, that eight percent of the Earth's adult population, that believed as his father had believed. A touch of awe at what their true power might be touched him. He went soberly back to his bed.

The next day he woke clear-headed. And when he went about the day's classes, he discovered a strange sort of minor miracle had happened. Before, he had pretended that none of the pressures, the words and actions aimed to trip him up, had been able to touch him. All at once, he found that this had actually come to pass. The attacks upon him had become shadow weapons, wielded by shadows. His gaze looked through them to the more important meanings and things in which they had their roots.

Once, filing in line past the glass doors leading to the dining room at a time of day when that room was dark, he caught a glimpse of his shadowy reflection in the dusk-backed glass. He was smiling.

CHAPTER NINE

At the end of the ten weeks Cal graduated from Contacts School along with Washun and the rest of the predicted ten percent of the entering class. The rest took their new Lieutenant's tabs off on an eight-day leave. Cal made an appointment to see General Scoby the following day.

The thin, clear sun of September was cutting squarely across the papers on the desk in Scoby's office as Cal stepped into it this second time. The year had turned the part of the planet

around Denver into mountain autumn, since they had first met;
and the point of that meeting lay many millions of miles back
along the Earth's path through that space which is also time.
Scoby sat as he had sat before, but the cheetah, Limpari, this
time lay alongside the desk, at desk-top level, forelegs stretched
out so that the light-colored puffs of her paws rested barely
against the sleeve of Scoby's shirt, feline head laid upon those
forelegs. Her animal eyes turned to Cal as he entered, but nothing else about her moved. Scoby looked up.

"Well, Lieutenant," he said. "Sit down."

Cal sat.

"You said to come see you, General," he said, "after I got
through Contacts School."

"That's right." Scoby reached for his pipe and began to fill
it, considering Cal coolly. "So you got through all right."

Something about the question operated against the relative
peace of mind Cal had discovered during the later days at the
Contacts School. An old defensiveness came back, an old, sharp
edge unsheathed itself in him.

"The General didn't expect me to?"

"Now there," said Scoby, striking a light to his pipe and
puffing on it, "is why I want you for the job I have in mind and
I'm afraid of you at the same time."

"Sir?"

"You're management training material," said Scoby. "I want
you as high up in my organization as you can climb. But I don't
want you coming along faster than you're ready to. Tell me about
the Paumons. What'd you learn about them at Contacts School?"

Cal frowned.

"Very humanlike," he said. "Human enough to get by in a
crowd of us, almost. Stripped, of course, you'd notice differences. But with clothes, they'd look sort of like eskimos with
sunburns."

"Ah. . . ." Scoby closed his eyes. "What's the name for
them?"

"Sir?"

"The mulebrains and anybody else who knows about them.
What're they calling these Paumons people?"

"Oh," said Cal. "Progs."

"Standing for what? What d'you call them?"

"Standing for what?" echoed Cal. "I don't know, sir. Myself, sometimes I call them Progs. Or Paumons. Depends on who I'm talking to.''

"Yeah," said Scoby. "You got a ways to go yet. What about their culture?''

"Industrial. They get their power from volcanic taps.''

"Art? Philosophy?''

Cal stared at the older man.

"Art?'' he said slowly. "Philosophy? School didn't give us anything on that.''

"And of course you didn't go look it up on your own. What's the job the Contacts Service is supposed to do? Can you tell me that?''

"Yes, sir,'' answered Cal. "Just as the Armed Services' job is to subdue the enemies of the human race, the Contacts Service's job is to lay a basis for future peaceful co-existence with those former enemies.''

"Oh,'' said Scoby, "but you're a great little quoter, Lieutenant. Now tell me how you're going to do it.''

"Establish workable relationships with Paumons leaders and enlist their cooperation in working out future patterns of co-existence.''

"Damn you!'' shouted Scoby, suddenly slamming the desk top with one hand. The cheetah's head came up like a striking cobra's. "I didn't ask you for chapter and verse! I asked you what you're going to *do!*''

"My job,'' said Cal, staring into the other man's eyes. "What I'm told to do.''

"And I tell you,'' snarled Scoby, leaning toward him, "that nobody's going to tell you what to do. You're going to do what you have to do, what you think you ought to do. You're going to have to work it all out for yourself!'' He glared at Cal. "You know why there's nothing about philosophy or art in the Paumons course: Because I told them there wasn't to be any. You want to find out about these people, you go find out about them for yourself. Far as the Assault Team's concerned, you're a goddam aidman, and a goddam interpreter and a goddam headache. Far as *I'm* concerned, you're a goddam substitute working Christ and I expect you to produce!''

He sat glaring at Cal for a long second. Cal looked back without moving his head.

"All right,'' said Scoby more calmly—Limpari put her head down again. "As I say, I expect something more of you than I do of what I ordinarily get for help. I've got a special assignment for you. Contacts Officer—with your old outfit.''

Cal felt a soundless shock. It was something like the feeling that had followed Walk's last words three months before.

"Want to back out?" jeered Scoby, staring at him closely.

"No, sir," said Cal.

"Then take off." Scoby went unceremoniously back to the papers on his desk. Cal rose and left.

He had been due for a several-week course with the Medics to fit him for his aidman duties. He had planned to meet Annie that evening when she came off shift at the Service Hospital. He had even sourly made up his mind to get to the library and do some extra-curricular reading on the Paumons, in line with what Scoby had said. None of these things took place.

That afternoon, even as he was walking out of Scoby's office, things were "breaking," as the News Services said, with the Paumons situation. The Cabinet on Earth was being called into emergency meeting. Six hours later he was collected by military patrol and confined to base with all other uniformed personnel on a general muster order. Seventy-eight hours later, he and the rest connected with the Paumons Expedition Assault Force were spaceborne.

Quarters on their ship, as on all ships of the Assault Force, were close; and all experienced Service people were on their best behavior with each other. Cal met the other officers of his Wing. Walk, as the only former member of the unit, was Section Commander of Section A of the Wing, and executive officer under Wing Captain Anders Kaluba, who now headed the outfit. Kaluba was a pleasant, dark-skinned man, who had been a lieutenant with the Seventy-second Combat Engineers against the Lehaunans. He did not seem unduly prejudiced against Contacts Officers. And Walk, when he met Cal, was almost subdued. He said little. Joby Loyt was Section Leader under Walk. Tack had been promoted to Wing Section for the outfit, and talked and acted older than before.

The Assault Force was on the jump for nine days—and fourteen hours out of destination. An order was posted for an orientation address by General Harmon, the Force Commander, to all officers and men on all ships at X minus 1200 hours. On Cal's ship they took down the hammocks in the main room and everybody crowded in, sitting cross-legged in ranks upon the cold metal flooring. At the far end of the room there was a viewing platform.

At 1200 hours precisely, the platform lit up with a three-dimensional representation of the Force Commander's office on the flagship. It showed a desk, a wall representation of the Paumons world, and a door. At a couple of minutes past twelve, the door opened, and the image of Harmon strode out before the audience. He was wearing combat coveralls with a field dress jacket over them and a light-weapons harness with, however, no weapons clipped to it. He nodded into the pickup; a warming current ran through the audience in Cal's ship. Harmon looked slightly tired, but confident.

"I won't keep you," he said. "I want you all to turn in as soon as I'm through and get as much rest as you can."

He picked up a pointer from the desk and turned to the wall representation of the Paumons.

"Here," he said, indicating a squarish-looking continent spreading south and west from the planet's equator, "is the high central plateau area which Intelligence had decided would be the most promising location for our initial drops. The weather is uniformly clear and good at this time of year. The terrain is both highly defensible because of its ruggedness, and adapted to our overland transport. It also overlooks the industrial centers of this key continent. You'll all be getting full details from your individual Commanders."

He laid the pointer aside and came to stand looking out over the desk at them all. There was a moment of silence in the main room of Cal's ship. Across the room, somebody coughed, and a couple of other barks answered from nearby.

"Fort Cota hack," muttered a voice behind Cal. He shifted his haunches on the hard metal plates. Around him the room was filled with the smell of still air heavy with the odors of clothing and other men's bodies. Jump boots squeaked on the flooring and coveralls rustled as those about him fidgeted and shifted.

Harmon cleared his throat.

"The alien enemy we will be facing in a few hours is tough. We might as well face that fact. But, being an alien, the alien is not as tough as we are: The Prog is going to find out that he's bitten off something he can't chew at all."

Harmon clasped his hands behind him and stood out from behind the desk.

"When a human being fights, he knows what he's fighting for. That's one reason we've got it all over the alien, the alien is not as tough as we are. The Prog is different. He doesn't know. All he knows is some other alien got him stirred up, or some sort of alien sacred cow got trampled on, or it just looks like a good opportunity for him to grab something. But it's a human being's right and duty to know what he's about. And so I'm just going to take a minute or two out here, and bring you officers and men up to date on the events that require us to be here."

Cal's underneath foot was going to sleep. He quietly uncrossed his legs, bringing the numb one on top.

"As you all know," Harmon was saying, "ours is an expanding culture and requires us to be continually on the lookout for additional living room. Three years ago, we made contact with the Bellatrix solar system and set down token bases on two of the empty, less habitable planets. At the same time we contacted the Progs to explain we were only interested in what they did not have, and didn't intend to bother them in any way."

"Move, will you!" hissed a man in the row behind Cal and off to his right. "You're crowding my goddam knee."

"Shove your knee!" retorted another whisper. "I haven't got any more room to move than you have."

"However, they withheld official acceptance of our presence in their solar system," Harmon's voice was continuing. "And shortly after that, less than six months ago, presented us with an official complaint against what they termed an offensive build-up of military equipment and personnel in these areas. We attempted to negotiate, but a month ago we were given what amounted to an ultimatum to pull out of the Bellatrix system. Ten days ago, the Prog attacked without warning and took over both our peoples and our property. Twelve hours from now, he's going to have to answer for that to us."

Harmon's glance swept from left to right in front of him.

"That's it, Assault Soldiers. Turn in now and get some rest—and tomorrow we give 'em hell!"

He threw a slight wave of his hand, turned about, strode back through the imaged door, and out. The stage winked blank and bare. The seated men rose, grunting and stretching, and the room was suddenly overcrowded. By orderly masses, they moved back along narrow corridors to their individual unit rooms, where the thick-hung hammocks drooped like white foliage from the low ceilings.

Pushing between the hammocks and the men climbing into them Cal heard his name called by Wing Captain Kaluba. He went toward the corner of the room that was Kaluba's.

Kaluba, because of the necessities imposed by rank and his duties, did not have a hammock, but a cot and a small folding desk. He was sitting on the cot behind the desk as Cal shoved past two filled hammocks to come into view.

"Yes, sir?" said Cal.

Kaluba was stacking reports in a neat pile. He looked up.

"Oh, yes. Lieutenant, you're not to go down with the outfit on the drop. You can come later with the medics."

Cal frowned.

"Sir?" he said. "I'm supposed to be aidman for this Wing."

"I know," said Kaluba. "I've picked a couple of the older men to fill in that duty." There was an awkward pause.

"Can I ask why, Captain?" said Cal.

"I suppose so," said Kaluba. His dark face looked tired. "You're an ex-mulebrain. And it's my commission if you take an active action in combat—you know the regulations. I think it'd be better all around if you weren't in on the drop."

"The Captain," said Cal, "doesn't trust me?"

"I don't trust your reflexes." Kaluba lowered his voice. "Fifteen hours from now, or less, some of these men will be badly hurt, and others will be dying. Are you dead sure you can just stand around and watch that happening?"

"That's right," said Cal.

"Well, I'm not."

"Captain," said Cal, "I think you may have just talked yourself into something. I'm aidman for this outfit, and you're going to need me on this drop." He kept his eyes steadily on Kaluba. "You're going to need every man on the list."

Kaluba chewed his lower lip angrily.

"I'm trained and I'm experienced," said Cal. "You leave me back up here and I'll write a letter of complaint to the Service accusing you of a personal bias against me. I don't think the reviewing board will think your reasons strong enough."

Kaluba's eyes flickered up at him. Then he looked down at the reports and swore.

"All right," he said. "Get some sleep."

Cal went back to his hammock and climbed in. Beside him, Wajeck, the Lieutenant officering B Section, was lying on his back on his hammock, gazing at the ceiling ten inches away.

His hairy-backed hands were gripping the edges of his hammock.

"Think of six beautiful women," Cal said to him.

"I'm all right," said Wajeck, not taking his eyes off the ceiling. "I'm just not sleepy."

They made their first wave landing thirteen hours later, the assault glider that carried Cal along with A and B Sections screaming in at five hundred feet of altitude to eject them right and left like tossed popcorn. Cal cut wide in his shoulder jets with a short burst and slid in to earth under a tree so like a terran cottonwood it was hard to tell the difference. The trees on windy hillsides on Lehaunan had been warped and strangely twisted like high-mountain conifers. On the world of the Griella, there had been no true trees. Only a sort of large bush. But here the trees were like trees and the cut-up rocky country all around and between them greened with a heavy moss that almost resembled grass.

Cal jettisoned his jets and checked his wrist scope. All the men of the two sections were down without trouble and already moving in on the red dot which marked the location of the senior Section Commander. That would be Walk. Cal took a bearing and moved, too.

He was two-thirds of the way to the twenty-foot-high cluster of rock where the red dot showed, when the first Paumons seeker torp came over the small hill at his left. It flashed black for a moment in his vision like a gnat flying right into his eye. And then the rocks he was headed for went up in a graceful, vase-shaped gout of brown earth and debris.

"Spread out! Spread out!" yelled Cal automatically. "Torps."

He had gone down without thinking at the black flicker in his vision. Now he rose and ran, changing direction, for the rocks. When he got there, he found a crater, five dead men, a boy with one leg blown off, and Lieutenant Wajeck. Wajeck was sitting up against a rock, apparently unhurt, but hugging himself as if he were cold.

"You all right?" said Cal to Wajeck. He got no answer. Cal turned to the boy with his leg off and got a shot into him and a tourniquet around the pressure point just inside the midthigh. He set the tourniquet to loosen at fifteen minute intervals—the boy was out cold—and turned to Wajeck.

"What's wrong with you?" he said, and pulled at the folded arms.

"Oh, God," said Wajeck, "I knew it. Right in the middle. I knew it, I knew it."

Cal got the arms apart and there was blood soaking through all over the stomach area of Wajeck's coveralls. There was a slit in the cloth like a torp fragment might make. Cal put his fingers in it, tore it wide, and looked inside. It was a bad hole. He got a patch on it and gave the other man a shot, but Wajeck's face was already beginning to go pinched and strange. Another torp came suddenly over the hills and Cal jerked Wajeck down with him to the ground, as the explosion went off not fifty yards from them.

"Oh, God," said Wajeck, quite plainly and clearly in Cal's ear as they lay on the ground together. "I knew it. I was sure. I knew it."

"Where's Walk?" said Cal. Another torp went off to their right.

"They switched him to Kaluba's glider. Last minute. He didn't come down with us. Oh, God . . ."

"Where're your Section Leaders?"

"There. There. Squadmen, too—" Wajeck twitched a hand and wrist toward the hole the torp had left and the dead bodies in and about it. "I told them to close when we ejected. So we'd come down ready to organize."

Cal stared along six inches of dirt at Wajeck's profile, staring up at the cloudless sky.

"Didn't you learn—" Cal broke off. "Somebody's got to get these men out of here. You must have a non-com somewhere still out there."

"No one. No one," said Wajeck's lips to the sky. They stopped suddenly. Jerkily his head turned sideways. He looked along the ground into Cal's eyes.

"You," he said. "You know what to do. Take over, for God's sake. You got to take over, Cal. Right now."

There was a shriek and a roar. A torp exploded so close to them it brought dirt raining down about them. The boy with the leg off had just come to, and he was hit again. He began screaming.

CHAPTER TEN

The men were dying, and someone was weeping. Looking around under the thunder and groundshake of the nearby exploding torps, Cal saw the one who wept was the boy with his leg off. He was lying on his back looking at the sky and tears were running out of the corners of his eyes, back into the blond sideburns in front of his ears. Cal looked back at Wajeck, who was trying to get the command scope off his wrist. But his fingers were already too weak to stretch the expansion band over his hand and the scope kept slipping back to his wrist.

"You got to!"

"I can't," said Cal. "Kaluba wasn't going to let me come on this drop because he figured I'd do something like that. It's my orders."

"You gut," said Wajeck, still fumbling like a baby with the expansion band. "You don't care about these men; you only care about keeping your uniform. Nobody lives by orders all the way, you know that." He was still fumbling with the scope band. "I'm going to make you do it, you lousy gut."

"Quit wearing yourself out," said Cal. He pulled the arm with the scope out of Wajeck's weak grasp of the other hand, and lifted arm, scope and all to his lips. He pressed the talk button. "All right, men," he said into it, "this is Lieutenant Truant. Lieutenant Wajeck is out of action, and so are all the non-coms. I'm a Contacts Officer and you know I can't take over. You need somebody in here to take over the command scope. I'll help all I can once one of you gets here. But that's my limit. Those torps'll have us all in another ten minutes, unless one of you forgets all he ever learned about not volunteering. Somebody better make up his mind and get in here fast."

For a moment there were no explosions. In the unusual silence that suddenly seemed all wrong, Cal looked about him. There were two or three large holes in the open space around him, but it looked like very little damage, just by itself. He had to remember that the seeker mechanism on the torps would almost certainly have found at least one man where every hole was now.

An assault soldier dodged out from behind a tree about eighty yards away and began running towards the rocks where Cal lay. Another broke cover off to the left about the same time, but, seeing the first ahead of him, dodged back again.

Cal counted the seconds, watching the man come on. But nothing happened. Only, the second after the man threw himself down beside Cal and Wajeck, a torp flitted over the hilltop and exploded to their left.

The man was in his thirties, small, with a sort of hazelnut-shaped face. Cal searched his memory.

"Mahauni?" he said.

"Yes, sir," said Mahauni. "What do I do?"

"What you think you ought to do," said Cal. "It's your show."

"Yes, sir. What would you do?"

"Get the men on the move. Keep them at least fifty feet apart." Cal pointed at the command scope on Wajeck's wrist. In a larger circle around the unit dots were the battalion signals, clustered now to their west. The two Sections under Wajeck had come down in this little area with a low, open hill to their east, scattered trees and, to the west, rising clusters of trees to a wooden horizon. Beyond that, about eight miles off, was battalion command.

"Perimeter's about five miles," said Cal. "When I was a soldier they had anti-torp defenses along battalion perimeters. I'll take the Lieutenant. You take the kid, there."

"Right," said Mahauni. He moved like an old hand, stripping the command scope off Wajeck's wrist and talking into it. He gave commands as if he might have been a Section Leader once. Or better.

"Ready to move," he said to Cal finally, the command scope now on his own thin, brown wrist.

They moved. The rest of it was simply horribly hard work, running and climbing with a wounded man apiece on their backs, shouting commands at the rest of the two Sections of men, and being lucky when the torps came over. They made it over the hill and safely at last within battalion defenses, with fifty-three men left out of a hundred and eighty-one that had been dropped.

By the evening of the day of the first drops, waves one, two and three of the Initial Assault Team were down on the Paumons ground, and regrouped. They formed a curving, staggered line of battalion fronts, arching around three Paumons cities and several hundred small settlements. The settlements were essentially housing centers, the cities essentially factory complexes for Paumons' heavy industry, which here was supplied by power from volcanic taps.

Cal, having checked in with Kaluba, had received permission to leave for a few hours and make contact with his own Contacts Service Command, for instructions. His supplementary and unannounced reason was to tell his story of the drop to someone like Scoby (who was in Contacts Service Command, along on the Expedition) before any other version of it should reach him. He had no idea where C.S. Command Headquarters was so he hunted up Expedition Command, where he would be able to get directions. He found it just a little before sunset—a camouflaged cluster of domes in a little clearing surrounded by tall trees of a cottonwood-like variety.

"Contacts Service HQ?" he asked a Wing Section who was passing between the domes.

"Check with the liaison desk, Command HQ, Dome Eight," said the Wing Section, brusquely, looking only at the Command Service patch on Cal's breast pocket and not at Cal's face. He pulled away and hurried off.

Cal found Dome Eight. He stepped through the vibration screen at its entrance and found himself in an outer office with several empty desks and chairs. A door in a thin partition led to an inner office from which the sound of a conversation came. It occurred to Cal belatedly that this would be the time for evening chow. The people belonging to the outer office, including the Liaison Desk Officer, would be off eating. He moved toward the inner office, then checked as he recognized one of the conversing voices as General Harmon's, the other as Colonel Alt's. It would hardly do to use the Commanding General of the Expedition and his aide as an information service. Cal took a seat beside the partition to wait for the return of the Liaison Desk Officer.

"—bismuth," Harmon's voice sounded thinly through the partition. "Their communications system depends on those thermopiles. We seal off this manufacturing area and they've got to come to us. Then we can make other drops. Here, hit them here, Zone Five. Zone Three. Around the planet here, in this mountainous section—Zone Eleven. By the way, we'll have to watch that spot for mop-up toward the end, Hag. It's natural country for a regular hornet's-nest of guerrillas. Put a strong-point out-side the mountains under somebody fitted for the work. But don't overload him with men. . . ."

Cal dismissed the voices and let his thoughts drift off to the subject of Annie. She would be with the Medics main unit, and that, too, would be locatable through the Liaison Desk. But he would not have time after finding Contacts Service HQ and tell-ing his story. . . .

". . . 4th Assault Wing, 91st Combat Engineers," Alt was saying. Cal came alert with a jerk, hearing his own outfit men-tioned. "A couple of sections, I understand."

"Yes," said Harmon's voice. "But outside of a couple of in-cidents like that, it was a near-perfect drop. Almost too perfect. We've got a fifty-year advantage in weapons on these Paumons, and it's making for too much complacency on our side."

"The men'll stiffen up as they get more action," said Alt.

"No doubt. But will it be soon enough? Soldiers aren't sup-posed to regard the enemy with good-humored contempt. They're supposed to hate 'em, and have a healthy fear of them. Anything else results in a lot of throats being cut the first dark night."

"I'll write up a general order."

"No good, Hag. Half the trouble's with the Progs. They're treating us as if we're halfway civilized, and we're treating them as if they were. Everybody forgets their fighting force outnum-bers ours six hundred to one from a mathematical standpoint. One of these days we'll wake up to find we've half-civilized ourselves into being completely surrounded and defeated." Har-mon broke off suddenly. "I've got it."

"Yes?"

"We've got about five hundred prisoners down below Head-quarters here, haven't we?"

"That's right, General."

"Pick a town behind our front here—say, this place here. What's its Prog name? Manaha? Get a good, stiff man and have him march those prisoners there, wounded and all. You under-stand, Hag?"

There was a slight pause. Cal suddenly sat bolt upright, lis-tening.

"I think so, sir," came Alt's voice.

"I'm not going to give any orders. Don't you, either. Just pick the right man."

"Yes, sir. I think I know who I can get."

"Handle that march right, and the word'll get out fast enough. It'll stiffen up the Paumons, and the Paumons'll take care of stiffening up our own boys. That's what—"

Quickly and quietly, Cal got up and out of the dome. He was in the new darkness of early night among the trees surrounding the Headquarters area, headed downhill, before he slowed. The little breeze among the trees felt abruptly cool on his forehead.

He kept going. The business of telling his story of the drop to Contacts HQ would have to wait, now. He stopped abruptly. He had headed off without thinking of direction. He would have to return at least to the edge of the HQ area to get his bearings. But he did not want to come back into the area by Dome Eight. He turned to his left and began to circle around the base of the hill on which the area was located.

A few moments later he came up against a steel fence. He turned and went down along it. A little ways further on he came out of the trees and saw Paumons standing behind the wire mesh of the fence. These must be the prisoners Harmon had been talking about. They stood silently in little clumps. The sun, Bellatrix, was down, but the western sky was still light. In the dusk what little light there was left glimmered here and there on light patches about the prisoners. The patches were bandages that they had put on the wounded by tearing up their own uniforms—dark green on the outside, and light green on the inside—and using them inside out. They stood silently, but he saw them watching him as he passed. In the dusk their figures were outlines, indistinct. They could have been Lehaunan—or human. He walked on.

"Bunnyrabbit!" said a voice.

The world rocked suddenly. One quick movement. Then it stopped and everything was just the same as it had been a moment before. Cal found he had stopped dead, and his hands were up at his chest, reaching to a harness that was not there. A great chill flowed over him. He turned sharply around.

The dim figures were still there. They did not seem to have moved. A single figure was standing closest to him, back a half a dozen steps, just on the other side of the wire. He went back and looked through the mesh at it. It was a Paumons with a large bandage all over one half of his face. It looked as if he had been badly wounded in the cheek and jaw. He saw the light-colored parts of the Paumons' eyes glitter at him in the gloom.

The Paumons said something. Cal had been taught the language. If what the Paumans had said had been understandable, he would have understood it. But it was not understandable. The other's jaw or tongue must have been damaged to the point of producing incomprehensibility. It was a mangled, bawling sound that made no sense. But it was directed at Cal, and there was a feeling behind it that matched the glitter of the eyes. Cal's ears had metamorphosed it into the recognizable human word.

Cal turned and walked off. After a moment, he stopped, turned and went back, but the prisoner who had spoken to him was no longer at the wire. He looked for a moment at the other motionless shapes, then turned for a final time and went up the slope in the darkness.

The outer office of Dome Eight was still empty, for which he was grateful. Harmon and Alt were still talking behind the partition. He walked up to the door in the partition, and knocked.

There was a pause inside.

"Who's that? Come in!" said Alt. Cal opened the door and stepped a half-step into the inner room. There was a desk at which Harmon was sitting, and Alt was standing half-turned toward the door, in front of the desk. There was a further door and, on the walls, maps and schematics.

"Lieutenant Truant, sir," said Cal. "Contacts Service. I thought I'd better speak to the Colonel. It's about the Paumons prisoners."

Alt turned his head a little bit and looked at Cal more directly.

"Prisoners?"

"Yes, sir."

"What about the prisoners?"

"I happened to pass the compound where they're being held, sir." said Cal. "And some of them spoke to me. You know they gave Contacts trainees the language."

"I know that," said Alt. "What about the prisoners?"

"I thought I'd speak to you, Colonel," said Cal. He looked directly into Alt's face. "The prisoners seem to think something's going to be done with them; they're going to be done away with, or something like that. I thought, as part of elementary Contacts, I might have the Colonel's permission to speak to them on his behalf and assure them they've got nothing to worry about; that they're going to be well treated."

Alt stared at him for a moment.

"You did, did you?" he said.

"Yes, sir."

From behind the desk, Cal could see Harmon also looking at him. The General was tilted a little backwards in his chair, and he had been gazing at Cal all this time with no expression on his face except a sort of steady interest.

"Tell me, Lieutenant," said Alt. "Did you just come in to the outer office, there?"

"Well, yes sir," said Cal. "I did. There was no one out front, so I took a chance and knocked on your door. I didn't realize you were busy with the General."

"That's quite all right," said Harmon. Cal turned his head toward the seated man. "Tell me, aren't you the officer I sent over to see General Scoby, back in Denver?"

"That's right, General."

"I thought so," said Harmon. "I've got quite a good memory for certain things." He sat up straight and businesslike. "Well, Colonel, I think the Lieutenant here should do what he suggests, don't you? We want to make an early start on good Contacts with the Paumons. Wait outside, will you, Lieutenant? The Colonel will have some more specific orders for you as soon as we're done here."

Cal went out into the outer office and took a chair well away from the partition. He heard the conversation begin again between Harmon and Alt, but the voices were not so loud now and it was not possible to make out the words. After some minutes, the officers and men belonging to the outer office began to come in.

"Did you want to see me, Lieutenant?" asked the Captain at the Liaison Desk—a tall young man with blond hair already veering back at the temples—as he sat down.

"I wanted to locate Contacts HQ," said Cal. "But Colonel Alt asked me to wait on another matter."

"Oh," said the Captain. "Well, Contacts is about three miles west by the Medics, at Grid four-five-seven-zero. I imagine Colonel Alt will be calling you shortly."

The lights were all turned up in the outer office, now, and the four enlisted men and three officers were all busily at work. Over the noise of their occupation, Cal heard a door close beyond the partition wall. A minute or so later, Alt put his head out of the partition door.

"Truant," he said.

Cal got up and went into the inner office. Alt faced him inside, his legs a little spread apart, his shoulders hunched.

"Lieutenant," Alt said. "We're going to get some orders cut for you. You won't have to go back to your assigned outfit. Those Paumons prisoners you saw are going to be walked to a Prisoner of War center we're setting up about forty miles from here at a town called Manaha. General Harmon suggested, and I agree, that since POWs generally are handled as a part of Contacts Service business, you might be the very man to manage moving them there. The General wants them there by tomorrow night. We'll give you four armed enlisted men. You can move out at dawn."

CHAPTER ELEVEN

Nothing happened in a hurry, of course. Cal's outfit had to be notified, and the Contacts Service HQ, and then his orders had to be printed up. It took several hours and as they were just getting into it, the Liaison Desk Captain, who did not seem to share the popular prejudice against Contacts people, suggested Cal see about food and billeting for the night, sending him over to Officers Quarters. Cal got himself allotted a bunk and served some field rations and coffee. The Duty Officer, a young Lieutenant, came in and sat down and had a cup of coffee with him in the empty messroom.

"We'll roll these Progs up in three months," said the Duty Officer. "They've never been hit like this before. It stuns them; and they just give up. I saw them bringing them in all day today."

The Lieutenant was wearing the patch of the Administrative Service.

"Yeah," said Cal. "Can I get some more coffee?"

"Urn's over there. Help yourself," said the Lieutenant. "Of course, they're aliens. They can't help it. But it may well be practically a bloodless conquest."

As soon as he had his printed orders, Cal went back down to the compound where the prisoners were. He showed the orders to the Section Leader in charge of guarding them.

"I want to talk to their leader," said Cal. The Section un-locked the gate and let him in. There was no illumination inside the fence, but they had set up searchlights outside, and the harsh glare of these cast back a sort of bare stage-lighting over the Paumons standing around in little groups inside. Now that it was illuminated, Cal could see the extent of the compound, which was about five hundred feet on the square. The only structures inside it were a sanitation dome, and a small office dome.

"I want to talk to your ranking officer," said Cal in Paumons, to the figures nearest to him. Without waiting for an answer, he went on into the office dome, which had a table and a few chairs, and sat down behind the table.

After a few minutes the door opened and two unwounded Pau-mons came in and stood before the desk. At first glance they looked alike as all the others did. But Cal, searching hard for differences, saw that the one facing him on the right was a little taller and stood straighter. The one on the left, without any particular identifiable sign of it, gave an impression of greater age. They both wore the piping on their trousers and jacket battle dress that identified them as officers.

"Sit down," said Cal in Paumons, indicating two chairs he had arranged on the other side of the desk.

"No," said the one on the right. "I am General Commander Wantaki. This is my aide, Leader Ola Tain."

"All right," said Cal. "I'm the officer who is going to be responsible for moving everybody in this compound to more permanent quarters tomorrow. We will move out at dawn."

"Everyone?" said Wantaki. "A good quarter of the men here are walking wounded, and there are close to seven sixes of men who cannot walk."

"That's why I am talking to you tonight," said Cal. "It is a very long day's march to where we are going, even for your well people. But I have my orders and I must carry them out. I will do what I can, but you must all travel. So I tell you now."

"What good does that do?" said Wantaki harshly.

"Listen," cautioned his companion, Ola Tain, who had not spoken up until now.

"I suggest you make preparations," said Cal. "Rig litters and assign those who are well to help the walking wounded. I have already arranged to have litter poles and fabric for the litters and for bandages to be given you."

"You show an unusual amount of courage to come in here

without at least a sidearm," said Wantaki. "Some of my people, and I do not exclude myself, might not be able to resist the temptation."

"I belong to a branch of the human army known as the Contacts Service," said Cal. "The Contacts Service never bears arms or joins in the fighting."

"They would be well advised to change their ways in the seasons to come," said Wantaki. "If you supply us with poles and fabric, we will use them. Is that all?"

"That is all," said Cal. They went out. He himself went out and returned to the gate. The Section Leader of the Guard let him out.

"I've made arrangements with Quatermaster to have some litter materials and stuff delivered to the prisoners," Cal told him. "Let it through to them when it comes."

He went back to Officers Quarters and turned in to his assigned bunk. He went off to sleep immediately, but several hours later he was awakened by the Duty Officer.

"What's up?" said Cal thickly. Ugly dark half-remembered shapes were still thronging the back of his brain.

"You were yelling," said the Duty Officer. "Some kind of a nightmare or something, about rabbits."

In the pale light of predawn, near the fence, Cal could see the four armed men he had been given to control the five-hundred-odd prisoners on the march. He imagined Alt had personally selected them. Two were youngsters. One had his hair cropped to a stubble and a thin, wide, sharp-looking mouth in a thin face. The other was small and large-eyed. One was of the same type and age as Mahauni, the mulebrain who had taken over command of the outfit under the torps. These were all buck soldiers. There was a non-com, too, a Squadman. He was lanky, black-haired, and tall. He did not call the men to attention as Cal came up, but stayed lounging against the fence above the other three seated on the grass. They were all wearing full harness and weapons.

"You the prisoner guard?" said Cal as he came up.

"That's us," drawled the non-com, not moving, glancing at Cal's Contacts Service patch.

"What's your name?" Cal asked him.

"My friends call me Buck," said the Squadman. Cal waited. "Allen," said the Squadman.

"All right, Allen," said Cal, in the same tone of voice. "You report back to your outfit and tell them to send me somebody else. Tell them you impressed me as being sloppy, unreliable and insubordinate, and that I said I couldn't use you.''

Allen straightened up with a jerk.

"Hey, wait a minute—'' he began. But Cal was turning to the other three.

"On your feet," he said. They scrambled up. Behind him, Cal heard the Squadman talking.

''. . . senior man of the Combat Services gives the orders in the field. You don't tell me—''

Cal looked around. ''I thought I gave you an order," he said.

"Listen, Lieutenant, I—''

"Get in there," said Cal, turning back to the three others. "Start counting the prisoners, and see that all the wounded who can't walk have litters." They went off.

Cal watched them go down the fence, in through the gate and out of earshot. The Squadman was still talking. He stopped when he saw Cal's face.

"Listen," said Cal, holding his voice down. He could feel his arms beginning to shake from the tensed muscles in them. "Listen, soldier. Get one thing clear in that head of yours. You're here to do what I tell you, and exactly what I tell you in getting these prisoners to Manaha. You can just forget anything else. Never mind rule books or the kind of Contacts Officers you maybe ran into in the past. Just remember that on the official papers it's just you and me, all alone on this trip. And if you think your two stripes can play games with these—Cal jabbed a rod-stiff finger at his Lieutenant's tabs—"just you try it. And I'll hang your hind end, boy. Remember that. No matter what happens to me, when the dust settles you're going to find yourself in front of a long table with five officers of the rank of major or above behind it.''

Cal quit talking. He was shaking all over now. He knew Allen could see it, but he didn't give a damn.

"Well?" he said. Allen was not moving. He stood stiff and stared straight ahead. His face was pale. ''All right," said Cal, almost in a whisper. "I'm going to take you along and you're going to see that you and those other three do the job they're supposed to do. Now, get in there and get them organized.''

Allen turned and went. Cal watched him go, and gradually the case of shakes he had picked up began to leak out of him.

They actually got the Paumons prisoners moving by half an hour after sunrise, which was even better than Cal had hoped. He had figured it would take a full hour to get the march actually on the road. What helped was the authority of Wantaki and Ola Tain. They had taken over internal command of the march; and Cal wisely let them be.

He and his four soldiers wore jump belts; and he had a man pogo-sticking along on each side of the column, one at the rear and Allen up front. He jumped back and forth from tail to rear of the marching column, himself.

It was a good-weather day; there was that much in its favor. They were in the southern latitudes of the northern hemisphere and high up. The air was dry. To begin with, the column made nearly three miles an hour, but that could not last, Cal thought. He moved back and forth along one side of the column, then in the opposite direction along the other. The Paumons prisoners marched steadily, in a rough column of fours, two whole individuals on each side of a wounded, two frequently changed on each litter. Their eyebrowless, dish-shaped faces seemed to show no expression. They talked little among themselves. He found himself getting curious about them.

There was an atmosphere of numbness about them, a leaden quality. They marched like people in a dream, or about some dreary, routine task. Only up at the head of the column were exceptions to this to be found. There, Wantaki strode with heavy, jarring footfalls, staring straight ahead like a thwarted wrestler. Beside him, Ola Tain paced soberly, but apparently calmly.

Now that Cal had time to study the two leaders, he found himself puzzled by Ola Tain. Wantaki he could understand to a certain extent. The Paumons Commander had the ring of the military about him. But Ola Tain did not seem to belong at all. He was almost like a priest.

They had been stopping at Cal's order ten minutes out of every hour. They also stopped at noon. Nobody had known anything about rations for the prisoners, or even what the Paumons ate, when Cal had asked about it back at HQ before leaving. So the column was without food. They did not complain about it, but sat quietly in the brilliant, high-altitude sunlight from small, bright Bellatrix, like a white coin in the sky. Glanced at for just a fraction of a second, it left a black after-image burning against the closed eyelid, floating about with the hidden movements of the eyeballs.

When the order came to move on, they took up their march again. But they were definitely slowing. It was the wounded who were holding the rest back. They went through several small towns, but the white, low buildings on either side of the narrow, winding streets were locked up tight and no Paumons civilians showed themselves. By mid-afternoon, Cal was forced to call another halt and the prisoners, particularly the litter-bearers, went down where they stood as if they had been so much grain cut by a scythe.

Cal sat on a little rise of ground at the side of the road and let them lie. After about twenty minutes, Allen came up to him.

"How long we going to leave them here, Lieutenant?" the Squadman asked. Cal looked up at the man without answering, and Allen wet his lips and went away.

It occurred to Cal that he had no idea how much endurance the Paumons might have. It might be less, or more, than humans in the same position. He got up and went up to the head of the column. Wantaki was there, sitting on a roadside boulder, looking back over the column of men. One muddy, rust-colored hand was on his knee, curled up into a fist. His face was as hard and washed clean as a stone seen under running water in a mountain stream fed by glaciers. He sat alone. Ola Tain was a little ways off, also alone, lying on a hillside. Cal turned and went toward Tain.

They had come to a wide open area of the plateau now, with only an occasional clump of the cottonwood trees. In between the heaved up rock, in the stony soil, the green moss was everywhere. There was a faint, sweet odor to it, like lavender.

The moss deadened the sound of Cal's footsteps, and Ola Tain evidently did not hear him approaching. The Paumons aide was lying on one elbow, the forefinger of the hand belonging to that elbow tracing out the small, feathery stems of the moss-plant directly underneath it. His face was absorbed. Cal's steps slowed as he watched the other. For the first time, now, he saw that there were tiny yellow blossoms hidden among the cone-shaped leaves of each miniature stem, and that Ola Tain's finger was counting these.

Cal felt a constriction in his guts and his throat tightened. There came to him suddenly a strong and desperate longing to know what sort of feelings moved inside the breathing, living being just a few feet from him; a sort of terrible loneliness. He opened his mouth to speak, but all that happened was that he made a sound in his throat. Ola Tain looked up.

"I need some information," said Cal, in Paumons. "I did not think now would be a good time to ask the General Commander."

Ola Tain's glance slid past Cal to Wantaki, and back to Cal again.

"No," he said.

"I want to know," said Cal, "how your people are standing up to the march. We have still over half the distance to go."

"You see," said Ola Tain, nodding toward the column. "Can you tell us what our destination is?"

"Manaha. I have no means to take care of stragglers."

"I had noticed that." Ola Tain looked at him for a moment. "You are doing the best you can for us within your orders?"

"Yes."

"I had thought so, myself. I will help as I can."

"If we take until tomorrow dawn, will all make it?"

"We will pray so."

Cal lingered, looking down at him.

"You pray?" he said.

"Sometimes," said Ola Tain. "I am praying today."

"What to?"

"Does it matter?" said Ola Tain.

"I guess not." Cal looked back over the column, then down at Ola Tain again. "You're a strange sort of soldier."

"I am not really a soldier. I teach—" the term he gave did not translate well. Something between philosophy and anthropology, in the Paumons sense.

"*He* is a soldier," Cal nodded toward Wantaki. "He hates us, doesn't he?"

"Yes," said Ola Tain.

"Do you hate us?"

"I try not to. Hate gets in the way of clear thinking. But . . ." Ola Tain hesitated. "Yes, I hate you, too." He looked back down at the flowers of the moss.

"Well," said Cal, after a second, "we're only ensuring the safety of our bases and our people, you know."

"Please." Ola Tain did not look up. "Do not make it harder for me to try not to hate you."

Cal went back to the column, and to Squadman Allen.

"Get 'em moving," he said.

With the declining of the sun, the air cooled quickly. At first that seemed to have a good effect on the prisoners and revived the column. But as Bellatrix sought the horizon, what had been merely a pleasant coolness now began to approach a chilliness. With the long night ahead of him, Cal faced the fact that the only way to keep the most of his prisoners moving was to get some food and drink into them.

He took Ola Tain and went ahead up to the next town. Together and alone, they came on the small place by surprise. There were lights in the windows and female Paumons and children moving about the streets. They stared for a moment at the sight of Cal, then scattered to their buildings. Ola Tain left him and went on into the heart of the town, alone.

He was some little time getting back. When he returned, he was followed by a female driving a civilian balloon-tired transport carrying food and drink of the Paumons variety.

"Well, you got it," said Cal to Ola Tain, as they headed back toward the column with the truck going ahead.

"With your people attacking, they did not want to spare it," said Ola Tain, looking ahead to the truck. "It is not easy." After a moment, he said, "I had to threaten them with you."

They got back to the column, which had built fires. After the prisoners had eaten, they appeared stronger. But at the next halt, Allen came up to Cal.

"There's five of them dead," he said. "They've been carrying them all this time in the litters so we'd think they were wounded."

"If they can keep up, let them," said Cal.

But during the long night, the column began to straggle. Cal ordered the dead left behind, and in the process found that there were now twelve corpses in the column. They left them behind and went on, the exhausted, four to a litter now, carrying the near-dead, the staggering wounded helping each other. Cal increased his halts to one every half-hour.

Dawn found them straggling through another small town. Word of their movement had gone ahead of them over the civilian Paumons communications system, which was still operating. With Manaha, their destination, only a little over two miles off, the civilians had grown bolder and more in sympathy with the prisoners. They said nothing, but they peered from windows and rooftops, and dodged up side streets out of the way, as the column reeled forward.

As they emerged from the last village before Manaha, they found the road ahead lined with the old, the female and the young. They moved back from the road as Allen, leading the column, came toward them, but they waved in again toward the plodding prisoners as he passed. Looking ahead now, along the semi-open country ahead, Cal could see the distant glint of sun on windows that would be Manaha. He looked back at the reeling column; at the civilian Paumons, leaning in toward it as if over some invisible barrier rope. Wantaki and Ola Tain still moved ahead of the rest.

There was a slight bend in the road, and, as Allen reached it, the crowd of Paumons children there shrank back. But as he passed on, they bulged forward. There was a sudden flurry in their ranks, and a small, male youngster darted toward Ola Tain, who was closest.

The thin young soldier with the wide mouth snapped up his machine pistol.

"Hold it!" shouted Cal, as the youngster darted back again into the safety of the crowd, leaving Ola Tain holding a green and leafy branch from one of the cottonwood-type trees. For a long moment Ola Tain looked at it in his hands; and then, holding it upright before him, took up the march again.

A moment later, another child, a little older this time, darted out with a branch for Wantaki.

Soon, branches were being delivered to prisoners, all along the column. Allen came back to Cal.

"Sir?" he said, looking at Cal.

"Leave them alone," said Cal harshly.

Allen went back to the head of the column. Soon all the prisoners had branches. Each carried his own upright before him, their shoulders straightened, and stepping out. As they came into Manaha at last, they looked like a forest on the move. And they were marching like soldiers.

CHAPTER TWELVE

Cal rejoined his outfit after that, and for the next six months he worked with Battalion as Interpreter, questioning prisoners.

The Expedition made large advances, conquering most of the planet. It went as Harmon had predicted. The Paumons had to come to the Expedition on the plateau, and the Expedition made large-scale drops of fighting forces elsewhere around the world.

But it was not a bloodless conquest. It took the Paumons some time to learn not to fight head-on battles against the vastly superior equipment of the Expedition, that whenever they did they suffered heartbreaking losses. The Expedition also suffered losses. At the end of six months they had received three sets of replacements for the Combat Services; their casualties were over seventy-five thousand. Estimates of the Paumons casualties put those at over two million dead and wounded. Cal was promoted twice, to First Lieutenant and then to Captain, and was brought back to take charge of the big new Prisoner-of-War center next to Expedition Headquarters and Expedition Main Hospital at Manaha. This gave him a chance to be with Annie, who was stationed at Main Hospital. He heard occasionally of Walk, who was making a name for himself as commander of a newly formed guerilla-hunting group. Promotions had been faster in the Combat Services, and Walk had made major.

One day Annie called Cal from over at Hospital Receiving to say they had just brought Walk in with multiple wounds of the arm and leg from a Paumons mortar. Cal juggled his schedule for the day and went over to the hospital. He found Walk had already been put into a room by himself. In the anteroom outside were Annie, who was charting up the readings of the preliminary checkover the Medical Officer had given Walk, and a Public Relations Officer from Administrative, who was there to write him up for a news release back on Earth.

"Can I go in and see him?" Cal asked Annie.

"In a minute," she said, coding up results of the checkover, with her fingers hopping over the machine keys. "I'll take you in. I asked to be his nurse."

"Are you a buddy of his?" asked the PR Officer, a neat First Lieutenant with a mustache. "The officers and men of his outfit idolize him, I hear. And to the Paumons he's almost a legend they tell to frighten their children into being good. Maybe we can get some pictures of the two of you together. His story is one long string of heroic exploits after another. They say even the aliens respect him."

"You can come in now," said Annie to Cal. They went in together. Walk was lying in a hospital bed, under a light top sheet only. He was so tanned and thin he looked like a sun-blackened corpse against the white sheets. His eyes focused crazily on Cal as he came up to the side of the bed.

"Cal . . ." he muttered. "What're you doing here? Get out . . . Get back to base. . . ."

"He's out of his head," said Annie. She folded Walk's arm up and put a hypodermic syringe gun against the side of it. After a moment his eyes began to clear. He recognized Cal sensibly, and his lips twisted in a hard line.

"Captain Truant," he said.

"How're you feeling?" asked Cal.

"Like a million," said Walk. "Just like a million." He made an effort to pull himself up on his pillow. "Nurse—" He recognized Annie. "Annie, they got any liquor around here for the casualties?"

"I'm sorry," said Annie, "but they've got to do some operating on you."

". . . them," said Walk. His tongue was beginning to thicken. Annie had evidently given him some fast-acting sedation. ". . . you, too. All of you . . . The universe. That's all it's good for. . . ."

His eyes closed and he passed out. Annie put a gentle hand on Cal's arm.

"That's all right," said Cal. "It doesn't matter. I was figuring he'd be like this."

He went back to his office at the POW compound. There was a message that General Scoby wanted to see him, but Ola Tain had been waiting in his outer office for half an hour. In the large Manaha POW Center that now held over eighty thousand Paumons, Ola Tain was Cal's most valuable connection. It was as Scoby had implied in his talk with Cal after Cal had graduated from Contacts School, back in Denver. There were no rules for building a basis for co-existence with those you had conquered. You could only feel your way.

Cal felt it mainly through Ola Tain. Wantaki had escaped early. He and five of his officers had broken out and got clean away the second week of their internment at Manaha. Cal was convinced that Ola Tain could have gone at that time, also, if he had wanted to. But he had chosen to stay and speak for the other prisoners. The other prisoners seemed to respect him, but not absorb him. It was as if he was alien to them, too. Cal had asked once if he was never lonely.

"No," said Ola Tain. "One can only be lonely within walls. And I have never built any."

Now Cal stopped in the outer office to explain that he would have to get over and see Scoby.

"There's no hurry about my business," said Ola Tain. "I have only promised to ask again that the recreation area be enlarged."

"I'll ask General Scoby about it," said Cal.

He went on over to Contacts Service HQ. Scoby, busy at his desk as Cal came in, looked as if he, his office, and Limpari the cheetah had been transported all in a package from Denver, without even disturbing the papers piled on the desk. Cal repeated Ola Tain's request.

"No," replied Scoby. He leaned back in his chair and stared at Cal, seated opposite him. "They don't really want more space. They just want to find out if the rumor's true."

"What rumor?"

"That if peace is signed next month, they'll all be released."

"I hadn't heard that."

"It's circulating," said Scoby. "What do you think we ought to do about it?"

"Do?" said Cal.

"That's what I said."

"Nothing. The whole thing's crazy. In the first place we're a lot more than a month from signing peace, anyway. Wantaki's still back in those mountains of Zone Eleven with better than thirty thousand men."

"Thirty thousand isn't much," said Scoby with one of his sudden spasms of mildness. "They can be ignored. The main civilian Paumons representatives are ready to ignore him and sign."

"You mean they'd leave him in the position of an outlaw—the Commander that fought harder for them than anyone else? Him and thirty thousand men, to say nothing of all the other guerrilla groups around the world?"

"They're a lot like us," said Scoby. "Or hadn't you noticed?"

"I noticed," said Cal bitterly.

Scoby gazed at him for a moment.

"Trouble with you, Cal," he said, "is you're still expecting miracles from people—and I mean people of all sorts, Lehaunan, Griella, Paumons, as well as human. That's the trouble with most of us. We quit expecting the worst from people, so right away we've got to swing over and start expecting nothing but the best."

"If the General will forgive me," said Cal. "I'll try to do better next time."

"And don't get sarcastic. You've learned a lot this last year but I still know a few things more than you do. One of them is how particularly important this particular race is to us. Or can you tell me that too?"

Cal thought a moment.

"No," he said, finally, "I guess not."

"They're important just because they are so damn much like us," said Scoby. "Long as the races we were knocking over were covered with fur, or had prehensile noses, we could go on calling them Pelties or Anteaters. We could shut our eyes to the fact that they had about as much brains, or probably about as much soul as we had. But an alien we got to call 'Prog,' now— that's getting a little like 'God' or 'Nigger.' You're sort of straining to point up the difference. And yet it stood to reason if we were going to bump into other thinking races out among the stars, sooner or later one of them was bound to be pretty human."

He stopped. He looked at Cal for a reaction.

"I guess you're right," said Cal.

"Of course," said Scoby, "I'm using the word *human* in only its finest sense."

"I guessed you were," said Cal. "So being like us is what makes the Paumons so important?"

"That's right," said Scoby. "What would you do if you were a Paumons and this was Earth, and you had eighty thousand 'Humies' out behind that wire when peace was signed? Would you want to turn them loose?"

Cal straightened up in his chair.

"Hell, no!" he said. "I see what you mean."

"Not unless you wanted to start the conquest all over again, that right?" said Scoby. "How far would you say these people are from being re-educated into living side by side with us?"

"Twenty years," said Cal. "Do something with the next generation maybe."

"Don't kid yourself. Five generations'll have a hard time wiping out the fact we started things out by coming in and trompling them."

"Can you talk General Harmon out of releasing them?"

"No."

"Then we're helpless," said Cal. "We're just giving them back an army. This and the other POW camps—they'll have three-quarters of a million men under arms again in half a year. And we can't do a thing."

"Not quite," said Scoby. "Once peace is signed, Contacts Service Head can interdict any step taken by Combat Services Commander, if Contacts Head thinks it'll lead to a breach of the peace."

"Ouch," said Cal. "But you wouldn't want to do that to Harmon."

"No. But then I won't have to," said Scoby. "You will."

Cal sat up straighter suddenly. He stared at Scoby, but Scoby was not smiling.

"Me?" Cal said.

"I told you I'd been grooming you," said Scoby. "I've got men here who've been with me sixteen years. But you've got the Combat experience, and you've got the guts. You've got something else, too."

"But me—" said Cal, and stopped.

"Every Expedition the mulebrains in the field talk about how they should all hang together and go back as a unit to straighten out the ex-mulies in Government. The man on the spot always thinks he knows best. Rubs Government the wrong way. It's happening now—politics, boy. Now's the time for me to get things from Government. I've got to go back to Earth and fight for our team."

"I'm not sure I can do that," said Cal slowly.

"I'm sure for you," said Scoby. "I'm having orders cut now, giving you a double jump to Lieutenant Colonel. You'll have as much authority here as I would—just not the reputation to back it up. That you've got to make yourself." Scoby grinned. "Be happy, boy. You're going up in the world."

CHAPTER THIRTEEN

Cal saw Scoby off from the Headquarters field just outside Manaha. The field had been leveled and poured only six months before. But the green moss could grow anywhere, and where it was not burnt away daily by the ascending ships, it had flung long arms across the concrete. It was destroyed by a puff of heat, the touch of a human foot. But it grew again overnight. Standing with Scoby, waiting for boarding orders to be announced on the slim, small courier ship that would take the older man home, Cal could see, less than forty yards away, the great tower of the Expedition's flagship black against the morning sky. It had not moved since landing on this spot eleven days, local time, after the first drops in which Cal had come down with Wajeck and the others. It carried the sheathed sword of nuclear explosives under its armor, that could potentially devastate the world it stood on for half a thousand miles in every direction from where it stood. It could wound a planet; and from four hundred and twenty-six feet above Cal and Scoby, in the observation room, the single caretaker soldier aboard it could be looking down on them all. From the main screen he could be seeing the lesser ships below him, and the field, and Manaha, with all the main strength of the Expedition laid out like a toy scale model below. And even on this lord of space and war, the moss at its base was already beginning to lay its tender, green relentless fingers.

The hooter sounded, announcing boarding orders.

"Hold hard, Cal," said Scoby, one fist clutching the handle of Limpari's harness. He put his hand out blindly, and Cal took it. In the last moment one of his blackouts had taken him and he could not see. They shook. "Now, girl," he muttered to Limpari. And smoothly and powerfully, she led him away from Cal and onto the ship.

Cal went back to Contacts HQ and a work day that in the several months following stretched to better than ten hours as a routine matter. He had little time even to see Annie. He had come to depend on her heavily, but when she suggested that they might get married—he had never mentioned it—the violence of his reaction startled even him.

"No!" he had shouted at her. "Not now! Can't you see that? Not now!"

He had turned and flung himself three angry strides away from her, from the hospital desk where she was sitting on duty, at the moment she had mentioned it. Down the hall, an ambulatory patient had turned, surprised, to stare. Ashamed suddenly, he came back to the desk, but muttering under his breath, still, "Not now. Now's not the time, Annie. Can't you see that?"

She did not press him.

The peace was signed. Wantaki was now an outlaw in Zone Eleven, with now nearly twenty thousand Paumons. Walk, recovered, was also back in Zone Eleven, harrying the Paumons leader from a series of strong posts encircling the base of the mountains. Harmon signed the order releasing all Paumons prisoners of war, and Cal stood at his office window and watched as the waves of prisoners celebrating their release literally tore the gates from their hinges and ripped half the compound to shreds along with it. For a day and a night, riot threatened in and around Manaha. Three mechanized battalions were ordered in to patrol the area. Subdued, the Paumons ex-prisoners melted away to their own home area. Five days later, Cal looked out at the torn and empty shells of the buildings in the compound as rain began to fall.

The initial drops of the Expedition had been timed to come at the earliest possible date after the winter season on this plateau. Now a new winter season—a time of rain—was upon the high, arid country about. Day in and day out, the gray curtains of the rain obscured the landscape as Cal went back and forth between Contacts HQ, Expeditions HQ, the Medical Center, and his own quarters.

For two months the rainy season continued. Meanwhile, elsewhere about the planet, the yeast of the returned Paumons fighting men was beginning to ferment. The Paumons civilian authorities made apparently honest attempts to comply with the plan for reorganization and re-education of their people. But the whole planet now was beginning to quake and gasp from unexpected fumaroles, like cooking oatmeal before it comes to an active boil. The Paumons people were torn, divided and violent. On the one hand there were outlaw resistance groups even in the large cities, haunted by human soldiery and their own police as well. On the other hand, in Zone Eleven, Walk commanded one whole fighting unit made up of Paumons enlistees and ex-soldiers. Ugly stories began to emerge from Zone Eleven, and from the activities of resistance groups elsewhere. Prisoners were not taken so often; and those who were taken by both sides were liable to turn up later as corpses in not-so-pretty condition.

Cal, trapped in a snarl of paperwork and tripped up on every hand by inefficiency or petty resentment on the part of Contacts

Officers over whose heads Scoby had promoted him by putting him in Paumons authority, saw a crisis approaching. He messaged Scoby back on Earth, saying that the greater authority of the older man was badly needed with the Expedition. Scoby sent back word that he could not possibly come before six weeks. Talk to Harmon, he advised. Cal made an attempt to do so, but his appointments with the Commander of the Expedition had a way of being canceled at the last moment. Harmon messaged that he would have his office set up time for a talk with Cal at the first opportunity. Time slipped by.

The six weeks came and went. Harmon remained incommunicative. Scoby had not come, or sent word he was coming. Cal, working alone in his office early one evening—he understood better now why Scoby's desk had always been loaded with papers—at endless reports and explanations of reports, heard the single snap of a fire rifle close under his window. And then two more snaps.

There was a commotion in his outer office. His door burst open, and a Paumons whom he suddenly recognized as Ola Tain half-fell inside. There was a babble of voices beyond in the outer office as Cal jumped up and helped the other into a chair. Ola Tain was burnt clear through the body twice. He could not live. The office door banged open again, and Cal, looking up, saw a hard-faced and shoulder-scorched man in the entrance whom he did not recognize—and then with a sudden shock did recognize. He had looked a little like Walk, but he was Washun, the Contacts Cadet who had shared Cal's second tour of Basic at Fort Cota. The Contacts shoulder patch on his jacket now was stained and ancient.

"It's Walker Blye, in Zone Eleven," said Washun. "He's planning a massacre."

CHAPTER FOURTEEN

The two-man atmosphere ship fled westward at forty thousand feet of altitude. It caught up with the retreating sunset, passed it and came down half a world away in late afternoon at Garrison Number Three of Zone Eleven—Walk's Headquarters.

The garrison was drained empty of men. The senior man was a non-com, a Wing Section. It was Tack. He and Cal looked at each other like close relatives that have been raised at far distances from each other, and to different customs, as Cal questioned him.

"He left six hours since," said Tack. "He took twenty-eight hundred men and all equipment back in the hills. To that place they call the Valley of the Three Towns—how did you know?"

"A Paumons named Ola Tain," said Cal. "Wantaki knows about Walk's plan. Was he crazy? He could be court-martialed for this."

"He *is* crazy," said Tack, lowering his voice, and glancing at Washun, who had made the trip with Cal, and now stood at the long end of the Headquarters Office, out of earshot. "He doesn't care—about anything. And he's always drunk, now. But you say Wantaki's laying for him?"

"Yes," said Cal. His body felt heavy and tired and old. "Tain came to your own Contacts man in this area"—he gestured at Washun—"to try and stop the whole thing. But your tame Paumons caught him and shot him up. Washun rescued him and got him to me. But he couldn't even talk by that time." Cal felt bitter inside. "He was shot again outside my office by some fool."

"Can you get to Walk in time?"

"Give me a combat-ground car. I'll try."

The sunset caught up with Cal once more as he shoved the little round car, alone, along an unpaved roadway back into the jagged, tree-covered young mountains of Zone Eleven. In the darkness, the trees looked even more like Earthly trees, the dirt road like some back-country trail of home. The combat car, fleeing a few inches above the pounded dirt of the road on the soft, shushing noise of its countless tiny jets, seemed to be pouring itself into the pit of the quickly falling darkness. And there came on Cal suddenly one of those seconds of strange emotion he had been used to calling "inside-out" moments when he was a boy—while his mother was still alive. For the first time he recognized that he had never had them after her death. But now one was with him once again and he saw himself with a strange, still, twilight clarity, as if from a little distance, a different viewpoint just outside his body. And what he saw had a sadly comical lack of sense and yet a sharp understanding.

What, he wondered suddenly, was he doing here in this heavy, adult body? In a complicated vehicle, on this strange world, upon this alien soil? To what dangerous explosion of things were the steel bars of events channeling him? He was bound to save some lives, to avert some kind of disaster. But was that really the purpose, was that really the meaning? For a moment he found himself storm-tossed on a sea of endless mystery. And then the road curved suddenly and his own automatic hands, jerking the combat car into the turn, snapped things sharply into pitilessly clear and unambiguous focus in his mind.

It was not any faceless duty that he was facing here, but the sharp spectre of his own guilt. It was not the Paumons villages, but Walk he was rushing to save, so that he might still save himself.

For it was Walk, his dark twin; Walk, his other self, for whom he was responsible and had always been responsible. Annie had seen it, when she had burst out in the hospital back on Earth after the Lehaunan expedition, that Walk was the weak one. Weak he was not, in the ordinary sense. But when they had gravitated together instinctively as boys—two motherless half-orphans—Walk had been the one with greater need and less initiative of imagination. Cal had taken the Services' side in revenge against his father for his mother's death. But Walk, following Cal's greater imagination into the glory-land of a military life which Cal had fashioned as a club against Cal's father, had had no buried knowledge of its unreality outside Cal's mind. Walk had believed. He had followed the sound of the trumpet, expecting to find the home and the kin he lacked behind it. And Cal, who had known his lie for what it was from the beginning, deep inside, had escaped his own mirage—but left Walk behind with it, stumbling in the desert.

Walk had pursued the mirage of love, and, not finding it, had grown more savage and murderous. He would *force* the mirage to be real. He would *force* his cause to be just, his fighting noble, his life, when it came to an end, to be a worthy price paid on a purchase of value. And all the time he was doing this, the undeniable realization grew stronger and stronger in him that his god was an empty shell, his purposes false, and he faced no final dedication, but the closed-in grave of a brain-mad wolf.

But the sin in this, it came home to Cal now, was on Cal's head. For whatever small credit, he might try to count work he had done with the Paumons prisoners of war. For whatever Pau-

mons soldiers he had saved on that march to Manaha, or eased
in better conditions of prison camps, or protected during questioning by Combat officers; for whatever he might count to his
benefit from this—he must also count his share in the Paumons
whom Walk had harried to an exhausted end, to those prisoners
who had died from indifference or cruelty while in his hands, to
those he had slain outright, or killed for no necessary reason. If
Walk massacred tonight, Cal massacred also.

Cal's hands were wet with sweat on the wheel. Night had
completely fallen. As recklessly as Walk himself might have
done, Cal flung the combat car into the turns and twists of the
unknown and narrow road, toward its destination.

Through the darkness, with only the narrow beam of his head-
lights, he fled. Finally, he nosed upward over a little rise and
saw abruptly down into a valley where lights glowed and clustered about three main areas. He swooped down upon them. But
as he entered the first of these, he found the lights came from
the broken windows of damaged homes. There was rubble in
the streets, but no movement of living beings. But when he
stopped in the little open space at the center of the town area
where he was, dark bodies moved in around his car.

He got out. They were all Paumons laden with weapons.

"Come," said one of them. Cal followed him. They walked
across the open space, and Cal's guide stood aside at a door to
a low building. Cal pushed open the door and stepped inside.
He found himself in a low-roofed room with a dirt floor. There
was a wooden table, two cots, some plain chairs, and several
heavy, square wooden timbers holding up the roof. Wantaki stood
beside the table, and between two of the pillars, slumped with
the cords about his wrists only holding him upright, his shirt
torn off, was Walk.

"Ola Tain?" said Wantaki. Cal, who had started to go to
Walk, stopped. He had thought Walk unconscious when he first
stepped in, but he saw now that although Walk's head slumped
between his bare shoulders, his eyes were open and watching.
His body showed a bad wound low on the left side.

"Dead," said Cal. "He died reaching me."

"Yes," said Wantaki. He did not say anything more for a
moment. "I would have saved him, but . . . that is the way it
goes for people like him."

Cal came up to the table. Wantaki looked squarely at him.

"I have no good word to say for you," said Wantaki. "People

like you are—'' the Paumons expression he used was untranslatable. ''With him''—he used the verb form that made it clear he was referring to Walk, the only other person in the room— ''it is different. He is as good as a man any day. If you had been all like that, you might even have eaten us up the way you have tried to. But you were not. I would not even have him tied up like that, but many of my soldiers hate him, and something had to be done.''

He waited. Cal waited also, saying nothing.

''I am a military man,'' said Wantaki. ''This is the beginning. For a while your weapons gave you an advantage; but we have stolen some of them and made more. Today was the beginning. We are going to rise all over the world. We will wipe out your Expedition. And then we will go hunting you in your own home planet.''

''No,'' said Cal. ''Any uprising will fail. The Expedition has weapons it has not used.''

''I do not believe you,'' said Wantaki. He stared at Cal for a long moment. ''Besides it does not matter. Weapons can eventually be duplicated. If we fail this time, we will not fail next. The Paumons spirit will never endure to be a tame beast. And right is on our side.''

''That can only end in a stalemate,'' said Cal.

''How can it end in a stalemate when we are superior to you?'' said Wantaki. ''Given equal weapons, our spirit will conquer— I do not know why I talk to you.''

''I do,'' said Cal. ''You're thinking of all the Paumons that must die before you win your victory.'' He stepped to the edge of the table. ''If the humans would negotiate with you, face to face, as equals, and not as conquerors talking to conquered, would you hold off your rising?''

Wantaki said nothing.

''If you could walk into Expedition Headquarters with sufficient force to feel safe, and there talk, would you?''

''You cannot do this,'' said Wantaki.

''I can. Give me three days.'' Cal looked over at Walk. ''And him.''

''He is dying.''

''Still.''

Wantaki stepped away from the table and then stepped back again.

''I have a responsibility to save lives, as you say,'' he said.

"I don't believe you . . . but it's a bargain." He went to the door. "When you are ready to go, you may go."

He went out. Cal turned quickly to Walk and untied the rope on one side. Walk came heavily down into his arms. Holding him, Cal got the other rope untied and laid Walk on one of the cots. Walk's eyelids fluttered and he looked up into Cal's face.

Walk's lips moved. He did not seem to be saying anything. Then Cal realized he was whispering. Cal bent his ear down close to the lips.

"Cal," Walk was whispering. ". . . lucky . . . lucky, go out . . . in . . . time."

"You're going to be all right," said Cal. Then he realized from the shadow of a look on Walk's face that he had misunderstood. It was not the present moment Walk was talking about.

". . . lies," whispered Walk. ". . . trumpets . . . drums. Liars . . ."

"Lie quiet," said Cal. "Rest a bit. Then I'm taking you east to the Hospital."

Walk sighed and closed his eyes and lay still. Cal sat quietly beside him for perhaps half an hour. Then he realized Walk had opened his eyes and was looking at him again.

"What?" said Cal. He bent down to hear. Walk's faint breath tickled his ear.

"Annie . . ." whispered Walk, ". . . hates me?"

"No," said Cal. "Hell, no! Annie likes you. We both like you a lot. So does Tack. So does everybody."

"Good," Walk whispered. ". . . know . . . somebody. You . . . never . . . ?"

"Hell, no!"

"Promised me . . . good . . . feeling. Noble . . . Liars. Feel lousy . . . dying. Nothing but . . . damnservice. . . ."

"Hey, boy," said Cal. His throat hurt. He reached out and took hold of Walk's hand. "You got nothing but family. Annie and me and everybody. What're you talking about?"

"Lousy . . . Knew . . . liars, long . . . time ago, Didn't get out . . . time." He closed his eyes once more and lay still.

Cal continued to sit. About an hour later, Walk spoke once more.

"Don't . . . mind . . . being killed," Cal was barely able to make out with his ear right at the pale lips. "Just . . . don't want . . . to die. . . ."

A little while later, when Cal lifted an eyelid, the eye beneath stared straight and unmoving and fixed.

CHAPTER FIFTEEN

Cal brought the body of Walk into Hospital Receiving, back at the Hospital at Expedition Headquarters.

"But the man's dead, Colonel!" said the First Lieutenant in Receiving. "What do you want us to do with him?"

"Give him a Services funeral," said Cal. He went in search of Annie.

"I'm going to see Harmon," he said. "I want you to get off duty here, now, and do something for me. Can you do that?"

"Yes," she said. "What is it, Cal?"

"Get a ground car and follow me over. Wait until I go in to Headquarters, then park it around by the side entrance to the Files Office. Leave the motor running and clear out. Can you do that?"

"Yes, Cal, but—"

"I'm not telling you any more," said Cal. "If you have to ask questions, don't do it."

"All right," she said. "Give me a minute to get somebody up here to take over the ward desk."

Cal drove a ground car of his own to Expedition HQ. In the scope he could see Annie's car following. He pulled into the official parking lot, and went in.

"Colonel?" said the Wing Section behind the small wooden fence that separated staff from visitors in the outer office.

"Contacts Service," said Cal. "Colonel Truant. I'm to talk to General Harmon." And without waiting for an answer, he pushed open the small gate in the fence and strode past.

"But Colonel, just a minute. *Colonel!*"

He heard steps behind him but kept going. He passed through another door into another, smaller office, where a Captain looked up, startled, from a wide desk.

"Colonel Truant!" said Cal. He kept traveling. The farther door in this second office was closed. He opened it and stepped through.

Harmon and Colonel Alt were standing together by a desk, within.

They both turned as the Captain from the outer office and other staff members reached the door behind Cal.

"General," said Cal. "I think it's time for your talk with the Contacts Service."

"I'm sorry, sir," said the Captain, from behind Cal's shoulder. "He just walked by—"

"That's all right," said Harmon. "Close the door." Cal heard them leave and the door close behind him.

"Alone," said Cal.

Colonel Haga Alt came around the desk, walking on his toes like a boxer.

"Truant," he said, "I've waited one hell of a long time for—"

"Hag," said Harmon. Alt stopped. He looked back at Harmon. "It's all right, Hag," said Harmon gently. "You can leave us."

Alt's nostrils spread. "All right, sir," he said. He walked on, looking squarely into Cal's face, passed him, and Cal heard the door shut a second time behind him.

"All right, Truant," said Harmon, in the same gentle voice. "What is it?"

"The Paumons are rising."

"I know," said Harmon.

"I know you know," said Cal. "I know you planned it this way. There was a time when I thought you just didn't know any better. But I found out different."

Harmon walked around the desk himself and stood in front of it. They were only a few feet apart. Harmon put his hands together behind him, like a lecturer.

"Back in Denver," he said, "I sent you to General Scoby because I was under the impression that whatever had happened to you with the Lehaunan, you were a soldier."

"I was," said Cal. "I was one of the prettiest."

"But you aren't any more?"

"Yes," said Cal. "I'm a soldier. I'm a hell of a soldier. But maybe you wouldn't recognize the kind I am."

"No," Harmon said. "You're wrong. I would recognize what kind you are. In fact, I do. That's why I'm talking to you, instead of having you thrown out." He sat down on the edge of the desk. "You're the best kind, Cal. That's why I sent you over to

Scoby in the first place. Because you're the kind that has to fight out of a sense of conviction. Men like that are too valuable to lose.''

"Only, I am wrong."

"Yes," said Harmon. "You got in among people like General Scoby who talk about fine things like peace and understanding and no more war. It impressed you. I think you may have forgotten that those sort of things don't come about naturally. They have to be imposed by a strong hand from the outside." He looked at Cal, and his voice was almost pleading. "I want you to understand. Damn it, you're the sort of man who *ought* to understand."

"I should, should I?" said Cal.

"Yes. Because you've seen both sides of it. You're not like these half-baked glory-preachers that think we're going to have Heaven next Tuesday. I tell you, Cal, I've got more use for a Prog like Wantaki, than I have for these Societics-Contacts choirboys."

"It's mutual, no doubt," said Cal. "You're both generals."

Harmon frowned at him.

"Something in particular seems to be eating on you," he said.

"Major Blye's dead—you know, Zone Eleven. I brought his body back with me."

"I didn't know. That's too bad," said Harmon. "There's a man who was a soldier clear through. I'll bet he died like one."

"He sure did," said Cal.

"I want to hear how it happened. But the point right now is something different: You, not Major Blye, good man though he was. I'm fighting for your soul, Cal. Do you believe I'm an honest man? Tell me."

"Yes," said Cal. "I believe you're honest. I believe you believe every word you say."

"Then believe me when I say nobody wants peace more than I. That I agree with Scoby one hundred per cent about these Paumons being the nearest thing to human we've ever run across, with brains and soul and pain-reactions to match. He's told you that? I see he has. But from that point he gets idealistic, and I get practical. He thinks this qualifies them to be great friends. I know it qualifies them to be great enemies. It's one thing to make a pet out of a dog; but don't try to make one out of a wolf."

"Or a cheetah?" said Cal.

Harmon stopped talking. The whites of his eyes showed a little.

"I'm talking seriously," he said.

"So am I," said Cal. "Don't you know why that cheetah does things for Scoby?"

"I don't know and I don't care," said Harmon. "I'm concerned with the future of two races, not with a brainless animal. I'm concerned with making you see that just because these Paumons are what they are—because they're so much like us—that we can't ever trust them. We've started something and we can't stop now. Now we've got to break them; teach them with a bloodbath that they'll remember to the ultimate generations, that the human is master. We can't stop now."

"Why'd we start in the first place?"

"History," said Harmon, "forced our hand. We're an expanding people." He stood up. "Cal," he said, "can't you see that what I've arranged for isn't only the right thing, it's the most humanitarian thing? We treated the Paumons humanly in the original conquest. Because of that they took the enough rope we gave them and now they're going to hang themselves. They, themselves, are insisting on being taught a lesson. And, like a good surgeon, I save lives by cutting now instead of later, when a more extensive operation would be necessary. I save human lives. You might say, I even save Paumons lives. Because, if they grew to a real threat to us, we might have to exterminate them completely."

"Yeah," said Cal.

"You understand, then," said Harmon. "Believe me, Cal. You were one of the ones I had hoped could understand."

"No," said Cal. "Put me down with Scoby. No, put me down a notch below Scoby, because I'm still ready to fight and kill if I have to, in spite of this shoulder patch. I just don't have to pretend there's anything right or noble about it."

Harmon sighed. He shook his head slowly.

"I'm sorry, Cal," he said.

"So am I," said Cal. "I just finished talking to Wantaki. I told him he could come in here with sufficient force to protect himself. Then he could talk over this Paumons situation—not as conquered talking to conquerer, but as a couple of equals meeting face to face, with the object of avoiding any more fighting. I gave him my promise."

"That was foolish," said Harmon. "It was even a little ridiculous."

"No," said Cal. "Because as Contacts Service Head on this planet, I'm interdicting any military action by the Expedition during the time of the talk."

"I see," said Harmon. He stood for a moment, then turned to the desk behind him and pressed a button. Holding it down, he spoke to the desk. "Will you send in a couple of Military Police?" he said. He let up the button and turned back to Cal. "As I say," he said. "I'm sorry. I would rather have made an ally of you than arrested you."

"Yes," said Cal.

He hit Harmon suddenly in the stomach, and, as the other man fell toward him, hit him again behind the ear with the side of his hand. Harmon fell to the floor and lay there quietly. Cal went out through the back door of the office, down a flight of stairs and into another office banked with the metal cases of microfiles.

"Sit still, sit still," he said to the startled workers there. "Just taking the short way to my car."

He went out a further door onto the street. The car Annie had been driving was parked across from him. He sprinted for it. As he dived inside behind the control stick, he heard someone shout from the door he had just come through.

He floored the throttle and the car jumped away from the Headquarters Building. He shot down the street, out onto the road to the Expedition Landing field and pulled up at the base of the towering flagship. Thirty feet up the service ramp, the rear port was open to the ventilation of the warming day. He was through the hatch and throwing over the hand control to close and lock the port when he heard somebody breathing hard behind him.

He turned. It was Annie.

"You crazy fool!" he said.

The port slammed shut and locked with a clang. A second later the inner door closed also.

Chapter Sixteen

"You've got to get out of here," said Cal. "You don't know what you're in to."

"I won't," said Annie. "I know very well. And I won't. You can't put me out bodily, either, without leaving the controls here. And you can't risk that."

"I'll manage it."

"No," said Annie. She was quite pale. "I won't let you. I can fight that hard."

They were up in the observation room, where the standby controls of the ship were. The duty caretaker was locked in the projection room behind the wall chart. Cal had the standby power on. It did not take an engineer to do that much; and the house-keeping energy flow it gave him was all he needed. Outside, above the entry ports at three levels, the red lights were glowing to warn anyone back beyond a hundred-yard circle. From the outside screen Cal could see the field below, and the other ships like models, the little buildings of the field, and Headquarters, the hospital, and beyond those buildings the limits of Manaha. Beyond this he could see the green and open hills, with here and there the darker green of trees.

The ground phone buzzed. Cal answered, and the screen lit up with the face of Colonel Alt.

"Truant," he said. "Come out of that ship before I send in MP's to haul you out."

"I wouldn't try that if I were you," said Cal. "I'm prepared to blow this ship and half the plateau if I have to."

Alt hesitated. He looked aside for a moment, then back into the screen.

"You'd do better to cooperate," he said. "I'd be justified in having you shot on sight. You killed General Harmon when you hit him."

"Don't lie to me, Colonel," said Cal. "I know when I kill a man. Tell the General I want to talk to him as soon as he's up to it."

He cut the connection. He sat down in the operator's chair by the little desk below the screens. His head swam; his body felt several gravities heavy. He put his head down for a second on his arms and immediately felt Annie shaking him.

"Lie down," she was saying. "There's an off-watch cot in the Communications Room. Here . . ." She was tugging him to his feet. "You've got to rest. When did you sleep last?"

"No—" he said. And all the time, he felt his will-less, stupid body being steered by Annie toward the cot. "Harmon'll call back. . . ."

"Let him call. I'll answer."

"No. You get out. . . ." The words were thick on his tongue. The edge of the cot struck under his knees, and he fell into it. The world made a sort of half-turn around him, as if he were very drunk. And then it suddenly winked out.

His head hurt. It was the amber light from the barber poles, street lights of the Lehaunan town, that was dazzling his eyes and giving him a headache. And he had never been so tired. He wandered through the town with his fire rifle in his hands, letting his feet take him among the dome-shaped buildings. Now and then he shot perfunctorily at what might be Lehaunans. He was so tired that he could not think exactly what he was doing there. Something had not worked out, and he had decided to do something else. But just at the moment he could not remember what that was. He was tired and looking for a place to sit down.

He came at last to a little open space between the buildings, and there was one of the small protuberances like a half-barrel sticking up out of the pavement. He sat down on it and rested his fire rifle across his knees.

There was a building a little to his right and another a little farther off, up ahead of him and to his left. Almost directly ahead, about thirty yards away, was a third building. A barber pole by the building to his right spread its crackling light impartially over the scene.

He sat, not thinking of anything, and after a little while, a Lehaunan ran across the open space before him, saw him, hesitated, and then ran on. A little later, he saw another one run between two houses farther off that could be seen dimly beyond the building to his left.

He did not move. He felt a sort of numb oneness with his surroundings, as if he had grown to be part of the object he was sitting on. The thought that was in his head, like a title on a movie screen frozen in position, was that if he rested for a little while he would remember what he was to do next. He sat still.

Some little time later, a family of three came out of the building directly before him, out of its triangular-shaped entrance. They were evidently an adult male, a female adult a little smaller, and a small young one. He sat so still that they were only about a dozen feet from him when they saw him, and stopped short. They were carrying some small packages.

He and they remained motionless, staring at each other.

It's quite all right, he said inside his head, in normal human speech, *go ahead. I won't bother you.* It was too much effort to say the words aloud. So, having said them mentally, he merely continued to sit there.

The female adult made a small noise and pushed slightly at the young one. The youngster hesitated; she pushed again. Reluctantly the young one ran off, past Cal and out of sight. The two adults stayed facing him.

That's all right, he said in his head. *You go, too. You're obviously civilians. Besides, I have taken your town. I've got no need to shoot you.*

They did not move for a moment. Then, as if they had heard his thoughts, they began to back cautiously away from him.

There, you see? he thought. *You're quite safe. I'm not going to do anything.* They were like ants, he thought; afraid of being stepped on. He watched them back away. They were quite handsome in their black fur. He must look like a monster to them. An incomprehensible monster that killed or did not kill for no sane reason.

Still holding their packages, they were backing away from him, back toward the house from which they had come. Sudden pity flooded him.

Go in peace, he thought. *Go in safety.*

They were almost halfway across the open space between him and the house, now. The male turned and, turning the female, urged her in front of him. They broke suddenly into a run for their own doorway.

They're getting away, thought Cal suddenly.

He raised his rifle and shot the male, who fell immediately. The female dropped her packages and put on speed. His second shot dropped her just inside the doorway. He could see her lying there.

The packages lay scattered about in the open. He wondered,

idly, what sort of valuables might be in them. They should be saved, he thought, so the young one could claim them at some future date. . . .

Annie was shaking him. It was a terribly hard thing to wake up. He struggled into a sitting position on the side of the cot, but he had come to with only half his mind. The other half was still back in the circumstances he had been reliving in the dream.

". . . General Harmon," Annie was saying. "He wants to talk to you. I didn't want to wake you, but you've been sleeping there almost nine hours."

"Nine hours!" He staggered to his feet and lurched into the observation room. Annie made to help him to the ground phone, but he shook his head. "He can wait." He laid sleep-numbed hands on the controls of the outside screen. It was late afternoon now and on the far hills, the light of Bellatrix had turned the covering moss to chartreuse color, and the clumped trees to a deeper green. He ran the magnification up to the limits of the scale and saw, as from a dozen or so yards away, armed Paumons soldiers standing under the trees.

"Wantaki," he said. "He made it."

"What?" said Annie.

He did not answer, swinging across the room to the ground phone. He punched the receive button, and the image of General Harmon sprang to life on the screen. He was standing half-turned away from Cal. The call buzzer at the other end must have sounded then, for Harmon turned back and approached the screen. He looked as calm and unharmed as ever.

"Colonel Truant," he said quietly, "I'm ordering you to come out of that ship."

"No," said Cal. His legs were still weak from sleep. He sat down in front of the screen. "I'm staying here until you commit yourself to a meeting with Wantaki, by letting him into the Headquarters area with enough men to match your Headquarters forces."

"I'm not the kind of man you can blackmail, Colonel," said Harmon.

"I'm not blackmailing you," said Cal. "I'm holding you up with a loaded gun at your head. If I blow this ship, you, Wantaki and everything goes. If it goes, there's nothing left of the Expedition on this world but a lot of small scattered garrisons.

They wouldn't last twenty-four hours with the real power of the outfit destroyed here."

"Rather a strange way to go about saving lives, isn't it?" said Harmon gently. "Have you counted the people that'll die—the Paumons, as well—if you blow up that ship and its armaments?"

"You don't understand me," said Cal. "I told you I wasn't up on General Scoby's level. I know what I am, if I blow this ship. But if I have to blow it the Paumons'll come out of it better than if I hadn't. The only way I can get you to meet with them properly is to threaten to blow it. And I can't threaten it without meaning it. And I mean it, General!" Cal looked into the imaged eyes of Harmon, but what he saw was a small black-furred figure tugging and murmuring at a larger, black-furred figure fallen still in a triangular doorway. "You better believe I mean it."

"I'll give you thirty minutes," said Harmon. "If you haven't started to come out thirty minutes from now, I'll order the other ships on the field here to open fire on you."

"You know," said Cal, "you can't destroy this ship before I can blow it. And you're just as liable to blow it yourself trying to destroy it. I'll give you until sunset, about two hours. If Wantaki and his men aren't entering the Headquarters area by sunset, I'll blow the ship."

"Thirty minutes," said Harmon.

"Good-by," said Cal. He cut the connection. He stood up, turned, and saw Annie standing a little across the room from him.

"Annie," he said, "there's an escape pod in the nose of this ship that'll kick itself fifty miles up and six hundred miles out. You get in it and get out of here."

"No," said Annie. "I told you I wouldn't."

"I am too dead to argue with you. Don't you understand? Two hours from now, I'm going to press the arming connection and destroy every living thing for five hundred miles. Can't you get that through your head? I'm going to have to do it!"

"The General will give in."

"No, he won't," said Cal. He looked grimly at the blank screen of the ground phone. "He can't. Not while there's a chance I might not press the button. And by the time he knows for sure there's no chance, it'll be too late."

"I'll wait till the last minute," said Annie. "But I won't go a second before."

Cal felt suddenly weak all over. He realized suddenly he had been standing with every muscle tensed to the limit, as if he had crossed his fingers with all the strength in his body, against the possibility that she would refuse to go and he could not get her out before the end.

He let out his breath suddenly and sat down in the chair.

"Good," he said. "Good."

She came quickly over to him.

"Cal," she said, "are you all right?"

"Fine," he said. "Fine." She had her arms around him. He grinned a little shakily and reached up and patted one of the arms that held him. "It's just that I love you." The words came out quite easily. He had never been able to say them before. He said them again. "I love you."

She held on to him. They did not say much. After a little while she excused herself and was gone for a few moments. And then she came back and they sat together, watching the sun moving toward the horizon.

When it touched the tops of the hills, he felt a strange, cold, feeling thrill suddenly all the way through him. He turned to her.

"It's time," he said.

She did not move.

"You've got to go now," he said.

"I lied to you," she said. "I never planned to go. When I went out just now, I went up to the pod and smashed the control board. I couldn't leave if I wanted to."

He could only stare at her.

"Don't you see?" she said, almost composedly, "I *want* to stay with you."

He said, through stiff lips:

"I can't blow it with you here."

"Yes, you can," she said. Her voice was very quiet, very certain. It was as if she had moved into a shell of peace from which nothing would be able to take her, neither death nor sorrow. "I know you can."

He got heavily to his feet, and looked once more to the hills. The light of the sun was now resting on them and it made the whole horizon seem ablaze with horizontal rays shooting all at him. He walked slowly over to the arming button. He looked at her again and put his finger on it.

"All right, Cal," said a voice from somewhere above his head. "You win."

It was the voice of Harmon. Cal stared foolishly around, for a second he half-expected the General to walk into the observation room.

"We've been listening to you," said Harmon. "We fired a contact mike into the skin of your ship eight hours ago. If you'd left that room for five minutes, we'd have had you. Look out to the hills, there. I've had Alt standing by to pass the word to Wantaki. You can see the Progs already starting to come in."

Cal looked. Against the glare of the sun he had to shield his eyes. But when he did he made out dark masses moving in, close to Manaha. They were already in below the range of Headquarters' heavy ground weapons.

"All right," said Cal. "I'll come down."

He waited until the approaching Paumons forces were actually into the city. Then he went down in the ship, with Annie beside him. When they stepped out onto the ramp and started to the ground, he saw that there was quite a gathering waiting for them. There were Military Police, both male and female, Colonel Harry Adom of the Military Police, and Cal's own Contacts Service aide, Major Kai. Major Kai was fifteen years older than Cal and looked like a bank clerk. He represented the old guard over whose head Scoby had put Cal in charge. Kai was looking embarrassed and unhappy, but Cal was glad to see him there.

"Major," he said. "You take over Contacts until orders can be got out from General Scoby. He'll want—"

"He's here, himself," interrupted Kai. "Or rather, he's coming in right now." He pointed off to their left and upward. Cal, glancing in that direction, saw the sudden flash of a pinpoint of reflecting surface, high enough up to still catch the sunlight.

"When did he send word he was coming?" said Cal.

"Yesterday," said Kai unhappily. "The message came in. We couldn't get hold of you."

Cal had reached the bottom of the ramp now. The MP's waiting there closed about him. He saw the female MP's moving in on Annie.

"Wait a minute!" he called. "She didn't have anything to do with this. I—"

They paid no attention to him. The MP's were searching him for weapons.

"All clean," said one.

Across the field, the courier ship bearing Scoby was now down and landed. There was quite a crowd around it, and as the hatch opened and the small figure preceded by a small cheetah came out, another small figure walking like Harmon stepped forward to shake hands.

"Cal," said Annie's voice.

He looked over at her, as the cold metal of handcuffs closed around his wrists. They were doing the same thing to her. For a second, they could look at each other. Then the MP's closed around Cal once more and he and she were led off in different directions.

CHAPTER SEVENTEEN

The Military Police took Cal to the Stockade and locked him in a cell by himself in an unoccupied section of the building. It was so quiet and isolated that it was almost as if he were in a hospital instead of a prison. At the end of four days they took him in a closed car to the field and put him on a ship for Earth. It was impossible to tell what had happened since he had been arrested. Fighting might even have been going on without his being able to know it. And they made it a point to tell him nothing. Scoby did not come to see him.

Back at Earth, he was taken to the Fort Shuttleworth Military Prison outside Denver and housed in separate quarters that were a little better than a cell—a room and a half. It was like a small, compact apartment, and through the bars of a fairly wide window Cal could see a section of perfectly kept green lawn, some tall, pyramidal pine trees, and beyond that the white top of a mountain. He thought that it was Longs Peak, but he could not be sure and a small, irrational stubbornness kept him from asking anyone, so he never did establish its identity from that window for certain.

Shortly after he was placed there, a Captain from the Adjutant General's department came to see him with a folder of papers. The Captain identified himself as Cal's legal representative. He explained something to the effect that they were pondering charges against Cal. It would probably be treason and lesser crimes, but nothing was established yet. For some reason it was a matter of jurisdiction. The Captain took himself and his work very seriously, and most of what he had to say Cal found fairly unintelligible. The Captain wanted an account in Cal's own words of what had led up to Cal's arrest, and took it down in recorder and on paper. He and Cal were pretty well up against it as far as the book went, he told Cal. They would find it hard to deny the statements of prosecution. Their best bet, considering the Lehaunan background, might be to make their claim one of temporary insanity.

Cal was uncooperative on that point. He would not claim temporary insanity. Otherwise, he paid only slight attention to the Captain's flow of words. He was more interested in pumping the other man for news. Annie, said the Captain, was under arrest elsewhere. He did not know exactly where. He, himself, was not representing her. About the Paumons, he had very little information. The human and native Alien forces there were certainly at peace at the present moment, though the situation was touchy, as always. Yes, he believed the Paumons authorities had had some sort of official talk with the human Command, but there had been no more than a mention of it in the news services and he had heard nothing from official sources.

"It's a long ways off, there around Bellatrix, you know," he said to Cal.

After the Captain's visit, they began to allow Cal the news services and he got a sudden supply of backed-up mail. There was nothing from Scoby and only a handful of letters from Annie—and these had been censored almost into unintelligibility. Cal wrote her back, but with no great hopes that his letters would not be treated the same way.

It was July on Earth. There were seldom clouds on the mountain peak Cal could see from his window. He read a good deal and thought and walked around his locked quarters. The Captain came occasionally with papers for him to fill out or sign. July went into August and August drifted into September. He felt the leaking away of the valuable days of his life. He had found again the serenity that had come to him in the later days of Contacts School, and he did not worry too wholeheartedly over what would eventually happen to him. It was a curious thing that while the death penalty was not now imposed by a civilian court, the Armed Services had retained it for certain crimes. For himself, his conscience was clear and it was no worse an end than Walk's had been. But he worried about what would be done to Annie.

Then, the third week in September, his Captain was able to tell him that Annie had been released without charges. He felt a great relief and even hoped that she might manage to visit him after that. But she did not come, and even her letters stopped coming. He told himself that this was good, that she was well out of it.

He was able to face the fact that he loved her now, and understand why he had been unable to tell her so before. He had been shackled by the old fear of a reenactment of his mother's death, with Annie in his mother's role, and he in his father's. Just so, he had been able to face the fact that he had always wanted to be the sort of man his father was, but had gone against him because he had blamed his father for his mother's death. Looking at his father through the stripped eyes of a child, he had taken his father's refusal to be vindictive against the Armed Services and the officer indirectly responsible for his wife's death, as a sign his father did not really *care*. Now that his father was dead, it came to Cal that his father must have cared very much.

Not only cared, but loved!—and been right about many things. He had been right about the uncertainty of that thin line that marks off the soldier from the murderer, that thin line that is also the edge of the precipice over which the spirit of a man falls to its final destruction. Cal could face this, too, now, as he could face the fact that with the Lehaunan in that village he himself had crossed the line and fallen. A man, he told himself now, can kill and go on living. But if he murders, he erects a barrier between himself and life; a barrier behind which he dies alone.

And a man begins, thought Cal, to murder when he begins to tell himself that it is all right to kill; that there are practical or moral justifications for it. Because there are none. Sometimes it happens and things afterwards are better than they were before. But it is never good, it is always bad. There was always a better way if someone had had the wit to find it.

I suppose, thought Cal, leaning against his window and looking out through the bars at the grass and the pines swayed by the wind that seemed to be always blowing, and the far-off mountain peak with a small white cloud near it—I suppose it should be pushed right to the point of holding insects and microbes sacred, to hold water. But that's a trap, too. To say, if I can't be perfect there's no point in my being good at all. I didn't have any qualms back there on the Paumons about blowing up Harmon—no, of course I did. But the point is: how much more readily I would have put my own head on the block to pull Walk out. And Harmon by his own standards is an upright and honorable man, while Walk was something to frighten Paumons babies with and better off dead.

No, Cal corrected himself again, I'm wrong about that. Nobody is better off dead, not in that sense. No. There are always miracles. There is always hope. If you deny miracles and hope, you're playing God—and that's the insects and microbes bit all over again. If I can't shoot par, I won't pick up a golf club. Wrong. You stick by what you believe, and go on doing what you can in your own clumsy, imperfect way, trying to hack out Heaven by next Tuesday, even though practical people like Harmon are sure it can't be done. And damned if you don't make some progress now and then.

Christ, yes, thought Cal! Otherwise we might as well have stayed in little family ape-bands, wandering around and trying to tear out the throat of every other living thing that stood up to us. The thing is not to kid yourself. Just because cutting a man open to get out his ruptured appendix has a way of saving his life doesn't mean that it's a good thing to cut a man open. It's a very bad thing, a destructive, immoral wrong being done to the living body. And you must never lose sight of that fact, either through long custom or need to justify your own emotional reactions to the cutting. And one day you may be moved to the point of finding some way to save the man's life without cutting him open.

And it's that way with us, thought Cal. We mustn't lose sight of the fact that it's wrong to go up against each new race we meet with all guns blazing. The only right way in the end is to go naked to the stars. Without weapons, because we don't need them. You never find a way until you try. And you don't try as long as you kid yourself that it's okay to—

The sound of a door opening behind him broke off Cal's train of thought. It was one of his guards with the noon meal on a tray.

"No mail today either," said the guard, as he put the tray down. "They seem to be losing your address these last few weeks."

Two weeks later, Cal was taken from his cell to the office of the Director of the Prison, where an Administrative Services Captain told him he was released. There was no explanation. He was given a small plastic container in which to carry his possessions, a sealed manila envelope, and escorted to the gate of the Prison.

As he walked to the gate, he opened the envelope and drew out a sheet of paper inside. It was his release from the Services. He was discharged, he read, without honor but with prejudice, and not recommended for reservice. The gate opened before him and he stepped out into the wide parking lot beyond.

He had to look twice to believe what he saw. It was Annie, and Scoby with the cheetah, and beyond them a convertible flyer. Annie ran and put her arms around him, but Scoby stood impatiently with one foot on the step to the open door of the flyer.

"Oh, Cal!" said Annie, holding tightly to him. "Cal, will you ever forgive us? We couldn't. We just couldn't!"

"Come on, come on!" said Scoby.

They got into the flyer and Scoby sat down at the controls with Annie and Cal on the curved seat behind him. Annie would not let go of Cal; she sat pressed close against him.

"Oh, Cal!" she said. She was trying not to cry and it was making her nose red.

Scoby touched the controls and the flyer went straight up about nine thousand feet, then made a half-turn and streaked eastward. Cal caught one last glimpse of the mountain peak to the north of his prison window. It apparently had put aside all clouds in honor of the occasion. It stood sharp and white against the perfect blue of the sky.

"Where are we going?" asked Cal.

"Washington," grunted Scoby.

"Darling," said Annie. "We couldn't even write. We had to make them think you weren't at all important, that we'd forgotten all about you."

Cal shook his head. The whole thing had happened so quickly everything had an unnatural feel to it, as if it was a trick of some sort.

"But what happened?" he said.

"Politics," said Scoby, not turning his head. Limpari swung cat's eyes about from where she sat staring out the window, and then yawned at Scoby.

"He had to wait. I had to wait, too. Until it looked as if nobody cared what happened to you any more. That's why I stopped writing you. Only I didn't stop writing, Cal. I wrote anyway. I just didn't mail the letters. I've got them all for you."

The flyer had been continuing to climb and to increase its speed as it did so. They were now at a hundred thousand feet with the sky black overhead. Their speed would be about two thousand miles an hour, Cal noted automatically from the instruments before Scoby. After sitting still for so many weeks it was an odd sensation to have sprouted wings and be hurtling to some distant destination. Below him, he could see the line of the sunset, flowing toward them across the earth below. He felt the beginnings of a slow return from numbness, like a leg that has gone to sleep and is just now beginning to wake up.

"I thought you were well out of it," he said to Annie.

"Oh, *no!*" she said. "You knew I'd never just give you up. You knew Walt would never abandon you, either!"

"Walt?" he said. And then he remembered that this was Scoby's first name. It was a small shock, after all this, to realize Scoby had a first name. "I don't understand. I don't understand it," Cal said. "That Captain assigned to my case said the charge was probably going to be treason." He looked at Scoby. "And here I am."

"Matter of jurisdiction," said Scoby. The ship had leveled off now. He put it on automatic pilot and swiveled his chair around, pulling out his pipe. "That's what I went back about. The time was just right for squeezing on the home front. I squeezed." He got the pipe going. "I got the Contacts Service made a separate civilian branch. Not under Armed Services any more."

"So you were really acting under civilian authority when you interdicted Harmon and tried to make him talk with Wantaki," said Annie. "Even if you didn't know it, or Harmon didn't."

Cal looked from one to the other.

"What difference did that make?" he said.

"Just one," answered Scoby, uttering rich puffs of smoke from his pipe. "Harmon didn't have the authority to order you arrested. On paper, since a peace had been signed with the Paumons, you as head of the Contacts *Department*, were his superior, not he yours."

Scoby leaned back around to the automatic pilot and set the speed-and-distance clock.

"Of course," he said, swinging back to face them, "he had a case to make. The fact orders hadn't arrived; and you threatened human as well as Paumons lives, and so forth. So what I did was wait and let things cool, until it wasn't worth the Combat Services' while to make an issue out of you. Early this week I tacked your release onto a list of little minor demands I was dealing with from the Services. And here you are.''

Cal sighed. He felt abruptly small, and insignificant.

"No fuss," said Scoby. "Or wasn't that what you were thinking?''

"Not exactly," said Cal. He looked ahead out the window of the flyer. They were almost to their meeting with the sunset line moving toward them over the relief map of the earth below, and beyond that edge of light he saw only darkness. "I was thinking it's all over, now.''

"Over?" said Scoby.

"Finished! Wound up," said Cal.

"Finished!" said Scoby. "What d'you mean *finished?* You think you brought eternal peace to the Paumons by having Wantaki and Harmon hating each other's guts?''

"No," said Cal, "they admire each other.''

"Hating each other's guts and admiring each other, what the hell's the difference," said Scoby. "But just the two of them sitting down across a table from each other? You think the Lehaunan're all set up, now, or there's no rebuilding to be done with the Griella? That what you think?''

"No," said Cal. There was a slow, heavy weariness creeping into him. He was looking out the window now at the rapidly approaching darkness—and remembering. It seemed there was always a darkness for him. It had been dark on the Lehaunan hillside before they had gone in to take the town. It had been in darkness that Walk had called him a Gutless Wonder; and in the Paumons darkness, Walk had died. Night had been falling as he reached for the arming button on the flagship, that meant the end for everyone there; and darkness was falling again, here, now.

"Don't you think there's work to be done?" Scoby was saying. "Why do you think I worked so hard to get you loose? This is what I've been after from the start. My own Department, independent, where I can get the kind of men I want and train them the way they ought to be trained, instead of having to let good people go by the board because they couldn't pass Services' physical, or couldn't make it over an obstacle course!" He glared at Cal.

"What do you think I've been driving at all this time, but an army of my own—a Contacts army which'll go on growing and getting more effective until the Combat Services can't do without us? Until we get so good at last, that the day comes they let us go in *first*, to see if we can't make it without fighting at all. *That's* what I've been working for all these years. *That's* when I'm going to need the sort of men this race of ours has only written philosophies about before. *That's* why I want you—for my right hand man, to take over for me when the time comes—just as I planned it from the first time I discovered you.''

The twilight line was under and past them, now. It was all a dark world ahead.

"It's no use," said Cal. He leaned forward and passed his manila envelope to Scoby. "I'm discharged with prejudice. Not recommended for reservice."

Scoby slammed the envelope to the floor of the flyer.

"Bonehead!" he snarled. *"Department,* I said. Not Service! You had so many coats of varnish you think that if the Services turn you down, the Civilian Departments can't hire you either?''

Cal lifted his head, startled.

"I thought—Government—" he began, and got stuck.

"Oh, the personnel don't like hiring Service bad cases. They don't *like* hiring ex-cons or reformed alcoholics, either. But I'm in charge of my Department. And *I* say you're hired. And you're hired!''

Cal sat, letting some of the sense of it sink in.

"I want men!" Scoby was muttering furiously. "Men, not recommendations on paper!" He was simply blowing off the last of his head of steam. As proof of the fact, he was glaring not at Cal, but ahead out the windscreen of the flyer. "Christ! it's hard enough to handle things as it is. It's hard enough to do the job I have to do—and that's double the job I ought to be doing at my age—with the sort of men I want, anyway. Let alone . . .''

Cal looked ahead out of the flyer's windscreen, himself. Annie was sitting close beside him and had slipped an arm through his left arm. He felt the living and continual warmth of her body, close. A sort of hope stirred in him. The thrumming vibrations of the flyer hummed through him down to the furthest tips of his fingers. He could feel the lift of the ship's wide wings, spread now at this altitude to their greatest, hawk-like, soaring dimensions, bearing him up. On those wings they here in this ship sailed against the night, at speeds of which no flint-axed caveman had ever dreamed.

Far up ahead, on the darkened horizon, a sprinkling of lights rose into view around the curve of the world. They rose and multiplied as the flyer dropped toward them, until they looked like jewels of all colors scattered more and more thickly upon a cloth of black velvet. Together, the spectrum of their many-colored rays made up the white light of a city. It was the city toward which he and Annie and Scoby—all of them together in the flyer—were now heading above the primitive darkness, as to an inevitable destination.

And to that city, now, they stooped.

THE ALIEN WAY

CHAPTER ONE

. . . Turning in his sleep, Jason Barchar rolled over so that the weight of his head was upon the right side of his skull, under which the receiver had been implanted. The area was still tender, even two months after the operation, so that he rolled a little farther, until he was almost on his stomach, and went back to dreaming about the bears.

He was dreaming that he was again out on the hillside in the Canadian Rockies, where he had actually been six years before. He was lying very still in the spring sunlight, with the wide-angle binoculars at his eyes, looking down into a small natural meadow with only a few birch and spruce scattered through it. The stiff, broken stalks of winter-killed grass among the new growth pricked his wrists where his leather jacket had pulled back to expose the skin, and his elbows were sore from contact with the rock under the damp surface skin of earth, but he paid no attention. Below there were about two dozen of the bears, and the spring fury of mating and battles was on them. The brown and black cubs were mostly already up in the trees, and the females were hanging back. But just below him, in the weedy lists of a little open arena, two males stalked each other, up on hind legs, necks arched snakelike and heads thrust forward in rage.

They were lost in their rages. They did not see him up on the hillside, or the females hanging back, or the cubs in the trees, and they did not care. There was nothing left for either of them but the other bear facing him. They were almost formal and completely honest, in their advancings and their shuffling retreats. Jase's heart beat with theirs. It was what had made him a naturalist—which like all important work was a way of thinking, not just the application of a lot of book knowledge as people thought—and thinking that did not understand things like this spring fighting of the bears.

They thought the urge to fight, the fighting and the winning or losing, was a simple matter of automatic instinct and easy reflex. But it was not so. There was custom to it, and a complex of experience operating on the part of each combatant. There was desire, and decision, and courage required from each bear. There was hope and fear, and the need to tell a bluff from a true threat. There were many factors entering into each situation in the meadow, each combat—and no two combats were ever alike.

So Jase dreamed that he watched and learned from the bears. While the hum of the insects in his dream blended with the hum of the air-conditioner in his bedroom window, and in the window of his living room beyond. The whole dark, brickwalled apartment in the stifling, rainy June night was a cool cave of isolation set off from the unsleeping, night-time streets of Washington, D.C., outside, where the cabs rolled all night long over the glistening asphalt, past the traffic signals and the neon signs of restaurants.

In the sleeping apartment, nothing moved. The air-conditioners hummed. The bedroom was shadowy. The distant light of a street lamp glowed faintly through the drawn blinds and touched the opposite wall beyond the bed with two ghostly faint rectangles of light. They seemed on the verge of merging, so uncertain they were, and pale.

Jase's clothes lay lumped on the chair by the bed. The carpet beneath the chair was a plane of darkness, reaching toward the open doorway and through it into the larger space of the living room. There the walls were lit by three more ghosts of windows. The light showed bookshelves and a glass case crammed full of the study skins of small animal specimens, carefully sewn, preserved with borax, and tagged. The number of them piled in the case made them look like a horde of prisoners. Pent by the invisible glass walls as the bears were pent by invisible instinct and desire. On the bookshelves, filling the walls of the room from floor to ceiling, the faint light through the blinds barely showed some of the titles: P. Chapin, *Preparation of Bird Skins for Study;* H. Hediger, *Wildgere in Gefangenschaft;* K. P. Schmidt, *Corollary and Commentary for Climate and Evolution,* magazine pages extracted and bound; W. K. Gregory, *Evolution Emerging*. . . .

On the desk full of papers the still-uncashed last paycheck made out to Jason S. Barchar by the newly formed Wildlife Studies Section of the U.S. Department of the Interior lay shadowy and still. It was a half-paycheck, since Jase had been on sabbatical leave the last two months. Under the check was a birthday card two weeks old on which was scribbled, "With no apologies whatever to A. A. Milne—*Hippy Pappy Bithunday,* love, Mele."

Isolated, dark, the apartment slumbered—all but the receiver, the tiny microdevice implanted under Jase's skull, with its hair-thin wire reaching into certain areas of his brain. Unsleeping, unisolated, the receiver reached outward through a tight, invisible channel of collapsed space to a cold, dark fragment of earth manufacture, so far distant that it was just being touched just now by the same sunlight that had shone on those condemned in the Salem Witch Trials in 1692.

Close now, approaching—though he did not know it—that fragment in a vessel no larger than a thirty-five-foot motor launch on earth, came another dreamer. A dreamer who had never breathed spring mountain air, or the damp air of a Washington night, or any earthly air. Neither stuffed and preserved study specimen nor human book nor neon restaurant card could have spoken to him intelligibly. No birthday card would have made sense to him, no signed check supported him, no brown bears' battle stirred him inwardly.

Still—he dreamed also. He sat with his hands on a sloping table covered with studs and switches. His hands, like his body, were covered with black fur. But his flesh was warm. A vital fluid, driven by a heart-like pumping organ, flowed through veins in his body, refreshed by oxygen from an atmosphere that Jase also could have breathed.

His mind moved on its own desires. He felt heat, and cold, desires, and fear, and the necessity of making decisions. There was courage in him, and hope.

And now, approaching the fragment he did not know was

there, as Jase slumbered back in the humming stillness of his Washington apartment, the other dreamer dreamed. A dream of a white palace with many levels below ground but only three above in the light of a star he had not yet found. And on the topmost level, the mothers of his sons, and his sons—straight and strong and honorable and dreaming as he did then.

But it was a waking dream he dreamed. And it was the dream of Founding a Kingdom.

CHAPTER TWO

Therefore it happened that before the sleeper woke, Kator Secondcousin, cruising in the neighborhood of a Cepheid variable down on his charts as 47391L, but which the sleeper would have called *Ursae Minoris* or Polaris, the Pole Star, suddenly found himself smiled upon by the Random Factor that all seek.

Immediately, for although he was merely a Secondcousin, it was of the family of Brutogas, he grasped the opportunity that offered itself and locked the controls. Before him shone his chance of Founding his Kingdom. Therefore he planned carefully and swiftly. He fastened a tractor beam on the drifting artifact presented by the Random Factor. It was a beautiful artifact, even in its fragmentary condition, fully five times as large as the two-man scout in which he and Aton Maternaluncle, of the family Ochadi, had been making a routine sampling sweep of debris from the galactic drift.

Kator locked it exactly in the center of his viewing screen and leaned back in his pilot's chair. A polished bulkhead on the left of the screen threw back his own image, and he twisted the stiff, catlike whiskers of his round face thoughtfully and with satisfaction as he reviewed the situation with all sensible speed.

The situation could hardly have been more convenient. Aton Maternaluncle was not even a connection by marriage with the family Brutogas. It was true that he, like the Brutogasi, was of the Hook persuasion, politically, rather than Rod. But on the other side of the summing up, the odds against the appearance of such a Random Factor as this to two individuals on scientific survey were astronomical.

It cancelled out Ordinary Duties and Conventions automatically. Aton Maternaluncle—had he been merely an observer outside the situation rather than the other half of the scout crew—would certainly have approved of Kator's attempt to integrate the Random Factor positively with Kator's own life pattern. "Besides," thought Kator, watching his own reflection in the bulkhead and stroking his whiskers, "I am young, and my best years of life are before me."

He got up from the pilot's chair, loosened a connection in the body of the internal ship's recorder, and extended the three-inch claws on his stubby fingers. He went back to the sleeping quarters behind the pilot room. On a larger ship the door to it would never have been unlocked. But on a small ship like this the scouts must endure their work without benefit of a Keysman. Aton was sleeping on the lower bunk, his back turned.

Skillfully, Kator drove his claws into the spinal cord at the base of Aton's round, black-furred skull. Aton sighed and lay silent. He had felt nothing, Kator was certain. The stroke had been swift and sure. Kator pulled the heavy body from the bunk, carried it tenderly to the airlock, and released it into the wastes of outer space. He returned to the recorder, tightened the loose connection, and recorded the fact that Aton had attacked him without warning in a fit of insanity, knocking the recorder out of commission in his attack. Finding Kator alert and resisting, the insane Aton had then leaped into the airlock and committed suicide by discharging himself into the airlessness of the void.

It was true, thought Kator, gratefully, reflecting on his ancestry as he finished recording the account. *While others think, I act!* had been the motto of the original Brutogas. Kator stroked his whiskers in thankfulness to his forefathers.

He suited up in his spaceclothes. A little over half an hour later in the time-equivalents of Kator's people, who called themselves the Ruml, Kator had a close-line magnetically fastened to the explosion-ruined hull of the artifact and was hand-over-hand hauling his spacesuited body along the line toward the hull. He reached it without difficulty and set about exploring his find by the headlight of his spacesuit.

It had evidently belonged to a people very much like Kator's own kind. The doors were the right size, the sitting devices Kator could have sat in comfortably. Unfortunately, most of the original material of this obviously space-going vessel had been blasted away by an explosion of the collapse field that had destroyed it. This was important, highly important, for the type of faster-than-light drive system used by Kator's people also utilized a collapsed universe theory, and contained a field such as this one, which in exploding had left rainbow-colored streakings on the ruined walls of the artifact.

Of course, nearly everything not bolted down aboard the artifact had been expelled outward and lost into space as a result of the explosion. . . . No, discovered Kator—not everything. He discovered a sort of hand carrying case with a semicircular handle wedged between the legs of one of the sitting devices. Kator unwedged it and took it back to the scout with him.

After making the routine safety tests on it, Kator got it open. The find within was magnificent. Several items of what appeared to be something like cloth—shaped like a one-piece, continuously solid, thin, allcovering body harness set—if you could imagine such a thing. There was no provision on it for fastening either honors or weapons. Nevertheless, there were honors present, in various shapes and sizes of metal in the box, mostly ring-shaped and of a size to fit perhaps fingers or arms. And what was evidently a writing utensil of soft red wax with a sharpened point and a screw device to project it from its case.

Enclosed in a clear wrapping material of plastic properties and artificial construction were two oddly shaped containers, which perhaps were foot protectors. Soil still adhered to the bottom of them, and Kator's breath paused in his lungs as he discovered it. He detached the earth, carried it to a microscope to examine it minutely.

The Random Factor had not failed. Amid the crumbling soil he discovered and separated out the tiny dried form, the body of a dead organic creature.

A dirtworm it was, almost indistinguishable from the primitive form of the dirtworms at home.

Kator lifted it carefully from the dirt with a specimen clamp and sealed it into a small cube of transparent preservative material. This, he told himself, slipping it into his harness pouch, was his. There was plenty of material in the rest of the artifact for the examiners to work on back home, to discover the location of the race that had built the artifact. This small form, the earnest of his future Kingdom, he would keep close by him. And if the Random Factor continued to associate with the situation, there could be a use for it . . .

Kator logged his position and the direction of drift the artifact had been taking when he had first sighted it. He headed himself and the artifact in tow toward Homeworld, and lay down himself on Aton's bunk for a well-earned rest.

As he drifted off to sleep, he began remembering some of the sweeps he and Aton had made together in the scout ship before this, and regret was like a hollow pain within him until the shades of slumber came to soften it.

They had never been related, it was true, even by the marriage of the most distant connections. But Kator had grown to have a deep friendship for the older Ruml, and Kator was not the sort who made acquaintances easily.

Only, he thought, drowning sorrowfully in the well of sleep, when a Kingdom beckons, what can you do?

CHAPTER THREE

The sleeper woke and found himself weeping. For a moment he lay without moving, face buried in the pillow he clutched under the maple headboard of the bed in the shadowy room. He could think only of the fact that Aton was dead, that he had killed him.

Then, gradually, the undeviating, comforting hum of the air-conditioner began to intrude upon the memory of Aton. The softness of the strange thing that was a pillow next to his face, the yielding, flat surface that was the bed beneath his horizontal body, began to make themselves known as things he recognized as belonging to a place where there was no empty space, no artifact, and no Founding of Kingdoms. Remembrance of another life woke in the back of the sleeper's brain and flooded once more through his consciousness. Wiping his face on the thin white sheet that covered him, the sleeper sat up in bed.

He was in his own bedroom. On the nightstand beside him the yellow, luminous figures and hands of his alarm clock glowed in a circle of obscurity that was the clock's face. It was one-twenty-three in the morning. He reached out, fumbling for the black shape of the phone on the bedstand, behind the clock. His sleep-clumsy fingers knocked the receiver from its cradle before they closed on it. But he got it to his ear, pulled the cradle forward into the dim light from the windows, and dialed Mele's number. It rang, and rang again . . .

"Hello—" It was her voice, sleep-fogged, suddenly answering.

"Mele . . ." he said, and his voice seemed to have trouble getting out of his throat. "It's me. Jason. I'm through. I connected just now, while I was sleeping."

"Jase—" She seemed to be waking up to the information at the other end, fumbling for a moment. Her voice came suddenly, stronger. "Jase? Are you all right, Jase?"

"Yes." He wiped his face with a shaking hand clumsily and breathed deeply. It was ridiculous to feel like this, under the circumstances. But he did.

"Your voice sounds strange. Jase, are you sure you're all right?"

"Yes," he said. "It's just something that happened at the other end. That's all."

"What?"

"I'll tell you later." He was getting control of himself now. Even to his own ears his voice sounded more in control, stronger and more sensible. Businesslike. "I'll get dressed right away and come down to the Foundation. You'll phone the Board?"

"Right away. . . . You sound better now."

"I feel better," he said. "I'll get dressed and packed now. I'll be leaving in about fifteen or twenty minutes. I'll take a cab. Want me to pick you up on the way?"

"Do that." Her voice came back. It was a bright, warm voice now that it was waking up, and he loved it very much. "I'll call the Board people now and phone you back as soon as I have. 'Bye, sweetheart."

"Good-bye . . . sweetheart," he answered and heard the phone click down at her end of the line. He hung up himself and got out of bed. Standing in the lower half of his pyjamas in the dark room, feeling the furriness of the rug underfoot and the wind of the air-conditioner chilling his perspiration-damp chest, he came all the way awake.

He palmed the switch on his bedside table that turned on the lights of the room. The sudden, yellow brightness of them made the disordered bed, the familiar walls seem to jump out at him harsh and unnatural. He shook his head to get rid of the last of the feeling of being in the mind of Kator Secondcousin—but did not succeed. Taking fresh shorts and T-shirt from the dresser drawer, he walked through the door to the bathroom, opposite the door to the sitting room, which still lay dark.

He showered, and the hot water revived him. He began—and he was awake enough now to smile at the thought—to feel human again. He left the shower, lathered, and began shaving automatically. He was beginning to forget he was anything but a normal, earthbound zoologist in his twenties.

But as he rinsed off the lather, the shock returned. And with it the fear he had been pretending was not there. He lifted his face dripping from the water in the bowl and confronted it suddenly in the dark depths of the mirror with the fluorescent bulbs on either side of the mirror harshly lighting it.—And for a second he did not know it.

It was not merely strange to him. It was alien as the face of some unknown animal.

It was a lean face, he saw, and dark. It was narrow-boned and long. The bones were slight for a body his height, and the skin was brown from the constantly being outdoors that was part of his work as a zoologist and naturalist. His black hair, disordered now, curled down on a high forehead from which it was already beginning to retreat slightly. Below that forehead his eyebrows were black as jet and straight across as the bar of a gate.

Below these again, his eye sockets were deep, so that his brown eyes were shadowed normally. Women—not Mele—had told him on occasion that he had beautiful eyes. The term had always jarred on him. It sounded as if they were saying that his eyes gave him a look of softness. Now, in the pitiless light of the fluorescents, there was nothing beautiful about the eyes he saw. Their color was hard—like brown, weathered granite—but he remembered the literal jet blackness of eyes reflected from a polished metal bulkhead.

He turned sharply away from his image, walked swiftly back into the bedroom, and began dressing. When he was dressed, he pulled the gaudy plaid shape of a pullman bag from under his bed and began packing. As he did, the phone rang.

He picked it up before its first ring was finished. "Hello."

"Jase?" asked Mele's voice.

"Yes," he said. "I'm dressed and just getting packed now. I'll get a cab and be at your place in twenty minutes anyway. . . . Wait upstairs, though. If there's any delay, I want to be able to get you on the phone."

"You can call me if I'm in the lobby. The night clerk's always at the desk there. Just ask him to call me to his phone."

"Oh, yes." He rubbed the fingertips of his right hand across his forehead. "Of course. I wasn't thinking. You called the Board?"

"Yes. They'll all be there but Wanek. He's on the west coast.—Jase?" she said. "How do you feel now?"

"Fine," he said. He made himself smile into the phone. "Just fine."

"All right. I'll be waiting for you."

"All right. Good-bye."

" 'Bye."

She hung up. He called a cab, was told one would be at the front of his apartment house in five minutes, and finished packing his bag.

When he got downstairs and stepped out through the front door of his apartment, the cab—a yellow skimmer—was already waiting at the foot of old-fashioned granite steps. The air was still muggy with dampness and heat, but the street and sidewalks were drying back to their normal dullness. He maneuvered the pullman bag into the rear seat with him.

"Four-twelve North Frontage Road," he said.

"Right," said the driver. The cab whined more loudly and pulled away from the curb. They whined down the night-time street. From the back seat Jase could see hair in need of a haircut curling out from under the cap the driver wore, and he felt a moment's distaste, as at the sight of some uncared-for and messy animal. He looked away, out the open window of the cab and watched the lights of Washington sliding by, instead.

When they stopped at last before the wide, twin glass doors through which he could see the lobby of the resident hotel where Mele lived, he could see her standing inside. She was wearing a light blue summer dress that fitted closely on her tall, slim figure with its brown hair. She had white gloves on her hands, and her gloved fingers held a slim purse of a lighter blue than the dress. She did not wait for him to get out of the cab and come in to get her but came directly out at the sight of the cab.

He opened the door for her, looking up at her. And she stepped down and in to settle on the seat beside him. A faint scent of cologne—which he did not find distasteful but strange—entered the cab with her. She sat straight, her back barely touching the seat, and her eyes looked comfortingly into his.

"Twelfth and Independence Avenue," he told the driver, without turning to look at him. Mele kissed him. Her lips felt cool and strange, as the smell of cologne had seemed strange to him.

The cab pulled away from the curb once more. She moved over to sit close to him, slipped an arm through his, and held his right hand with the hand of the arm she had slipped through his. They sat close together without talking. He felt strangely like a man who has been ill for a long time and is now recovered, but who continues to feel the habits of his sickness clinging to him. The memory of being Kator Secondcousin—from the moment when Kator picked up the earthworm body that infected him with the virus-sized mechanisms making contact between him and Jase possible—stayed wrapped around Jase like a sheet. Like a sheet of plastic, transparent, but through which all the world with which he was familiar seemed blurred and distorted.

Mele was not only his observer in this experiment; she was the woman he intended to marry. She loved him. But now, feeling her beside him, touching, close as she was, she was made somehow removed and strange.

And there was nothing he could do about it. From here the experiment plunged into an unknown area. And there was no going back.

CHAPTER FOUR

They stopped before the wide steps and heavy bronze doors of the granite-fronted building that was the headquarters of the Foundation for the Association of Learned and Professional Societies. Jase paid off the cab, took his bag, and with Mele mounted the steps and rang the bell. The night janitor, Walt, let them in.

"They're all here already," Walt told them. "They're in the Library, waiting for you."

Jase and Mele went down the wide, green-carpeted hall, past the foot of the curving stairs with their wide polished balustrade of dark and on down a narrowed hallway to the point where it turned to the right. They turned and passed the first closed door to their left and entered the second. They stepped into a lighted room, walled in by bookshelves reaching to the ceiling and equipped with tracked ladders, one on each side of the room.

In straight chairs that looked out of place near the over-stuffed furniture elsewhere around the room, the eight members of the Board sat about a polished table at the far end of the room. Beyond them the tall green drapes had been drawn across the high windows looking out on the walled garden of the Foundation.

Jase and Mele went forward and took seats at the table.

"Here you are," said Thornybright.

Jase looked around at them. He was coming out of it, he thought. Here, in this familiar room where the whole thing had been planned and decided on, the business with Kator was taking on proper perspective. The eight men he looked at—none younger than their mid-thirties, and at least one, Wilder, as old as the mid-sixties—had all the look of men who have climbed hastily out of bed in the middle of the night. Their hair stuck out over the ears. Most of them needed a shave, and not all had their ties straight or shirt buttons buttoned.

They were all good men, top men in the sciences. Jase knew them all. James Mohn had taught him biology at Wisconsin as a sophomore—for a moment the sharply pitched streets and wooded campus at Madison rose in Jase's mind's eye, and then vanished. William Heller had aided him in getting his present position with the Department of the Interior. And so forth. But only two of the eight were important at this moment. One was Joe Dystra, and the other was Tim Thornybright. In his early fifties, heavy-bodied and powerful, Dystra dominated the table just by sitting at it. Across from him, the slim, forty-year-old, half-bald Thornybright looked frail and unimportant.

But this was an illusion. Tim was hard as tool steel. As Secretary of the Board, he headed up most of its decisions. He and Joe Dystra complemented each other. Like everybody else in the room—with the exception of Mele, who was Librarian here at the Foundation—Tim and Joe were scientists. But both bulged outside their fields, which was psychology for Tim and physics for Joe. Tim had a flair for politics, Joe a literal genius for business and organization. And they were both drivers.

"You're still in contact, Jase?" Dystra asked now, the hard fat of his face looking bunchy from lingering lines of sleep. Jase nodded.

"I still feel . . . different," he said. Thornybright held up his hand.

"I'm going to turn on the recorder," the thin psychologist said. "The sooner we get started the better."

He put his hand on the square, polished wood mount rising slightly from the table top in front of his chair, and everybody in the room heard the click as it was turned on.

"All right," said Thornybright, "this recording is being made on the third of June at—" He glanced at his watch. "Two-oh-eight A.M. It is the forty-sixth meeting of the Board for Independent Foundation Action, of the Foundation for the Association of Learned and Professional Societies. Present are Lester Wye, Joseph Dystra, William Heller . . ." he ran on to list everyone about the table.

". . . Miss Mele Worman, Foundation Librarian and Observer for our Subject connected with Bait Thirteen, Jason Lee Barchar," he wound up. "The reasons behind the action of the Foundation in allowing members to volunteer for the founding of this Board and this project are a matter of record. However, now that we've come to a point of decision, I think it'd be wise to recap." He glanced about the table. "Accordingly, I move that a rough outline of events leading us to this moment should be dictated to the recorder now by the Secretary, before this meeting proceeds any further."

He paused.

"Second," said Dystra.

"All in favor?" Thornybright looked around the table and a chorus of ayes responded from all but Mele, who had no vote.

"Motion carried unanimously," said Thornybright. He reached into the inside pocket of his sports coat and took out several sheets of typed paper, which he unfolded. He began to read from them.

"This Board," he read, in a brisk, dry voice, "was founded a year ago by volunteer members of the Foundation to invite other volunteers to join in an independent effort financed by the Foundation to protect our world of Earth against possible contact and destruction by one or more inimical alien races originating elsewhere in our galaxy. The basis for fearing such contact is to be found in the Report on the Likelihood of Alien Contact, issued five years ago after nearly ten years' work by members of this Foundation and its constituent societies and organizations. This report, made at Foundation expense and published for public information, was compiled for the purpose of awakening the Government of the United States and all other concerned governments of this planet to a situation brought about by the construction of vessels capable of reaching the neighboring star systems at speeds in excess of the speed of light—utilizing the Collapsed Universe Theories of Joseph Dystra, a member of the Foundation and of this Board.''

Thornybright paused and cleared a slight hoarseness from his voice with a dry rattle of his throat.

"These vessels," he went on, "were put into service and have been in service for nearly a dozen years now, in spite of strong warnings by this Foundation. The Foundation, it may be repeated at this point, was originally founded twenty-three years ago to coordinate the opinion of those in all countries of the world engaged in pure scientific research and development. The purpose behind its founding was to bring to public, and particularly governmental, attention the fact that almost since the beginning of the twentieth century, technological development has been using up the reservoirs of pure, basic or disinterested research and the search for knowledge, faster than these reservoirs have been refilled.''

He paused to clear his throat once more.

"The reason for this situation, the Foundation has been pointing out for the twenty-three years since its founding, lies in the fact that economic competition and public interest have made available large sums of money for the application of scientifically trained people and scientific facilities to immediate technologically profitable problems. So that, while the public standard of technological living has been growing apace, the world fund of new knowledge out of which this technological advance was made possible has been dwindling.''

He paused and turned to the second sheet of those in his hands.

"The recommendation of this Foundation," he read on, "from the first has been that the governments of this world counter this situation by making available a large fund and organization which can compete in facilities and salaries offered with private industry. So that those qualified to engage in pure research may be enabled to do so. In the past twenty-three years the Foundation has implemented this point of view with no less than six major reports, fully documenting the steadily worsening situation and setting forth those measures which must be taken to repair it. In spite of this—''

Thornybright broke off and reached under the table for a glass of water. He sipped at it, put it back, cleared his throat, and continued to read.

"In spite of this, and in spite of the fact there has been a great deal of public and even governmental support for such action in all of the major governments of the world, no such funds and organization have been provided."

Dystra grunted, grimly. Thornybright glanced at him and then went on.

"With the putting into use of the Collapsed Field Theory Drive and the penetration of space vessels of human origin beyond the immediate star systems within a fifty-light-year radius from our Sun, the situation, in the opinion of this Foundation, has become critical. As the Report on the Likelihood of Alien Contact stated three years ago, such contact has become—in the light of present scientific knowledge—a statistical certainty within ten years from the publication of that Report. Also, as the Report states, we must face such contact while possessing a scientifically unbalanced civilization, far overdeveloped in the technology which provides creature comforts for our own people. And a civilization which is woefully inadequate in knowledge and science which would equip us for contact, understanding, coexistence, or conflict with another, intelligent space-going, and technological race. A race such as our Report of three years ago estimates we must encounter within a decade of space exploration such as was then, and is still, going on."

The lean psychologist paused to change sheets of paper again. Jase glanced to look at Mele, seated at his right, to see how she was reacting to this rehash of what they all knew. But her profile was as calm as the profile of the statue of an Egyptian princess of four thousand years ago. Jase looked back at Thornybright. Inside Jase these old facts were echoing now with a new effect. He felt chilled and lonely.

"Accordingly," Thornybright was reading, "this Board was set up to direct a project in which the Foundation would independently finance and put into space apparent sections of destroyed earth-constructed space-going vessels. And these sections were to be sent into yet unexplored areas of surrounding interstellar space where contact with other intelligent technological space-going races was considered to be a high probability. These sections, referred to as Baits, were sent out equipped with a recent discovery by an independent researchist financed by the

Foundation. This discovery, utilizing the Collapsed Universe Theory together with recent developments in interpreting, transmitting, receiving, and associating the electrical activities that accompany activity of the brain, whether human or belonging to a postulated intelligent alien, would be embodied in virus-sized mechanisms. These mechanisms would seek out the circulatory system of any alien contacting them, travel by means of that circulatory system to his brain, and set up a transmission link, embodying no time-loss, between this alien and a volunteer subject responsible to this Board.''

He changed sheets of paper for the last time.

''These subjects, Foundation members and members of this Project who have volunteered and been chosen from among the volunteers as being those best suited for the duty, have been twelve in number. This morning, for the first time, one of them, Jason Lee Barchar, has reported making an alien contact.''

He broke off and turned to Jase.

''He will now describe that contact as fully as possible in this moment, although a more extensive report will be made by him later at a more convenient time.—Jase?''

Jase leaned forward with his elbows on the table and began to talk. He began with the moment a few seconds after Kator had taken off his spacesuit and handled the dead earthworm he had brought back to his own scout ship. He confined himself only to Kator's actions after that, keeping to himself all the strange half-understood emotions and desires that had also reached him at the time of the murder of Aton Maternaluncle and afterward as Kator was falling asleep.

His conscience chewed at him for this holding back. But he told himself that what he did not tell now could go in his more extensive written report later. Right at the moment he was too exhausted, he was too hard hit by the contact with the alien mind of Kator, to judge what else he had felt or had not felt and understood.

''That's the story?'' said Dystra finally when he had finished. The eyes sunk in the fleshy face across the table from him, were penetrating in their glance.

''That's all that happened,'' said Jase.

''All right,'' said Dystra. He had slumped down in his chair, listening. Now he straightened up and looked across the table to Thornybright, beyond Mele on Jase's right. ''Now we vote on whether to turn this whole project over to the U.S. government or whether we want to wait a little longer.—Jase, you aren't voting on this one, unless you have to break a tie. All right, I move the vote.''

''Second,'' said Heller, thinly, down the table. His bony face smiled at Jase.

They voted. For waiting were Dystra, Heller, Mohn, and the single physician on the board, Dr. Alan Creel. For informing the government and turning over all information and equipment now were Thornybright and the three remaining board members.

''I think,'' said Thornybright, precisely, after the vote was taken, ''anyone with any doubts about holding off ought to reconsider. After all, we've gone as far as private citizens can be expected to go.''

''On the other hand,'' Dystra, ''the work of a great many good men and the cost of a great deal of expensive equipment is tied up in something that's working for us now. We've turned things over to the authorities before, only to watch them fumble it and mess it all down the drain because one branch of the government won't play ball with another branch.'' He looked around the table. ''Once we turn it over, we can't take it back. And what we set out to do isn't done. I say, wait until we can be sure the work will be carried on right, before we turn it over. If we've contacted the Ruml, they've also contacted us. They can examine our Bait and learn a lot.—How about it? Anyone want to change their vote?''

He looked around the table again. No one there spoke or moved.

''All right,'' he nodded at Thornybright. Thornybright turned to Jase.

''All right, Jase,'' he echoed, ''it's up to you. Which way do you want to break the tie?''

''Hang on to the project ourselves,'' said Jase.

He saw them all watching him. He had spoken quickly, so quickly that Thornybright had hardly had time to finish the question.

''You forget,'' he said. ''Our original idea was that the earthworm infected with transmitting mechanisms would be passed from hand to hand, so that we'd have a number of contacts, not just one. So far my contact has kept it to himself, and his partner is dead. Let's hang on at least until Kator gets home for it and we have a number of contacts with Ruml minds.''

Thornybright looked around for a final time at the Board members.

"That argument make any of you want to change your vote?" he asked.

Again, nobody moved.

"Nor does it make me want to change mine," said Thornybright. "I still believe that now contact has been made matters belong in the hands of the authorities. Anyhow, Jase's vote has decided the question. According to previous arrangements, Jase will now move here into the Foundation building, where he can be kept under constant observation and guard by one of the Board members, and a constant record of information received from his alien contact can be maintained.—Do I hear a motion to close this meeting?"

"I so move," said Dystra.

"Second," said Heller.

"It being moved and seconded, this meeting is closed," said Thornybright and turned off the recorder.

Its click sounded strangely loud in the ears of Jase and seemed to echo on and on as if it reverberated over an inconceivable distance—a distance as far as from where he sat now to the scout ship of Kator Secondcousin, with its artifact in tow, heading back toward the experts of the Ruml Homeworld.

CHAPTER FIVE

Jason was installed in a room already prepared for the first of the subjects of the Project to make contact with an alien mind. The room was in the basement of the Foundation building, between the billiard room and the bottom level of the library stacks. The library room in which the Board had met with Jase and Mele actually held only a few of the Foundation's many and valuable volumes. The rest were in a five-story stack running from basement to roof in the space formerly used by three of the four elevators that had served the building when it had contained offices, before the Foundation had taken over and remodeled it. Connected by a door to the library room was a small room that was Mele's office, and a further door in this communicated with the stacks, which managed to cram two levels of stacks into each of the fifteen-foot floors of the building.

Jason's basement room had a door leading into the stack, but this was locked by Thornybright, who took the first shift of keeping him under observation.

"Sorry, Jase," Thornybright had said, locking it, "but we've got to stick by the rules. Everything we do will be gone over with a microscope when the authorities take over."

He settled himself in an easy chair, with the light turned low, while Jase gratefully turned in to get some sleep on the bed provided. He had been provided with seconal to knock out the intellectual centers of his forebrain and insure that he slept rather than contacting Kator again. The moment he touched the pillow, he felt himself going down into slumber.

The last thing he remembered was watching Thornybright seated in the lamplight, reading. The lean psychologist's coat was open, and something dark and heavy was suspended under his armpit. It took little imagination to deduce that it was a gun, and loaded. Still, in his alien-sensitized brain, a little fear moved Jase at the sight of that weapon, before he went on down into sleep.

After all, the Foundation member responsible for the development of the virus-sized contact mechanisms had been emphatic about stating that certain things about them were unknown. They had been tested and observed to cause no harm, physical or psychological, between human subjects, or even between human and animal.—But how could anyone anticipate what would happen in the case of a linkage between the minds of a human and an alien . . . ?

Sleep put a period to that thought.

Jase woke about ten the next morning, feeling much more rested and cheerful. He had breakfast brought to him, went for a walk around the various floors of the Foundation and out into the walled garden with Dystra, who was then on shift guarding him. Afterward he came back into the library to start writing his full report of the initial contact between his mind and Kator's.

He worked at it through the rest of the morning and the afternoon. When he was done, he found he still had not mentioned the vague but powerful emotional feelings that had been part of the contact. He told himself they were too hard to define, and that succeeding contacts would probably focus them in to the point where he could justifiably write them up.

He ate dinner in Mele's office that evening. He thought he noticed her eyeing him covertly from time to time during the meal, but he paid it little attention. That night he contacted Kator again. But in this contact, and in those that followed it for the next ten days, Kator was still in process of returning to the Ruml Homeworld, the original birth-planet of the race and capital of the worlds of four star systems to which the Ruml had spread.

In spite of this, Jase was busy. One of the reasons he had been picked from the mass of volunteers to be one of the subjects on the Project was that he could draw. He had trained himself to sketch accurately and quickly as a tool to aid him in the observation of wild animals in their natural habitats. He had found that if he sketched an animal, bird, reptile, or insect, he not only observed it more closely than if he photographed it, but remembered the observation so that he could recall details at a later time. Now he spent his days sketching for the Project the instruments and tools and devices of the Ruml scoutship's interior. This in addition to recording all the information he was able to absorb.

He found that he had no real thought-contact with Kator, any more than humans using the tiny mechanism contact device had been able to read each other's thoughts. He saw with Kator's eyes, he felt with Kator's body, and the stronger of Kator's emotions moved him to parallel emotions. In addition to this, he would occasionally be able to catch and interpret memories of Kator's, when the Ruml concentrated strongly on them. These came through to Jase not as pictures seen by the human, but in terms of remembered light, shade, muscle tensions, emotions and conversations.

Conversations were what disturbed Jase most at first. So far Kator had had no one to talk to, and no reason to speak. The remembered conversations that rose to the surface of his mind from time to time came through to Jase in an odd sort of double sensation. Jase would hear in his human ear the memory echo of strange sounds in the gruff, lower register of the Ruml. The jaws of the Ruml were longer and narrower than those of the human, and there were other, more serious differences toward the back of the mouth and throat. Particularly, there were no palatal or nasal tones to the Ruml speech at all. English m, n, c, and j, for example, were completely missing from their language. On the other hand, their narrow, thicker tongue was capable of rolling English t, d, and l in a manner that a human could not accomplish. Jase would, in contact, however, hear himself in memory making these sounds and at the same time get a certain impression of their meanings.

It was necessary to qualify the word "impression" even to himself. Because what bothered him was something that had never bothered any human speaking a foreign tongue of earth. To put it clearly, if confusingly, Jase understood perfectly what Kator remembered saying. But his human mind was often unable to relate that understanding fully to human terms.

For instance, when Kator was hungry, he thought of himself as "permitting" himself to hunger. And yet he had no more conscious control over his body's sensation of a desire for needed food than Jase did. The difference was buried in a maze of instinctual and social differences of the Ruml culture from the human culture.

"I understand, but I can't always translate. And I can hardly ever translate perfectly," said Jase to Mele, one evening ten days after the original contact. They were in her office, and he was showing her the sketches he had made that day while she had been out of the building on Foundation business. "Not merely the signs and labels of the instruments on the control panel of the scout, there—" he pointed at the sketch before her. "But the instruments themselves don't seem to come out quite right when I sketch them.—Maybe Kator's eyes see a slightly different spectrum than we do."

"It fascinates you, doesn't it?" she asked, unexpectedly.

Something jumped inside him, uncontrollably. He looked up and saw her brown eyes—lighter than his own—watching him intently.

"Yes," he said, keeping his voice calm, "I suppose it does. They're like a new species of animal—"

"No," she interrupted him. "I don't mean the Ruml. I mean the process of contact fascinates you."

"Not . . . fascinates . . ." he said, slowly. Inside him an inexplicable fear was beginning to beat.

"Does it frighten you, then?" she asked.

"Frighten . . . yes," he admitted. "A little."

"It does something to you," Mele said. "I've been watching. Jase—"

"What?" he said, sharply, shuffling the sketches back into a stack.

"Maybe you shouldn't go on."

"No!" The harshness of his own answer fascinated him. He lowered his voice and softened it to a reasonable tone. "There's something here more important than anything we've run into since fire was discovered and controlled.—I think. I just can't pin it down. Anyway," he added, "we can't stop now."

"If it was really dangerous for you, the Board would agree—"

"No," he said. "It's not dangerous. Anyway, we can't think of stopping. We have to go through with it now.—I'll know better about the limitations of contact after Kator lands. He should be landing tomorrow afternoon at In Point of the Homeworld."

But Kator landed, not the night after that, but the same night he talked to Mele. Jase had misunderstood the time interval somehow. In fact, by the time Jase fell asleep that night and his mind slipped into contact with Kator, the Ruml was already landed and making his report to the Ruml authorities in a building near the forty-mile-square landing area from which the Homeworld sent forth and received its space vessels.

If Jase had not made that mistake—if he had gone to bed, or even closed his eyes early, as he had planned to do the following day—he would have gained invaluable data on the landing area and its defenses. Now that chance was lost.

Lying suspended in a pool of darkness in the basement of the Foundation building, Jason drifted into the slightly stooping, harnessed, black-furred body hundreds of light years distant that stood facing three older Ruml on a platform, seated behind something like a desk. It was Kator who stood there, but it was Jason who stood within him. Jason-Kator stood before the Panel of Inspectors. Jason stood there, proud and triumphant, but hiding the double-beat of his warm heart beneath the formality of his posture.

He had just come through the door on the order of the Inspector's clerk. He stood now, harness bright, feet solidly planted, knees as close together as he could bring them and body so stiffly erect that it barely slanted forward from his hips at all. His whiskers never moved. His expression was imperturbable, for he, like the Inspectors, was playing the game that his return was no different than thousands of others that monthly took place in this building.

"I trust I am among friends," he addressed the Inspectors.

"You are among friends," said the presiding Inspector on the right of the panel. But the tone of his answer was ironic. Jason did not blame him. The Inspectors were all men of age and Family. Their harnesses were heavy with inherited honors, while Jason, in addition to his small Scouting Honor, had only the small Honor of a lesser Brutogasi: and the new, if large, Honor of the Random Factor fixed to his harness. And this last Honor was brilliant in its shininess, almost cheap looking, so new it was. While the inherited honors of the older men behind the desk were respectably dull with tarnish and dust.

The polite forms were required before this Panel, where people of all Honor stood at times—but of course that did not mean that the Inspectors must actually react toward young Jason as if he were an equal.

"We have examined your report, Kator Secondcousin Brutogasi," said the Presiding Inspector. "The artifact you brought back is, I believe, being gone over already at the Examination Center. Have you anything to add—particularly about the death of your partner on the scoutship."

"It happened so quickly," said Jason. "One moment I was fighting for my life—the next he was gone, and the airlock inner door was closed behind him. I couldn't open it against the air pressure inside the ship in time to stop him from opening the outer door."

"Indeed!" said one of the other Inspectors. There was a faint tone of respect in his voice, which paid tribute to the coolness of Kator's answer. It was something for someone just two seasons adult to answer so well. "Young man, you may even live out a respectable man's lifetime if you keep on like this."

Kator bent his head in acknowledgment of the compliment. He saw that the Inspector who had just spoken wore the badge of the Hook party—like himself and all the Brutogasi. The Presiding Inspector, as well as the other senior, wore the emblem of the Rods. It occurred to Jason for the first time that perhaps the whole Panel had wished to express its approval to him—naturally, the Rods could hardly make such an expression. Jason glowed inside, and his lungs felt filled with fire

"Then," said the Presiding Inspector, "if there's no other

questions, we won't keep you. You'll be called to assist Examination Center if any questions come up about the artifact.''

Jason inclined his head again, back to the door and went out. Outside the clerk handed him the short, ceremonial single-bladed sword he had been holding, and Jason reslung it in his harness. The clerk had not been particularly respectful, but Jason unclipped the top piece of money from the bandoleer strap of his harness and tipped the man anyway.

''May you found a Kingdom,'' said the clerk, bowing his head.

The poor lad did not know. Jason went out and took a seat on the overhead belt into the inner city and the section containing the Castle of the Brutogas. It was a short walk through narrow shell-paved streets to the Castle, and many older women who had had their children were at work in gangs, raking the shell. The shell fragments glittered in the blue-white light from the pinpoint of the sun, now above the roofs of the eastern quarter of the city. The little ornamental pools along the way glittered also with clean blue water, like Honor settings for the crystals growing in the center of the circular, or oval, or other-shaped pool bottoms.

The women sang as they raked—the house songs and the Songs of the Kingdom Founders. How beautiful, thought Jason, was this city of his people with the early sun on it and the women singing. At the curve of one steep, narrow road, he stopped to drink from a double-curved pool about as wide as his outstretched arms and as deep as his waist. Magnified, the center of its bottom of white, small tiles, the random shape of a growing crystal was ruby-colored. It shone like some great Honor in the clean water.

''Shade be with me, water be with me, strength be with me,'' whispered Jason, lifting his dripping whiskers from the water, speaking the invocation. He got back to his feet.

A solitary woman was raking nearby. She was of an age to be Jason's mother, though that was unlikely. Jason's mother was undoubtedly still in the palace of the Brutogasi. Someday he must look up the records and see. It was a matter he had always meant to get around to. An honorable man should know the identity of the woman who bore him and carried him sleeping in her pouch for seven years.

An impulse—perhaps it came to him from the Random Factor—moved Jason. He unclipped a coin from his bandoleer and gave it to the raking woman.

"Will you sing a song for me, fruitful lady?" he asked. "The song of the founding of the Kingdom of the Brutogas?"

She took the coin, leaned on her rake, and sang. Her voice was high-pitched and sweet. She was older than he had thought. She sang how the Brutogas had gone on the great expedition to the third planet of the second system the people had expanded to. That planet which, full of jungle or poisonous seas, had destroyed two expeditions before that. How, with twelve companions out of all those who had gone, the Brutogas—then Brutogas Thirdcousin's-Firstchild of the Leechena—had returned with a settlement planted. How he then had accused the other eleven of crimes against the expedition and dueled them, one after another, killing all eleven between sunset and sunrise of one day—so winning the worth of the settlement for himself and Founding the Kingdom of the Brutogasi for himself.

The song came to an end. The woman went back to her raking. Jason stood, filled with the pictures the song had painted in his imagination. Like himself, the orginal Brutogas had been only a distant connection of an illustrious blood line.—Not that that had anything to do with it. Great men appeared in all places—but quality bred quality, there was no denying that. . . . And quality was in Jason's ancestry, though he was several orders of relationship removed from the main line.

He came at last to the gates of the Brutogas Castle and was passed in by the porter at the gate, who was required to know by sight all those of the Family. He entered the ground-level courtyard, beneath the second story, where the immediate members of the family lived, and the third—the highest legally permissible level of dwelling—where lived the current Brutogas himself. He, and all the mothers of his sons, spread out through the nearly half square mile of corridors and rooms.

Jason's room, as a Secondcousin, was on the top of the fifteen basement levels of the Castle. He went down to it. It felt good to shut the door behind him on this small, square, blank-walled room with the image of the first Brutogas in one corner. It was as he had left it go on scout work, half a season before. The sunlight slanted in through the high half-window just at ground level above Jason's head, and the light fell familiarly upon the small washing pool beneath it, the circular sleeping pad, and the cabinet of Jason's possessions.

He had just taken off his harness when the door spoke to him, saying there was someone outside. He opened it and saw the tall shape of Bela Firstcousin, one generation older than he and one degree of relationship closer to the present Brutogas. Bela handed him a small, gold-glinting object.

"This to you from the Brutogas," said Bela. They were relatives and almost friends, and so they looked at each other with hardly any guarding tension. "And you are to move up to a room on the ground level tomorrow."

He saluted and left Jason. Jason looked down at the gold object in his furry hand. It was a half-Honor, the smaller of two Family tokens which the Family head could bestow on his lesser relatives. Jason's chest swelled, and deep feeling moved him. It had not passed unnoticed—the fact that he, one of the Family, had encountered a manifestation of the Random Factor like the alien artifact and had then returned alone.

True, there had been only one other man on the scoutship with him . . . And it had been with eleven others that the original Family head had fought that past day—to say nothing of those who had been original members of the expedition from which the original Brutogas and his companions had returned. But his own modest case had not passed unnoticed.

His chest expanded with love and pride. He turned toward the picture of the original Brutogas in the corner and shrank slowly down on his haunches before it. He crossed his forearms upon his unharnessed chest. A joy and pain too great to bear moved through him. He stayed in the reverential position as the sun mounted outside his room and the light moved across its floor.

"Give me shade . . . give me water . . . give me strength . . ." he prayed.

Back in his own basement room on earth, Jason-alone woke to find once more his pillow wet with tears.

CHAPTER SIX

"—But why," demanded Thornybright at the next meeting of the Board, "isn't he passing the worm along so that we can get the mechanisms into the bloodstreams and brains of some others of them?"

"You can't influence him in any way?" asked Heller.

Jase shook his head.

"I'm only a passenger," he said to Heller. "I know there was hope that just by sheer chance, with an alien, a subject like me could exert some mental pressure, or domination." He smiled for a moment, wryly. "Just like nobody's ever really given up the fear that maybe Kator is subtly starting to dominate me. But I give you my word, neither of these things is happening. It's just as it was when I tested with another human, before the Program got under way. The sleeping or inactive subject is simply carried about by the contact. He experiences what the contact experiences. And that's all."

"You didn't answer my question," said Thornybright.

"I don't know the answer." Jase turned to the lean psychologist, looking past Mele at him. Mele, as usual, was sitting in on the Board meetings although she remained officially unconnected and unvoting, her only duties being that of observing and helping Jason with his paperwork and written reports on the Ruml during the daylight hours. "He's hanging on to it for some purpose of his own. He thinks of it as 'Founding a Kingdom.'"

"Maybe he plans to use it as some sort of symbol?" said Dystra, looking shrewdly at Jase. "To start an uprising against the Family Heads? To put himself in power through a Revolution against the established procedure on that Homeworld of his?"

"No. Nothing like that." Jase shook his head. "You can't see their society as I see it. Any kind of Revolution is . . . unthinkable. I don't mean impossible. I mean . . ."—again he fumbled for a word—"unthinkable. The Ruml are complete individualists. The structure of social authority among them is an instinctive, not a sociological, arrangement." Inspiration came to him. "If you had Kator here right now and you could explain to him what you mean by 'revolution,' he'd stare at you finally and say, 'against what?' You see, even if a Ruml should for some—to them—insane reason, gain the power of life and death over his fellow Rumls, it wouldn't mean anything."

"Wouldn't mean anything?" echoed Thornybright.

"I mean—" Jason fumbled. "The authority he gained would have no meaning in terms of desirability to the Ruml nature. What are desirable are Honors—which are abstract things. It's true they call the badges they wear on their harnesses, Honors. But the badges are actually just like our medals—they represent the actual Honors. And the actual Honors have some deep, basic connection with the instincts of perpetuation and evolution of the Ruml race.''

''You mean?'' Thornybright pounced. ''That they represent actions showing survival qualities, or actions leading to the continuance and evolution of the race?''

''Yes . . .'' said Jase, reluctantly. ''But I hate to just say yes and let it go at that. What you say is true, and still—it's more than that to a Ruml. There's something religious, mystic, deeply noble and emotionally moving to a Ruml about these Honors. We think of something like, say, the Congressional Medal of Honor, as something apart from the man who won it. But to the Ruml, somehow, the man—pardon me, I suppose I ought to say 'individual,' but they think of themselves as 'men,' just as we do—the man *is* the Honor. It's as if the awarding of the Honor merely recognizes something that was already in him—that's been in him, or of him, or part of him, since the moment of his birth.''

He looked around at them with the helpless feeling that he was not getting through to the human brains behind their human faces. Even Mele was looking at him without real understanding.

''The Congressional Medal winner—,'' said Jase. ''We'd be shocked of course, but we wouldn't consider it impossible that someone who'd won it should later turn out to be a coward, a thief, a murderer—somebody utterly reprehensible. To the Ruml, that couldn't happen. If a man—individual—there should receive an Honor as a brave person, it simply could not happen that at some later time he could prove to be anything but brave. It never happened in the known history of the race, it never could happen. Even if it happened, it couldn't happen. If he should turn out to be a coward, it would be because he was only *apparently* being a coward.''

''You mean they wouldn't believe it, even if it was true?'' said Dystra.

''I mean it wouldn't be true. It actually would be because he was only apparently being a coward,'' said Jase. ''He just—'' He stared around at them, helpless to explain it, ''wouldn't be a coward. He couldn't be.''

''What keeps mistakes from happening?'' demanded Thornybright. ''What keeps a coward from getting an Honor for bravery through official mistake?''

''The one who received it wouldn't accept it if it didn't fit him,'' said Jase. ''But it wouldn't go that far. Long before it came to the point of granting an Honor, it would be clear to those who granted it and the one who received it whether it was deserved or not.''

"These Rumls can't make mistakes, then?'' asked Thornybright. The psychologist's eyes were sharp as hypodermic needles through which the man's disbelief sought to pump itself into Jase.

"They can make mistakes, but—This is a matter of instinct, I tell you!'' said Jase. "They don't go wrong about Honors. They just don't!''

Thornybright sat back in his chair.

"Move we turn this Project over to governmental authorities now,'' he said. "The alien contact is holding on to the mechanism-infected worm, and our single human contact is having too large a load of responsibility laid on him to interpret these aliens to us. Meanwhile those Rumls at their 'Examination Center' will be deducing more about us from that Bait every day, in spite of all the precautions we took. We've got no right to assume the responsibility of contact with a possibly inimical alien race this way.''

"Second,'' said Jules Warbow, the Board member next to him.

"Discussion?'' asked Thornybright, looking around the table.

"We shouldn't, that's all,'' said Jase. "I can't explain that to you yet, any better than I can explain the Honors or the Founding a Kingdom business. But I give you my word as the subject involved that we should continue to keep control of this project a while longer.''

They voted. As usual, it was four-four, with Jase casting the tie-breaking vote that put off the moment of informing governmental authorities about the project and releasing it from Foundation control.

The Board meeting was adjourned.

The Board members returned to their individual busy lives outside the walls of the Foundation building. Jase followed Mele back into her small office adjoining the room and sat down in a chair, as she sat down behind the desk with the recorder, prepared to type up the minutes of the meeting.

"They can't quite discard the notion,'' said Jase, wryly. "They can't forget the possibility that I might be slipping under the domination of Kator's mind—turning into a sort of TV horror science fiction monster. That's what's behind most of the opposition. All but Tim Thornybright. He isn't afraid of man or monster, but he wants to see the project in government hands and ten times as big as it is now.''

He watched Mele.

"Mele," he said, "you don't think I'm coming to be dominated by an alien mind, do you?"

She had been just about to begin typing, her hands poised. She dropped them and looked squarely across the desk at him. She took a deep breath.

"No," she said. "But I think you're wrong, Jase."

"Wrong?" Startled, he stared at her.

"Wrong to keep voting so as to break the tie and keep the Project in Foundation hands," she said. Her brown eyes were almost hard. "You're too cautious, you're too conservative. It ought to be going on with the finances and facilities something like the United Nations can put behind it, not just be confined to one man in a basement and eight scientists—even if they are some of the best minds in the world—sitting around a table making decisions."

He looked back at her grimly. She was younger than he was and adventurous. She had read a great many books, and the books were full of solutions to things. He had felt the same confidence in book solutions until he found himself lying out on a mountain hillside watching the spring fighting of the bears, or following a gang of killer whales through the icy Antarctic waters for days in a two-man submarine.

"Once you turn it over to the authorities, you can't turn it back," he said.

"What makes you so sure you're liable to want it back?" she counterattacked. "You haven't come up with any real reasons, any real, logical reasons that outside authorities wouldn't understand what you're doing, as well as the Board and the Foundation."

"The situation there on the Ruml Homeworld," he said stubbornly, "goes beyond logical reasons. Logical reasons are a part of logical thinking. Logical thinking is a part of the intellectual processes developed in a civilized, complex society—"

"And the Ruml Society isn't civilized, or complex?"

"Yes, of course it is," he said. "But—"

"Honestly, Jase," she said, "honestly now, can't you recognize the fact that you're dragging your heels about turning the project over not because of anything to do with the situation of those aliens on their world? It's nothing more or less but your old play-it-safe, cautious attitude that makes you want to hang on to being the only contact with the Rumls until you know everything about them—even if that means forty years more of study. You won't trust anyone else!"

Decisively, almost angrily, she began to type. Her fingers rattled on the keys.

"No," he said—so harshly she stopped typing after all and looked up in faint surprise. "You don't understand, any more than anyone on the Board does. The instinctive basis of the Rumls' civilization is drastically different than the instinctive basis of our civilization. Make a mistake about that and we could find ourselves fighting for our lives against them when it's the very thing we want to avoid."

She leaned forward with her elbows on the desk, staring levelly at him from beneath her two arched brows.

"Now it comes out," she said. "You *don't* trust anybody else to make contact with a Ruml. Only yourself!"

"I seem to be the only one who understands that instinct can be a greater determining power than intellect, in matters of survival and nonsurvival!" he said. He heard his voice raising but was without the will to control it. "My God, you're a woman. Don't you have any faith in instinct?"

"I have a good deal of faith in instinct!" she said, icily. "But I happen to have been born now—not five hundred years ago when men like you thought women didn't exist outside of the four walls of their own houses! I've got all the normal, womanly instincts, thanks, but that doesn't mean I can't control them with the higher centers of my brain when a conflict comes up."

He sat looking at her. Calmness had come back to him.

"I think," he said, after a moment, "maybe it's your personality that's the problem here, not mine."

She began to type.

"Or, let's say, as much as mine," he said. "And one thing more. If you think you can control your instincts, every time, you're as wrong as everybody else around here seems to be."

He got up and went out, hearing the typewriter continue to rattle unceasingly behind him. Outside, in the now deserted library room, the sun had descended, even during his short argument with Mele, into a lean bank of dark cloud streaking the sunset horizon. Earth's star flooded the empty room now, with a cold red light that left dusky shadows lingering in corners and behind the overstuffed chairs. For a moment Jase leaned against the bookcases along one wall, feeling against the back of his hand the leather binding of old and honorable books.

He had not meant to fight with Mele. It was bad enough that the Board did not understand the unexplainable, powerful, emotional force he had felt in his contacts with Kator. A crisis was bound to come when their lack of understanding and the possibilities of this force, directed toward the human race, would bring about a moment of dire peril.

Subconsciously, in that moment, he had counted on the support of Mele. Now whether it was his fault or hers did not matter, but she, too, had deserted his standard.

He stood on watch alone, like a single armored and sworded soldier of the Roman legions in a pass at night, facing north toward the German wilderness, the darkness and the sound of stirring hordes. The legions he guarded were all asleep in the camp behind him. He had never felt so alone in his life.

Chapter Seven

". . . And you're positive," said the Examiner, "that there's nothing you've forgotten to tell us about this artifact, nothing you may have done and forgotten in the process of your boarding and searching it?"

"I've forgotten nothing," said Jase, in Kator's body. "Nothing."

He stood before the Examiner in the Examiner's interview room of the Examination Center. The Examiner himself was heavy and gray with years. He was the Aton, an honorable man known to all the worlds of men, head of a numerous Family, expert in his field of study of space-found alien fragments and artifacts. He had lived the long lifetime of an honorable man, and his harness was heavy with Honors. He looked down on Jase now not only from the raised platform of his padded tuft, but from the pinnacle of that long lifetime.

"You are only two seasons adult," he said, now, glancing at the papers of the artifact report on the small table hinged to one side of the circular tuft, uncurled himself slightly, and straightened up to look down on Jase "And that's why you're certain. *I* wouldn't be certain—not after all these years. No matter how careful I had been, if I'd been in your place."

"The Random Factor—," began Jase.

"Young man," interrupted the Examiner, but not harshly, "the Random Factor is a dream, a fantasy. Oh, it exists—it exists. But as part of the statistical mass of the universe, not as something to be appreciated and integrated with the individual lives."

He fell silent, staring at the papers of the report. Jase felt emotion move him, at the sight of this man of age and Honor, lost in the question of the artifact Jase—Kator, that was—had found. He pulled himself together.

"Is there something—," he ventured, "something unaccounted for about the artifact, sir?"

The Examiner raised his eyes from the papers and looked down as if surprised to see Jase still there.

"Nothing," he said. "Nothing apparent, young man. Only, it seems to me we're getting surprisingly little information from it. It's almost as if the explosion that destroyed the craft it was originally had been intelligently designed to rid the artifact section of as much information-producing elements as possible."

Jase felt sudden anxiety speed up his heartbeat.

"You mean, sir," he asked, in a calm, controlled voice, "you won't be able to discover the planet of its origin?"

"Oh, that—yes," said the Examiner. "But there's so much else we ought to know before we send an expedition to the originating planet—much of which we ought to be getting from this artifact. And we're not." He looked again at the papers of the report. "That's why I called you in. I thought we might get some clue from you . . . Incidentally," his gaze swung back to center on Jase. "You aren't scheduled to leave on another Scouting Survey Sweep, I hope? We want you here to answer questions if need be."

"Sir," said Jase, "I have withdrawn myself from the Scouting Duty Lists."

"Good . . ." the Examiner nodded. His eyes ranged from foot to head of Jase's black-furred figure, as erect as the skeletal angle between the Ruml pelvis and backbone would allow. "By the way, do you think you might find Honor working on my staff, here?"

"You are too kind, sir."

The Examiner nodded.

"I guessed not," he said. "This work here is too slow and dull for the energies of young bodies. Men your age want active duties like your Scouting work. Well, I'll leave the offer open. Always provided you remain a man of adequate Honor, you can come back later on if you want."

He stared down at Jase.

"You may surprise yourself and do just that," he said. "When we're young we want to do everything overnight. We have wild dreams of great Honors and the Founding of Kingdoms. And that's the way it should be, of course. But after a few years it becomes time to remember that for everyone who founds a Kingdom and a Family, there must be the millions who care for all the other responsibilities of Honor. For there's a greater responsibility on all of us even than that of being an honorable man— you look surprised, young man?"

"I—" Jase stumbled. "I am a Secondcousin only."

"That makes no difference," said the Examiner. "Even an orphan is a member of the race. And he, too, has his greater responsibility than that toward his own honor—his share in the responsibility to see that in the end he is part of an honorable race." He stared at Jase in surprise, and not without kindness. "—Why do you mourn, young man?"

"—I am not fit!" choked Jase.

"Come!" said the Examiner. "Didn't I say that dreams and fantasies are proper to the young?—And where would we be if ever and again, at great, rare intervals, a Founder should not grow out of such dreams? I only warned you not to forget everything else in the search for personal Honor. Come—" said the Examiner, again kindly, "I see you're a very sensitive young man. If you live another five seasons, you may be the sort of whom we can all be proud.—You may go now."

Jase inclined his head and backed away. He went out, still deeply affected by what the honorable old man had said. It was not until he was actually clear of the huge complex of structures that was the Examination Center, that he got his feelings under control. He headed toward the Brokerage offices in the city center, wondering about himself. It was so strange—at one moment his ambition was such that he seemed to look down on all men, past and present; then, in the next minute, a word or two like those he had just heard was enough to make him feel less worthy than the meanest orphan cripple in a charity ward. He shook his head, baffled.

By the time he had arrived at the Brokerage Center, however, he had put the emotion behind him and was once more in the vein of the determination that had dominated his life since the moment when the artifact had first registered on his Scout Ship instruments. He found the Broker that Bela Firstcousin had recommended to him and gave the Broker his list of worths.

The Broker ran a practiced eye down the list and then turned to his computer connection and checked out the current values of the items on the list, worth by worth. When he was done, he nodded thoughtfully, typed out a total, and passed the list back to Jase.

"Not bad at all for a Secondcousin in his second season," the Broker said. He was a Rod, of the family Machidae, who had always been friendly to the Brutogasi—it went back to a gift of water made by the original Brutogas to the young Founder of the Machidae. "Of course, it's that credit devolving from your public reward for finding that artifact that boosts the total out of the ordinary. What was it you wanted to do with the list?"

"Liquidate it," said Jase. The Broker raised his eyebrows.

It took some little conversation for Jase to convince the Broker—a sensible man already well on his way toward an honorable age—that he meant what he said. And even more talk to convince the Broker that the final item of emergency demand upon the Family coffers of the Brutogasi was to be included in the liquidation.

"That," said the Broker, finally, "you can't do—or rather, I won't do it for you. Probably, if you can try hard enough, you can find some unscrupulous individual who'll liquidate it for you—but I won't. What I will do is lend to you against it—up to three-quarters of its value. At that, I'm trespassing against my own Honor and the friendship between our two Families. You realize what'll happen if you can't pay back that loan within one season, don't you?"

"Yes," said Jase.

"Well, I'll repeat it to you, anyway," said the Broker. "If you haven't paid it back by due date, it becomes payable against the Brutogas coffers. And you know what that means. Your family head will pay it immediately, but the minute he does so, you become a potential liability to the family—since any further indebtedness would also have to be paid, but you would have no personal credit with the Family coffers to absorb the payment. In self-defense, your Family will have to disavow you. Do you know what it means to live without the protection of your Family?"

"Honorable men have lived that way before," said Jase, stoutly.

"Honorable giants! Honorable geniuses!" said the Broker. "Hardly anything as feeble as ordinary honorable men. Most ordinary men, no matter how individually honorable, either suicide shortly afterward or are killed by some Familied individual, knowing it is quite safe to do so for private purpose without question—as is only right, of course. There'd be little point in our having Families if it was easy to exist outside them. But the point is a disavowed man seldom lasts more than a matter of days, at best. And it's a purposeless, unrewarding way to come to death.—You still want to do it, though?"

"Yes," said Jase, though his stomach contracted. His imagination was so strong that he could almost feel the horrible loneliness of being without Family or name.

"All right," said the Broker. "—And you won't tell me why you want the money?"

"I'd rather not," said Jase.

"Very well. I've said as much to you as my conscience required, and as much as manners will let me. That concludes our business then. It'll actually take an hour or so to put the papers through, but for practical purposes you can start honoring drafts against that sum I've written down immediately."

Jase thanked him and went out.

Outside the office, once more in the white sunlight, Jase wasted no time taking a shuttle bus through the tunnels to the far side of the city, where the pools and gymnasiums were. In the Center for the *Salles d'Armes*, Jase found and entered one of these establishments where the instructor specialized in teaching the use of the duelling sword. He almost passed the entrance at first, for it was a simple, bare room with only a small pool in the center of it and some bare seating platforms around the walls. Then he saw the sign, small above the entrance, announcing that this was the school of Brodth Youngerbrother Clanth, Swordsmaster. He went in.

Once inside he heard the shuffle of feet and the ring of metal on metal from an inner room. There was no door to this inner room, which was surprising—or rather, would have been sur-

prising with anyone but a Swordsmaster of Brodth Youngerbrother's reputation, Jase (or rather, Kator) reminded himself. It would
be a matter of Honor with such a Swordsmaster to employ neither public nor private Keysman.

Jase stepped into the inner room. The scene he entered on
was of a high-ceilinged, brightly lit, rectangular chamber, with
three pairs of fencers fencing, and a lean, tall Ruml almost ab-
normally erect of back, moving from group to group and giving
instruction. Occasionally he clapped his hands together for several seconds to get a fencer back into the steady rhythm necessary for swordwork.

"—Lean into it!" his harsh, rather high-pitched voice was
saying exasperatedly to one of the fencers in the pair farthest
from the room's entrance. "Lean into your stroke! And again!
And again! —The stroke comes from the hips—so!—And
again!—"

Catching sight of Jase, he broke off and came over toward the
entrance, walking with the swift metronomic balance of a trained
swordsman—his footfalls steady as the ticking of a superb piece
of clockwork.

"Sir?" he said, looking down at Jase. "I am Swordsmaster
Brodth."

"I want to enroll as a student of the sword," said Jase.

"An Honor to have you—" Brodth inclined his slightly gray-
ing head. "You are undoubtedly aware that my rates are somewhat higher than the ordinary—?"

"Yes," said Jase. "I know. I don't mind paying triple rates
to study under a Racc Champion."

"Thank you," said Brodth, inclining his head again, with no
change of expression. He turned slightly and indicated the fencing couples. "All three of my assistants are engaged at the moment, so you can pick the one that you'd prefer. All three have
openings in their schedules. If I might make a suggestion . . .
How experienced are you with the duelling weapon?"

"I've worked steadily with it for two seasons," said Jase. "Of
course . . . on my own. And with others in my Family."

"I see. Well, if I might suggest Lyth Cousincousin. He may
be a little too strong for you to begin with—he's my best assis-
tant—but if you're willing—"

"I wanted," said Jase, "to study with you."

"But you are studying with me—" Brodth broke off. The skin
around his nose tightened, and his eyes narrowed. "Sir," he

said dryly. "I am not for hire. If you wish to study directly with a Swordsmaster, there are other *salles d'armes*—"

"Sir," said Jase. "My last desire as an honorable man is to offend you in any way. My situation is unusual and severe. Within a matter of days I'm going to have to fight and beat a man as skilled as the average Swordsmaster."

Brodth looked at him.

"And who," he inquired, still dryly, "might this man be?"

"I don't know," said Jase. "But he'll probably be a Champion of one of the Heads of Family."

Brodth stared at him for a second longer. Then the tightening about his nose relaxed, and his eyes relaxed to let humor enter them.

"At least," he said, "you're not some young puppy who thinks he can buy the right to boast that he has Brodth Youngerbrother for his personal fencing instructor."

"Sir," said Jase humbly, "I would even be glad to keep it a secret if you want it so."

Brodth chortled. Like most Swordsmasters, Jase saw, he had long ago got over being touchy about his personal Honor—which no ordinary layman was liable to challenge in any case. Jase's hopes lifted. He had hoped for much, but he had not dared hope that Brodth would be possessed of a sense of humor.

"Well, well," said the Swordsmaster. "Come here." He led Jase across to a rack of the long, twin-bladed, basket-hilted duelling foils—identical in all save edge and point with the actual weapons used in an affair of Honor. "Choose one," he told Jase, "and run through the first twenty-six beats of the primary drill. I can tell all I need to know by watching you."

The fur matting a little with perspiration under his chin, Jase scanned the rack of swords. There were weights and lengths there for all sizes of man. As Swordsmaster, let alone the man who had won the supreme Championship in the interworld competitions of the best of the Ruml race, Brodth would have unhesitatingly chosen the heaviest and longest for himself. But Jase, only two seasons adult, was barely average height for a Ruml and no more than average weight.

He reached out and chose a sword that he judged to be even a few ounces lighter and shorter than the one he exercised with back at the Brutogasi Castle. He balanced it in his fist, point up, then swung it a few times to get the feel of the particular suppleness of its long, narrow twin blades. Then—he stamped once on the floor to give himself the beat and lunged into the first of the primary drill movements.

He attacked in five movements, retreated in four, attacked in six, retreated in two, attacked in two, retreated in two, attacked in four . . . and was suddenly overwhelmed by self-consciousness. His fifth attack movement, the concluding lunge, saw him stumble and almost lose his feet.

He pulled himself erect, his neck-fur soaked with the sweat of self-hatred and misery. He replaced the sword in its rack and turned to face the expected cold invitation by Brodth to leave the establishment.

But it did not come. Brodth was looking at him curiously.

"I don't know what . . ." Jase was beginning to stammer, when Brodth cut him short with a negligent wave of one hand.

"That fault?" said the Swordsmaster. "Nothing. You suddenly remembered I was watching. In an actual duel you'd have had no emotion left over to make a fool of yourself. No . . ." He considered Jase, rubbing his chin. "You're not bad. You didn't choose a sword too heavy for you to show off in front of me. Your reflexes are really excellent. And when you faulted just now, you didn't try to blame it on an unfamiliar weapon or the polish on the floor."

He fell silent, rubbing his chin and studying Jase.

"Then . . . ?" asked Jase. "You think it's possible? I could be trained to win—"

Brodth dropped his hand from his chin.

"Against Family Head's Champion?" he said, frankly. "Never in a thousand years. As I say, your reflexes are excellent. If that were all—" he twitched his head, shruggingly, "but you're too small, my young friend." He looked at Jase almost with sympathy. "A Family Champion will have half an arm's length reach on you, and a third again the weight—to say nothing of experience, and possibly reflexes as fast as yours."

He shook his head.

"No," he said, "Take my advice—and I won't even charge you for it. Just don't challenge this man."

"I'm afraid . . .," said Jase, "there's no choice."

"No choice?" Brodth stared down at him, "What do you mean? He can't have challenged you—that wouldn't be possible. And he can't crowd you into challenging him. Look here," said Brodth, "if somebody's been taking advantage of you on the strength of his position or ability as Champion to the Head of a Family—"

"No. Nothing like that," said Jase. "As I told you, I don't even know who I must challenge. But I will be challenging someone like that before long." He hesitated. "Sir, I repeat the last desire I have is to offend you, but if you could give me a little help with the sword, even though you know it's hopeless . . ." He reached and got the list of worths from his harness pouch and handed it to the Swordsmaster. "I have an adequate drawing account, and even the instruction of one of your assistants—"

"Sword and my Honor!" exploded Brodth, staring at the list. "You've pledged your Family coffer-rights?—To pay for fencing lessons?"

Jase's neck trembled. He caught himself just in time from reaching out to pluck the list back from the Swordsmaster's grasp. He had only intended to show the other man the total. His eyes burned with embarrassment. The fencing room seemed to rock around him. He looked right and left, expecting to see the assistants and pupils all having ceased fencing and staring at him. But, he saw suddenly, except for himself and Brodth, the room was empty. The others had concluded their efforts and gone.

"I plan . . ." Jase's voice was husky. "I plan a great effort . . ."

"But you young idiot!" said Brodth, with a Master Swordsman's indifference to the need for respecting other men's touchiness about name-calling. "Don't you realize you could be disavowed if you can't pay the pledge in time? And where's someone your age to get a sum like that? What are you counting on—Founding a Kingdom?"

"Yes," admitted Jase, miserably. "I—"

He broke off, seeing Brodth staring at him, and became belatedly aware that the other man had not meant his question seriously.

"You . . . *are!*" said the Swordsmaster, finally. "You actually think . . . Do you know what the odds are against one man . . . ?"

Jase nodded grimly.

"That's why I didn't intend to mention it to anyone," he said, stiffly. "May I depend on you as an honorable man to keep my inadvertent admission to yourself—"

"Yes, yes, of course . . ." muttered Brodth, still staring at him. "What's your name?"

Jase told him. Brodth stared for a second longer, then his eyes lit with recognition.

"You're the scout that encountered that artifact in space some weeks back!" said the Swordsmaster.

"Yes," said Jase, shortly. He turned toward the entrance. "Well, sir, if none of your assistants are able to take me—"

"Wait!" said Brodth.

Jason turned about. The Swordsmaster was looking at him strangely.

"You may not think it," said Brodth, slowly. "But I was a young idiot myself once. I had thoughts of Founding a Kingdom—" For a moment emotion lighted his gaze. "And it was not farfetched at that . . ." he muttered, "Race Champion three seasons running . . . I might have gone one step farther." He raised eyes and voice together and spoke sharply to Jase. "Come with me."

He led the way back into the anteroom with the pool and by a closed door Jase had not noticed there before into a room that was half office, half the lounge of a suite of living quarters. He led Jase on through another door off the lounge into a room set up like a small, bare gym. On the walls of it hung various weapons, ancient and modern.

"Our present duelling sword's no good for you," muttered Brodth. "Gives all the advantage to the taller, stronger man. But here—" He stopped before a section of the wall. "Look at these."

Jase looked. He saw two twin-bladed swords crossed on the wall. But they were practically hiltless, and the blades were several times as wide as the blade of a normal sword and half the length. Between the X formed by these swords hung two round circles of metal that Kator recognized suddenly as shields. He was looking at weapons as they had been used nearly two thousand years before.

"Here," said Brodth, indicating them with a wave of one gray-furred hand, "are weapons that favor your abilities as the present duelling swords would favor your opponent. The time is short to make an ancient Ruml warrior out of you, but—are you willing to gamble, Kator Secondcousin?"

CHAPTER EIGHT

The days and nights of the Ruml Homeworld were shorter than the days and nights of earth. But, because Kator thought of the Ruml day as a day in his own terms, Jase found himself thinking of it in that way as well. So that Jase found himself oddly, as it were, living in two different time systems—The hours, days, and weeks of the human world and the time divisions of the Ruml Homeworld, which went by half again as fast.

The result was not so much confusion in the mind of Jase as an odd type of schizoid perception, like double vision—or perhaps, Jase thought, it could be called alternate vision—without unpleasant effects. In any case, the practical effect of this was to find Jase unconfused but confusing the others at the Foundation with the frequent fact that something which was to happen about a week of Ruml time away would actually be taking place the day after tomorrow by earthly standards.

One case of this was the matter of the duel for which Kator was training. This by Ruml standards was roughly a month of days away. In earth time it was little more than two weeks distant. Jase's sleeping hours were spent living with Kator through the practice under Brodth's instruction with the archaic Ruml sword and shield, and Jase's daytimes in recording and sketching what he had seen, and his own attempts to relate it to earthly parallels.

Like most people who end up as zoologists, he had been fascinated by creatures other than human ever since he was a small boy and had pulled back to health his first wounded squirrel with an airgun-pellet broken leg. The mystery of the little universes of life and death existing in hollow trees and earthy burrows—as in upland, African ranges of the elephant, and the ocean-wide hunting grounds of the killer whale—had always fascinated him. His dream of remembrance, of how he had laid out on the hillside in the springtime Rockies, watching through his field glasses the spring fighting of the brown male bears, had been a dream of anticipation once, when he had been a boy.

It seemed to him that there were identities between all creatures, including man. They were all related. They were like people without speech, with different needs and wants and customs. With a little—only a little—understanding, it had seemed to him that it should be possible to get through to at least all of the higher mammals.

As a boy, he had imagined himself actually discovering a way to speak to wolf, tiger, and bear. Growing up, he had put the fantasies aside—but in spite of that, they had almost led him into the fields of psychology and communication instead of into his first love, naturalism.

Now, in contact with Kator and the life of the Ruml, the old dream had come back. Only he was a man now, and it was an obsession, not a dream.

He spent what time he could spare from recording and sketching in the Foundation library. The uncertain, foggy figure of a great discovery seemed to be fleeing just before him out of reach, like some veiled promise out of a story as wild as the Arabian Nights. He roamed the stacks where the old elevators had risen and descended, his nose and attention together buried in W. Köhler's *The Mentality of Apes,* C. Loyd Morgan's *Animal Behaviour,* Warden, Jenkins, and Warner's *Comparative Psychology*—until Mele had to come and find him to bring him back to matters of food, drink, sleep, and the very alien experiment itself in which they were engaged.

One day, nearly two earth weeks after Brodth had begun his tutelage of Kator, Mele came looking for Jase and found him seated on the floor on the sixth level of the stacks. A sixty-watt light bulb under its soup-plate reflector shone down on the shelves of books and Jase himself. He was seated cross-legged, absorbed in his reading. On the floor, open beside him, was Theodore H. Hittell's *The Adventures of James Capen Adams, Mountaineer and Grizzly Bear Hunter of California.* But the book he was reading, balanced on his knees, was Chalmers' *The Childhood of Animals.*

"Here you are," said Mele. "It's past lunch time—and did you forget? There's a board meeting after lunch."

"Oh!" Jase looked up and climbed to his feet. "Sorry." He picked up his books. "Haven't you eaten, either? Lead the way."

She stared at him, made a half-unconscious gesture toward him with one hand, then checked herself.

"You might brush some of that dust off!" she said angrily. "There'll be other people in the bar and the dining room."

"Oh—?" He flicked at his trousers with the one hand not holding the two books. Mele turned sharply and led the way through the narrow aisle between the bookshelves, where only one could pass at a time. Jase followed her to the stack stairs, down the stairs, and through her office into the main part of the Foundation building.

The bar and dining room of the building—for the Foundation was more than half club to its scientific members scattered all over the world—occupied the first-floor space that had been a cafeteria back when the structure had been an office building. But the business tenants of the original building would have been startled by the difference. The dining room that now was, was a place of heavy tables, carved chairs, fine carpeting, and panelled walls.

The bar, a short, heavy curve of oak, occupied one corner of the room to the left of the entrance. And when the big double doors of the entrance were pulled back, there was a little area containing three tables almost partitioned off, with the bar on one side, the wall on the other and the inward-opened, heavy door providing a screen on a third.

Jase and Mele, since Jase had moved into the basement of the building with the start of the experiment, normally sat at one of these three tables—the one in the corner by the end of the bar. And the waiter on those tables normally held it for them.

He had held it today as usual, and it had evidently been no great task this time. The dining room had only three other tables occupied—none of them among the three in the corner. Jase and Mele sat down and ordered. Jase put down his books on the table and immediately opened Chalmers' *The Childhood of Animals*.

"No you don't," said Mele "—He'll have a drink," she told the departing waiter. "An old fashioned. So will I."

Jase opened his mouth to argue, shrugged, and closed Chalmers. He put both books on the floor.

"There," he told her. "Out of sight, out of mind. Better?"

"Yes," she said. But she did not smile. Her eyes searched his face. "Are you losing weight?"

"I don't know. Why?" he asked. "You could ask Heller. He's been keeping the physical charts on me."

"I think you ought to have a drink before every meal," she said. "And no books."

"How about a night off?" He grinned—but then he sobered.

"I don't think you understand about this reading I'm doing," he said. "I'm an observer in this business—and I have to have some knowledge of what to look for."

"You act as if you've got to do it all yourself," Mele countered. "There'll be lots of people going into the subject deeply later on. Why can't you just stick to doing what you were originally supposed to do—just observe and report, and let it go at that?"

The argument they got into then was old territory. It was interrupted by the coming of the drinks. But they went back to it again.

"You keep saying I don't understand," challenged Mele. "Well, if I don't understand, tell me. Explain what I don't understand." The plates holding their lunches were placed before them, but they both ignored the food, leaning toward each other across the table.

"I've been trying to," said Jase. "You don't seem to listen. There're more critical elements to this situation than anybody but me seems to believe. You see, we really didn't know what we were getting into. It's a matter of instincts, both on our side and on the Rumls. And instinctive—or, actually, early imprinted—patterns of behavior are more powerful than the Board members, and particularly you, seem to realize—"

"That again!" said Mele. Her eyes flashed. "Now you're going to suggest again that I'm something less than a woman as far as instincts go, is that it? Well—"

"No," said Jase, grimly, but keeping his voice down. "No! You're deliberately misunderstanding me. I'm just saying that you're typical of our present times. And our present times—from early twentieth century on—have been loaded over with the notion of how-to blueprints for living. It started with popular psychology and spilled over to infect the whole pattern of man and civilization. I don't say you—or anyone else—is lacking in natural instincts. I say you and everybody else seems to have forgotten how much more of a determining factor they are when the chips are down than intellectual pattern, from Dr. Spock to automation—"

"Hi, there!" broke in the voice of Thornybright. "Can you stand being interrupted and intruded on at the same time? I've got someone here I want you to meet, and he can't wait around until after the meeting this afternoon."

Jase and Mele straightened up almost guiltily. They had been talking in fiercely low voices, with their heads almost touching. Now, as they sat back, Jase saw that standing beside the thin psychologist across the round table from them was a tall, extremely erect, athletically slim man with hair so neatly and closely cut it was impossible to tell whether it was gray or simply blond. This companion of Thornybright's was wearing a light-weight, gray summer suit, but he wore it on his active figure with a difference on which Jase could not at the moment put his finger. The man's face was tanned, sharp-jawed, and he smiled pleasantly.

"Certainly," said Jase. "Sit down. Both of you." He indicated the other side of the round table and the two chairs there that were normally never used. "We'll get the waiter over with the menu for you."

"Thanks, we've eaten," said Thornybright, as they pulled out the chairs and sat down. The waiter, seeing them, came over anyway. "Nothing for me. How about you, Bill?"

"Nothing, thanks." The other shook his head, smiled at the waiter, smiled at Mele and Jase, and looked back at Thornybright.

"Oh, yes—," said the psychologist. "Jase, Mele, I'd like to have you meet Bill Coth. He's one of our Air Force generals—a three-star man, currently tied up with the White House on special matters. He and I have been working together on this nationwide mental health program."

"You're a psychologist?" Mele asked him. Coth laughed.

"Sort of left-handedly a psychologist," he said. "Right-handedly I'm a dedicated military sort."

Jase, who had been about to make a light remark about young Air Force generals, changed his mind about the color of that short-barbered hair. The pleasantness and self-possession of the man was a social tool honed smooth by years of practice. Now that he looked closely, there were faint lines in the bronzed skin at the outer corners of Coth's eyes, radiating in a quarter-circle. They deepened and showed when the general smiled.

"I was telling Bill," said Thornybright, "—go ahead and eat, you two; don't mind us—I was telling Bill about your paper on the seasonal combativeness of the brown bear."

"Left-handedly a zoologist, too?" asked Jase, hastily swallowing a gravied piece of beef stew that—he now discovered—was growing cold.

"I don't have an extra left hand for it," laughed Coth. "No,

I'm just interested. I was always interested in animals when I was a boy. I thought of zoology just as I thought about psychology. But an appointment to the Academy at Denver came through—" He shrugged cheerfully. "Also, anything concerned with fighting falls into my right-hand department. I thought I'd like to read a copy of your paper, but I haven't been able to get hold of a copy."

"It was read, not published," said Jase. "I don't have an extra copy myself, but I think the Foundation has a copy to lend out. I had the typescript of it photocopied at the time." He looked at Mele. "Does the Foundation have a copy?"

"I can find out." She smiled back at Coth, and Jase felt a slight touch of anger. He knew her well enough to know that she was smiling for his annoyance.

"I'd appreciate that," said Coth. He launched into a wryly humorous account of the misadventures that apparently befell him when he tried to find materials in the Library of Congress from time to time. Jase returned to his beef stew. By the time he was done, Thornybright was looking at his wristwatch.

"Well," said the psychologist, "Bill, I guess the three of us are going to have to take off and leave you. The other people will be waiting for us to start the meeting back in the library room, now." They all rose, and Coth shook Jase's hand warmly in parting.

"Don't think I'm trying to butter you up," said the slim general. "But I've read some of your articles in *Natural Science* magazine—and I was fascinated by them." His smile was genuine, and his handclasp was warm. Jase felt momentarily ashamed of the resentment that had burgeoned in him following Mele's smile.

Thornybright was right. The rest of the Board was already in the Library Room waiting for them when they got there. Waiting and seated around the table.

"I declare this meeting open," said Thornybright, sitting down, starting the recorder beneath the table, and taking some typewritten notes from his pocket. "Present are . . ." he read and went on to read other current information about the date and number of the meeting into the minutes. ". . . Shall the minutes of the last meeting be read at this time? Do I hear a motion?"

"Move no," grunted Dystra. He was looking more like a bull than ever, a monolith of solid flesh seated between the two arms of his chair.

"Second," said Heller. "Vote," said Thornybright. All voted aye.

"Reading of minutes of previous meeting are therefore dispensed with," said Thornybright. "The Volunteer in this experiment, will now bring this meeting up to date on his experiences while in contact with the Ruml Kator Secondcousin Brutogasi."

He sat back in his chair. Jason leaned forward and began talking, beginning with the interview between Kator and the Examiner at the Examination Center, through the business with the Broker, and so on through the Ruml Homeworld "days" of practice in Brodth's *salle d'armes* since.

When he was done, Thornybright declared the question period open.

"This business the Examiner mentioned—about sending an expedition," asked Heller. "What's meant by 'expedition,' Jase? And did your contact, Kator, know about an expedition being sent in advance, or suspect it?"

"He seems to have taken it for granted," said Jase, frowning. "As far as what it means—he thought about it for just a second there, but the impression I carried away was that it was a sort of single-ship-go-and-look thing, rather than an attacking or occupying force of any kind."

"Correct me if I'm wrong," said Thornybright. "But wasn't the word 'expedition' mentioned before? Wasn't this what the original Brutogas went on and from which he returned only with the twelve companions he later killed? I got the impression that 'expedition' was definitely an occupying or conquering force."

Jase frowned again and searched his memory. It was a curious process, to have a question draw a complete blank from his human store of memories and then be able to dredge up an answer out of his remembered alien experiences as Kator.

"—I'm sorry," he said after a minute. "That's my fault. It wasn't the same word. I simply used the term 'expedition' to translate both of them into English. The words are almost the same, and they both mean essentially 'expedition,' but there's that difference between them. The Brutogas's expedition was an expedition to take possession. What the Examiner spoke of was an expedition to explore and report back. The confusion comes—" Jase searched his mind for a minute. "The confusion comes because both expeditions would be the first sent out to that particular destination."

"What's the difference?" demanded Dystra. "Why an occupying expedition to the Brutogas's world and an exploring one to earth?''

"There was no native intelligent life on the Brutogas's world!" said Jase, disgusted with himself. "Of course! Why didn't I think of it?''

"Then," said Thornybright, interestedly, "perhaps this expedition to earth is merely preliminary to establishing something like diplomatic relations with us?''

"No—" the word was hardly past Jase's lips than he realized he had been tricked by the thin, sharp-minded psychologist.

"Why do you say no?" Thornybright pounded. "What else could it be for?''

"To spy us out," said Jase, grimly.

"With a view to conquering us?''

"—Yes," said Jase.

"You sort of hesitated over answering that," said Thornybright. "Why spy if they aren't considering conquest—or isn't 'conquest' the right word?''

"I don't know if I can answer that," said Jase, carefully.

"Maybe you better try," said Dystra. They were all looking at him. Jase felt bitter inside. There was no use trying to avoid the answer with men like this interested in getting it out of him. And Thornybright—as well as Dystra, now—would keep after him until they got it.

"Whenever they've come across intelligent or semi-intelligent other races in the past," said Jase, harshly, "they've either eliminated them in taking over their worlds or reduced them to a more or less domestic animal status. But—"

"Why didn't you tell us this before?" demanded Thornybright.

"But—," Jase went on, "as I was going to say, they've only encountered worlds so occupied twice before. And in neither case were the intelligence of these races, or their civilization, anywhere near level with our own. The higher of the two was perhaps on a level with Pithecanthropus of over two hundred thousand years ago on earth, with a brain two-thirds the size of present-day man. There's nothing in the Ruml gestalt so far that leads me to believe that they're incapable of nonviolent contact and association with their mental and cultural equals, such as us. The business of sending an expedition is merely normal procedure with them—"

"Jase," interrupted Dystra, quietly. Jase fell silent. "I think," said the physicist, "we've cleared up the meaning of the word 'conquest' in this context. Anyone anything more to say about that?" He looked around the table. "All right, suppose we get to a question that I think is considerably more to the point. Jase—" His eyes under their tangled and bushy brows swung back to center on the face of Jase. "You seem to be assuming that your contact, Kator, is going to win this duel."

"I think he will," said Jase.

"You *think*," said Dystra. "This fencing master—Brodth—doesn't seem to share your confidence, and he's supposed to be their expert." He turned to face down toward the blond-headed, brilliant young man who was the only physician on the Board. "Alan, what about it? If Jase's in contact with this Kator, and Kator's killed in the duel, what happens?"

Alan Creel pursed his lips.

"I can only guess," he said. "We weren't exactly in a position to kill off one of our human volunteers when we were testing this linkage equipment to find out what would happen to the other. If the Ruml's killed . . . well—" He hesitated.

"I'll put it bluntly," said Dystra. "Would Jase die, too?"

"Well . . ." said Creel, "there's no definite reason why he should. . . . On the other hand, the psychic shock would have to be extremely severe. Someone with a weak heart, say, would be inviting a fatal result. Jase, of course, is in top physical condition or we wouldn't have picked him for this work. But, even at that, he's going to share Kator's reactions. He'll die, psychically, at the same time Kator does. Of course, maybe the linkage between their minds will fail just before the actual moment of death, in which case there'd be no psychic shock at all. Jase would just find himself out of contact."

"But on the whole," Dystra pounded softly on the table with one heavy fist, "you wouldn't advise staying in contact with a mind as it dies?"

"Advise it? Certainly not!" said Creel. "I'd advise against it. In fact—" He turned to look at Jase. "That's what I do right now. Advise against it."

"I don't think," said Jase, deliberately, "Kator's going to lose that duel."

"But if he does?" Dystra demanded.

"If he does—" Jase broke off and then started again. "Well, if he does, we still can't risk losing what we might learn from my contact with him between now and then. Once broken, chances are the contact can't be renewed—you remember we established that on our tests with humans. And if two humans can't get back into contact again after breaking it, what's the chances of a human and alien managing it—when the alien doesn't know he's contacted and they're two hundred light years apart?''

"I don't think," put in Thornybright, "that we've got the right to decide to risk Jase's life, or whatever damage might come to him."

"You don't have to—," began Jase. But Thornybright broke in on him.

"I'm not through, Jase. What I started to say—" The psychologist tapped deliberately on the polished surface of the table with a spatulate forefinger. The ticking of his fingernail against the table was emphatic in the quiet room. "—And I don't mean to insult or blame Jase in any way when I say this—the situation in this experiment is getting completely out of hand."

"Completely?" asked Heller, raising his eyebrows.

"I chose the word deliberately." Thornybright glanced at the biologist who had been Jase's teacher before turning back to address the gathering as a whole. "All of us here—except Mele—sit in a position of responsibility toward an experiment that involves not only a human guinea pig but possibly the future of the whole human race. As it stands right now, there's a chance our world may be attacked by an alien race many times our number and with a longer history of space travel and experience. Our single human contact with this race—our peephole on their Homeworld—is showing signs—forgive me, Jase, but it's how I feel—of being at least partisan, if not actually subconsciously influenced by the alien mind with which he is in contact—"

"Just a minute!" broke in Jase. "I can't let that go into the record without saying something. I deny any influence, subconscious or otherwise. As for any desire to be partisan—"

"You wouldn't have to be consciously partisan," said Thornybright. "Merely sharing Kator's emotional drive toward his own goals could cause you to identify with those goals to the point where your human judgment might be biased. Can you look at me right now and guarantee me that nothing like that can have happened to you since you first made contact?"

Jase opened his lips and closed them again. Then he spoke.

"I'm positive," he said, "nothing like that has happened."

"You don't guarantee it, however," said Thornybright. "I'll

go on. In addition to what I've already mentioned, we've got a situation coming up in which our human guinea pig may be risking his own life, if not lesser damage. Now," Thornybright looked deliberately around at all the faces at the table, "I don't say we ought to vote to make Jase break contact before the danger of the duel threatens him. I do say, as I've said before in this room, that it's time to turn this experiment over to the proper authorities. It's not for us to decide—either on matters of Jason's life or on matters of possible attack on our world by an alien civilization."

"As far as my own life's concerned," said Jase, "I claim the right to make the decision about that."

"The other half of the decision remains, in any case," said Thornybright. "Now—" He leaned forward. "I brought in a man for lunch today at the Foundation building here. An Air Force three-star General, William Coth. I introduced him to Jase and Mele just now. He's a good man, he does special jobs for the Administration, and he has a strong background in the sciences combined with a proper respect for the research process. If we move now—instead of waiting until the last minute—to turn this project over to the government, I'm sure our wishes as to the man to take authority over it will be respected. Coth is ideal for the job, from our point of view."

He swung about to face both Jase and Mele.

"You two met him," he said. "I leave it up to you. How did Bill Coth impress you?"

"I—," began Mele hesitantly, but Jase cut her off.

"He impressed me a good deal," said Jase. "I believe he's everything Tim here says he is. But the question before us here isn't yet *who* to turn the project over to. It's whether to turn it over. Probably—and I trust Tim in this—we couldn't find a better man than Coth. But I still say we ought to stay independent on this experiment until the very last minute. I repeat—there're elements and qualities to the Ruml culture which I haven't been able to render to you. There's just no way of getting across what I've felt in the process of being Kator. Maybe, once I completely understand these things I can explain them to you. At least I'll be able to let you know that I can't do anything with them. Now, this upcoming duel with Kator is crucial. I want to go through with it. With no one but the Board behind me."

"Move we put the matter to a vote," said Dystra.

"Second!" said Heller, quickly.

"Object," said Thornybright. "I move for further discussion of this point."

"Vote on the prior movement," said Dystra. "All in favor. . . ?"

The vote was straight down the middle. Everybody looked at Jase.

"I vote," said Jase, slowly, "to keep control of this experiment in the hands of this board and to go through the duel with Kator, whether he is killed or not.—I vote aye."

He looked at Thornybright. The eyes of the psychologist were unreadable in a poker face. Turning away from them, he came face to face with the staring eyes of Mele.

Those eyes were harder to turn away from. He remembered what Creel had said about the possibilities for him if Kator should die while Jase was in linkage. And he remembered what at times he came close to forgetting—that Mele loved him.

CHAPTER NINE

The day the Examination of the Artifact was completed, Jase was standing in his room, adding the ceremonial kilt for official functions to his weapons' harness, when the door spoke to him.

"Bela Firstcousin wishes to enter," it said.

Jase turned toward the door.

"Enter," he said.

The door opened, and Bela Firstcousin came in. He looked at Jase with a strange new combination of liking and respect.

"I'm sent to you with a message," he said. "The Brutogas wants to see you in his office, before you leave the Castle."

"The Brutogas?"

Jase's hands hesitated on his kilt. He understood now the reason for the sudden, almost shy, respect in his older cousin and occasional companion outside the Family walls. A sudden bitter sadness of superstition assailed him. He had liked Aton Maternaluncle, his scout partner—and he had been forced to kill Aton. Bela, here, had been his one close acquaintance within the family, and now he was leaving Bela behind. *Solitary are the great men*, said the proverb; and it was true. He became aware that Bela was watching him in surprise.

"Why do you mourn?" Bela asked. "It is a great Honor as Family Honors go."

"I know. It's just—I feel the passage of time, suddenly," said Jase. His hands finished adjusting the kilt.

"You talk," said Bela, watching him, "like a man who has already achieved an honorable age."

"That, too?" said Jase, a little bitterly. "I'm ready. Are you conducting me?"

"I'll take you to the top level of the Castle and point the way for you," said Bela. "I can't go any farther with you, and none of the immediate family can honorably be the guide of a Secondcousin. Come on."

He led Jase out of the room, along corridors, and up two sweeps of curving ramps to a heavy, tall, white door with a golden handle. Bela took hold of the handle, turned it, and with effort pushed open the door enough to admit the body of Kator.

"The Brutogas has four attendants to open such doors," said Bela with a grimace. "Hurry through."

But Jase hesitated for a moment. Through the partial opening of the door he looked down a long, lofty corridor of white marble pierced with tall windows along its right wall. The morning sunlight through those windows lost its white harshness upon the marble and became soft and glowing.

"Hurry!" repeated Bela, straining against the weight of the door. "Water, shade, and peace go with you."

"Thank you, cousin," said Jase, gratefully—and walked through into the sunlit corridor. Behind him he heard the door close with a solemn boom, but now he did not look back. Bela had told him the route to the office of the Brutogas. Jase followed it.

Early in the morning as it was, he passed over the whole route without encountering any of the immediate family. When he came at last to the smaller, white door with a gold handle that was his destination, memory awoke in him. He did not remember how he had got here, but he remembered being here on the single previous occasion of his life—and the single only occasion normally allowed to those not of the immediate family. It had been on his naming day, the traditional third hour after he had left his mother's pouch. Of course, he had seen the Brutogas on a number of Family ceremonies and occasions since then—

though never close up. But now, raising his hand to the golden handle of the office door, it all came back; and he remembered the Head of his family not as the grayed and stooping man of honorable age he had seen at ceremonies, but as a mysterious towering figure who put a hand on his head and rumbled some deep, incomprehensible sounds that he was later to learn were *"Kator Secondcousin Brutogas."*

Jase's neck trembled under its black fur with the memory. He put his hand to the handle, opened the door without speaking—for here on the top level there were no Keysmen, locks, or door speakers—and entered the office.

It was a smaller room than Jase's memories pictured it. Before the tall window and behind a desk on a low pedestal, squatted rather than curled the Brutogas. He was now in person as Jase remembered him from the Family occasions and ceremonies—a gray, stooped Ruml of honorable age. Kator approached the desk and inclined his head.

"I am Kator Secondcousin, sir," he said.

The Brutogas considered him, almost ponderingly.

"Yes," said the Family Head, at last, "you were an active youngster. They could hardly keep you still in here on your Naming Day. Well," he pushed the papers on the desk aside. "We understand you have ambitions to lead the expedition shortly to be sent to the Homeworld of the Muffled People."

"Sir?" said Jase, blankly.

"You don't know? That's the name they've pinned on those aliens who originated that artifact you found and brought back because they evidently wrap themselves in cloths. But you haven't answered my question about wanting to lead the expedition?"

"Sir," said Jase, carefully, "I've no idea what the Examination Center has discovered and deduced about the artifact—"

"Quite right," the Family Head nodded approvingly. "Don't go off half-cocked until you know what you're getting into. As it happens, I've got a copy of the report here. Would you like to know what the Center found?"

"Yes sir," said Jase, standing as stiffly straight as the hinging of his spine with his pelvis allowed. "I would."

"Well," said the Brutogas, flicking back the top sheet of a sheaf of papers lying before him on the desk, "the conclusions are that the aliens are about our size, biped, of a comparable level of civilization—"

A small sound of excitement escaped Jase in spite of himself.

"That's right," said the Brutogas, looking up, and repeating himself, slowly. "*A comparable level of civilization.* The challenge of a race like that will be greater than anything in the history of man. But to go on. . . ." He resumed reading, "A comparable level of civilization but probably loaded with taboos from an earlier, more primitive stage which would take the place of a system of Honor. They—you have a question?"

"Sir?" asked Jase. "Can any intelligent beings grow to a level of civilization without developing a concept and system of Honor?"

The Brutogas nodded approvingly.

"The report considers that question," he said. "The conclusion is: No, of course they can't avoid the concept of Honor. Development of a civilization requires a racial self-awareness, self-awareness means that they must become conscious of the duty of racial survival as an intellectual matter, and the evolution of a concept of Honor to insure that survival would be inescapable."

He looked thoughtfully at Jase.

"On the other hand," he said, "it is almost as much a foregone conclusion that our own system of Honor would be utterly incomprehensible to them. The chances of it occurring spontaneously in an alien race are too small to be reckoned in any sensible numbers. What the Examination Center considers most likely—as I repeated to you—is that this race will have a system of primitive taboos elaborated to fit the complexities of a technological civilization. So that while they will, in effect, operate within a sort of system of Honor for the sake of survival, they will not understand it."

"But, sir," said Jase, "that means that any expedition sent against them stands a very good chance of success!"

"Secondcousin, Secondcousin," said the Brutogas, shaking his head. "Do you think one advantage insures success? They may have either personal or technological advantages of their own over us."

"But, surely," said Jase, "no material or characteral advantage could compare with an advantage a system of Honor has over any system?"

"Abstractly speaking, of course not," said the Brutogas. "But practically speaking, there may be serious stumbling blocks in the matter of mere alien numbers or ability of alien weapons. It is an honorable endeavor to die to a good purpose, but it is not honorable to risk bleeding the race dry. If all the fathers are killed, who will engender the sons?''

Jase stood silent, feeling rebuked.

"There remains as well," said the Brutogas, after a pause, "the possibility that they do have—not the same system of Honor as ourselves—but a comparable one we cannot yet identify. Possibly even a superior one."

"Superior?" Jase stared at the Head of his Family.

"Theoretically, it's possible," said the Brutogas. "Remember how it's said, ''Honor is without limit, effort is without limit. Only Man has a limit.' ''

Jase inclined his head.

"Now," said the Brutogas, "will you answer me about your desire to lead the expedition to this Homeworld of Muffled People?"

"Sir," replied Jase, "I desire it very much."

"Yes. I was sure you did." The Brutogas breathed out softly through his nose and stroked the stiff, gray whiskers around his mouth and nose, which were twice as long as those of Kator Secondcousin. "And, of course, it would do our Family reputation no harm to have a member of our name Keysman on such an expedition."

"Thank you, sir."

"No, that's all right. However," said the Brutogas, slowly, "there's something you have to understand. It's the reason I called you here today. The political climate at the moment is such that I cannot in Honor risk the prestige of the Family in attempting to help you capture the Keysman post in this expedition—or even the post of Captain—"

"Sir—," began Jase.

"I know, I know." The Brutogas waved his incipient protest to silence. "Being a Secondcousin, you didn't expect Family assistance in this endeavor. Nevertheless, I want you to know that I would be disposed to give it to you, for the sake of the vital spark of ambition I see in you, if it were not for the political situation. Something perhaps you don't know is that the selection board will be a seven-man panel, and it is a practical certainty that the Rods will have four men on it, to only three of our Hooks."

Jase felt his stomach contract. But he kept his neck stiff and his posture erect.

"That will make my possible selection a far chance, sir," he said.

"Yes," said the Brutogas. "I'd say so. Wouldn't you?"

"Yes, sir."

"But you're determined to try, anyhow?"

"I see," said Jase, making formality a stiff armor to hold him erect in the face of this disastrous news, "no reason to change my present view about the situation, sir."

"I guessed as much." The Brutogas squatted back on his platform, gazing at him. "Every generation or so one like you crops up in a Family. Ninety-nine per cent of them end up as disasters. Only," he added softly, "one in a million is . . . remembered, as a success."

"Sir," said Jase, his head spinning. He had never dreamed that his ambition would become known to the Head of his Family.

"The Brutogasi," said the older man, "can have no official concern in this ambition of yours, and no interest in officially backing you for Keysman of this proposed expedition. But, if by some miracle you should succeed, I imagine I can trust to your Honor to give credit to the Family for counsel and guidance, and other assistance."

"Sir—how could you think otherwise?" Jase almost cried out.

"I didn't, really. It's my duty to mention it, only." The Brutogas breathed out through his nose, sighingly. "It's also my duty to mention now that if your attempt should somehow end up with you in a scandalous or other than honorable position, you must expect that mortgage you pawned on your Family coffer-rights will be immediately called in for payment."

The contraction of Jase's stomach increased.

"I understand, sir," he said.

"Well," said the Brutogas, "that's all. But my personal wishes go with you. Shade be yours, water be yours, peace be yours."

"I honor the Head of my Family, now and ever," said Jase.

Slowly he backed to the door and went out. The last sight he had of the office showed the gray head of the Brutogas bending once more above the papers on his desk.

He hardly knew how he found his way back through the sunlit marble corridors. But once away from them and once outside the palace, he took the shuttle toward the Examination Center and made a definite effort to shake off the emotion of his interview with the Head of his Family. Such emotion was an honorable thing, but he needed all his faculties for what was coming.

Twelve invitations for the post of Keysman had been sent out in response to the, naturally, hundreds of applications for interview. Only those with some claim to consideration would be allowed before the Selection Board. Jase's claim was that it was he who had found the Artifact, and that he could therefore claim that the Random Factor favored him over all other candidates. To anyone not acquainted with politics and selection boards, this claim undoubtedly would have seemed so paramount as to make the act of selection a formality.

Actually, Jase had received only the eleventh of the twelve invitations distributed by the Board. It could, Jase told himself on the shuttle bus, be worse. He could have been the twelfth invited.

When he was finally at the Examination Center's Headquarters Building, and had finally been summoned in to face the six-man board—in the room from which he had watched the ten previous candidates depart—he discovered the faces behind the table to be exactly as cold-eyed and gray-whiskered as he had feared.

Only one member looked at him with anything resembling approval. And that was because this member happened to be himself a Brutogasi—Ardolf Halfbrother. The other five board members were—in order from Ardolf at the extreme right behind the table—a Cheles, a Worna (both Hooks politically and therefore possibly votes for Jase), four Rods, a Gulbano, a Ferth, an Achohka, and the Nelkosan himself. This last could hardly be worse. Not only did the Nelkosan, as a Family Head, outrank everyone else on the board, but it was to his family that Aton Maternaluncle, Kator's dead scout partner, had belonged. The board of inquiry on Jase's return had found him not chargeable with Aton's death. But the Head of Aton's Family could hardly in honor accept this verdict with grace. As an honorable man, it would be his duty to damage Jase if he possibly could.

Jase took a deep breath through his nose as he halted before the table behind which the six were ranked and saluted with his claws extended from his right fingers over his heart region.

"I am Kator Secondcousin Brutogas, sirs," he said, "responding to your kind invitation to be here at this time. I trust I am among friends."

"Here, Secondcousin," said the Nelkosan, responding as Senior board member with the traditional guarantee, "you are among friends."

Jase breathed more easily. The guarantee was honorable, but not required. Evidently the Nelkosan was a man of strict customs. However, if strict in fairness, he was strict in duty as well. Without pausing for breath he plunged into the procedure of the board.

"The candidate," he said, "may just as well start out by trying to tell us of what reasons he may have, in addition to the one stated in his application, to justify us in awarding the post of Keysman on this important expedition to one so young."

"Honorable board members," answered Jase, clearly and distinctly. "My record is before you, attached to my application. May I point out, however, that training as a scout, involving as it does work on both a scientific and ship-handling level, as well as association at close quarters with a scout partner . . ."

He talked on. Jase had, like all the candidates, carefully prepared and rehearsed beforehand the speech he would present to the board. The board itself listened now with the mild boredom of a body that has heard ten such speeches already. The single exception to this air of boredom was the Nelkosan, who sat forbiddingly alert.

When Jase finally concluded, the board members turned and looked at each other.

"Well," said the Nelkosan, briefly, "shall we vote on the candidate?"

Heads nodded along the table. Hands reached for ballot chips—black for acceptance, red for rejection—the four Rod members automatically picking up red, the Hooks reaching for black. Jase licked his whiskers furtively with a dry tongue and opened his mouth before the chips were gathered in.

"I appeal!" he said.

Hands checked in midair. The board woke up suddenly, as one man. Seven pairs of black eyes centered suddenly upon Jase. Any candidate might appeal—but to do so was to call the board wrong or unfair upon one of its actions, and that meant somebody's Honor was to be called in question.

For a candidate without Family backing to question a board of elders such as sat on a board of selection like this was to lay his whole future life upon the outcome of the appeal. The board sat back on their platforms and considered Jase.

"On what basis, if the candidate pleases?" asked the Nelkosan in far too pleased a tone of voice.

"Sir, on the basis that I have another reason to urge for my selection than that of past experience," said Jase.

"Interesting," rumbled the Nelkosan. He glanced down the table at the other board members. "Don't you think so, sirs?"

"Sir, I do find it interesting," said Ardolf Halfbrother, the Brutogas, in such an even tone that it was impossible to tell whether he was echoing the Nelkosan's hidden sneer or taking issue with it.

"In that case, candidate," the Nelkosan turned back to Jase, "by all means go ahead. What other reason do you have to urge? I must say—" He glanced down the table again meaningfully. "I hope it justifies your appeal."

"Sir, I think it will." Jase thrust a hand into his harness pouch, withdrew something small, and, stepping forward, put it down on the table before them all. He took his hand away, revealing a cube of clear plastic in which a small figure could be seen as if floating there.

"A dirtworm?" The Nelkosan raised his whiskers.

"No, sir," said Jase. "The body of a primitive life form from the planet of the Muffled People."

"*What?*" Suddenly the room was in an uproar, and there was no board member not on his feet. For a moment everyone seemed to be talking at once, and then all the voices died away as all eyes fastened on Jase, who was standing at attention before them.

"Where did you get this?"

It was the Nelkosan speaking. And, for all the fact that the question could not be other than rhetorical, his voice was like frozen rock.

"Sirs," said Jase—and inside him he glowed with the knowledge that under his neck fur he was not even sweating. Now that the final moment had come, he felt elated, lifted up and carried forward by the great endeavor to which he had committed himself. His voice was calm. "Sirs, from the artifact I brought back to Homeworld."

"And you've never turned it in to the proper authorities here at Examination Center? Or reported the fact you possessed it?"

"No, sir."

There was a moment's dead silence in the room.

"You know what this means?" The words came spaced and

distinct from the Nelkosan. The face of the Family Head was as stiff as a mask. While he had been honorably committed to frustrating or discrediting Kator Secondcousin, this development went beyond honorable reprisal. It was a matter of the most delicate Honor, and the Nelkosan was now as impersonal as a judge.

"I realize," answered Jase, "what it would mean ordinarily—"

"Ordinarily!"

"Yes, sir. Ordinarily. However, my case," said Jase, "is not ordinary. I did not take this organism from the artifact for the mere desire of possessing it."

The Nelkosan squatted back down on his platform, and the other board members, as if this had been a signal, followed his example.

"You did not?" asked the Nelkosan.

"No, sir."

"Why did you take it then—if we may ask?"

"Sir," said Jase, "I took it after deep consideration for the specific purpose of exhibiting it to this board of selection for the post of Keysman on the Expedition to the planet of the Muffled People."

His words went out and seemed to fall dead in the face of the silence of the watching members of the board. A lengthening pause rang on and on in his ears as he waited.

"Why did you decide this?" asked the voice of the Nelkosan.

"Sir," said Jase, "and members of the board, you whose responsibility in Honor it is to select the Keysman, the man of final authority on ship and off of this expedition, know better than anyone else how important the expedition is. It is an honorable and common trait to feel sure of ourselves in the face of a great endeavor. But confidence is only part of what is needed for command of this expedition. The Keysman in charge must not only be confident—but *certain* of his ability to succeed in this first contact with a race which may turn out to be nearly the equal of our own."

He stopped and looked at them for some sign of reaction. But they were all men of honorable age. Their expressions were unreadable.

"I searched my mind," Jase went on, "for some proof of the certainty I felt inside me that I was the man to succeed in this important work. I felt it was necessary to perform some act symbolic of that certainty, so that when the present moment of selection came, you—sirs of the board—could feel justified in choosing me to be Keysman.''

He paused again.

''Go on,'' said the Nelkosan, in a perfectly level tone of voice, watching him through slitted eyes.

''Therefore I took and kept the dead alien organism,'' said Jase. ''And I now offer it to you in evidence of my own commitment to the task of the expedition. So highly do I regard that commitment that I've put my financial worth, my Family ties, and, finally, my personal Honor at stake in order to make one gesture that will convince you that in me you would have a Keysman who will place a successful return from this expedition above all else. I'm in your hands, sirs of the board. If you reject me for the post to be selected here, you should be sure that whoever you pick has a dedication to the purpose of the expedition superior to my own.''

He stopped talking. They looked back at him from behind the table without commenting. Then the Nelkosan spoke.

''You take property that should belong to the Examination Center here,'' he said, ''and, not content with that, you presume to instruct this board whom to choose for Keysman of a vital and unique expedition. The question is—'' He leaned forward toward Jase. ''Is this all mere effrontery and bluff? Or are you actually putting everything in the balance for this appointment.''

The tone of voice in which he spoke was serious and honestly inquiring. Jase's stomach lifted. He had, at least, succeeded in carrying the Nelkosan beyond the area of small reprisal into the open questions of honor. Now was the moment. The die was cast.

''So strongly,'' Jase said, ''do I regard my actions in taking the alien organism as correct and honorable evidence of my right not only to the post of Keysman by virtue of the Random Factor that brought the artifact within my ken in the first place, that—'' He had to pause to draw a breath in spite of his self-possession. ''—I challenge your right to take the organism from me now!''

And, suddenly, to Jase's eyes, the scene before him whirled, blurred, and disappeared. . . .

CHAPTER TEN

He woke, struggling and crying out. Hairless faces were all around him. Hairless hands were getting him to his feet and guiding him down fantastic corridors and into a cage that rose upward.

". . . No!" he said, struggling. "My Honor. The duel . . ."

"Jase! Jase!" One hairless face was shoved close to his. "It's all right! This is Alan Creel—don't you remember? I gave you a posthypnotic suggestion to wake up when the time for the duel came. Now, we're just taking you upstairs where I have my equipment handy in case of trouble."

Jase's mind whirled. What he heard made sense—and it did not make sense. Everything was mixed up.

"You can go back to sleep just as soon as we get you to the other room . . ." said the voice of the face called Alan Creel.

Jase stopped struggling and let them lead him along, out of the cage and along another corridor, this time darkly walled with some strange substance. The part that sounded all right was all right, and for the other, he was going to get back in time for the duel, so that would be all right too.

They were taking him through a door into a brightly lit room. The room was full of mechanical equipment that was familiar. There was a long, narrow, white-surfaced table with a head-rest. They were helping him up on it.

He lay on his back. The light was in his eyes blindingly for a moment; then someone said something and tilted it away. Shadow shielded his eyes. He felt a prick just below the inner elbow of his right arm.

"You'll be all right. You can go back now. Go back. . . ." It was the voice of the man—man?—called Alan. Jase felt his senses swirling. This scene, this nightmare dissolved. . . .

He was back again in familiar surroundings. It was a gymnasium of the Examination Center. At the other end of the gym were the six members of the selection board. One of them—the Nelkosan—was talking to a tall and powerfully built man whose black coat of fur was shiny with health. In a sling over his shoulder the tall man, who could be no other than the Nelkosan's Family champion, wore a long, twin-bladed dueling sword.

"Here he comes now," said a familiar voice.

Jase turned and saw Brodth the Swordsmaster. Abruptly, all confusion cleared from his mind. He remembered Brodth offering to meet him here and act as his weaponsbearer. Looking back across the room, Jase saw the Nelkosan champion approaching him. He was a pleasant, calm capable fellow, if large; and he saluted both Jase and Brodth as he stopped before them.

"I am Horaag Adoptedson," he said to Jase. "Champion for the Nelkosan. You are Kator Secondcousin Brutogas?"

"Sir," said Jase. "I am."

"Then, sir," said Horaag, "I find that as deputy for the Nelkosan, Honor requires me to charge you with arrogance and defiance directed toward my principal."

"Sir," said Jase, "you must either withdraw that charge or fight me with the weapons of my choice."

"In Honor I will fight you," said Horaag. "What weapons did you have in mind?"

Jase licked his whiskers.

"Double-sword," he said. Horaag started to nod. "And shields," said Jase.

Horaag stopped in mid-nod. He stared at Jase, and there was a slight stiffening to the skin around his nose.

"Are you serious?" he asked, still even-voiced.

"My principal," put in Brodth, "is entirely serious."

Horaag's eyes swung to Brodth and apparently recognized him as another Swordsmaster. He stared for a moment.

"Sir," he said. "May I ask—are you Brodth Youngerbrother?"

"I am," said Brodth. Horaag saluted him.

"It's an honor to meet you, sir." He turned and called past Jase and Brodth to a different corner of the room. "Match Umpire?"

A lean man, only just beginning to gray about the ears, came over to them.

"Sirs?" he asked courteously.

"May I introduce," said Horaag, "the match umpire of this gymnasium, Bolf Paternalnephew Cheles. Bolf, these are my opponents."

"I've already met them." Bolf saluted Jase and Brodth. "What's the question?"

"My principal opponent," said Horaag, "wishes to fight with double-blade—and shield. Is this within the honorable canons of combat?"

"I'll check the records." Bolf went off. Horaag made polite conversation with Jase and Brodth. He was evidently interested mainly in talking to Brodth, but to devote a majority of his attention to the weapons bearer of his principal opponent would have been discourteous, when Jase was directly in front of him. Horaag made, therefore, general conversation, complimenting Jase on having encountered the artifact and discussing the size of the expedition that would be sent out.

Bolf Paternalnephew came back across the gym floor to them.

"Shields," he announced, "are archaic and generally out of use, but still permissible. However, if the Nelkosan Champion wishes to enter a demur on the grounds that he is unfamiliar with shields. . . ."

"Not at all," said Horaag. As Champion he could not honorably demur, although it was his legal right. As Family representative, it was his responsibility not to be unfamiliar with any sort of weapons. "If you can find me a shield, Bolf—I'll use my own sword, since I'm familiar with it. . . ."

"Certainly," said the match umpire.

"I'll get my principal's weapons," said Brodth. All three went off. Brodth had been required naturally to check the weapons with the entrance gatekeeper of the Examination Center, while Horaag had a permit to carry his. While Jase waited, he saw Horaag experimenting with the round, target-shaped shield Bolf had found for him. It was a blank circle of metal designed to be held with the left arm through two handles on the inner surface, while the right hand used the sword. Horaag was trying fencing lunges with his long, twin-bladed sword and trying to decide what to do with the shield Honor required him to carry. At arm's length behind him in normal fencing position, the shield threw him off balance. Held before him, it restricted his movements.

Jase's weapons came—the same with which he had practiced so assiduously during the days past. He took them from Brodth. The shield was like the one found for his opponent, but the sword he now grasped was as archaic as the shield. Guardless, wide-bladed, and short, it was one of those Brodth had kept hanging on the wall of the room to which he had taken Jase that first day.

Jase slid his left hand and arm through the handles on the

inside of the shield and grasped the forward handle in his fist. He took hold of the hilt of his sword with almost an underhand grip and, instead of adopting the fencing position, took up a position like a boxer—left shoulder and shield forward, instead of right shoulder forward and sword extended.

The members of the board and a dozen or so other spectators who had gathered murmured at the sight of this. A voice commented on the similarity between Jase's fighting position and that of figures in old carvings depicting ancestral warriors who had used such ancient weapons. Horaag, with the remarkable adaptability of the trained athlete, fell into a duplication of Kator's stance, but with some clumsiness evident. Bolf Paternalnephew signalled to them both and they approached each other in the center of the gym.

"You are met here," Bolf Paternalnephew began as they stood facing each other, weaponed and ready, "in the interests of Honor and according to the code of honorable combat to resolve a situation for which other solution cannot be found. . . ." Jase listened with only half an ear. His eyes were wide, and it seemed to him that he could smell every person in the room, and every scent of the room itself. And every sound in it, no matter how tiny, came clearly to his sense of hearing even through the drone of Bolf's voice.

He thought that in a little while, a very short space of time, perhaps a long enough time to listen to the song of the first Brutogas, he would be successful or he would be dead. He repeated again to himself that he would be dead—but he could not seem to believe it. Never had he felt so alive. His heart beat steadily and strongly, but not rapidly. The breath moved smoothly in and out of his nostrils. He was sweating lightly under the fur at his throat, but it was not so much the sweat of fear as of exultation.

He looked at the tall, massive figure of Horaag Adoptedson, and the long, twin-bladed sword the other held. He saw them with such clarity that he could pick out little nicks and scars near the cross-piece of the hilt guard and count the scars marking the smooth pelt of Horaag's fur-like little lines, where the hairs lay all one direction on one side of the line and all the other direction on the other. He could even see the dark lines of the veins just inside the openings of Horaag's nostrils.

". . . and this case is a case of the thirty-ninth case," Bolf was saying, "in that it is provided that if a man have a thing and it be denied him that he keep it, he may honorably challenge the right of the one who withholds it from him—the right to claim Champion by either party notwithstanding as in the withholding party in this case. Therefore, as match umpire, I declare this combat to be authorized, to be taking place before witnesses, and to be honorable—*go!*''

The starting word shocked Jase from his thoughts. Had it not been for the days of training, he might have hesitated—but reflexes responded for him.

He and Horaag moved together, and Jase got his shield up just in time to deflect a thrust from Horaag's long sword. As the impact jarred him backward, a thrill ran through Jase. Suddenly, it seemed that he and Horaag were alone in some far place where not merely the sight but the sound of all that was around them had faded away. They were caught up together in a moment that excluded all else, partners in a dance which only one of them would finish. Over the edge of his shield he could see Horaag's eyes narrowing as if thoughtfully as their swords clanged on each other and on the opposing shields.

A distant shout penetrated the isolation that surrounded them. For a second Jase almost closed his ears in annoyance. Then he recognized the voice. It was Brodth, shouting at him in warning. Jase had been giving ground. The gray-furred swordsmaster had warned him of this, repeatedly during the days of practice that had led up to this. The advantages of the ancient shield and short, archaic sword lay in the field of attack—going in under the long blade of the opponent. Jase crouched, struck upward with his shield at Horaag's blade as it came in again, and stepped forward, bringing his sword up from under.

Horaag gave ground. Jase felt sudden exaltation. Then, without warning, the taller man circled to his left. For a moment Jase's own shield held his vision—and Horaag drove in an attack. Jase, turning hurriedly, tripped and almost went down. Horaag was instantly on top of him. Jase thrust the taller man back with his shield. Horaag, quick to learn, struck back with his own shield, using it as a weapon.

Jase slipped under the blow, took the full force of a second blow from the much stronger man, and was driven to one knee.

Horaag struck down with his sword. Jase caught it with his shield, struck with his own sword upward from the kneeling position, and missed. Horaag shortened his sword for a death thrust downward—and Jase, moving his shorter double blade in a more restricted circle, came up inside the shield and sword-guard of the bigger man and thrust Horaag through the shoulder. Horaag dropped the sword from his nerveless fingers and threw his good arm around his smaller opponent to break his back. Jase, letting go his sword hilt now that there was no longer room to use the weapon, reached up and clawed the throat of his opponent.

They fell together.

When a bloody and breathless Jase was pulled from under the body of Horaag, he saw only an arms length away, the Nelkosan standing, holding in one fist the ring of keys to a ship of the line. The keys to every room and instrument of the ship which would carry the expedition to the planet of the Muffled People.

He handed them to Jase.

CHAPTER ELEVEN

Jase slept without dreams.

It was not the sleep in which he was in the body of Kator. It was the dreamless sleep brought on by heavy sedation, which had followed on his waking from the successful conclusion of the duelling incident, and recognizing, this time, that he was back on earth among friends of his own kind. It was also the sleep of exhaustion. But, drugged as it was, and deep as it was, a feeling of confusion seemed to exist through it, stirring and troubling him so that he seemed to feel dark shapes approaching and threatening him in strange fashion.

At moments he felt that these shapes were the shapes of Ruml. At other moments he was equally sure they were human. —Finally they left him and he slept without dreaming and without stirring. . . .

When he woke, his basement room had no one seated in its armchair keeping him under observation. He rose on one elbow and looked at the clock on the bedstand beside his bed. Its yellow, luminescent hands stood at a little after three o'clock. He sat up, shaking the sleep from his head, and swung his legs over the side of the bed.

He thought of coffee. Heavy with the lethargy that follows

such deep slumber, he fumbled into his clothes and headed for the door. But the knob jarred against his hand when he tried to turn it, and the door itself stayed closed.

Frowning, he twisted hard on the knob and shoved the door. It quivered but did not open. He began to come awake. He jerked and rattled at the door—and woke at last to the fact that it was not meant for him to open it.

"Locked!" he said out loud, looking over at the empty chair where an observer should have been sitting. So, since there was no one handy to watch him, they had locked him up like a criminal or a maniac?

Rage suddenly boiled up in him. He took hold of the knob, threw his shoulder against the door above it, and—much more easily than he had expected, for he had never broken open a door before—the latch socket tore out of the door frame, and the door swung open. He stumbled into the basement corridor.

His rage had mounted rather than diminished with the breaking of the door. He headed at a fast walk for the basement stairs to the floors above, ignoring the slow and creaky elevator. Turning the corner at the far end of the corridor to reach the foot of the stairs, he ran head on into a young man in army suntans and wearing a gunbelt with a pistol holstered to it.

"Just a minute," said the young man, catching his arm. "You can't go up there. You have to go back to your room—"

Jase, redly angry, tore his arm from the other's grasp.

"What're you going to do, shoot me?" he said—and, shouldering roughly past the young man, went up the stairs two at a time.

When he emerged on to the dark green carpet of the ground floor carpeting, he found the hall there full of men and officers in uniform. They stared at him, and some of them moved toward him or tried to speak as if they would stop him, but he charged past them all, down the corridor around toward the back of the building and the library room. The door to the library room was open. A man in plain clothes was standing in the entrance. Jase thrust past him into the room.

Inside, the room was half full. Present were Mele, all the members of the Board, and Bill Coth, the general Tim had introduced to Jase and Mele just a week previously. Today he was wearing his uniform, and with him were a short, bullet-headed middle-aged man in a gray suit of European cut and a bookkeeperish looking man, slim, about fifty, and wearing old-fashioned glasses rather than contact lenses over pale blue eyes, under blond hair and faded eyebrows.

The sound of Jase's entrance, to say nothing of the shout immediately given by the man he had passed in the doorway, brought all their eyes around.

"What're you doing up here, Jase?" asked Coth. "—No, let him go, Hobart." The man in the doorway, who had grabbed Jase from behind, let go just in time to avoid having his instep smashed by Jase's right shoe heel. Jase stared savagely at Coth.

"Was it your idea to lock me in?" Jase said fiercely. "What're you doing here with all this gang?"

"I brought him, Jase."

It was Thornybright, standing a little removed from Coth and the other strangers. The psychologist stood slim and erect in a blue business suit, and his manner was as sharply self-possessed as ever.

"You?" Jase stared at him. "Why!"

"That's just what Bill and I have been in the process of explaining," said Thornybright. "Things with this project had reached the point where I felt we couldn't go any longer without informing the proper authorities and turning control over to them. We held a meeting, and I gave the rest a last chance to vote that the project be turned over. When we split down the middle again, I called Bill in." He glanced over at the slim, tanned military man. "He'd been waiting outside."

"Oh?" said Jase. He stalked over to stand looking down at the psychologist. "And what were you doing, calling a meeting when I wasn't there?"

Thornybright stared back up at him, a thin whip of a man four inches shorter and only two-thirds the weight of Jase. His gaze was as cold and unintimidated as ever.

"Maybe I ought to remind you, Jase," he said, "you aren't actually a member of this Board."

"And maybe I ought to remind you—"said Jase. "If we're going to start acting on our own, maybe I ought to remind you that I'm the project. Me!" Jase drove his own forefinger against his chest. He felt as though there was fire in his skull. "I'm the one who's necessary to what we're doing here—not the rest of you. And I'm an American citizen—" he broke off, looking around at the rest of the board members, seated in their chairs. Dystra sat solidly, looking back at him with no apparent emotion. "That reminds me," Jase said grimly. "We seem to have been illegally invaded. Why isn't anyone calling the police—or a lawyer?''

"That's not necessary—,'' Thornybright was beginning, when Coth interrupted him.

"I think Jase will see that, all right,'' he said, smiling at Jase. "It's just that no one's explained the situation to him, yet. Jase, I'd like you to meet a couple of people.'' He turned to the bullet-headed man. "This is—'' The name he spoke baffled Jase's ear with its foreign pronunciation. "He's here to more or less represent the foreign members of this Foundation of yours, and their governments. You might think of him as the man from the United Nations.''

"How do you do,'' said the man from the United Nations, without a trace of accent but with an intonation that rang strangely on Jase's ear. Jase nodded shortly.

"And,'' said Coth, looking over at the tall, spectacled man, "this is Artoy Swanson, from the White House. If you need a lawyer, he can get you the Inspector General.'' Coth smiled.

"I'll take him up on that,'' said Jase.

Coth's smile did not so much fade as become slightly grim.

"You aren't being particularly reasonable,'' he said slowly.

"No,'' said Jase. "Why don't you and the others just get the hell out?''

"No,'' said Coth, meeting his eye but still speaking pleasantly.

"Then I will,'' said Jase. He turned and headed for the door.

"Hobart,'' said the thin, bespectacled Swanson. The man in civilian clothes moved to block the exit. Jase stopped and turned. He looked sardonically at Thornybright.

"Now, wait a minute, Bill,'' said Thornybright. "There's other ways—''

"I'm afraid not,'' said Swanson. The spectacled man, for all his air of mildness, was definite. His interruption of Thornybright was a little like stopping a tiger with a feather, but the psychologist stayed stopped. Swanson took off his glasses and began to clean them with a paper tissue he took from a side pocket of his suitcoat. "We're all volunteers here, Mr. Thornybright. The situation was all talked over this morning—in quarters elsewhere. It was clearly accepted that any legal way of controlling you people would be too slow. We'd have to start out by finding cause for an injunction . . . all sorts of red tape. And meanwhile, things would be happening to and with Jase here.''

"To and with," echoed Jase. "I thought that would be the first thing that would come to the top of your minds when you heard about the project—the notion that I'm being controlled by aliens." He looked grimly across at Thornybright, who looked back with no change of expression. "So you're just skipping our legal rights, is that it?"

"Now look here!" said Swanson, with a touch of exasperation. "Be reasonable. You people have gone ahead on your own without any authority from this government, or any government on earth, for that matter, and made contact with an alien race, an alien civilization bigger, better, stronger than ours and evidently containing individuals intent on wiping us out. Did you expect us to subpoena you to a congressional investigation?"

"There wasn't any particular secrecy about the project!" said Thornybright sharply. "It, and the equipment we were using, has been written up in a dozen technical journals. And from there it got into the newspapers via the science writers."

"Who reads technical journals, with a million articles a year being published in nearly a thousand different languages?" said Swanson. "And who believes science writers—or if they believe, remember for ten minutes afterward what they've read?" He looked at Jase. "No one who knew of what you were doing seriously thought anything would come of it."

"No," said Jase, bitterly, "they never do."

"But you did," said Swanson. "And for my money you ought to have had more of a sense of responsibility. To your—to the world, and the rest of the people on it. At any rate, as I say, all of us here are volunteers. You can sue us afterward, if you want—and if there's any courts to sue in. For me, that won't make much difference. For General Coth it's a pretty bad finish to twenty-eight years of military service. But none of us are worrying about it. The thing is, we're in charge here now—and from here on out."

He looked around at the board members.

"We're going to have to hold you all—at least for the present. We'll move you all now to an Air Force installation, a small one, not too far from Washington here. When we get this project of yours under control, we'll turn you loose, and—" He grimaced. "You can try suing us or getting us sent to jail or whatever you like. But for now—"

"No," said Jase.

Swanson looked at him.

"No, I don't think so," said Jase. He backed up and sat down on the edge of the table, around which the board normally sat and where, with the exception of Mele and himself, they were sitting now. "You're not going to move them, me, or anything else out of this building."

Swanson took off his spectacles.

"Oh?"

"That's right," said Jase. "You must have missed hearing me when I was talking To Tim Thornybright, just now. I reminded him that I was the project. And I am—and you can't force me to move from here, or do anything I don't want to do. And I don't want to be separated from the library in this building."

Swanson put his spectacles back on.

"I think you'll do what we want. And, after all," he said, "we only want you to go on doing what you have been doing, contacting this Kator and reporting what you experience."

"What if I don't?" said Jase. "Don't report, I mean?"

"We can make it uncomfortable for you," said Coth, seriously. Jase looked over at the general.

"What if I lie about what I experience?" he asked.

"Oh," Coth laughed, answering immediately, "we could tell, of course."

Jase stared at him for a moment. Then he too laughed—but not lightly, grimly.

"You're good," said Jase. "For a second you sounded so certain of yourself to me, I was almost ready to believe you. No, you couldn't tell. And you know you couldn't tell." He looked from Coth to Swanson and the other man. "I'm the only link you have with the Ruml, and you need my willing cooperation—you need it more than anything else, because without me, you've got nothing left but your nightmares about invading aliens."

He paused.

"So," he said, slowly, "I'll tell you how you'll get that cooperation. You can stay with the project now you've joined it, but if you think you're going to run it, you're wrong. The board will go on acting like it always has. You three can sit on it, that's all. And I'll go on as I've been doing—without any interference from you, or the Board either."

There was dead silence in the library room. He and Swanson stood watching each other. After a moment Swanson took off his spectacles.

"Temporarily," he said, calmly, "all right."

Jase nodded slowly and turned around to Mele. He was about to say that now that the excitement was over, he wanted something to eat. He was about to ask her to join him in the dining room while the board sat down with its three new members to heal the smart of Jason's declared independence with talk. But he did not ask her.

Her eyes were gazing at him with as much shock as if he had made a Jekyll and Hyde switch before her eyes into the alien form of Kator. As if she did not know him.

He went out of the library room toward the dining room, alone.

CHAPTER TWELVE

Kator moved aboard the Expedition Ship immediately. The outfitting of such a ship could draw on past experience of the Examination Center, and the aim was to have the ship ready to leave the moment investigation of the artifact was completed. The selection of Kator as Keysman had taken place the morning of completion of the artifact Examination. And the Captain and crew of the ship were completed in the next few days.

Jase, in Kator's body, sat in on these later selections. In theory, he could veto any candidate. In practice, the selection boards knew their business, and it would have been impolite for him to have interfered. So he sat silent on the board and watched his crew chosen. It did not, Jase learned from Kator's thoughts, matter very much who were chosen to go on the ship as far as Kator's private intentions were concerned. And Kator had his own plans to consider.

So had Jase. In the Ruml's body, he was swept along by Kator's feelings and imagination. In his own body, surrounded now by the eyes of not only the board but Swanson, Coth, the man from the United Nations and their assistants, he tried to wall out everything else but his recording of what he experienced as Kator and his personal search for the meanings behind it.

Secretly, he had lost part of his earlier confidence. It was one of the reasons he had blown up when he found the door of his room locked, and later when he found Swanson and the others attempting to take over upstairs. Swanson and the rest wore like open badges on their coat fronts the belief that Jase was falling— if he had not already fallen—under the domination of Kator's alien personality. The unspoken implication roused Jase to fury. Such domination would be as fantastic as superstition.

But, he was no longer sure it was impossible.

This he kept to himself. From the beginning there had been a side of Kator he could not translate to the board members or any other earthly observer. This was the whole area of Kator's feelings as a Ruml. It began with Kator's pride in himself as a member of the Ruml race—a pride that was comparable to the unconscious and unstated feeling of superiority in a human when he thought of himself in comparison to an animal. But it went on—far on—from there. Into an area of the Ruml racial personality for which there were no human equivalents. And it was all completely unconscious. The Rumls did not put it into words even among themselves. Why should they? It was a part of the unconscious knowledge of all of them.

As a race, they *assumed* certain things. They took for granted certain things—things no human would imagine, let alone take for granted.

Where the human mind and personality was duplicated by the Ruml, there was no danger that Jase might be disturbed by the contact. But in this other, this truly alien area. . . . Jase had begun to feel the first stirrings of fear. For the first time he admitted to himself that Kator, without knowing even that Jase was there, might by simply existing be able to attack and destroy certain human elements in Jase. It might be that Kator's personality could infect and conquer Jase's personality *unconsciously*.

It was the duel that had brought Jase finally to this conclusion. Up until then, he had been approaching the truth without seeing it, as a man might be going up a mountain without realizing he was already on its lower slopes. The essential difference between the human and the Ruml was something that Jase had appreciated from the beginning in a way no one else could do. But even he, he thought now, might have been led astray. He had realized how different were the Rumls—but even he had thought of that difference as the sort of difference that there is between—say— a man and an intelligent black bear.

He had forgotten that where there was intelligence, there had to be a history—and a culture—even a soul.

Both man and Ruml were such that they would fight and die for certain concepts. What if those concepts were not understandable by each other?

What if they were diametrically opposed?

Men and Ruml could rush at each other in mutual self-destruction. Both utterly convinced of their rightness, both committed to fighting to the death with no compromise—over a difference of unconscious opinion they could not verbalize to themselves, let alone to each other.

And there was only one person on either side who could do anything to avert this Armageddon of two races. Jase. If only, somewhere in the books and technical and professional journals through which he searched, he could uncover some mutually understandable concept in this unconscious area. Something non-human, non-Ruml, but recognizable by both. Something in biology or zoology that both races could understand.

Meanwhile, since the duel, the sneaking fear of infection in him by Kator's personality stayed always in the back of his mind. There was no way of resolving it into concrete terms, any more than there seemed to be of getting rid of it. Once he could have used Mele for a touchstone. But now there was a wall between them. Since that day in the library room with Swanson and the others, she had carried what was almost a fear of him, a conviction of his unreasonableness. She seemed, thought Jase bitterly, to feel that he was being arbitrary out of sheer love of power.

She did not, thank heaven, share the feeling that Kator might be infecting him. But the fear rode Jase in spite of this. It was his fear and his secret. In the duel, for the first time, he had found himself sharing Kator's point of view when that point of view was exactly opposite to his own.

Kator had not disliked Horaag Adoptedson. But he had joyfully, pridefully, almost gleefully killed him when Horaag could have been defeated short of death. Doing so had made Kator feel noble in his own eyes, successful, and admirable. And for a moment there, Jason had felt so too.

And that trace of an alien attitude had been part of what had been behind him in the library room where he had faced down Swanson and the rest, after breaking the door and bulling his way upstairs. That had not been the way Jase Barchar would normally act—he did not think so now, afterward.

But it had been very like the way Kator Secondcousin would

have acted, if he had woken to find himself locked against his will in a room. Was Jase becoming alien in the way he thought?

Searching the stacks of the Foundation building late in the night, under the swinging, bare sixty-watt bulbs below their halo-like reflectors, Jase asked that question of himself as he caught sight of his face reflected in the night-black windows between the shelves.

And his image had no answer to give him.

CHAPTER THIRTEEN

The ship of the Expedition carried fifty-eight Expedition members, including Captain and Keysman. Shortly after they lifted from the Ruml Homeworld, Jase addressed all Expedition members over the intercom system of the ship. He stood in the controls room up in front of the ship, with the quarters of Captain and Keysman opening off from it. The Captain stood beside him.

"Expedition members," he said, speaking into the intercom pickup screen. "You all know that we are engaged in an effort together to bring this Expedition successfully to the world of the Muffled People and Home again with information that will allow us to successfully settle that world. For all of us it is a great opportunity. As members of the expedition, once the world is open for settlement, all of us will be able to colonize there and Found Families of our own. Just so was each of our six worlds, other than Homeworld, colonized and its leading Families Founded."

He paused. He could imagine them, all about the ship, standing honorably erect and listening.

"The success," he went on, "of this expedition therefore must in Honor be more important to us than anything in our lives. I, your Keysman, dedicate myself to this importance. I promise you all the order of impartiality from me which you might expect from the Heads of your own Families. And I commit myself to return to Homeworld with the scouting report on the planet of the Muffled People that will justify this expedition. I pledge myself, in fact, to the accomplishment of a perfect operation—"

He paused again. He was conscious of a singing in his veins, an upsurging of that power and confidence which had first come to him with the Random Factor in the discovery of the artifact and which had carried him successfully through the duel with Horaag.

"—I direct you," he said, more loudly, "to remember that word I've just used—the word *perfect*. I have dedicated myself to a perfect expedition. I refer you to the later writings of the Morahnpa, leader of the first Expedition ever sent out from our Homeworld. The statement written by the Morahnpa was: *If all things are accomplished to perfection, how can failure find lodging place in that operation in which they are so accomplished?* I will expect a like dedication from you all."

He turned away from the screen to see the ship's Captain, standing, leaning a little more forward from the hips than was perhaps normal, his arms folded before him, his feet spread a little apart. The Captain's eyes were on him.

"Keysman," said the Captain. "You haven't ever been Keysman on a voyage before?"

"As you know," said Jase.

"I have been Captain on thirteen voyages," said the Captain, "and I have learned a few things about men in ships, whether that ship is on Expedition or not. You can command men and expect them to follow, in two different ways. You can command as a man, and they will obey you as a man—that is, not perfectly, but reliably. Or you can command as a Founder, and they will follow you blindly and to the death without question. But as a man, you can make mistakes. As a Founder, you can't."

"I follow," said Jase, "where the Random Factor leads me."

"If you lay claim to the Random Factor in your commands and actions," said the Captain, "there is no alternative to failure. You know that yourself, Keysman. One who lays claim to the Random Factor in his actions and later fails must be destroyed so that what is apparently the Random Factor may only be experience, trying again and winning the second time. There can't be a second time if the race is to evolve from the best of its stock."

"I know that," said Jase. "I've known it since I sighted the alien artifact."

The Captain inclined his head.

"Then," he said, "is it a man or a Founder we have for Keysman? I have a right to know—the crew will learn for itself in due time."

Jase looked the grizzled features of the older man squarely in the eye.

"A Founder," he said.

The Captain's face showed no expression. He inclined his head again.

"Sir," he said, "may I attend to my duties now?"

"Yes," said Jase.

The Captain turned away toward the instruments of the control panels covering the walls of the room.

Jase himself turned away and left the Controls Room. He went back through the corridors of the ship, inspecting everywhere. As Keysman it was part of his job to make sure that no locks at any time had been tampered with. There must be no acts not honorable aboard, no fights or crimes that remained mysteries because of clever tampering with the security of any man aboard. Those on this ship, of course, were men handpicked and of great previous honor, so crimes were all but unthinkable. As for acts not honorable, their possibility was also remote, though it was hard to believe anyone on such a crew would be interested in such petty things as personal advantage and gain. But as for fights—there could be no Honor in a Ruml man if he had no sense of himself. And where many men were cooped up together, such individual self-recognitions must conflict.

The few crew members he encountered saluted him and kept on with their duties. The ship was fully manned with three men for each position, and only a third of them were therefore on duty now. Jase examined the gym, the cargo space in the bottom of the ship, the Construction Section, whose machine tools took up most of the middle section of the ship outside of the crew's quarters. Finally, he went down the two corridors flanked by the crew's staterooms and tested the lock on the door of each member.

Every four or five doors, he unlocked one at random, to check the workings of his keys. It was not a violation of privacy and protection when the Keysman did this. The first half-dozen doors he opened had no one in the staterooms. Most of the crew were up in the gym, recreating themselves. But within the seventh door he opened he caught sight of a crew member curled up and reading on his sleeping pad.

The crew member was on his feet and saluting instantly. Jase stared at him.

"Bela!" he said. It was his Firstcousin among the Brutogasi.

"I was an alternate," said Bela. They looked at each other, and Jase felt a fierce surge of affection for this familiar member of his own Family sweep through him. But with the rank and regulations of shipboard between them, he could not express it.

"Good to have you with us," said Jase and went out, carefully locking and testing the doorlock behind him. Of all those aboard, Bela should not be attacked in his sleep as poor Aton Maternal-uncle had been by his scoutpartner.

Jase returned to his own quarters. There, on a small table, he had laid out the dirt worm in its plastic cube, and a model of the artifact. He added the ship's keys to the two other objects and sank on his haunches before them. He felt the Random Factor illuminating him like a great light within him. In the blaze of it, his dedication reached out and touched Bela, Aton that had been, this crew, his Family, and all the Ruml. Swept up and carried away in the ecstasy of his dream, Jase crouched on the floor and gave himself up to it.

In the few days that followed, the ship leaped in one jump to the three light-year-wide area in which the planet of the Muffled People had been calculated to be. There were only two possible star systems in this area—both remarkably alike in that their suns were small, yellow stars, and they both had over half a dozen planetary bodies circling them—to judge by magnetic readings of their space area.

Only one planet of the nearer system could possibly support the evolution of a race in any way similar to that of the Ruml, and at the orders of the Keysman, this was examined and found uninhabited and all but uninhabitable—being essentially waterless. It was sampled and recorded in case future scientific developments should discover a way to make it habitable for Ruml colonists, and the ship jumped to the near vicinity of the other sun with its possible system of habitable worlds.

It was at the conclusion of this jump that the Captain's signal rang. Jase, in his quarters at the time, answered the screen.

"There's been a fight between two of the men," said the Captain's face from the screen.

"I'll come at once," said Jase, jumping to his feet. "Assemble the Expedition's members in the gym."

When he got to the gym, the men aboard were drawn up, standing, in two units, with a little space between them. Before these two units stood the two brawlers, and facing them was the Captain, with a portable table set up before him, holding those papers which would be records of the speedy investigation already held.

Jase came up beside the Captain and glanced over the desk at the two men who had fought. His stomach tightened up inside him: One of the two was Bela.

"The papers?" he asked, turning to the Captain.

"Here, sir." The Captain passed him the sheets of paper which had been obviously all this time before Jase on the desk. Jase took them and ran his eye over them. The two involved, he read, were Bela and one of the Antoniti. Neither had claimed any need to be reticent. Both had freely told their stories, and the stories agreed. The Antoniti had considered that Bela wished to discount the Antoniti's work aboard the ship. Therefore, the Antoniti had attacked Bela without waiting to challenge the other. Bela had fought back.

Jase's stomach relaxed. Bela had clearly had no alternative. Once attacked he could not in Honor do otherwise than fight, even if as a normal man he could have restrained himself. It was simply a matter of condemning the Antoniti and excusing Bela from guilt.

But—on the verge of opening his mouth to do just that—an idea occurred to Jase. An idea so sudden and so convenient that it could only have sprung from the Random Factor which had caused the fight to involve Bela in the first place. That some fights should take place on a voyage of this length with fifty-eight men within the walls of a single ship, was inevitable. But it was far from inevitable that the Random Factor should cause the first fight to involve Jase's Firstcousin. Jase looked up from the desk at the assembled members of the Expedition.

"The Antoniti," he announced, "is self-admittedly the instigator. Ordinarily, he alone would be condemned. However, I find it necessary to remind you now that I announced at the inception of this voyage that I expected all of you to work for perfection on this Expedition. To execute only the Antoniti would be to leave one of those that had marred this expedition by fighting still among us. Accordingly, while I hereby absolve Bela Firstcousin Brutogas of any guilt in the incident, and enter into the ship's records my judgment that he acted honorably in all respects, in the interests of undeviating and unyielding perfection of action—to which I committed myself at the voyage's beginning—I hereby condemn him also."

He looked at Bela and the Antoniti. Bela's eyes met his squarely.

"My judgment as Keysman is given," he said.

He stepped back and turned away from the table, hearing behind him the roaring of the crew as they swarmed over the two condemned men and tore their throats out. He walked slowly back through the corridors alone to his own quarters, and only when he was once more behind the locked door of his own room did he give way to the feelings of grief that threatened to overwhelm him.

He sank into a crouching position before the table on which the dirtworm in its transparent cube sat silent and still. The violence of his mourning shook his whole body and made his jaws gasp for air. First it had been Aton Maternaluncle. And now Bela. Who else would the Random Factor require from him—his Family Head, the Brutogas himself?

The door spoke behind him, announcing that the Captain was outside wishing to see him. Jase pulled himself together and got to his feet.

He admitted the Captain, locking the door behind the older man. The Captain saluted.

"Yes?" said Jase.

"Sir," said the Captain, and there was a profound respect in his voice. "I wish to offer you my condolences on the necessary death of your kinsman."

"Thank you," said Jase, woodenly.

"And sir—" the Captain hesitated. "I am charged by the members of the Expedition to convey their condolences as well."

"Thank you."

The Captain still hesitated.

"Something more?" asked Jase.

"Yes, sir." The Captain's face was stiff with emotion. "Something I wished to say, Keysman. I believe this crew aboard this ship will follow you anywhere now, Keysman. I said when you first lifted ship that there were two sorts of leaders whom men would follow. One was a man, and the other was a Founder. Sir," said the Captain, "it is a great Honor to me and to all of us aboard to have a Founder for our Keysman on this Expedition."

He saluted and went.

Jase locked the door behind him and fell once more into a crouch before the table with the cube and the model of the artifact. Two great, conflicting emotions—sorrow and triumph—fought within him. It was, he thought, a wonderful but lonely thing to move with the Random Factor. He hid his eyes in his hands and let the emotions toss him as they would.

Mourning and exulting, safe behind his locked door in the exalted loneliness of a keysman, he fell, at last, asleep.

CHAPTER FOURTEEN

". . . I tell you," Swanson was saying, "we know they've landed. On the far side of the moon. Why didn't you tell us?"

Jase swayed a little with weariness and decided to sit down. He dropped into one of the heavy, carved-wood armchairs that belonged around the meeting table in the library room, but which was now scattered back away from it. In the library room now, Coth was seated at that table, as was the man from the United Nations. Swanson was standing in front of the table, talking to Jase. Neither Mele nor any of the members of the original Board were present. Somehow they had ceased to be part of the discussions—arguments rather—between Jase and Swanson's associates. Their place had been taken by several unidentified individuals—men in business suits of various ages—who sat around, listening intently but not intruding on the verbal duel between Swanson and Coth on one side and Jase on the other.

"—Didn't I tell you?" Jase passed a hand over his jaw. He needed a shave. Even Alan Creel had disappeared, to be replaced by some physician with what sounded like a trace of French accent and a neck thick with the fat of middle age. "I've been so busy in the stacks. . . ." He searched his memory, sorting it out from the Kator-memories that competed for attention in his head. "I must have forgotten."

"Don't forget," said Coth from the table. "That's what makes you valuable, your not forgetting to tell us everything."

Jase looked exhaustedly at him.

"Don't threaten me," Jase said. "I'm too worn out to be threatened. Let me keep my strength for necessary things."

"Yes," said Swanson, without turning around. "Perhaps we'd better be gentle, Bill. Jase does look shaky. But Jase—that's because you're wearing yourself out in those library stacks. Why don't you give that up for a while?"

"It's our only chance," said Jase, leaning his head back against the top of the backrest of his chair and closing his eyes for a second. What Swanson was saying became a meaningless jumble of words as sleep plucked at him, trying to drag him down into unconsciousness. He opened his eyes and Swanson's voice came clear again. "—What have you learned, anyway?"

"A lot," said Jase. "A lot."

"Such as?"

"I'm on the track," said Jase, "of what it is—that wellspring that their instinctive reactions come from. It's that we've got to understand. Not what they do, but why they do it."

"Be reasonable!" broke in Coth, suddenly—almost angrily. "They've landed on the other side of the moon and dug in there somewhere. We'll have them on top of us any day now. Is there time for that sort of scientific poking around and nonsense?"

"Nonsense!" Jase straightened up in the chair, taking his head away from the backrest. "It's because the world didn't have any time for what you call nonsense—yes, the same sort of nonsense, and the same sort of people like yourself having no use for it—that we're in this spot. Our neck stuck out into space ready to be chopped off, while the body of our race's still back down on plain earth, living and thinking in terms of it's a long way from here to Tokyo. And the world lying naked to a globe of space six hundred light years at least in radius around us—"

He broke off suddenly. He had lost his temper like this before with these people. It did no good; it did not even begin to open up their closed minds that thought of the Ruml as something between a horde of black-furred foreigners and a composite of all the science-fiction movie monsters they had ever seen on their home screens.

". . . What do you want from me now?" Jase asked, wearily.

"We know they landed on the other side of the moon," said Swanson. "We don't know where. You can tell us where."

"Why?" said Jase. "So you can send one of our space-going vessels over the spot to drop a nuclear bomb on it?"

"Of course not!" said Swanson. "We'd try to take them alive if at all possible."

"It wouldn't be possible," said Jase. "In any case, you're to leave them alone." He closed his eyes again, tempting himself with the thought of unlimited slumber. "I won't tell you."

"Won't tell us!" the voice of Coth jerked Jase's eyes open. "*Won't* tell us?"

"No," said Jase. "As long as you ignore them, they've got no reason to think you know they exist. They'll go on trying to scout us, instead of messaging back for an invasion team from their seven worlds. Once they do that, there's no hope for any of us. As long as they hold off, I've got time to go on searching for what moves someone like Kator. What makes what he does noble—"

"Noble?" said Coth. "This mindpartner—this Kator Second-cousin of yours—killed his scout partner in his sleep, lied about that, stole part of the artifact-bait from his own authorities, took an unfair advantage to kill another of his own kind in a duel—and he's just finished executing the one close relative he liked in order to make his crew on the ship admire him." Coth breathed sharply for a second. There were two points of color in his face, high on his narrow cheekbones. "—And that's, according to what you've seen fit to tell us about him and his race, noble!"

"Noble by his standards, not ours," answered Jase. He looked around the room at all of them. "Isn't there one of you who's willing to be openminded about the difference between Ruml and humans?"

"Of course," said Swanson. "Just tell us what those differences are. And what they mean."

"But that's what I'm breaking my neck to find out!" said Jase, furiously. "I'm not asking you to listen to a set of differences and then conclude the Ruml aren't like us! I'm asking you to believe they're not like us to start off with and use the fact of their not being like us as a starting point to understanding their differences of beliefs and thoughts and actions!"

"And after we've understood them, what then?" asked Coth. "Will understanding them stop Kator and his expedition? Or the Ruml that come after them?"

"No," said Jase. "But if we understand, we can maybe explain to them why they needn't or shouldn't try to kill us and take over our world the way they want to. Don't you understand?" he glared at Swanson. "They don't know any better.

Neither do we—yet. But we've got a chance in me, and my contact with Kator's mind, to find out better. So it's *our* responsibility to find the answers, not theirs."

One of the men present, who never spoke, grunted.

"Cut it out," said Jase looking over at him in disgust. "I'm as human as you are. No alien's speaking through me." The man who had grunted got out a cigarette, studied it, and lighted it—not looking at Jase or showing he had heard.

"Go on," said Swanson patiently. "Go on. Explain it to us."

"Look—," said Jase, leaning forward in his chair. "J.P. Scott, in the early nineteen-sixties, did some research on the critical periods in behavioral development that was printed in *Science* magazine. I've just been reading over that article he wrote, again. It points out that there's an amazing amount of flexibility in behavioral development. In humans and dogs, for example, the periods can actually occur in reverse order—"

"What periods?" asked Swanson.

"Well, they vary from species to species. The song sparrow, Scott points out, for example, has six developmental periods. The dogs—puppies—have four. There's neonatal, the nursing period, first. Then the transition period, in which the puppy makes the transition to adult methods of feeding and moving about. Third, there's the socialization period, in which the puppy first begins to socialize with his equals, playing and forming primary social bonds. The fourth and final stage, juvenile, is characterized by the beginning of final weaning—independence."

Jase paused and swallowed. His throat was dry with the effort of explaining.

"What about it?" demanded Coth.

"Don't you see?" asked Jase. "Think how different a dog is from a human. And yet those four periods correspond—though not in that order—to similar periods in human development. But of those four periods, only one is comparable to a period of Ruml development. The others are either unconscious, or not there at all in the development of a young individual as Kator was to begin with."

"What do you mean?" asked Swanson, taking off his spectacles and beginning to clean them with a tissue.

"Didn't you read my earlier reports?" demanded Jase. "Kator wasn't even conscious until, by human standards, he was about ten years old. He was born after being carried for three years inside his mother, then transferred to a pouch where he spent the next six years, developing physically but hardly growing and as unconscious as a human in a deep sleep, nursing and breathing and all else by instinctive reflex. Then, suddenly, in his tenth year, he started to grow. Within a week he was too large for the pouch that had been his home for six years. He awoke to consciousness, struggled out of the pouch, and left his mother. Within an hour or two after leaving her, he was walking erect, physically able to care for himself—in fact, a young adult in miniature, already weaned. Left alone, he would have wandered away from his mother. Under civilized Ruml conditions, he was first taken to the Head of the Family, named, and given a room of his own. In the next two years he grew to nine-tenths of his adult size and took his place in Ruml society."

Jase stopped at last, worked his dry throat, and looked around him. None of the faces looking at him showed any sign of understanding the implications of what he had said. The silent men, in fact, were actually showing signs of restlessness and boredom.

"Don't you—*can't* you understand?" Jase appealed to Swanson. "All the things a human child learns from ten years of conscious association and growing up with its parents or other adults are completely unknown to a Ruml. Mother love is unknown; juvenile play and socialization is unknown. In place of those things are reflexes, or instinctive conditioning we can only guess at. Kator's reasons for what he does literally don't make sense in our terms—but they make sense to him. And we've got to understand why they make sense if we want to stop the Ruml attack!"

Jase ran down finally. Swanson stood looking at him.

"I'm sorry," said Swanson, at last. "You haven't made any sense to me, or convinced me that all this studying and searching of yours is leading to anything vital. Let alone that it's more important than sensible, realistic action to surround that Ruml expedition up there on the other side of the moon. Now, will you tell us where they are?"

"No," said Jase. He stood up, swaying a little, and reached back to catch hold of the top of the chair to steady himself. "And you won't go ahead without my telling you because what I will tell you is that you can't get close to search the other side of the moon without them spotting you. And if they spot you, word will go back immediately, by collapsed universe field relay, to the Ruml Homeworld, and the invasion by the Ruml will be started. So—I won't tell you, and you'll leave them alone."

He turned and started toward the closed door of the library room. Halfway there, he stopped and faced about.

"I'll tell you," he said, "what comes now that they're dug in on the moon. They'll be sending down little relay devices on to the earth's surface to relay back pictures of what it's like and we're like. I'll keep you informed of where each one of these devices is sent—and if there's something there you don't want them to see, you can arrange to have some accident ruin the device." He paused, swaying a little. "And meanwhile," he said, "I'll keep on with the important work, and you'll let me. Because I'm the only pipeline you've got into the enemy camp, and you can't force me."

He laughed—or, rather, he had intended to laugh. It came out as the harsh barking of an exhausted man.

"Because," he said, sharing the joke with them, "I'm just as ready to die to save the world in my way as the rest of you are in yours. . . ."

He turned around, fumbled the library door open, and went through it, closing it behind him. Outside he staggered and caught himself with a hand against the wall.

From within the room he had just left a voice penetrated the relative thinness of the door panels. It was not a familiar voice, and he assumed it belonged to one of the men who were always present but never spoke.

"That ivory tower bastard!" it said. "He probably never had to work for a living!"

CHAPTER FIFTEEN

The ship of the Expedition was down and safe under forty feet of lunar rock. Jase, considering the situation, felt satisfied. The rest had worked like dedicated men, and if the Muffled People were anything comparable to the Ruml, their instruments—even if their suspicions had been aroused—would have a difficult time finding the Expedition.

Jase walked through the Construction Section. In the rooms

of this section the other fifty-four members of the Expedition—excluding only himself and the Captain—were working around the clock to construct the simulated shapes of alien objects and creatures that would house the tiny but powerful relay transmitters. "Information collectors" these were officially called—"collectors" plain and simple in the speech of the Expedition members themselves.

These were of three types, two of which had already been sent out. The initial type were simply lumps of nickel-iron with a monomolecular surface layer sensitized to collect up to three days' worth of images of the surrounding environment. In addition, these collectors had been furnished with tiny internal drive units to get them down to the surface of the planet of the Muffled People and back to the ship—and to explode either on order from the ship or if the collector should be trapped or investigated in any way.

Several thousand of these, looking like meteorite fragments, had been sent down on to the planet and recovered with less than a twenty per cent loss through accident and necessary self-destruction. To the knowledge of the Ruml aboard the ship, not one of the primary devices had been even recognized as anything but a chunk of rock—let alone handled by one of the alien natives. Five weeks had been consumed in this, and now the Expedition had a complete and detailed map of the world of the Muffled People, including the streets of its cities and the contours of its deepest ocean bottoms.

That had been phase one of the scoutwork to be done by the Expedition. Marking it up in his Keysman's private log, Jase had written against its final entry, *Completed to perfection*.

The next stage had been the sending down of the secondary type of collectors. These were almost identical lumps of nickel iron, but somewhat larger, and with cargo-carrying space inside them. After four more weeks spent in this and careful study by the xenobiologists among the Expedition's members, the xenobiologists had recommended three types of small native, alien life be used as tertiary collectors. And after consultation with the Captain, Jase had agreed to go ahead using them.

Against the phase two section of his private log, Jase wrote, *Completed to perfection*.

The three types of native life chosen were a small, flying, blood-sucking insect known to the natives as the mosquito; a crawling, six-legged pseudo-insect, one of the arthopoda in the

Muffled People's classification, an arachnid or "spider"; and a small, sharp-nosed, long-tailed gnawing and scavenging animal which evidently lived largely off the discarded foods and what it could steal in the warehouses and pipings of the Muffled People's cities. It was the duplication of these living creatures that the Expedition was busy on at the moment.

The duplications the crew were making now were far from ideal imitations—they could hardly be so when constructed under such cramped and hurried conditions as those aboard the ship. But, like the earlier collectors, they could be destroyed before they were investigated or captured by the natives, and so it was not necessary that they stand up to close examination.

These duplications were already beginning to be sent down into the cities of Earth. Jase stopped by the monitoring screen of one of the crewmen to examine a filmed report sent back by a collector already in one of the native hospitals. Jase stared at the interior of a room with two sleeping platforms, each set up on four high legs, in fascination.

The natives were most amazing, most incomprehensible. They certainly possessed locks and keys. But those among them most resembling Keysmen operated only at night and usually in areas where other natives were absent. It was almost as if the Muffled People regarded property rather than life as something to be guarded. It suggested that the concept of Honor here on this planet was markedly different from that of the worlds of men. The women did not carry their children in pouches in normal fashion—but the young were born very tiny and crippled, and a good section of the mother's lifetime seemed devoted to nursing them into health and size to face their responsibilities as individuals.

It was all a little disgusting. But, Jase reminded himself, to the Muffled People it was perfectly normal. The Expedition members had all been briefed before leaving Homeworld, and the xenobiologists there had been emphatic about cautioning them not to adopt a provincial attitude toward the native life. Such things confused and biased the reporting and observing faculties.

"—You can expect them to be different," in sum, was how the xenobiologists had advised the Expedition, pointing out that the Ruml had encountered alien creatures before this on the six earlier conquered worlds they had now colonized.

Oh course, this was only right. Still, thought Jase, it was one thing to view an alien *animal* without emotional reaction. Another to view an alien who was an intelligent being like yourself. You tended to expect him—or it—to measure up to proper and intellectual standards of cleanliness, morals, ethics, and so on.

It was fortunate, he went on thinking as he turned away from the screen, that the Ruml had not encountered this planet of the Muffled People first before landing on the other planets with alien, semi-intelligent creatures on them. The first, unsophisticated reaction of a race of men unused to the sight of alien life would have stimulated them to exterminate the Muffled People out of sheer revulsion. And that would have been other than honorable action.

Looking ahead now to the time when he would be the supreme authority on the planet below, after its conquest, Jase made a strong mental note to the effect that he would allow no killing of the natives except to reduce their numbers to regular conservation levels. It was criminal, if not outright dishonorable, the way whole, remarkable, alien species had been wiped out on the first few planets colonized by the Ruml.

In fact—Jase's thoughts ranged ahead—the matter might go merely beyond the conservation of the species. The Muffled People were truly intelligent, with an amazing technology. Moreover, they were—judging by their indifference to proper privacy and individual security—evidently a generally gentle, friendly species. The collectors had sent back out of there millions of filmed scenes and actions, but almost no instances of fighting at all. And the only possible approach to a duel had been a glimpse, by one collector, of two of the natives fighting without weapons. For surely handmufflings could not be considered weapons—in fact, undoubtedly just the opposite. They were probably designed to keep the duelists from hurting each other. And judging by the number of spectators, this had been an unusual occurrence.

It might even be possible that the natives—provided they could be trained to do so and did not smell too badly, or anything like that—could be eventually used as assistants and workers in the Ruml culture. Perhaps—

"Sir!" The voice of the Captain interrupted Jase's thoughts.

"Yes, Captain?" he said, turning about.

"I wanted to speak to you, Keysman." The Captain drew him aside where none of the others could hear, into the corridor without. "It's amazing, and I can hardly bring myself to believe it, Keysman. But outside of what seemed to be a few ornamental surface and atmosphere devices, the collectors haven't turned up any weapons at all. Oh, they have hand weapons, which they used for hunting the local game—"

"It is amazing," said Jase. "But perhaps we shouldn't be too upset by it. We knew they were bound to be different."

"But it's unbelievable. An intelligent race. A technology like this—"

"Oh, I don't doubt you'll turn up their war-making potential eventually," said Jase. "Have you tried underground?"

"Not intensively, sir."

"Try it intensively. Divert—say—fifteen per cent of the imitation live collectors to search for underground installations. As I say, there's no doubt we'll find war potential eventually. They could hardly exist without some concept of Honor."

"Yes sir," said the Captain, inclining his head. "I'll go see about diverting those collectors right now."

Jase watched him go. It was true, in spite of what he had said. The lack of fighting instinct apparent in the aliens of the world below him gave him a creepy, uncanny feeling.

It was not natural. How could the Muffled People have emerged as dominant over the other native species of their world without an honorable instinct to begin with? And how could they have survived after that to build this civilization of theirs without building a system of Honor upon that instinct?

Perhaps, thought Jase, pacing in the direction of his own quarters, there was something here that neither the xenobiologists back on Homeworld nor he himself had suspected. Best, undoubtedly, if he kept the sudden suspicion that had flashed into his mind just now—the suspicion of a completely honorless society, unimaginable as that was—entirely to himself.

If that was the case with the Muffled People—that they were a species without Honor, like the beasts that were born and lived out their lives and died unpurposefully—then there could be no conserving their species. In that case they would be worse than the beasts—for the beasts knew no better. But a people who had intelligence and yet had no Honor would be an abomination. In Honor the Ruml themselves could not endure that such should exist. It would be a duty, all other considerations aside, to cleanse the universe of such.

The skin of Jase's face stiffened.

This was something he had better quietly look into on his own at the first opportunity.

Chapter Sixteen

In one corner of the library stacks, in one of a dusty pile of cardboard-bound old magazines, Jase found at last what he had been looking for all this time. His legs gave way with relief and exhaustion, and he sank down crosslegged on the dusty floor of the stacks.

He had been living with the shelves of publications containing abstracts of scientific articles in the zoological and biological fields. Just a few days before he had given up on these and begun searching through the periodical indexes, such as the *Reader's Guide to Periodical Literature*, for the past fifty years. What Kator had thought less than a week before about the possibility that the human race did not possess the concept of Honor, had finally sparked in Jase's mind. It illuminated for the first time the answer toward which he had been groping ever since he had felt the first shock of being in contact with Kator's alien mind.

It was a half-forgotten memory of something he had read years ago. An article by someone authoritative in the zoological or biological fields. What the name of its author was, he could not remember. He could not even remember the shape and message of the article itself—but the intricate, innate computer of his mind had made the connection between the Ruml and this piece of writing from a time long before contact with anything like the Ruml had ever been imagined by man.

The thinking process of his brain insisted that in the article lay the key to the mutual understanding between human and Ruml that he was after. It was like a voice continually nagging at him. Like most men who have lived long years with books and the process of research, he trusted such a voice. If he felt it, it was there, just as the memory of a tune that will not return to the tongue to be sung still clings to and haunts the back of the mind, which *knows* that the tune is there—if only it could be pinned down.

The day before yesterday, on sudden impulse, he had given up the abstracts of past published scientific articles and turned to the periodical indexes. For two days he had drawn blanks. Then, just an hour or so since, a sudden hunch had sent him to checking titles rather than subject indexes. He had been thinking of what he sought as the key to his solution, and the word *key* had stuck in the forefront of his brain. For a long time he had paid no attention to it. He had thought that Kator's concern with Keys and the position of Keysman was making the word intrude on his search.

Then, yielding a little before the pounding of his search, the mists of his memory seemed to thin for a moment, and he was ready to swear the article he had been after had the word *key* either as part or whole of its title.

He turned to title searching through the back indexes, hunting through the one he had in his hand at the moment, which was dated away back in the mid-nineteen-sixties. Fuzzily, he ran his fingers down a list of titles beginning with the letter *K*.

A title jumped at him.

He turned, scrambled through the stacks to this area of storage of ancient magazines—and found the issue he sought. The minute he saw the cover the mists of his memory rolled back and he remembered where he had read the magazine. It had been in college, before he went that summer to the Rockies to observe the spring gatherings of the black bear. He opened the cover and turned to the page indicated for the article he sought. It was there before him.

"A Key to Ferocity in Bears," by Peter Krott. And it was in *Natural History Magazine*, the January, 1962, issue. Now that it was before him, he remembered clearly and without any difficulty that the January 15th issue of *Newsweek* magazine for that year had also dealt with the Krott notion.

Hands shaking a little under the glaring, reflectored, overhead bulb, Jase skimmed through the article. It all came back to him as if he had read it only a day or so before. Krott, with his wife and two children, had spent a couple of years in the Italian Alps. While they were there he had raised two young bears and observed them. What he had observed was that the young bears were gentle, even shy or timid in their play with his own children, but that they did not play a good deal simply because they were too busy searching for food—an activity that took up most of their time, since the Krotts left them to forage for themselves.

The only interruption to this perfectly amicable partnership was one day when Mrs. Krott was carrying some test tubes of alcohol in the pocket of a leather jacket. One of the bears attacked her, clawed the jacket off, tore open the pocket, pulled the corks from the test tubes, and swallowed the alcohol in them.

This first set Peter Krott, a Finnish zoologist of repute, to thinking. And his conclusions, after a good deal more observation of the same two bears and relating this to past accounts of people who had associated with bears under wilderness conditions without trouble, was given toward the end of the article. Jase flipped over to it.

. . . *To summarize:* he read, *a herbivore can be fed because its body is not in any way adapted to the movements necessary for seizing prey. Many carnivores, in turn, acquire the ability to be fed as a result of parental attention.* . . . Jase paused, checking through his memory for something else that intruded. What was the book—oh, yes. *Born Free*, about a lion named Elsa, raised by a woman and her husband under similar conditions in the African bush. . . . What was the authoress' name? Jase's foggy mind retreated from the effort of producing it. Anyway, it only corroborated what was here—he turned back to Krott's summary.

. . . The bear lacks this ability and evidently cannot acquire it. That, I believe, is the deciding factor in the danger of bears living in contact with men. The way to the bear's heart is not through its stomach; that is what is hard for us to understand, since we ourselves are capable of being fed as are others among the true predators. . . .

Clutching the magazine, Jase clambered groggily to his feet and set off through the stacks down to the door that entered one side of Mele's small office between the stacks and the library room. He and Mele had not been close since the day that Swanson, Coth, and the rest had taken over the project, but now success, compounded by his state of exhaustion, burned from his mind and sent him to her. He blundered down the stairs and burst in through the small door.

She was seated at her desk, transcribing on her typewriter from a tape recording. The sound of her fingers on the keys broke off as she stopped, staring up at his sudden appearance. In the little silence, he could hear from beyond the farther door the voices of Swanson and the rest in conversation that could not be resolved into words through the door's thickness.

"Mele!" he shouted. "I've found it."

He discovered his knees suddenly ready to give way beneath him. There was no place in the little office to sit down. He pulled the door to the stacks closed behind him, recklessly seized the wastebasket in the corner behind Mele, dumped its contents on the floor, and turned it upside down. He sat on that, dropping the opened magazine on the typewriter before her.

"Look—," he said eagerly.

"Jase . . ." She put her hand up to move the magazine away. "I've got a lot to do."

"Listen!" he said fiercely, catching her hand. "You've got to listen!"

She looked at him then, and her face changed. She shook her head a little, and her eyes grew dark with unhappiness.

"You're covered with dust," she said. "And you're ready to drop. Jase, why don't you go and lie down? Then later, after you've had some rest, we can talk about whatever it is . . ."

"Mele!" he leaned forward toward her, tapping the surface of the open page before her with a grimy forefinger, "This is it! Can't you understand? Now we can do something!"

She stared at him, her eyes wide and brown.

"About what?" she asked.

"About the Ruml—the Ruml and us!" He stared at her. "What I've been driving at from the beginning. A bridge between their basic character and ours. It's here—in this article."

"This article?" She stared at it. "But that was written . . ." She turned back the cover to look at the date of issue of the magazine. "Years ago."

"Doesn't matter," said Jase. He grinned a little lightheadedly with his fatigue and having a chance to explain to her, finally. "It's a bit of honest basic research—the kind those people in there—" He nodded at the library room door, from beyond which the voices muttered. "Never saw the use for. 'Who cares what the reason is for ferocity in bears?'" he mimicked savagely. "Can't you hear them saying it? 'Who wants to go to the moon?' 'What difference does it make whether there's anything smaller than the atom—the atom's so small now we can't see it anyway?' You've heard them talk like that all their lives. So've I. Well, for once a piece of basic research is going to save their lives—all their lives!"

"Jase . . ." she said, pityingly.

"No, listen," he said. "Let me tell you what Krott found out. There's always been a problem with bears—wild ones— sometimes attacking humans, at other times just ignoring them.

Take Yellowstone Park. Every year tourists feeding the bears would get clawed, and other tourists would get away with it. Well, Krott found an explanation.''

"Jase . . .''

"No, listen." He went on in a rush. "You see, just a matter of a handful of years before this article, they were beginning to get interested in what they called feeding patterns. A barracuda, for example, will strike at a flashing, shiny object, whether he's hungry or not. A shark in a feeding frenzy will slash at anything and try to feed—even on his own entrails if he's been slashed by the blind frenzy of the other sharks around him. He'll try to feed even when he's dying.''

Jase paused to take a breath. The words had been tumbling out of him.

"Krott uncovered part of a feeding pattern in some bears he raised. Bears are omnivores. Midway between herbivores and carnivores. Herbivores aren't fed by their parents when they're young. Carnivores are. But herbivores don't attack to get their food. Bears do. The bear has a herbivore's feeding reflex and the offensive equipment of a carnivore—so he *attacks* any moving food he encounters. And it's not a conscious thing. It's a reflex, one that will operate even against a human he likes if the human waves, say, a chunk of bacon before him. If he does, the bear will attack—the bacon and coincidentally the human holding it. And the fact of the attack will have nothing to do about the bear's higher feelings or thoughts about the human.''

"Well, what if that's true?" said Mele. "You're talking about bears, not Ruml—or human beings.''

"But human beings have reflexes, too!" said Jase, desperately. "Not feeding reflexes comparable to the bears—but a young human child, able to walk but not yet able to defend itself, will run to and try to climb up on the nearest adult in case of out and out danger. In large groups or crowds, the herd instinct to escape—such as from a burning building—or to attack—as in the case of mob riots—will override the intellectual processes that otherwise would check such behavior.''

"Oh, Jase . . .'' Mele opened a drawer of her desk and exposed a box of paper tissues. She took several from the box and gently began to wipe Jase's forehead, where the sweat of exhaustion was mingling with the dust of the stacks. "Jase, you're exhausted. Why can't you leave such things to those men in there—'' She nodded at the next room. "They're experts. Let them handle it—"

"But they're handling it all wrong!" said Jase. "Our confrontation with the Ruml isn't a situation that's political—or even sociological. We're right back for practical purposes a hundred million years ago, meeting like two primitive, different animals on a hillside! I tell you in a case like this, the intellectual process of civilization gets swept aside. It's the root character of one race—the animal character of one race—face to face with the animal character of the other. And these animal characters override the decisions of our upper brains. We don't act like thinking individuals. We act like primitive representatives of our own particular kind of being. These basic reflexes are tied in directly to the survival instinct—the racial survival instinct—and they override, I tell you, the intellectual, individual decision—"

"Well, they don't override mine," said Mele, firmly, throwing the dampened, soiled tissues into the pile of waste paper Jase had dumped from the wastebasket. "Now, Jase, you're going to get some sleep—"

"They will," he interrupted her grimly. "You'll see. Someday—"

"No, I won't," said Mele with decision. 'I'm not some silly ground-down woman out of the nineteen centuries, thank you. I'm in control of myself like any modern woman, and I'll continue to be so—"

"It's got nothing to do with being modern—"

Jase's desperate voice was cut off sharply, as the door from the library room banged open and Swanson stood filling the entrance, his spectacles dangling from one hand.

"Mele!" he said. "Have you seen Jase anywhere—Oh, there you are, Jase. Come in here. Both of you come in!"

Jase pulled himself up, his legs trembling with tiredness, by gripping a corner of Mele's desk. He went into the library, blundering against the frame of the door. Mele's arm caught his elbow and steadied him from behind.

"Sit down," she said to Jase. Over his shoulder, as she steered him into a chair, she spoke angrily to Swanson. "He needs to sleep. Can't you see that? Can't you talk to him later?"

"No," said Swanson, briefly without exaggeration. From the chair, Jase looked up at him, seeing behind him the face of Bill Coth, today not wearing his Air Force uniform, and the faces of the other men who never spoke when Jase was in the room.

"What is it?" asked Jase.

Swanson looked at him for a second as though debating what—or how much—to say.

"They've found something," he said, finally. "Kator's bunch. With their collectors. They've penetrated into an area we didn't want them to get into."

"When?" asked Jase.

"Twenty minutes—half an hour ago," said Swanson. "One of their rat-shaped collectors got right onto the threshold of a secret installation. They blew it up before we could capture it."

"What installation?" demanded Jase. "What's at it that's so secret?"

Swanson hesitated.

"I'm not authorized to tell you," he said. "I'm sorry."

Jase stared at him for a second, speechless.

"Why, you—incredible people!" he burst out, when he found his voice. "Are you going to play coy with me? I'm the one person who can save your necks. In fact, I've just found something—"

"I'm sorry," said Swanson, doggedly. "I'm simply not authorized to tell you."

Jase felt the fury in him burn his foggy brain clear for an instant and give him strength, for which he was grateful.

"Not authorized!" he said. "I can probably guess—what else could it be but something you could use against the Ruml. What is it—ground to air missiles? Something to do with telescopic observation of the Ruml area of space? Space warships of some—"

Swanson's eyelids flickered uncontrollably. His face, like Jase's, was haggard with tiredness.

"Space warships!" repeated Jase, staring at the man now fumbling his spectacles back on to his nose. "You *do* have such things! I was just striking out at random."

"It's an underground installation. Under what looks like an abandoned factory," said Swanson, harshly. "I don't understand how they found it."

"They knew what to search for," said Jase, "—probably. How much did the collector's filming device see?"

"It didn't get into the underground ship parking area—just into the elevator shaft leading down there. Then it blew up before any of our people could get to it to stop it. That's what makes us think the Ruml knew what they'd found. There was no reason to destroy the collector, otherwise. They just didn't want to take chances on our finding out they knew about it.''

"Yes . . ." said Jase. He pushed himself up out of the chair on to his feet. Thoughts were racing through his brain. "That's what he'd do.''

"He?''

"Kator." Jase thought hard. His mind was working furiously and brilliantly, like the mind of a man in a high fever just before the collapse into delirium. Jase was conscious of the abnormal clarity, like the final upflare of illumination before a light bulb burns itself out. But grateful for it. "This couldn't come at a better time.''

"Better time?" said Coth. Jase saw the faces of the men staring at him. Mele, behind his back, was no doubt staring also.

"I told you—I just found what I've been hunting for from the beginning of my contact with Kator—" Jase looked down at his hands for the copy of the magazine containing Krott's article, and then remembered he had left it on Mele's typewriter. "I've got the key to the basic Ruml character. Now I've got to meet one of them.''

"Never mind that," interrupted Swanson. "Let's get back to the important problem. How do we keep further collectors from getting down into the warship parking area itself? There must be some detection device the Ruml themselves know about that will warn us when one of those damn gadgets gets close—"

"Why don't you want their collector to see that the human race has space-going armament, too?" asked Jase. "They already know from the artifact what the stage of our spaceship development is—I see," Jase broke off, the final, brilliant clarity of his mind giving the answer. "You've taken the ships out of there—that's what you don't want them to see, isn't it? You think if they see what's obviously a place where space warships could be, and there's only a few broken down ones still there, that they'll realize we're aware of them.''

He felt the wideness of his eyes, blazing on Swanson and the others.

"You shortsighted—" He broke off. "Where are the ships, then?''

"I'm sorry," said Swanson. "I'm not in any position to discuss any of this—"

"You want me to guess?" snarled Jase. "You've sent them out where they'll be in space, within striking distance of the

Ruml Homeworld. It's the sort of thing you'd do. That's where they are, aren't they? Aren't they?"

"I can't—," began Swanson.

"Never mind," said Jase. "You don't have to admit it. It's exactly what the human basic pattern would drive you to do, just like their pattern— Never mind." Jase's mind was racing too fast for his tongue to keep up. "It doesn't matter. He'll come himself. Yes, that's what he'll have to do."

"What're you talking about?" demanded Coth, behind Swanson.

"Kator. He'll come himself," muttered Jase. "Yes, it all makes sense now.—It's all right. I can handle it now. Only, I've got to meet him."

"Meet who?" demanded Swanson.

"Kator. He'll be coming down to look inside your underground spaceport himself. I want to meet him when he comes. You've got to arrange it so I'll be there." He looked at Swanson. "You can do that, can't you? I tell you, I've got the solution now. I just found it in the stacks. We can handle both."

"Both what?" said Coth.

"Both the human and Ruml pattern. They'd clash head on otherwise. Well—" He stared at Swanson. "You didn't answer me. I said, Can you arrange to have me there?"

Swanson looked back and shook his head, slowly.

"No," he said, calmly. "You must know by this time that very few people—if any—think you're free from infection by the alien mind you've been dealing with. I'm afraid we don't trust you. I'm afraid you won't be allowed near the place—and particularly if your friend Kator is due."

Jase stared at him. The room seemed to rock suddenly, but he fought it back to steadiness. Got to hold on a minute longer, he thought.

"I'll make a deal with you," Jase said. "You'd like to do without me, wouldn't you? You'd all like to be able to keep track of Kator and the rest without using me?"

Swanson met his gaze unapologetically.

"Yes," said Swanson, briefly.

"See I'm there when Kator comes," said Jase. "See I have a chance to met him face to face and speak to him, on his way in. On his way out, I'll help you to capture him. I'll guarantee you'll be able to capture him alive and fit him with instruments without his knowing it. You can put your own transmitter on him and bypass me. You can even fit him with a device to blow him up if you want to stop him later.''

Swanson stood for a second without answering.

''I haven't got the authority to make that kind of agreement with you,'' he said at last. ''I'm not empowered—''

''You'll agree,'' said Jase. ''You'll all agree because it's part of your pattern, and, like the Ruml, humans react according to their basic pattern when the chips are—''

The room rocked once more around him. Only this time it kept going. It went all the way over. He was conscious of the faces of Swanson and the rest whirling, the room whirling circularly before him. And then nothing. . . .

CHAPTER SEVENTEEN

Jase allowed the Expedition a shift in which to celebrate. He did not join in the celebration himself or swallow one of the short-lived bacterial cultures that manufactured ethyl alcohol in the Ruml stomachs from carbohydrates the Expedition members had feasted on earlier. Jase wanted neither the momentary exhilaration nor the quick oblivion of unconsciousness that followed intoxication by such cultures. The intoxication that he desired most was a subtler thing that had sung in his mind and body since he had first made the great decision to try and Found his Kingdom. He called the Captain into conference in the Keysman's private quarters aboard the ship.

''The next stage,'' Jase told the Captain, ''is, of course, to send a man down to examine this underground, and obviously secret, area.''

''Of course, sir,'' said the Captain. The Captain, like the rest of the Expedition, had swallowed one of the bacterial cultures already but, because of his responsibility aboard, would not eat until the rest had recovered from their drunkenness. He thought of the rest of the Expedition gorging themselves now in the gym, and his own hunger came sharply on him to reinforce the anticipation of intoxication.

''So far,'' said Jase, ''the Expedition has operated without mistakes. Perfection of operation must go on. The man who goes down to the planet of the Muffled People in person must be the one man on whom I can absolutely depend to carry the job through to success. There's no question who that man must be.''

"Sir?'' said the Captain, forgetting his hunger suddenly and becoming alert. His stomach contracted. "Are you thinking of me, Keysman? If there's someone who can take over my job, here—''

"I'm not thinking of you.''

"Oh,'' said the Captain. The excitement left him, and his stomach expanded in disappointment. "Well, it was just a stray hope, sir. Naturally, I know you'd want a younger, more physically apt man—''

"Exactly,'' said Jase. "Myself.''

"Keysman!"

It was almost an explosion from the Captain's lips. His whiskers flattened back against his cheeks.

"I . . . I beg your pardon, sir,'' he said. "Of course, it's your responsibility and your authority. You can select whoever you want. But . . . do you want *me* to be acting Keysman while you're down there?''

Jase looked squarely at him.

"No,'' he said.

The Captain's face stiffened slightly. But his voice remained impassive.

"Then . . . who, sir?''

"No one.''

This time the Captain did not explode. He merely stared blankly, almost blindly, at Jase.

"No one,'' repeated Jase, slowly. "You understand me, I hope, Captain. I'll be taking the Keys of the ship with me.''

"But sir—'' The Captain's voice broke off. He took a breath deeper than usual. "For the record, sir, I must point out that it would be extremely difficult to get home safely with the ship's Keys in the hands of an acting Keysman who has already formed likes and dislikes among the other members of the Expedition Crew.''

"It would probably be impossible,'' said Jase. "For that reason, I intend to lock ship before leaving and take the keys with me. That way, there will be no danger of mutiny or riot destroying all hands on the return voyage. And the valuable information about the Muffled People we have already gathered will not risk being lost forever, on a dead ship drifting through space. In case

I and the keys are lost, a later ship will find this one of our Expedition safely buried here, with the information on it intact and available."

"Yes, sir," said the Captain. He saluted with respect.

"You'd better inform your officers about this decision of mine after I've left. Then you can inform the Expedition as a group."

"Yes, sir."

"I'll let you get back to the celebration then," said Jase. The Captain turned toward the door. "And, Captain—"

The Captain halted with the door half open and looked back. Jase nodded approvingly and with commendation.

"Tell them," said Jase, "to enjoy themselves—this shift."

"Yes, sir."

The Captain went out, closing and locking the door behind him. Jase turned and walked over to the table holding his Keys, his model of the artifact, and the cube containing the dirtworm. He picked up the cube and gazed at it for a moment, holding it tenderly.

"First of my Kingdom," he said to it, "you'll go back now to the soil from which you came."

Gently he returned it to the table. Sinking on his haunches, he sat gazing at it. And through his mind moved the pictures of his sons, his grandsons—all the members of his Founded Family, playing and growing under the alien sun. And from among them, perhaps, one day would come not one other, but several who in their time would Found Kingdoms too. . . .

The shift after the celebration, Jase set most of the Expedition Members to work constructing collectors who could burrow, examine, and report on the surroundings of the secret underground area of the Muffled People. But these, when they were sent down, were strictly programmed to avoid any movement critically close to the critical area. That would remain for him to penetrate alone.

Meanwhile, he himself, with the help of the Captain and two specialists in such things, attacked the problem of making him bear at least a passable resemblance to one of the Muffled People—not only in appearance, but in speech and action.

It was an ambitious task.

The first and most obvious change was the clipping off of Jase's long, stiff mouth whiskers. There was no pain or discomfort associated with this, but the emotional shock was considerable, since criminals, those suffering birth defects, and hospital patients requiring surgery in the facial area were the only male Rumls ever seen without whiskers. Oddly, Jase found that the fact he knew they would grow out again within a few months—if not a matter of weeks—did not help. Without his whiskers he felt emasculated.

The fact that the whiskers had been clipped by his own hand somehow made it worse.

The clipping and shaving of the fur on his face and head was otherwise a minor operation. After the shock of losing the whiskers, Jase had been tempted to simply dye brown the close, inhumanly glossy black fur covering the skull between his ears like a mat. But that would have been too weak a solution to the fur problem. Even dyed, his natural head covering bore no relationship in appearance to human hair.

Still, dewhiskered and shaved, Jase's reflection in a mirror presented him with an ugly sight. Luckily, he did, now, look like one of the Muffled People after a fashion—from the neck up. The effect was rather like that of a pink-skinned oriental with puffy eyelids over unnaturally wide and narrow eyes, and with a flat and unusually narrow jaw. But he was undeniably native-like.

The rest of his disguise would have to be taken care of by the mufflings he would be wearing, after the native fashion. These complicated body coverings therefore turned out to be a blessing instead of the unmitigated, hampering curse he had expected them to be. Without them it would have been almost impossible to conceal the Ruml body differences from the shape of one of the Muffled People.

As it was, foot coverings with built-up undersurfaces helped to disguise the relative shortness of the Ruml legs, as the loose-hanging skirt of the sleeved, outside upper garment hid the unnatural—by native standards of physique—narrowness of his hips. Not a great deal could be done about the fact that the Ruml spine was so connected to the Ruml pelvis that he appeared to walk with his upper body at an angle leaning forward. But heavy padding widened the narrow Ruml shoulders, and the wide sleeves hid the fact that the Ruml arms, like the Ruml legs, were normally designed to be kept bent at knee and elbow joint.

When it was done, he was a passable imitation of a Muffled Person. But these changes were only the beginning. It was now necessary for him to learn to move about in these hampering garments with some appearance of native naturalness.

The mufflings were hideously uncomfortable—like the clinging but lifeless skin of some loathsome creature. But Jase was as unyielding with himself as he was with the other Expedition Members. Shift after shift, as the rest of the Expedition made their burrowing scanners, sent them down, and collected the film strips from them back on the moon, Jase tramped up and down his own quarters, muffled and whiskerless—while the Captain and the two specialists compared his actions with tapes of the natives in comparable movement and action. And criticized.

Intelligent life, they all knew, is inconceivably adaptable, and Jase was working for great stakes. There came a shift, finally, when the three watchers could offer no more criticism, and Jase himself no longer felt the touch of the mufflings about his body for the unnatural thing it was.

He announced himself satisfied with himself. He went to the recordings room for a final briefing on the information the burrowing mechanisms had gathered about the Muffled People's underground and secret place. He stood—a weird-looking Ruml in his wrappings—while the Recorder informed him that the mechanism had charted the underground area completely and found it to be immense. A tenth of a native mile in depth, nearly five miles in extent, and half a mile wide. And the whole underground area was walled in by an extremely thick casing of native concrete stiffened by steel rods.

The mechanisms had been unable to record through the thickness of that casing and since they had been programmed strictly to make no attempt to burrow through it for fear of alarming the natives, nothing was known about the area's interior.

What lay inside the concrete shell, therefore, was still a complete mystery. If Jase was to invade the secret place, therefore, he would have to do so blind—not knowing what in the way of internal defenses he might encounter. The only open way in the mechanisms had discovered was down an elevator shaft through which supplies were sent down into the area.

Jase stood a moment in thought, while the Captain and the officers of the Expedition waited.

"Very well," he said at last. "I consider it most likely that this place has been set up to protect against invasion by others of the natives themselves—rather than by someone like myself. At any rate, I'm going to go ahead with it, on that assumption."

And he turned to the Captain and the officers to give them his final orders to cover the period while he would be gone. He did not bother to tell them what to do in case he did not come back. Such commands would be unnecessary to the point of dishonorable insult.

The face of the planet, hidden on beyond the body of the moon, was still in night when Jase breached the moon surface just over the site of the buried ship. Behind him, the hole in the dust-covered rock filled itself in again as if with a smooth magic.

His small ship lifted from the surface around the horizon of the moon and dropped toward the night darkness of the planet below him.

He came to the planet's surface just as the sun was beginning to break over the eastern horizon and the fresh chill of the post-dawn drop in native temperature was in the air. He camouflaged his ship, giving it the appearance of some native sumac bushes, and stepped from it for the first time on to the alien soil.

The strange, tasteless atmosphere of the planet filled his nostrils. He looked toward the rising sun and saw a line of trees and a ramshackle building blackly outlined against the redness of its half-disk. He turned a quarter-circle and began to walk toward the deserted native factory, which covered and hid the underground area.

Not far from his ship, he hit the dirt road running past the scattered farms leading to the isolated, abandoned factory complex that loomed ahead of him on the horizon like some monstrous jumble of enormous boxes. The Muffled People's habit of building to dizzying heights (even small dwelling places often reached to the full three stories above ground of a Family Palace, back home) made his destination visible from the time he left his ship. He continued along it with the sun rising strongly on his left, large and reddish-yellow; and after a while he came to a wooden bridge over a small creek. The creek was tangled with wild vegetation. No attempt had been made to border or beautify it in Honor to the life-giving fluid it carried. The bridge itself was a crude affair on which, as he crossed it, his foot covering fell with a hollow sound. In the stillness of the native dawn these sounds seemed to echo through the whole sleeping world around him. He hurried to get off the planks back on to dirt road again. And it was with an internal relaxing of tension that he stepped finally off the far end of the bridge.

"Up early, aren't you?" said a native voice, from only a few feet away alongside below the bridge.

Jase whirled like a swordsman. And saw—himself.

CHAPTER EIGHTEEN

Kator stood facing the native who had spoken. He stared at a figure seated on the sloping bank of the creek just a few feet below the end of the bridge.

Jase stared at himself.

Himself stared at himself. A container of burning vegetation was in his mouth, and smoke trickled from his small mouth. He was muffled in blue leg coverings, and his upper body was encased in a worn, sleeved muffling of native leather. His furless hands held a long stick of native vegetation out over the waters of the creek, with the line at the end of it dropping down below the water's surface. His lips in a furless face twisted upward in a native fashion that meant not excitement or rage, but friendliness.

But himself stood above at the end of the bridge. There was something both brave and pitiful about the small figure he looked at from his seated position. No human being could have been deluded for a second by the appearance of him at the end of the bridge. The clothes he wore were clumsy and fastened wrong. And the figure in them crouched like Groucho Marx in the old film comedies of the early nineteen thirties. The shaved face looked childlike without its fur and whiskers, and it was barely five feet tall.

It was fantastic for Jase to be at once five feet tall and a head taller. To crouch and sit erect at the same time. To be alarmed at the sight of himself and moved to pity at the sight of himself. . . . The point of view in Jase's mind jumped from his human body to his Kator body, from his Kator body to his Jase body—to his Kator body and mind—to his Jase body and mind—to his Kator mind—to his Jase mind—

He was Jase. He was Kator. He was Jase-Kator—or Kator-Jase—Kase—Jator—Jaskatore. . . .

He was both. The personalities blurred. Blended. Matched. He swayed.

"Are you ill?" he asked himself. Perhaps it was a native infected with a disease to which his race was prone.

"No," he said, catching himself. "What're you doing here? Out for a hike?"

"Yes," he said, wondering if the native noticed any accent to his words. "You are fishing?"

"Bass," he answered, waggling his pole. A small, colored object bobbed on the water where the line entered the liquid.

"I see," he said, not knowing what bass were. "There are some in this water?"

"Well," he answered, "never know what you'll catch. Might as well fish for bass as anything else. You from around here?"

"No," he said.

"City?" he asked.

"Yes," he said. He thought of the planet-wide city of the Homeworld. Yes, he was from a city.

"Where you headed?"

"Oh," he answered—he had rehearsed this speech—"I thought I would go around the buildings here and search for a large road and transportation to the nearest city."

"Keep going then," he told his small, crouching, self. "I'd show you the way, but I've got fish to catch. You can't miss it anyway. Ahead or back from here both brings you out on the same road."

"Thank you," he said.

"Don't mention it."

"Good luck then with your hunting in the water, here."

"Thank you, friend." The impulse came from deep inside him. He had been right—he had been right. But he had to come face to face with Kator as himself to put the two personalities one on top of the other, like cardboard cutouts. Now he had done it, and the overlappings on each part were finally plain and distinct. He spoke to the small, crouching, shaved-face figure. "We're a good deal alike—more than you'd think."

He stared at himself, unable to make sense of the words. They seemed to make sense, but they did not. It seemed that the native was referring to something taken for granted, something that he had not mentioned earlier in his conversation.

"Yes," he said, deciding to simply ignore the incomprehensible statement. "I must say so long, now." About to turn away, a strange feeling moved him. Perhaps it was an impulse of the Random Factor. The native had baffled him—it would not hurt to baffle the native a little. If the other became alarmed, he was carrying handweapons that could kill him silently and quickly.

"Perhaps," he said, on the wings of this strange impulse, "you can tell me—I am among friends, here?"

"Yes," said the native, "here you are among friends."

His stomach contracted. Surely it was the Random Factor that had caused him to speak—and the native to answer in polite, Honorable Ruml fashion. Possibly it was the Random Factor showing him that these natives of his Kingdom-to-be were not without Honor, as he had earlier feared when the reports from the collectors began to show their lack of weapons and duelings. Gratefulness rose inside him. He raised his hand in farewell, native fashion, as he turned away—but silently, inside him, he spoke the Blessing to this strange, native figure who could never have understood it, even if it had been spoken aloud—so many thousand years of Ruml history were behind it.

"Water be with you, shade be with you, peace be with you . . ."

His attention back now on the creek waters, the native raised his own hand unseeingly—almost as if he had somehow heard.

Turning, in the clumsy mufflings of his disguise, Jase in the Ruml body of Kator went on toward the factory.

Only a little way down the dirt road, around a bend and through some trees, he came to the wide wire gate where the road disappeared into the grounds about the factory buildings. The gate was closed and locked. Jase in Kator's body glanced around him, saw no one, and took a small silver cone from his pocket. He touched the point of the cone to the lock. There was a small, upward puff of smoke, and the gate sagged open. He pushed through, closed the gate behind him, and headed for the building with the elevator shaft to the hidden area underground.

The door to that building also was locked. Once more Jase felt himself glance around, but the watchmen of the deserted factory gave no sign or sound of their presence. Jase used the cone-shaped object on the lock of a small door set in the larger door that was wide enough for trucks to enter the building. He slipped inside.

Beyond the open space where trucks evidently parked when unloading supplies and material to be sent underground was the end of a conveyor belt wide enough to take large crates. It stretched off through a jungle of dark and idle machinery under the dim light of windows set several stories high in the corrugated iron walls of the building's skin.

Jase listened, standing in the shadow of the door. He heard

nothing. He put away the cone and drew his handgun. Lightly, he crouched and then leaped up in one bound onto the belt of the conveyor, five feet above the floor. Handgun ready, he began to follow along the belt back into the maze of machinery.

It was a strange, mechanical wilderness through which he found himself stealing. The conveyor belt was not a short one. After he had gone some distance on it, his listening ears caught a sound from up ahead. He stopped and listened.

The sound was the sound of native voices talking.

He went on cautiously. Gradually he approached the voices, which did not seem to be on the belt, but off it to the right a little distance. Finally, he drew level with them. Kneeling down and peering through the shapes of the machinery, he made out a clear area in the building about thirty feet off the belt where he stood. Behind the cleared area was a glassed-in cage in which five humans wearing blue mufflings and weapons harnesses supporting handguns could be seen, sitting at desks or standing about, talking.

Jase lowered his head and crept past like a shadow on the belt. The voices faded behind him, and in a little distance he came to the elevator shaft and the platform within it onto which the conveyor belt was designed to discharge its cargo.

Jase examined the platform with an eye already briefed on its probable construction. It was evidently controlled from below, but there should be some kind of controls on the platform itself—if only for emergency use.

Jase searched around the edge of the shaft and discovered some switches set in a line on a plate at the far end of the platform. Using a small magnetic power tool, he removed the plate and spent a moment or two studying the wiring going to the switches. Again, it was what he had been briefed to expect by experts among the Expedition crew. Amazingly—by sensible, normal Ruml standards—there was no lock on the controls at all.

He replaced the plate, reached out, and took hold of the switch that according to his briefing, should send the platform downward. For a second he hesitated. From this point on, it was a matter of calculated risk. There was no way of telling what in the shape of guards or protective devices waited for him at the bottom of the shaft. He had had his choice of trying to send the collectors in to get that information earlier, at the risk of alerting the natives, or of taking his chances now. And he had chosen to take his chances now.

He pressed the switch. The platform dropped beneath him, and the darkness of the upper shaft closed above his head.

The platform fell with a rapidity that made the claws extend instinctively from the ends of his fingers to keep a grasp on it. He had a momentarily alarming image of a device designed only for nonliving cargo beneath him. Then the thought of the damageable fruits and vegetables that would be transported down on this platform at times came to reassure him. Sure enough—after what seemed like a much longer drop than the burrowing scanners had reported likely—the platform slowed quickly but evenly to a gentle halt and emerged into light from an opening on one side of the shaft.

Jase was off the platform the second it stopped, and racing for the nearest cover—behind the door of the small room where the shaft had ended. And no sooner than necessary. A lacework of blue beams lanced across the space where he had been standing on the platform a moment before.

The beams winked out. The smell of ozone filled the room. For a moment Jase stood frozen and poised, handgun in fist. But no living creature showed itself. The beams had evidently been fired automatically as a defense against animal intruders. It would be part of the normal self-protecting machinery of the elevator shaft. However, he noted with a contracting of his stomach, the spot he had chosen to duck into was about the only place in the room the beams had not covered.

He came out from behind the door, slipped through the entrance to which it belonged—and checked suddenly. He had found it.

He stood in an underground area of enormous dimensions, his own figure shrunk by contrast to that of one of the small collectors. Here he was a pygmy. No, less than a pygmy. An ant among giants, dimly lit from an almost invisible ceiling, five hundred feet overhead.

He was at the end of what was no less than an underground spacefield. Towering close to him, too huge to take in without moving his eyes, were the Brobdingnagian shapes of great space warships. He had found it—the secret gathering place of the battle strength of the Muffled People; and inside himself some hidden corner of his spirit poured forth thanksgiving that they were now proved beyond any doubt to be not without Honor after all.

From between the titanic shapes up ahead came the sound of metal ringing against other metal and concrete. And the sound of feet and voices. Like a hunting animal of the Ruml Home-world, Jase slipped from shadow to shadow between the great ships until he came to a spot from which he could see what was going on without exposing himself.

He peered out from behind the roundness of a great, barrel-thick supporting jack and saw that he was unexpectedly at the edge of the parked ships. The discovery came as an abrupt shock.—Was that all there were of them?

There could be no more than a dozen at most in this space, which could have parked many more.

He looked ahead. Beyond stretched immense emptiness of floor, and only some fifty feet from where he stood hidden a crew of five natives in green one-piece mufflings were dismounting the governer of a collapsed-universe drive unit from one of the ships closest to them. A single native in blue with a weapons harness and handgun stood by them, watching—no doubt on guard.

As Jase watched, another native in blue with weapons harness appeared from between the ships closest to the working natives. Jase shrank back behind the supporting jack that shielded him. The second guard came up to the first who had been standing observing.

"—Nothing," Jase heard him say. "May have been a short in the powerhouse. Anyway, nothing came down the shaft just now. I've looked."

"A rat, maybe?" asked the first guard.

"No, I checked out the whole room. It was empty. Anything on the platform would have got caught by the beams. They're checking upstairs, though."

Jase slipped back among the ships.

The natives were alerted now, even if they did not seriously suspect an intruder like himself. Nontheless, a great exultation was welling up inside him. He had been prepared to break into one of the ships to discover the nature of its internal machinery. Now—thanks to the dismantled unit he had seen being worked on—that was no longer necessary. His high hopes, his long gamble were about to pay off. His kingdom was before him.

Only two things were still to be done. The first was to make a visual record of the place to take Home, and the other was to get himself safely out of here and back to his small ship.

He reached up and touched the top button of the sleeved, outer muffling which covered the upper part of his body in the native fashion. The button concealed the recording device, which had been running steadily, storing up picture and sound of all he had encountered. But adjustments were necessary to allow it to record the vast shapes and spaces about him now. Jase made the necessary adjustments with a touch or two on the apparently featureless outside of the button and for about half an hour after that flitted about like an entertainment-recorder, taking pictures not only of the huge ships but of everything else about this secret underground field.

It was a pity, he thought, that he could not get up to record a picture of the ceiling far overhead, lost behind the light sources beaming down on the ships and him. Such a picture would show the mechanism that would be necessary to shift aside the ceiling to let these ships out of here. However, that was a minor piece of information. The important information was what he was filming down here.

Finished at last, he worked his way back to the room containing the elevator shaft. Almost, in the vast maze of ships and jacks, he had forgotten where it was. But the sense of direction which his scout training in his first season as an adult had trained to a fine peak in him paid off. He oriented himself and worked his way at last back to the entrance of the room.

He halted there, just outside it, peering in at the platform sitting innocuously waiting at the bottom of the shaft. Crossing the room to it would undoubtedly trigger the automatic mechanism that fired the guns. He spent a few moments hunting around for controls, which the natives undoubtedly had for turning off the mechanism when they themselves wished to approach the platform. But he found nothing, and every minute he delayed here increased the chance of his being discovered. And to be discovered now would destroy all the advantage of the information he had gained—and warn the natives that his people had discovered their world. Whereas if he could get away without alarming anyone now, the invasion to come would have all the advantage of information and complete surprise. His Kingdom would fall into the hands of the Ruml and his own with hardly an effort.

He returned to the open doorway and gazed through it. For a

long second he stood, thinking with a rapidity and force he had hardly matched before in his life—even during the duel with Horaag Adoptedson. There had to be a way to the platform that avoided the beams.

Suddenly a farfetched but daring scheme occurred to him. He knew that the area behind the door was safe. The beams had not touched him there last time. From there two long leaps would carry him to the platform. Unlike the natives, his body was built for springing. If he, with that body the Muffled People could not have anticipated when they designed the automatic-beam circuit and this room, could avoid that single touching of the floor between behind the door and the platform . . . He thought. It might be possible then that he could reach the platform without triggering the defensive mechanism.

There was a way, he considered. But it was a stake-everything proposition. If he missed, there would be no hope of avoiding the beams.

The door opened inward, and it was about six feet in height, three and a half feet in width. From its most inward point of swing it was about twenty-two feet distant from the platform. Reaching in through the entrance, he swung the door so that it was at right angles to the entrance, projecting the distance of its width into the room. Then he backed up and took off his clumsy foot coverings, tucking them into pouches in his body mufflings.

He got down on hands and feet and arched his back. His claws extended themselves from his fingers and toes, clicking on the concrete floor. For a moment he felt a wave of despair that the clumsy mufflings hampering him would make the feat impossible. But he had no time to take them off, now. He resolutely shoved all doubt from his mind and backed up further until he was a good thirty feet from the door.

He thought of his Kingdom and launched himself forward.

He was only two seasons adult, his reflexes were superb, and the exercise under Brodth Swordsmaster had trained him into top shape. By the time he had covered the thirty feet he was moving at close to twenty miles an hour. He flung himself from the threshold of the entrance and flew to the inmost top edge of the door.

He seemed, even to himself, barely to touch the door in passing. But four sets of his claws clamped on the wood, making the all-important, slight change in direction and thrusting him forward with additional impetus. For a moment he flew above the deadly floor of the room. Then the platform and the shaft seemed to leap to meet him, and he slammed down on the flat surface of the platform with an impact that drove the breath out of him.

The beams did not appear. The room was silent—and safe.

Half-dazed, but mindful of the noise he had made in landing, which might attract the attention of any native nearby, he fumbled hastily around the edge of the platform, found the switches, and snapped over and down the one he had earlier marked in his mind as being the one to send the platform upward.

He shot up into the darkness of the shaft.

On the way up, he recovered his breath. He made no attempt to replace the clumsy foot coverings but drew his handgun and held it ready in his hand. The second the platform stopped at the top of the shaft, he was off it and running noiselessly back along the conveyor belt at a speed which no native should have been able to maintain in the crouched position in which he could contract his running, Ruml body.

There were sounds of natives moving about beyond the enclosing machinery through which the conveyor belt ran. But he closed his ears to them and ran on. Surely, after bringing him this far, the Random Factor would not desert him now. He clung to the feeling of confidence that his escape was almost already made—when a shout sounded from within the maze of machinery to his left.

"Stop, there! You!"

Without hesitation, he fired in the direction of the voice and dived off the conveyor belt into the tangle of gears and driving shafts to his right. Behind him came a grunt and the sound of a falling body. A blue beam lanced through the spot on the conveyor belt where he had stood a second before.

A dozen feet off the conveyor belt into the maze of machinery, he clung to a piece of ductwork and listened. His first impression had been that there was only one native in the area from which the shout had come. But now he heard three voices converging on the spot at which he had fired.

"What happened?"

"I thought I saw something—" The voice that had hailed him groaned suddenly. "I tried to get a clear shot, and I slipped down in between the drums here."

"You jammed in there?"

"I think my legs got broken."

"You say you saw something? Just a minute, we'll get you out."

"I thought I saw something. I don't know. I guess that alarm had me seeing things—there's nothing on the belt now. Help me out, will you?"

"Bill, give me a hand."

"Easy! Take it—*easy!*"

"All right . . . all right now. We'll get you in to the doctor."

He clung, listening, as the two who had come up later lifted their hurt companion out of wherever he had fallen and carried him out of the building. Then there was only silence around him, and in that silence he drew a deep breath. It was hardly believable, but once more the Random Factor had stood beside him.

Quietly, he began to come back toward the conveyor belt. Now that he could move with less urgency, he saw a clearer route to it. He clambered along and spotted a straight climb along a sideways-sloping, three-foot-wide strip of metal filling the gap between what seemed to be the high side of something like a turbine motor and a narrow strip of darkness about two feet wide alongside more ductwork. The strip led straight as a road, bypassing the conveyor belt, to the open area where the conveyor belt began.

Looking along it now, he could see the door of the building ajar and a little strip of sunlight outside showing.

Perfection, he told himself, attracts the Random Factor. . . . He began slipping along the strip of sideways-tilted metal, and his claws scratched and skidded. It was slicker than he had thought it would be. He felt himself sliding off sideways as he went forward. He increased his speed. Grimly, in silence, he tried to hold himself from slipping off into the strip of darkness alongside.

His claws blunted on the polished surface. From somewhere there was a single, odd, *putt*ing, sound. Scrambling at the metal, he felt a twinge as from a pulled muscle in his neck. He scrambled harder . . . and, unexpectedly, his senses started to swim.

A wave of dizziness swept over him. He felt his limbs relaxing, his body sliding, off into the strip of darkness.

He fell, and the darkness closed about him as his senses fled.

CHAPTER NINETEEN

Jase unscrewed the two halves of a small blowpipe and put the weapon back into an inside pocket of his leather jacket. As the two men in guards' blue uniforms came carrying the limp body of Kator out of the narrow space in which it had fallen, he moved after them. When they laid Kator down in a little open space, Jase reached down and removed a tiny, feathered dart stuck in the Ruml's neck, just behind and below the flat, pointed ear.

As he bent over the unconscious Ruml, his body shielding his left arm for a moment, his left hand closed over unhooked, and carried away the topmost of the large buttons on Kator's imitation jacket. Straightening up and turning away, he came face to face with Swanson.

"You can tell us now, can't you?" said the spectacled man. "What was the anesthetic?"

Jase smiled, wearily and a little ironically.

"Ethyl alcohol," he said.

"Alcohol!" Swanson stared at him, then exploded. "You mean their systems are that much like ours? We could have used alcohol ourselves!"

"They aren't that alike—not as much as you think," said Jase. "It just happens alcohol intoxicates them, like it intoxicates us. But just not the same way. Most of our drugs—chloroform, to take an example—would have killed him. Even alcohol doesn't affect them just the way it does us—" He gestured at Kator. "Did you see how fast he went out, when only a few drops were introduced into his veins? The same amount wouldn't have been enough for you or I to feel, probably."

"Yes . . ." said Swanson, without relaxing. He turned to look down at Kator himself. "Well, we'll start bugging him now. When he comes to and starts back to his ship, he'll be as full of miniaturized recording devices as a political convention. How long's he going to be out?"

"They swallow short-lived alcohol-producing bacterial cultures, the way we drink whisky, for relaxation," said Jase. "They get high in a few moments, go out almost immediately, and stay unconscious for about two hours, coming out of it gradually into a deep sleep that lasts about four of our hours.''

"Six hours then?"

"No, not if you want to cut it short," said Jase. "You can wake him up as soon as the actual unconscious period is over. With the sense of urgency I—he—'' Jase saw Swanson's eyes flicker at him momentarily as he made the verbal slip, ''was feeling, he may wake himself up as soon as he comes to. But, just to be sure, you can jar him or make a noise.''

"You're sure, are you?" Swanson stared at him in the relatively dim interior of the building, ''about all this information?''

"Yes," said Jase. "But why don't you get that doctor of yours in here if you want to check?"

"Good idea." Swanson turned away to speak to the guards. Jase slipped back into the shadows. From one pocket he took a small, brown cube the size of a jeweler's box for holding and displaying a single ring. Operating almost by feel in the darkness, he made some adjustments on the surface of the button he had taken from Kator's jacket and held it against a tiny aperture in the ringbox-sized cube. He pressed the cube.

There was a faint, almost inaudible whirring that sounded for a second just loud enough for Jase's ears alone to hear it. Then the whirring stopped.

Jase replaced the cube in his pocket and wandered back to the still figure of Kator, pushing between two of the three guards now standing above it.

"I'd better look at that spot where the dart stuck in, again," said Jase. Uncertainly, they let him through to the still body of the Ruml. Jase squatted down, rolled Kator's lax head to one side to expose the neck area where the anesthetic dart had stuck, and bent down to look closely at the area. He placed his left palm as if to steady himself on Kator's coat and palmed the button back onto the Ruml-designed hooks that held it.

None of the guards seemed to notice. The button fastenings were typically Ruml, and only someone who, like Jase, had been in a Ruml mind would think to look for them, or for the microscopic pack of sensitized surfaces just below the camouflaged exterior of the button that was the Ruml version of a miniaturized spy camera.

"What's this? Don't get in our way here!" he heard the voice of Swanson say behind him as he got to his feet. "Clear out of here, Jase. This is our business from now on."

The tone of the spectacled man's voice was brisk and impersonal. It was clear that what he said mirrored his thoughts—with the miniaturized recorders and tell-tales to be now implanted under the skin of Kator, the Ruml could be followed by mechanical snoopers, sending back pictures and sound through a collapsed universe field even from the Ruml Homeworld, if Kator should return to it. Jase was no longer important in the eyes of Swanson, Coth, and the men who did not speak.

Jase faded back into the shadows of the machinery. He had told Swanson when the capture of Kator was being planned that it was necessary for him to know the layout, not only of the underground spaceship parking area, but of the abandoned factory that served as ground-level cover for it. Now he picked his way smoothly through the factory—but not toward the side yard where the transportation back to Washington was waiting.

He threaded his way through empty rooms and between silent machinery to another end of the factory, and out a rusting, small door into a field of weeds some forty yards wide to a barbed wire fence and a little woods of maple and oak trees.

Casually, he strolled across the field. Once out of sight among the trees, he went at a fast walking pace. A little less than an hour and three miles later, he was boarding a bus at a small-town bus stop.

There was some delay about the bus starting. But some eighteen minutes later air finally sighed through its compressors, and it slid out of the bus terminal building. Jase leaned back his head against the pillowed backrest of his seat and closed eyes that were sandy with fatigue. He had done his part.

From now on it was up to Kator and the Heads of Families back on Homeworld.

CHAPTER TWENTY

. . . When he woke, he had to think for a moment to remember that he was not on Homeworld, to remember that he had been fleeing through a factory building on the world of the Muffled People—one jump away from capture—when something had happened.

Slowly it all came back to him; and slowly he began to take stock of his surroundings.

He was wedged someplace between narrow walls. Above him there was only silence and a dimness. It seemed to him he had been unconscious for some time, but far above him to his Ruml eyes the light still streaming through the high windows of the factory building seemed to come at almost the same angle. He lay staring at the light for a moment.

. . . No, he was wrong. Perhaps an eighth or sixth of the local sunlight period of the planet here had gone by while he had lain dead to the world.

His neck ached slightly behind his ear, and there were other sore spots about him. He must, he thought, have knocked himself out when he fell. But the guards chasing him evidently had not found him—

His thoughts broke off suddenly. Voices struck on his ears. The voices of two natives standing some little distance off. He raised his head slightly and saw he was lying in a narrow gap between the two walls of metal. The gap, like a roofless tunnel, ran toward the open space between the conveyor belt end and the door to outside.

". . . not possible," one of the speaking Muffled People was saying. "We've looked everywhere."

"But you left the place to carry Rogers to the ambulance?"

"Yes, sir. But Corry stood guard outside the door there while we did that. Then, when we came back, we all searched the whole place. There's no one here."

"Sort of a funny day," said the second voice. "First that short or whatever it was, downstairs, and then Rogers thinking he saw something or someone, and breaking his leg." The voice moved off, from the open area, back at an angle toward a further part of the factory building. "Well, forget it, then. I'll write it up in my report, and we'll lock the building behind us until an inspector can look it over."

There was the sound of the small door opening.

"What's anybody going to steal anyway?" demanded the first voice, now also moving away. "Put a half million tons of space warship under one arm and carry it out?"

"Regulations—" The closing of the door cut off the words. There was silence in the dimness, which stretched on and on.

Jase stirred in the darkness.

For a moment he was afraid he had broken a limb in his fall

into this narrow space. But all his arms and legs responded. It was as he had thought—he was only bruised. Gratitude welled in him for the fact that he was only two seasons adult. An older man, with brittle bones . . . it did not bear thinking about.

He was not wedged in here so tightly as to be trapped, he found. He wriggled his way forward between the two surfaces until some other object blocked his way. He climbed up over this—another section of ductwork, it seemed—and emerged a second later into the open area.

It was empty, clear of natives as if it was actually the deserted building it pretended to be.

The local sun was well up in the center of the sky as he slipped out of the building. No one was in sight. At a half-speed, limping run, he dodged along in the shade of a flanking building. Two minutes later he was safely through the gate and into the shelter of the trees paralleling the dirt road on each side—headed back toward his small, one-man ship.

The native fisherman was no longer beside the creek. No one at all seemed to be in sight in the warming day, with the sun now approaching the zenith overhead. He made it back to his ship, and only when he was safely inside its camouflaged entrance did he allow himself the luxury of a feeling of safety.

For—at that, he thought—he was not yet completely safe. He simply had a ship in which to make a run for it now, in case he was discovered. He throttled the feeling of safety down. It might lead to carelessness, and it would be nightfall before he could risk taking off. And that meant it must be nightfall before he took the final step in the securing of his Kingdom.

He got rid of the loathsome mufflings he had had to wear and tended the sore parts of his body. They were annoying, but a week or so would see them healed and forgotten. The button containing the recorder was intact on his jacket. The record of everything he had done would be available within it. No more would be needed back on the Homeworld, except Kator's own unique and valuable knowledge of how the Muffled People reacted. Now—if night would quickly fall . . .

He waited, schooling himself to patience and dreaming of the faces of the sons he would have. He would name the first one Aton, after Aton Maternaluncle, the second Horaag, and the third Bela. As soon as they were out of the pouch long enough to comprehend the concept of Honor, he would tell each of them, personally, of the man from whom the name they bore was derived. And of the part those three honorable men had played in the Founding of their father's Kingdom on the planet of the Muffled People.

He himself, the Kator, would live out his days and die here. But perhaps the second or third generation of his descendants would return, as was their right under his first son or grandson, to found a palace of the Katori on Homeworld. And, in time, from that palace of the Katori, would come one—perhaps several—more, to Found new Kingdoms of their own.

He would not know this. Long dust, his bones buried on this world of the Muffled People would never know. But his genes in the bodies of his descendants would know and Honor their name and call themselves truly of the Ruml. The Ruml, honorable as a race, ever growing, ever evolving toward that far and unimaginable future when man had burnt away all dross from his character and no longer knew anything but Honor.

. . . At last, the yellow sun, reddening and darkening, began to touch the horizon in the screen attached to the light collector outside the ship. Shadows flooded across fences and growing grain and under the clumps of trees. He sat down at the communications board of his small ship and keyed in voice communication, through an untappable channel via the collapsed universe, with the Expedition ship on the moon.

The speaker crackled at him.

"Keysman?"

He said nothing.

"Keysman? This is the Captain. Your channel is sending. Can you hear us?"

He held his silence, the skin of his face stiffened slightly with emotion.

"Keysman!"

He leaned forward at last to the voice collector of the transmitter before him. He whispered into it.

"No use . . ." His whisper broke and became a voice, strangled and husky. "Natives . . . surrounding me, here. Captain . . ."

He paused. There was a waiting silence from the other end, then the Captain's voice spoke again.

"Keysman! Hold on! We'll get a ship down to take you out—"

"No time . . ." he husked. "No way out. Destroying self and ship. May you have water, have shade, have . . ."

He reached out to his controls and sent the little ship leaping skyward into the deepening dark. As it rose, he fired a cylindrical object back into the ground where it had lain.

Seconds later, the tiny, brief, but incredibly violent glare of rainbow colors that was the explosion of a collapsed-universe drive field lit up the peace of the country evening.

But Jase at the controls of the small ship was drilling upwards through the darkness. He headed back toward the moon, but he did not hurry. He went on conventional drive until he reached the practical limits of the atmosphere; and only then did he use the unharmed collapsed field drive aboard the ship to return to the far side of the moon, in three timeless jumps.

He had taken four hours, local time, by the hour he returned to the buried ship of the Expedition. There was no response as he approached the surface above the hidden ship and its connected network of rooms excavated out of the rock beneath the dust. He opened the passage by which he had left the ship in his smaller vessel, and re-entered. The ship had been emptied of atmosphere, and he was forced to refill it before he went on.

There was no one in the corridors or in the outer rooms of the ship. But when he got to the gym, they were all there, as he had expected, lying still in their ranks, with the officers and the Captain a little apart. With no hope of returning to Homeworld, with the ship locked and the Keysman lacking, they had ended their lives in honorable fashion and lain down to secure the ship for those who would come after.

He looked at them with affection flooding through him and went to examine the ship's recorder log. He set it back to the moment of his call from the planet below and then played it forward. The Captain had recorded a full account of the conversation with him and the situation underlying the decision that was to follow. He had closed with the final word that completed Jase's unfinished blessing the moment before the small ship had apparently been destroyed on the planet below.

Jase read into the recorder a brief account of his escape and return, after all, from the forces of the Muffled People that had apparently had him trapped and then returned to the gym.

The ship of the Expedition had ample storage space in the cargo area. He carried the dead bodies down there, one by one, arranged them, and set the space on airlessness and subfreezing temperatures. The bodies would be returned to their Families on Homeworld. It was not a necessary but an honorable thing to do on his part. Then he returned to the Controls room, unlocked the Controls, and set to work.

There was no great difference between any of the ships utilizing the collapsed universe field as a drive. He could handle this larger vessel alone as well as the small ship he had taken down to the planet of the Muffled People. He set a course for the Homeworld. It was a simple matter, now that the position of the star of this world of the Muffled People was identified, and the distance and direction from it to Homeworld possible for the ship's computers to calculate. In contrast to the time they had taken coming, he should be able to return to Homeworld in three jumps through timelessness. No more than two days of Homeworld time—or a day and a half, measured by the turning of the Muffled People's world on its axis.

He broke the ship free of its hiding place under the moon's surface and took it well out from any solid solar bodies, before turning the programming of the first jump over to the computers. Then he went back to his own quarters.

There things were as they had been before he had gone down to the planet of the Muffled People. He opened a service compartment to take out food, and he lifted out also one of the alcohol-producing bacterial cultures. But when he had taken this last item back with the food to the table that held his papers, he found that he did not want to swallow the culture.

This was a moment that had its own intoxication—an intoxication that made small and petty the chemical drunkenness to be obtained from the culture. He threw the culture into a disposal slot in the desk. Doing so, he suddenly remembered something.

From a pouch in his harness that he had worn under the now discarded mufflings he took the cube containing the dirtworm. He had not remembered to return it to the soil of its birth, after all. Well, there would be another time . . .

He held it in its transparent cube up to the light above the table with the papers. In that light the worm seemed almost alive. It seemed to turn and bow to him, acknowledging his Kingship over it and the world from which it came.

He laid the cube down on the table and walked across to put the button containing his recording device in a resolving machine that would project its stored information of sound and pictures in life-size dimensions on a cube of the atmosphere of the room. He touched the resolving machine's controls. The lights of the room dimmed, and the morning he had seen as he emerged from his one-man ship came to life in the empty space in the room's middle. He retraced his steps to the platform before his table and settled down on it, curling up with a sigh of satisfaction.

He watched the story of the day's events, through the conversation with the native by the stream, the trip along the conveyor belt, the descent and return from the underground area. At the moment when he slipped and fell among the machinery, the picture suddenly blanked out and the sound ceased.

Evidently, he thought, the fall had broken the recording device, at that point. It would be blank from then on. It was too bad that had happened, but, after all, the important information had been safely recorded.

He was about to rise and turn off the recorder—when the cube of room atmosphere lighted up again. Facing him was the figure of the native he had seen by the stream, but with the walls of a room behind him instead of the outdoor scene.

The native took the container of burning vegetation from his mouth.

"Greetings. I trust I am among friends," he said in Ruml as perfect as the native mouth and lips could pronounce. "Greetings to Kator Secondcousin Brutogas and to all those honorable Heads of Families who will be viewing this back on Homeworld—"

Kator sprang from his platform.

CHAPTER TWENTY-ONE

Jase staggered a little, blundering against a high fence of black wrought-iron rods. The sudden pain in his bruised shoulder revived him a little. He made another automatic attempt to adjust his already turned-up raincoat collar against the steady draining of rain from the dreary skies above the capital city. He had been back in Washington, keeping steadily on the move, for over twenty hours now. As long as he kept moving and stayed away from his apartment or any place where he could be recognized, he thought he had a good chance of going uncaptured until the critical moment. He had made it this far—he calculated he had perhaps six more hours to kill.

Yielding for a moment to the seductive weariness of his legs, he paused now for a second, leaning against the hard vertical rods of wrought iron, and took the folded sheet of newspaper from his raincoat pocket. It was folded to show three columns of the front page, his own picture, and a portion of the headline SOUGHT BY F.B.I.

Below this a picture of him in shirt and slacks taken, luckily, a good three years before, looked out at him. With the automatic reflex of dull-mindedness, he found himself reading for the last of an unknown number of times, the opening words of the article.

By Will Uhlmann:

Still being sought today was Dr. Jason Barchar, wanted for questioning by the F.B.I. in connection with the alleged betrayal of government secrets to an unidentified foreign power.

Jase wrenched his eyes away from the damp lines of type. What was written was not important. His picture was. Luckily, he had lost weight in the last few weeks, and over thirty-six hours of beard stubble hid his jaws. Now, if he could just remember not to stand, move, or act in his accustomed manner. It was by habit, carriage, and actions that most people betrayed their disguises—he had read once, somewhere so long ago that he could no longer remember where it was. At some time in that remote past before he had ever heard of a race of beings called the Ruml.

"That's not you," he told himself, staring at the newspaper picture. "You don't look like that, you don't smile like that, you don't feel like that. You're twenty years older than that, stoop-shouldered, a bum . . . somebody unimportant. . . ."

He shoved the newspaper back into his pocket. Time to get moving again before he went to sleep leaning up against this iron fence. Wearily he pushed himself away from its support, grimly he started his enormously heavy and aching legs to moving again. "It's not true," he thought, "that people can't go to sleep on their feet." He had done it himself in army training school, when they sprang a night hike of thirty miles on top of a day hike of thirty-two. Stumping along in the moonlight, he had watched the white pack of the man ahead of him, bobbing, bobbing, bobbing. . . . Suddenly he would find himself stumbling, almost falling into the moonlit ditch beside the road and realize he had wandered out of line. He would pull himself back into line, look at other things for a while, and then the pack would start to catch his eyes again, bobbing and bobbing. . . . And the whole process would start over again.

"So I mustn't fall asleep walking here," he thought. "If I fall asleep walking here, I may walk into the path of a truck. Or get into trouble some other way and attract attention." His hand went to the pocket that contained the dexedrine, along with the other capsules with which he had filled the bottle when he had been planning for this time. But the dexedrine seemed to have had no effect on him the last two times he had taken it. Its only effect seemed to be to nauseate him, weakly.

The rain fell steadily from skies so dark that the streetlights had been turned on at midday. Thunder muttered in the distance from time to time. The lights in the office buildings of the city were on. The traffic signal lights glared through the mist of the rain when he came to corners.

His throat felt like dry sandpaper, his eyes were heavy and dry, and his face burned under the hat brim and inside the turned-up raincoat collar. This final exertion on top of the exhaustion of the past weeks had pushed him over the edge. He was sick, with something involving a high fever. At first he had been grateful for the fever, feeling that it woke him up and gave him additional alertness. But now he had swung full circle and hated it—it was draining his strength.

His feet tripped against each other, and he almost went down. A woman passing in the opposite direction looked at him with a passing glance that gave him a moment's glimpse of tight lips and narrowed eyes, as she circled out a little bit to pass him at more than arm's length.

"It's no good," he thought suddenly. "I'm not going to be able to make it, out on the street, trying to keep moving this way."

"Got to hole up somewhere," he thought.

He shook his head to clear it and looked around, to find out where he was. For a moment he did not recognize the street—and then he did. A stab of alarm brought him all the way awake. He had wandered back once more into familiar territories—this time again he was only a few blocks away from the Foundation building.

His mind working momentarily sharply with the impetus of the feeling of alarm, for the first time since dawn he considered the possibility of the Foundation building. His original plan had been to return there, sneak in and hide in the stacks. He had put the plan aside because of the danger that, once he was suspected to be there, he would be easily trapped without a quick and easy exit. While, continually walking like this, he had freedom to change his plans quickly.

Now, with a mind that no longer worked quickly and physical collapse threatening to betray him into the hands of the local police—or, probably just as bad, some good samaritan who would call the police—the Foundation building was safer than trying to stay on his feet outside like this.

He headed for the building.

It was about three blocks away. As he got closer to it, it began to loom in his mind with all the promise of comfort in a warm fireside to a man stumbling and freezing through a night of blizzard. Visions of the bed in the basement room he had occupied until the day before yesterday swam before him, like a pit of yawning, merciful oblivion into which his uncertain feet could stumble him. He fought off the seductiveness of the thought of sleep in bed.

Now, one hand brushing against the damp brick of the blank side of the Foundation Building to steady himself, he was coming up to the entrance of the alley that ran along behind it. He turned into the alley. About thirty feet in was the back entrance to the building—the entrance to the hallway opening on the kitchen of the old cafeteria and to the steps down to the basement. There would be people working in the kitchen this midday. With luck he might get past them. He had had a half-thought-out scheme. . . .

He came to the blank, metal-faced door set in the back wall of the building. In the dim light it was just possible to see the scratches and scribblings on its outer, sheet-metal surface. He paused, leaning against the closed door, which opened inward, and thought out carefully what he planned to do, so that it would be all clear in his swimming head.

He filled his lungs so that his voice would not sound cracked and exhausted. He swallowed a couple of times to moisten his throat. Thunder muttered off in the distance, and the rain streamed down. Straightening up, he beat on the metal surface of the door with his fist as he swung it open.

"Meter reader!" he shouted and went on into the hallway without stopping, letting the door bang shut behind him.

"Right downstairs!" shouted back a voice from the clattering, steam-bright kitchen entrance to his right. No one stepped out to look at him. He went briskly forward, so that his footfalls would sound natural. But as he clattered down the narrow, un-banistered wooden stairs, his knees gave suddenly and he almost fell.

But he kept on, and a second later the soles of his shoes slapped against the unyielding concrete of the basement floor. He was walking down a hallway in which the doors of storage and other rooms were set like green oblongs pasted against the white-painted walls.

His will power almost failed him as he approached the slightly larger, varnished-wood door among the green ones on his left. Behind that was the room and the bed that had been floating in his mind for hours now, as seductively as a dream of a fountain to a man lost in the desert.

However, he kept going, on down the hall and in through the narrow door leading into the bottom of the library stacks. Here, on this basement level, the windows that had been pierced in the outer walls of the stack higher up were not able to filter down enough light to see by. The artificial lights were off. He reached up, found the hanging cord of the first sixty-watt bulb inside the entrance and jerked downward. Yellow light revealed the shelves of books and magazines stretching away from him and the narrow, circular metal staircase to the levels above.

He climbed with great effort, turning on lights as he went. On the third level he left the stair and stumped heavily down aisles between bookcases until he came to the polished hardwood door that opened from the stacks into Mele's office.

Putting his ear to the panel of that door, gratefully for a moment leaning against it, he heard the faint, polite clicking of her typewriter-recorder. He sighed—it was almost an explosion of air in relief and exhaustion from his lungs. He put his hand on the doorknob, opened it, and tottered in and down the two small steps to her desk.

His hand pawed out in search of the wastebasket, to turn it up and sit on it as he had before. But the effort was too complex and too much for his strength. His knees gave way, and he dropped down heavily on a large tape video-audio portable recorder beside her desk. For a moment his head swam with the relief of being off his feet, and he had to catch the edge of her desk with both hands to keep from falling over.

He was aware of her face staring at him from behind the now silent typewriter. He stared back. He had—some uncertain, semi-idelirious time ago—figured out what he would say to her, how he would explain that the situation justified his involving her by asking her for help. But now, now that he was face to face with her, neither the strength nor the words would come. He simply sat, still dripping with the rain, leaning on the edge of her desk, staring at her with eyes burned dry with sleeplessness—silent.

Then the room began to tilt slowly on end. He was barely conscious of his falling, sliding off the tape recorder, and his feeble efforts to stop himself. Then . . . nothing.

When he woke, he was back in the stacks. He was not far from the doorway that opened on Mele's office, but he was back in a corner, and the light in the adjoining aisle threw shadows that would hide him from anyone underneath it. He was propped up in an angle of the corner and a heavy, gray wool blanket was covering him, wrapped around his shoulders.

Mele was kneeling before him, pouring something from a thermos bottle into a large coffee cup. He blinked at her uncertainly, collecting his scattered senses. How she had managed to lift or drag his hundred-and-seventy-five pound body up the two small stairs and back into the stacks here—to say nothing of getting him wrapped in the blanket and propped up in this corner—was more than his fatigue-drugged brain could imagine.

"Drink this, now," she said, holding the full cup to his lips. He started to swallow, then checked himself so abruptly that some of the liquid spilled on his chin. He had suddenly realized that what she was giving him might be coffee, and he had drunk so many innumerable cups of this in hamburger joints and from coffee machines in the last twenty-four hours that the thought of swallowing more of it gagged him.

But then the taste of what had touched his lips and the scent rising from the liquid reassured him. It was hot vegetable beef soup, and he tasted it in his mouth like some strange and wonderful dish from a foreign land. He was thirsty as well as hungry, and shivering now with a chill that seemed to be fast friends with the fever in his head. And he gulped eagerly at the soup, indifferent to the fact that it was scalding his tongue and the inside of his mouth and sore throat.

He swallowed a cup and a half of the soup—and was abruptly full. He found that he could not drink another drop from the cup, and he closed his lips against it, trying meanwhile to get his hand out from under the blanket to push it away. But Mele understood and took the cup away. She wiped his chin with a paper napkin, and the paper caught and snagged on the bristles of his unshaven beard.

". . . Better go now . . ." he said. "I'll be all right." He hugged the blanket around him in a new access of shivering. But she did not move. She continued to kneel there, staring at him.

"Swallow these now," she said, producing some capsules and another cup filled with water. "They're antibiotics, achrocidin." He took the capsules in his mouth and swallowed the cool water. "Jase," she said, putting the cup down. "Did you do it—what they said you did?"

"What?" he asked. "What—they say?"

"Did you add a film strip to the recording Kator made, telling the Ruml all about our knowing about them, and the Baits, and showing them a picture of our warships in space?"

"Yes," he said, huskily through his sore throat, which was now beginning to hurt steadily and fiercely, "I had to. You see—"

"You don't have to tell me." She was still staring at him, on her knees. "I don't care why you did it. When Swanson first came to see if I knew you'd been planning something like that, I first tried to think why you'd do something like that. Give away the only advantage we had to aliens that outnumber us ten to one. But then, when they didn't find you, and I began to see how everybody else felt about it—what they wanted to do if they could capture you—I woke up to the fact that it didn't matter."

He blinked at her. In his feverish head her words buzzed and sang without making sense.

"Jase—," she said. She took hold of his upper arms through the blanket. "Don't you understand me? You've got to understand. I don't *care* what you did! I was so proud of myself—I thought I believed in things being either right or wrong, no matter how I felt inside—but I don't!"

She leaned forward and flung her arms around his blanket-wrapped body, hugging him, pressing her head and the side of her face against the rough blanket over his chest.

"It's only you I care about! You!" Her arms tightened around him as if she would absorb and drown his shivering in her own body. "And they're not going to get you! I won't let them!"

He could see the dark hair of her head just below his chin. He opened his mouth to say something, but his lips trembled loosely and he could force no sound from his throat. Behind her he saw a black shadow move and obscure the light in the neighboring aisle. For a moment it passed away, and then it appeared again, like an occulting shape of darkness, at the end of the aisle they were in.

It came bobbing toward them and revealed itself into the shape of a man, then of several men, one behind the other. They stole up on them as Mele still clung to him and he sat, unable to speak.

She was not conscious of their presence until their hands reached down and seized her. Only then she awoke to the fact that they were upon her and Jase and began to fight.

CHAPTER TWENTY-TWO

". . . Why did you do it?" asked Swanson.

It was the same question they had been drumming at Jase ever since they had taken him and Mele from the Foundation building to this place—wherever it was. What they had done with Mele he did not know. What they had done with him was to bring him to this bare room with a few straightbacked chairs, where men he had not seen before kept asking him that one question.

The reason they could ask and expect an answer from him was that chemical miracles had been worked on his sick and exhausted body. Some capsules and two injections, one in each arm, had broken his fever, cleared his head, and pushed tiredness back as if behind some wall—so that he still knew it was there, but somehow it did not bother him. His heart pumped strongly, perhaps a little too rapidly, and there was a slight singing in his ears. Outside of these symptoms, and the fact that perspiration sprang constantly from him, so that he was continually mopping his face and feeding a raging thirst with paper cups of water, he felt almost normal.

But not quite. There was something unnatural about his alertness and lack of shivering and chills that made him feel as if he was made of delicate china, that any sudden move or emotion would shatter him into irreparable junk. He held himself tightly erect in his chair as if he was invisibly gripping himself together with will power, and their questions seemed to come from some place so remote and disconnected with him that they were not as threatening as they tried to be. He answered monotonously, unvaryingly, as he answered the new questioner, Swanson, who had come and gone from the room several times already and had just now once more returned to it.

"I can't explain so you'd understand," Jase said. "You'd have to have been inside Kator to understand, and none of you were. Only me. I can't explain."

"Try us," said Swanson. "If we don't understand, nothing's been lost, has it?"

"There're no words," said Jase. "Not until after you've experienced it. You see we're intelligent, and so are the Ruml." It was the same explanation he had gone over many times before since he had come into this room. "We've both got highly developed forebrains. But we aren't reacting with our forebrains, either race of us, in this matter. We're reacting primitively—" He stopped. It was no use.

"Go on," said Swanson, grimly.

"—Primitively," repeated Jase. "Emotionally. Instinctively. We're reacting against them as strangers, and they against us. Because the reaction's on that emotional level, we're not being reasonable. Reasonableness, understanding—these are intellectual things. Things we learn in the process of growing up in a civilized culture. A young animal—a young child—is not reasonable. He's not naturally understanding. His concentration is all on surviving, and growing. He takes any advantage that's offered, without considering abstract moral values or invisible differences. If we'd kept the avenue of basic research open—"

"Aren't you getting off from the subject?" said Swanson. "We're in a race against time, here."

"It's all connected. But never mind," said Jase. "I told you you wouldn't understand. Understanding's blocked out in your minds, just as it is in the Rumls', by primitive emotional reactions to the stranger. Basic research would have pointed out that this would happen before it did, before we contacted some race like the Ruml. We would have been forewarned and ready to keep from being crippled by the primitive reaction when we met our first intelligent alien. But we weren't. And now it's a case of one set of closed minds coming head on against another set of closed minds.''

"Point out," said Swanson, "where our minds are closed. Maybe we can open them."

"You think you mean that," answered Jase. "But you don't. You have to start out by understanding Kator. Start out by thinking of him as a man with a strict moral code—"

"Moral code!" said somebody in the room. Jase did not even look to see who said it.

"You see?" he said to Swanson. "You didn't say that, but you might as well have. That's the way you feel."

"We don't even have to consider how he's acted and thought, where we're concerned," said Swanson. "Against his own people he's shown us everything but a moral code. Hasn't he just finished lying to fifty-five of his own kind, deliberately tricking them into committing suicide? What's moral about that?"

"The greatest morality there is," said Jase. "The morality of survival, both individual and race. They died so that he could not only live but succeed. If there was one person of his own race and family he cared for it was Bela, and he arbitrarily had Bela killed to increase his prestige in the eyes of the Expedition—"

"When all the time he knew he was going to kill them off too," said Swanson. "I think you can see it's pretty hard for us to swallow that this was a noble thing to do."

"But he hadn't reached the point where he could safely kill them off, yet!" said Jase, stung at last out of his fragile, china-like detachment. "You think of his authority in human terms! You think of his obligations in human terms! You think of his goals in human terms—"

The door to the room opened. A man stuck his head in, and Jase broke off abruptly at the sight of the expression on his face, which was the expression of a man who has seen evidence of his own doom.

"It's starting," the man said to Swanson. "You said to tell you. If you want to come, you'd all better come now."

"Be right there," said Swanson. "Come along, Jase. Come on with us and see what you've done."

Jase got awkwardly and uncertainly to his feet. With men surrounding him and Swanson ahead of him, he walked out of the room, down several turns of corridor, and finally into a room with a large, three-dimensional viewing screen at one end and seats sloping toward it as in a theater.

In the row two back from the front, with a tall woman and two business-suited men, was Mele. They brought Jase down to the same row and moved him in. He sat down in the empty seat at Mele's right.

"Mele," he said. "How—"

"I'm all right." She smiled at him and took hold of his hand, squeezing it. She continued to hold on to his hand, and neither her attendants nor Jase's objected. Swanson sat down on the other side of Jase.

"Ready," said Swanson, turning his head to speak to one of the men behind him. The rows behind were filling in with as many as thirty or forty people.

A moment later the overhead lights in the room dimmed down to a deep twilight of gloom, and the cube before them lighted up with a scene. Instantly, Jase recognized it, although even Kator had never been in it before. But every Ruml knew what it looked like. It was the Gathering Room of the currently presiding Family Heads of the Ruml. Normally these consisted of fifty-one Family Heads chosen by rotation from among the more than five hundred thousand Heads of Families on all the Ruml worlds. Disability, disinclination to serve, or pressing business normally removed half of the list of available men from possible service. The rest took the turn of their Family when it came up and were members of the presiding group for ten days of a season.

The chance to serve came therefore never more than once in the lifetime of an eligible Family Head, if at all. And the responsibilities of the fifty-one members were two, as Jase knew. First, to order any necessary actions for the Honor of the Ruml as a race. And, second, to certify a Founder—whether only of a Family or of a Family and Kingdom.

It was for the last purpose the fifty-one were gathered here this day. The Brutogas was an invited member, without a voice in the gathering, making fifty-two in all. Just now, as Jase had sat down, the heavy-bodied, long-whiskered Rumls of honorable age were filing in to take their seats in a rising half-circle looking down on a small, circular amphitheater. When they were all seated, out by a low door into the amphitheater came Kator to stand and salute his elders with his right hand over his chest and the claws extended.

At the sight of him, Jase's brain, dreamy with exhaustion, sickness, and the stimulants that had been pumped into him, jumped the gap. Dreaming awake, he found himself as suddenly inside the body of the image of Kator before him as he had been when he had been asleep. The mental link between them was still operating—and in that second he left the room of the unknown building in Washington and leaped to the Gathering Room on the Ruml Homeworld.

His body continued to sit upright and open-eyed, watching the cube in the room on earth. But only those around him were watching. Jase was living the scene they saw. For a last time—he was Kator.

Jase looked up at the Heads of Families looking down at him, and when he saw the gray visage of the Brutogas among them, an instinctive thrill of pride ran through him—to be washed away almost immediately by a wave of shame and sorrow. He stiffened and spoke to the assembled Family Heads.

"Sirs," he said. "I am Kator Secondcousin Brutogas. I trust that here I am among friends."

"Keysman," replied the most honorable member, "here you are among friends. You have a report to make to us?"

"Sir," said Jase, "I have. The log of my voyage with the ship of the Expedition to the world of the Muffled People is already in your hands. You already know what is set down there. I have an additional recording to show you, but first I would like to put before this gathering a claim of a special nature."

"Your claim concerns yourself?" said the most honorable member, in the words which were always used to those who had stood where he stood now, under such circumstances.

"Yes sir. It is a claim for special consideration, of the fact that I am become unlike any other man, and therefore necessary and valuable to the honorable race of men."

"What," asked the most honorable member, "is the basis for your claim?"

"The basis for my claim," said Jase, "is that the Muffled People are unlike any other race encountered by men since the beginning of time. They have developed a civilization almost as great as our own, and it may be that their intelligence and Honor approaches equality with our own. In the face of such a departure from anything known in history, I claim a special consideration." He paused.

"What is this special consideration?" The question came down from the seat of the most honorable member above him among the ranked elders.

"Sirs," Jase said. "Of the Expedition that was sent to the world of the Muffled People, I alone have returned with the knowledge that would make any attempt to Found Families upon that world successful. Because of my unique and special value to the race of men, therefore, I petition this gathering to take special actions in my case."

"What special actions, Keysman?"

"I would like to point out," said Jase, "that as the Muffled People are new in our experience, the ways of Honor in dealing with them may also be new—including the importance of the knowledge of them I have within me. Therefore, I ask that this gathering not act at once upon my report once I have included it here, no matter how clear the path of honorable action seems to be. But that this gathering delay action for at least a day, during which it consider whether the clear path of honorable action is truly honorable, and whether it should be taken rather than a new path of Honor not yet suspected."

There was a little silence from the room when Jase had finished.

"Keysman," said the presiding elder, after a moment. "This is not in the usual manner. Let me make it clear—you ask this Gathering to refrain from any action toward you, any judgment of whether your actions were honorable or dishonorable, any response of reward or retribution? No matter how clearly the matter appears to us when you have finished your report?"

"For one day only," said Jase. "I want you to refrain and consider your judgment for one day only."

There was another hesitation.

"Does any among the elders wish to object?" asked the presiding member at the end of that time. There was a rustle of movement, but no voice spoke from the ranks of seats. "Very well," said the presiding elder. "One day's delay and our consideration during that time can make no difference if it is a question of Honor, since all questions of Honor must be clear to an honorable man. We grant you this, Keysman. Now, you will give us your report?"

"Yes, sirs, and thank you," said Jase, inclining his head. "I think I need say no more now than to repeat what I said earlier, that the Muffled People represent a new perception to us and possibly therefore require new ways of Honor to deal with them. And now I will show you my additional recording.''

Jase stepped to one side of the open space and touched the control at his harness.

"You have seen," he said, "how I escaped the Muffled guards and returned to the ship of the Expedition to find all the crew dead. Since they had thought me dead and return to Homeworld was impossible without the Keys of the ship and the Keysman, they had suicided—as was honorable for them under the circumstances. I had, as you may have deduced, tricked them into this action so that I might be the only one to return with the knowledge of the Muffled People necessary to colonize their world in the face of their native oppositions—"

He broke off and looked up at them for emphasis.

"As was," he said, "honorable for me under the circumstances. To a man committed to Founding his Kingdom, such actions which contribute to his success are honorable. Are they not?"

"They are," answered the voice of the presiding member of the Gathering.

"However," said Jase, slowly and sorrowfully, "once I was back aboard the ship and headed Home, I viewed what was in my recorder, up to and past the moment of my fall in the native factory. And what I saw there caused me to renounce my ambition—"

"Renounce?" It was half a dozen voices speaking at once from the seats. "Keysman! A man cannot renounce ambition once he has begun his actions to Found a Kingdom!" It was the voice of the presiding member, sharp and clear above the other voices.

"I know," said Kator, his face stiffening with anguish. "Let me show you my reason. You've seen the copy in the log of what my recorder recorded up until the moment I fell unconscious in the factory. Let me show you now what I found following that record, in my own recorder that was part of the Mufflings I wore as disguise. It was this I saw when I got back to my ship that not only caused me to renounce my ambition—but, in Honor, to refrain from joining the suicided members of the Expedition and return to you, here."

"Joining—," began the voice of the presiding member. But

Kator had already activated the control button on his harness. He was no longer visible to those in the seats. Instead, they saw a projection of sight and sound, filling the empty space beneath them.

For a second they saw only the bright flicker of an interrupted recording where some of the sensitized surfaces had been destroyed. Then this cleared, and the fifty-two of them, counting the Brutogas, looked down to face a native of the Muffled People—the native who had spoken to Jase earlier on the recording, when Jase had crossed the bridge over the creek.

Now the native took the container of burning vegetation out of his mouth, knocked the embers out and put the container away. He spoke in Ruml as perfect as the alien vocal apparatus could produce.

"Greetings," he said, "I trust I am among friends. Greetings to Kator Secondcousin Brutogas and to all those honorable Heads of Families who will be viewing this back on Homeworld. As you know, I am a member of that race of intelligent beings you Ruml refer to as the Muffled People, because of our habit of wearing body coverings, unlike yourselves. We are, however, correctly to be referred to as humans." The alien's lips pronounced the native word carefully for them in the way a Ruml would pronounce it, "*Heh-eu-mans*. With a little practice you should find it not too hard to say."

A babble of voices was beginning to rise from the seats of the Gathering when the voice of the presiding member spoke.

"Quiet!" he said sharply. "Listen!"

". . . we humans," the image of the native was saying, twisting his face in an odd fashion that lifted the corners of his mouth upward, "have a warlike history. But we prefer not to war. Our honor does not have the same basis as your Honor. Therefore, let me show you some of the means we have developed to do for us what your Honor does for you."

The scene changed suddenly. The assembled Ruml saw before them one of the small, long-tailed scavenging native animals Kator had used as a model for some of his collectors of information. This one, however, was smaller than the ones the Expedition had used as models, and white-furred. It was nosing its way up and down the corridors of a topless box—here being baffled by a dead-end corridor, there finding an entrance through to an adjoining corridor.

"This," said the voice of the native, "is a device called a 'maze' in the human tongue. We use it to test the intelligence of the experimental animal you see. This device is one of the investigative tools used in our study of a division of knowledge known as 'psychology,' which corresponds in some respect to what you Ruml call your system of Honor, which you believe is developed of necessity in any civilized, intelligent being."

The picture changed to show the native once more facing and speaking to them.

"Psychology," he said, "teaches us humans many useful things about how other organisms must react. This is because, like your system of Honor, it is based on primal and universal desires such as the urge of the individual or race to survive."

He reached to one side and picked up the stick he had held, with the string attached. He held it up for them to see.

"This," he said, "though it was used by humans long before we began to study pyschology as a conscious effort, operates on psychological principle—"

The view slid out along the rod, down the line attached to the rod, and—surprisingly—into some water that those watching had not been aware was there earlier. The line continued underwater until it terminated in a dirtworm like the one Kator had kept and sealed in a transparent cube. Then it moved off to the side a few inches and picked up the image of a native underwater-living creature possessing no limbs but a fan-shaped tail and minor fans farther up the body. The creature swam to the worm and swallowed it. Immediately it began to struggle, and a close-up view revealed a barbed metal hook in the worm. The creature, however, for all its struggling, was drawn up out of the water by the native, who hit it on the head and put it in a woven box.

"You see," said the native, once more imaged and speaking to them, "that this device makes use of the subject's—a so-called fish—desire to survive, on a very primitive level. To survive, the fish must eat. We offer it something to eat, but in taking what we offer, the fish delivers itself into our hands. It fastens itself to the hook hidden in the offering we placed before it, and we secure it by means of the attached line."

The native paused, as if to let his words sink in. There was silence among the Ruml of honorable age in the amphitheater seats.

"All intelligent," went on the native, "space-going races

conceivable to us must exhibit the universal desire to survive, like the fish, though on a much more complex level."

He seemed to lean forward toward those watching, confidentially.

"The worm on the hook," he said, "is known as 'bait.' Similarly, the worm Kator found on the space wreckage resembling part of one of our spaceships was 'bait.' It was intended to operate upon unknown races and cultures as the worm operated upon the 'fish.' The object on our part is, of course, to study whoever or whatever takes the 'bait.' Now, when Kator took the spaceship wreckage in tow, there was a monitor device following it at a distance of only a few thousand miles that followed it—and him—back here to Homeworld.

"When your Expeditionary ship came, it was allowed to land on our moon and an extensive study was made, not only of it but of your methods of gaining information about our world and people. Again, of course, our purpose was to learn as much as possible about you Ruml, on the basis that he who knows about a potential competitor when the competitor does not know about him has an undeniable advantage."

The native straightened up.

"After as much as could be learned by such observation had been recorded," he said, "we allowed one of your collectors to find one of our underground launching sites, and for one of your people—Kator—to come down on to our world and actually enter the underground area.

"We ran a number of maze-level tests on Kator while he was making his entrance to and escaping from the underground site. You may be glad to learn," once more the native's face twisted in the odd fashion that lifted the corners of his mouth, "that your racial intelligence tests highly in our opinion, although you aren't what we'd call maze-sophisticated. We experienced little difficulty in influencing Kator to leave the conveyor belt and follow a route that would lead him on to a surface too slippery to cross. As he fell, we rendered him unconscious—"

There was a collective sound, half-grunt, half-exclamation, from the listening Heads of Families.

"And, during the hour that followed, we were able to make complete physical tests and studies of an adult male Ruml. Then Kator was put back where he had fallen and allowed to get his senses back. Then he was allowed to escape."

The native put aside the stick with the string attached, to which he had been holding all this time. There was something about the gesture that signalled the end of his words.

"We know," he said, "all about your honorable race. And you, as a race, and with the single exception of Kator, know nothing about us. Because of what we have learned about you, we are confident that Kator's knowledge will not be allowed to do you any good." He lifted a finger. "I have one more scene to show you."

He disappeared. In his place, against a backdrop of stars none of them recognized in the Gathering room, there stretched inconceivable numbers of space ships, great shape beyond great shape, like dark, giant demons waiting.

"Kator," said the voice of the native, "should have asked himself why there was so much empty space in the underground site we let him enter. Come see us on earth whenever you're ready to discuss contact between our two races that does not involve violence."

The scene in the open space of the Gathering Room winked out. In the glare of the lights, Kator stood small and alone with the Fifty-two Heads of Families staring down at him.

For a moment, they sat silent and unmoving. Then, as if in response to some unconscious, instinctive, primitive signal—reflexive as the signal which causes the wolf pack to turn on a crippled member—they rose from their seats and swarmed down upon him.

"Wait!" cried Kator desperately. "Wait and think! You're throwing away your only advantage, just like the native said you would! Can't you see I'm your only chance, and this is different from anything we've—"

But they were already on him. He was young and strong, but there were fifty-two of them, including the Brutogas, and instinct fought against him as it fought for them. He went down, hardly feeling the claws piercing and tearing at him.

"I die in Honor!" he managed to shout while there was still breath in his body.

And, as he died, the body of Jase back on Earth rose fighting among the seats of the viewers around him, then fell lax and empty as Jase felt the darkness of death take him finally into her arms and bear him away from all that was, on Homeworld and Earth alike.

CHAPTER TWENTY-THREE

To die, thought Jase idly, is to stop. To experience stopping without dying is to go a long way away and have a long way to come back.

He did not know how long it had been since he had stopped, with Kator's death and the feeling of the claws tearing the life out of him, but it had been some days since he had first become conscious of the white ceiling above this hospital bed in which he lay. Daylight and dark alternated in coloring that ceiling. People came and went about the bed. Occasionally they spoke to him, but for a long time he did not bother to answer.

After you have stopped, he thought, nothing, not even stopping again, is very important. It is only necessary to let go a little in order to stop again—this time for good. Sometimes Jase wondered, vaguely, why he did not do so. There seemed to be some reason for not doing so, but he was too indifferent to inquire into it.

Then, after a while, Mele began to be among those who came and went. Gradually he became aware that she sat by the side of his bed for as much as several hours at a time. And, very slowly, after a while, he found himself answering now and then to the questions she asked about how he felt or what he was thinking. And in this way, imperceptibly, he drifted back into awareness of the world and conversation with her.

". . . No," he said, in answer to something she said, "Kator was a very rare, brave, and unusual man—Ruml I mean. For one like him there's a million among the Ruml who would never have tried what he did. That's one thing Swanson and the rest couldn't understand. Another—"

"You don't have to say anything if you don't want to," said Mele. "This room is wired for sound, you know. They just want to get information to help them try you for treason or something. That's why they let me come here, hoping you'll talk to me."

"That's all right," he said, indifferently. "I want them to understand. What was I saying? Another thing people here don't understand—but they will, eventually—is that neither Kator nor the other Ruml wanted to conquer earth, in the sense we think of it. Kator wanted to win the right to Found a Kingdom—which means he could start a family of his own and have as many sons as he could. Ordinary Ruml can only have one."

He saw Mele sitting close to him, watching him.

"You say you want people to know?" she said.

He nodded, absently. He was already drifting off on the receding tide of his indifference.

"If you really want them to know, I'll ask questions," she said. "Do you want me to ask questions?"

He considered the question idly. Slowly, as if from some sluggish reflex, came the response. He woke up a little.

"Of course," he said. "But I just told you."

"I know what you told me," she said. "But why did he want a lot of sons. Just so he could be proud of them?"

Jase shook his head.

"You're thinking like a human being," he said. "The chance he could be proud of one of his sons was very remote. But by having a lot he increased the chances."

"What chances?"

"Of having," he said, "another like himself—either among his sons or their sons, and so on. There might crop up one or more who would also Found Families."

Mele, gazing at him, slowly shook her head.

"Why?" she asked. "I don't understand. He Founds Families—or Kingdoms—"

"Same thing," murmured Jase.

"So that some descendants of his can do the same thing? It's a circle. The same thing repeating itself."

Jase shook his head upon the pillow.

"It's survival of the fittest, their way," he said.

For a moment she did not answer. Then she burst out, suddenly.

"I see! I understand!" she said. "So that finally all the Ruml will be descended from those who Found Families, the leaders!"

"Yes . . ." Jase said. He was beginning to drift off again.

"But Jase . . ."

However, he was already drifting beyond reach of her voice. The extended talk had tired him. In the next few days he grew stronger, but he resisted her efforts to get him to talk again. It was no use. It had been mere reflex telling her as much as he did. People were emotionally blocked against understanding

Ruml reasons—as the Ruml Family Heads had been against understanding Kator and letting him accept the shame of living. There was no point trying to explain.

Then, suddenly, he woke one bright morning to find Mele physically shaking him.

"Wake up!" she was saying in a low voice, but fiercely. "Wake up, Jase! The Ruml have come! A great fleet of them is in orbit around the world, right now. You've got to wake up! I wasn't supposed to know, but it was on the radio in the nurses' room and I overheard. And I heard you're going to be taken away—someplace. And probably shot. The night nurse was telling the day nurse! Jase—wake up! Maybe we can get out of here first, somehow. But you've got to wake *up!*"

He stared numbly up to her, irritated at the fact she continued to shake him. Then, understanding and consciousness of what she was saying returned to him like a smooth rush, gathering speed as it came. He caught at her arms that were shaking him.

"Help me up," he said. "Help me try to walk."

She aided him. When he was on his feet, his knees almost gave, but he forced them to move.

"Help me walk," he said. She guided him, and they went up and down the room. "Swanson," he said. "I've got to talk to Swanson."

"You can't, Jase!" she said. "We've got to get you away. Those nurses—"

"Never mind that. This is important!" he said, making his legs walk. "How do we get hold of Swanson?"

"We can't," Mele said. "Oh, Jase, don't be foolish, now! You're not in Swanson's hands any more. You've got to get away, somehow. They don't think you can leave your bed, so we've got a chance. If we go down the hall the other way, there's a fire escape—"

"No," he said. "Listen, Mele—. If they take me away, I want you to try to get to Swanson yourself. If the Ruml are here, you've got to get to him and make him understand how to deal with them. If he does the wrong thing, they'll attack. Just as surely as they killed Kator—"

"But they'll attack anyway—"

"No. Listen to me. Will you listen?" he said. "We probably don't have much time before whoever's coming for me gets here."

"I'll listen," she said. "If that's what you want, I'll listen. But, Jase—"

"Just listen, and remember this," he interrupted. "Tell Swanson—he may be ready to listen and believe this now, after seeing Kator die and the Ruml come—tell him the problem's with both races, ours and the Ruml. Both of us have an instinct to preserve our race and improve it through survival of the fittest, but because of basic animal differences, it's evolved two different cultures. Cultures whose individuals' instincts will bring them into a head-on clash unless they understand each other. Have you got that?"

"I . . . think so . . ." She was still guiding him up and down the room.

"There's no time to repeat it, anyway," he said. "I'll go on. The first protective unit was the family, among humans. Then the clan, the tribe, expanding out and out, to include the nation and the nation-group. Including more and more people in the not-stranger category. Until we finally began including the whole population of the world in one self-protective group. All right—"

He broke off suddenly; his legs were trembling.

"I better sit down for a minute, after all," he said. She steered him back to the bed, and he perched on the edge of it, feeling awkward in the ridiculous hospital gown with its ties in the back. "At any rate—the appearance of an intelligent, alien race kicked off, both in us and the Ruml, the ancient protective anti-stranger feeling that has its basis in the primitive association of the family, in human beings, but in something else in the Ruml."

"Something else?" said Mele.

"Yes. That's what I'm going to explain. The instinct that causes humans to band together in the face of danger from a strange enemy is based on the primitive bonds of affection not only in the human family but in the higher mammals. It's what causes elephants to try to hold up one of their number who's been shot by a hunter, or porpoises to support one of their number who's been hurt or knocked unconscious. This response grows out of the affection between mother and children, male parent and female parent—and so on. But the Ruml don't know that kind of affection."

"But they have Families. You were always talking about their Families."

"Not in the sense we do," said Jase. "A young Ruml spends

his formative years semiconscious in his mother's carrying pouch. Shortly after he leaves her pouch, at what would be the age of ten for a human child—they mature faster than we do—he's forgotten even what she looked like. The years of affection of a human child are lost to a Ruml. The only affection they're capable of on an individual basis is a sort of warm admiration between males and a momentary, transitory love between male and female that is entirely unrelated to the emergence of their child into the Ruml world ten years later.''

Mele's brow wrinkled.

''But— They have a society?'' she said.

''A different kind of society. I told you,'' said Jase, ''that the family wasn't the basis of their social response. But they have the same racial instinct for survival. In their case it finds expression in their concept of Honor.'' He stared earnestly at her. ''Do you understand?''

She shook her head.

''I don't see how Honor could compare to—''

''That's just it. A human being can't imagine it. Unless,'' said Jase, wryly, ''he's been inside a Ruml mind the way I have. You'll have to take my word for it. Everybody will have to take my word for it—but it's true. Believe me, a Ruml reacts as strongly, emotionally, to a possible threat to his Honor, or the system of Honor, as a human reacts to a threat to his child.'' Jase pulled himself off the edge of the bed. ''Help me try to walk again. He reacts as strongly, and as primitively.''

''But why?'' said Mele, helping him. ''How can he react to something so—so cold and abstract. I mean, why should he?''

''Because,'' gasped Jase, gritting his teeth and making his legs go, ''it's the way the Ruml system of racial survival, and the weeding-out process of survival of the fittest, works.''

''How?''

''The Ruml race—,'' said Jase. ''No, I want to keep walking—'' His knees had given way, and he resisted Mele's response for steering him back toward the bed. ''The Ruml race is exactly like an army waiting for a general, at all times. Any individual who wants to lead it to some exploit, the settlement of new lands or something that will make available room for more or better living conditions for the race, can have its services by just putting himself in a way to accomplish such an exploit.''

"But that doesn't make sense!" said Mele. "They'd all be trying—"

"Sure!" said Jase, mirthlessly and grimly, "but there's a penalty attached. Whoever leads them, whoever tries to Found a Kingdom, a Family, as Kator did, has to succeed or else. He isn't allowed the smallest, the most indifferent mistake. If he has anything but complete success, it's a sign the Random Factor wasn't working for him—he wasn't, that is, a chosen leader— and he must be disposed of, at once."

"Killed?" said Mele.

"You saw," said Jase, "what they did to Kator."

"But why kill him? To punish him for trying—"

"No," said Jase. "That's where the primitive, instinctive element of the reaction enters in. Socially, they think that they kill him as punishment—but the modern Ruml sociologist knows the real reason is something else." He turned his head to stare at Mele. "You see, if they let him live, he might go back and succeed after all. And that would raise a question. Did he succeed because of his innate, genetic genius for leading the Ruml to success or improvement? Or did he succeed, because he learned from his first mistake? It's to make sure of pure genetic talents that they kill off those who don't prove out all along the line. You see, evolutionarily, they're unconsciously working toward a super-Ruml, just as we're unconsciously striving toward a superman."

"But," said Mele. "That still doesn't explain why you said Kator was one in a million Ruml. Don't more Ruml than that try it?"

"No," said Jase. "That's the other side of the coin. The emotional block in the average Ruml against making the attempt is tremendous. The governor on this whole process is a countertrait of the Ruml character that works against trying to Found a Kingdom. The fear of failure is intense—and the fear of facing recognition of their failure is more so. That's why Kator was so noble in going back—but let's not get into that now. The point is, if the Ruml individual or the Ruml race has any reason to doubt success in anything they undertake, they can't be brought to try it, except as a last-ditch, desperate measure—"

He broke off. The door had opened. Two tall, quiet-faced men in gray suits had just come in.

"You've been listening to me!" said Jase. "You heard? Let me explain how this affected us—"

"I don't know what you're talking about," answered one of them. "We just got here. You're to come with us—both of you."

"He can't walk!" cried Mele. "He was just trying to take a few steps. He's been flat on his back for three weeks."

"I know," said the man who had spoken. "That's been arranged. We've got a wheel chair outside in the corridor for him. Come on." He took hold of Jase's arm.

"What do you want her for?" demanded Jase as he was propelled toward the door. "Where are you taking us?"

"You might as well not ask questions," said the man holding his arm. "You're not going to get any answers."

CHAPTER TWENTY-FOUR

The two men in gray suits escorted them down a service elevator of the hospital and out to the lawn behind the building. An air force helicopter was waiting for them there. And in this they all lifted from the hospital grounds and went swinging northward. Twenty minutes of flight brought them in sight of a large military installation, which after a moment Jase recognized as Fort Laud, halfway between Washington and Philadelphia. The helicopter drifted in and descended toward the spaceship pad in the northeast corner of the Fort.

However, before they reached it, the 'copter set down before a wide, rectangular building with a glass-sided control tower rising from it and beyond it, a reaching spread of concrete pad for spaceship landings. They were brought into the building and up in an interior elevator to the top level of the control tower. They found themselves in a nearly square, window-sided room. Across from him one window faced the pad, and among the spaceship shapes there he saw one, reaching skyward, that looked familiar, though he had never seen one like it with his human eyes before.

Just then, he saw Thornybright. Erect, in a blue suit, thin, sharp, and competent looking as the blade of an injector razor set on end. He was standing with Swanson, Coth, and some others in civilian clothes. They all turned to look as Jase and Mele entered. In the bright daylight through the windows all looked to Jase to be strangely pale. As they came up to Swanson, Jase saw the man's eyes were ringed with tiredness, and standing close, he could almost hear the beating of the other's heart.

"I told them," said Thornybright, behind Swanson, "that you were their only chance, Jase. For once they believed me."

"Never mind that," said Swanson without turning his head. He looked at Jase. "That spaceship out there? You recognize it?"

Jase looked through the window at it again.

"I don't know the individual ship," he said. "But of course it's a Ruml space vessel—of the type used for troop transport and assault."

Coth turned and said something inaudible to one of the other officers.

"The officers of the ship," said Swanson, sharply. "Can you pick them out?" The Ruml ship was about three hundred yards distant on the pad. Someone put a pair of wide-angle binoculars into Jase's hands, and as he looked over to take them his eyes met the eyes of Mele. Those blue eyes were perfectly calm and rested on him with perfect faith.

He lifted the binoculars to his eyes.

"Yes," he said, as the figures jumped into recognizable shapes before him. "That's the Captain standing to the foot of the ramp at the right there. The first and third officers are lining up the crew. The Keysman's inside. He won't come out until last."

He studied the furred and harnessed Ruml shapes a moment more through the twin lenses of the binoculars. The binoculars were a beautiful instrument, lighter and with an even wider range of vision than his own. He would have liked to have watched the autumn hawk migration southward over the hills of the west shore of Lake Superior, north of Duluth, Minnesota, with a set like these. He lowered them at last and turned back to Swanson.

"There's no one outside the ship yet I recognize," he said. "The crew seems to be split right down the middle. Half Hooks and Half Rods, politically."

"What're they here for? What do they want?" demanded Swanson. Jase looked at him.

"They're here to negotiate—if you'll let them," Jase said.

"*If* we'll let them!" said Swanson. "That's what we want them to do!"

"Then, go ahead," said Jase. "There's nothing more to talk

about, is there?'' He had been through a lot. He could not help sounding somewhat bitter.

Swanson stared at him for a long moment.

"We don't want to do the wrong thing," he said, at last.

"Finally," said Jase, with a great and weary sigh. "Finally—you don't want to do the wrong thing. It's time . . ." The room started to tilt and move slowly around him. He felt himself falling, hands grabbing him, easing him into a chair . . .

"Doesn't . . ." He found himself laughing, weakly and uncontrollably. "Doesn't want to do the wrong thing. . . . Doesn't . . ." Laughter spilled helplessly from him, getting in the way of the words. He felt himself going down like a drowning man for the last time, into hysteria—

CHAPTER TWENTY-FIVE

Mele was suddenly beside his chair. He felt her hands on his shoulders. He began to throttle back the laughter.

"He ought to rest!" she said fiercely to the men around her.

"No." Jase shook his head, sobering. "I'm just not used to being on my feet, that's all. I'll be all right sitting down." He smiled a little wryly at them. "Why doesn't everybody sit down."

Swanson pulled close a chair that was standing empty nearby and sat down. The rest remained standing.

"All right," Swanson said. "Maybe you told me before and I wasn't listening. I'll listen now. To anything you've got to say, anything at all."

Jase nodded.

"It's a matter of basic instinct, in us and the Ruml, too," he said. "You've got to understand that to understand how to deal with them. I was telling Mele—"

"What you told her in the hospital room just before we brought you here?" said Swanson. "We've got that." Jase blinked at him. "We were taping your conversations. When we called to order you sent to us, the monitor in charge of the taping read me what you'd said over the phone." He glanced out at the spaceship pad and the Ruml ship. "Go on. Don't waste time. Go on from where you left off telling her . . ."

"Basic research," said Jase. "If we'd had a decent program of basic research this last hundred years, we'd have been ready for the differences in the Ruml character, their differences from us, when we met them."

"How could we know anything before we met them?" said Swanson. "How could we know about them before we knew what they were like?"

"You don't understand how basic research works," said Jase. "It's a search after knowledge for the sake of knowing. There was work done right here on earth that could have warned us of the Ruml type of psychology and character. In fact, there was; I found it. I was looking for a bridge, some common understanding between their kind of being and ours. And I found it in an article written by a Finnish zoologist back in 1960."

"In 1960?" Swanson's voice trembled on the edge of disbelief.

"In a magazine called *Natural History*," said Jase. "I think in the January issue. It was called 'A Key to Ferocity in Bears,' and it was written by a man named Peter Krott. It told how he, his wife, and children raised two bear cubs under free conditions one year in the Italian Alps. And it gave some conclusions he came to as a result of observing the two bears."

"The Ruml are like bears?"

"No—" Jase was beginning, shaking his head, when one of the uniformed men interrupted.

"Some of the aliens are going back into the ship!"

"It's all right," said Jase. "They're just going to attend the Keysman. He won't come out without an escort in a situation like this—Where was I?"

"Rumls aren't like bears, you said," answered Swanson.

"That's right. Only," said Jase, "in one small way are they similar. But the way bears aren't like humans points up the way Rumls aren't like us." He paused, feeling his exhaustion.

"Go on," said Swanson.

"What Krott discovered," said Jase, "was that, after a certain period of growth, the bear cubs he observed began to develop a feeding pattern—" Jase looked around at the ring of faces. "Do any of you know about feeding patterns—like the sharks, for example? Do you know what a feeding pattern, so-called, is?

"When a shark," said Jase, "tastes blood in the water, instinct sends him into a feeding frenzy. In this frenzy, reflex action will make him snap at anything, a turning propeller blade or his own trailing entrails where another shark has slashed him. He'll go on trying to eat when he's dying. That reaction is part of his feeding pattern. It's below the level of conscious control.''

"But the Ruml—''

"Just a minute,'' said Jase. "Humans, although they pretty well have them buried nowadays for lack of use, have reflexes below the level of conscious control. Survival reflexes. A young child under a certain age will reflexively scramble up in to the arms of the nearest adult in the face of danger, or imagined danger. That's part of the survival pattern.''

He looked at Mele.

"Intellectually, Mele didn't think I ought to be doing what I did when I added that information to Kator's recorder,'' he said. "But that was intellectually. On the instinctive level, she obeyed the reflex to protect me, because she loved me.'' He looked over at Mele. She looked back at him with steady eyes.

"The bears, Krott found,'' said Jase, "developed a reflex that led them to attack any *moving* source of food. Though they were affectionate and gentle with all of the family, one day one of them attacked Mrs. Krott and clawed off her jacket to get at some test tubes of alcohol in her jacket pocket. The attack had nothing to do with how the bear felt about Mrs. Krott.''

"But the Ruml—!'' said Swanson, impatiently.

"That's it,'' said Jase. "The Ruml are carried for three years inside the mother's body, and for six years after in a marsupial-like—say kangaroo-like—pouch, during which six years they're only semiconscious. Then they start to grow suddenly, emerge from the pouch, and within a week they're on their own. They wander away from their mothers and pick up the language and customs during a few weeks of extremely rapid learning of the type we call 'imprinting' here on Earth, when we observe it in young babies and animals. Within weeks they're small adults, individually independent and responsible.''

"I see . . .'' said Swanson slowly. "They operate by reflex where we think, is that it?''

"And we operate by reflex in areas where they think,'' said Jase. "The young puppy, for example, on earth goes through four stages of very important development: neonatal, the nursing stage; transitional, when he starts to shift to adult methods of locomotion and feeding; socialization, in which he learns to play

and respond with his fellows; and juvenile, a final weaning stage
of achieving independence. By contrast, a song sparrow has six
stages. The Ruml have none—that correspond. When the young
human child is learning and responding to the affectionate social
structure of the human family, the young Ruml is still unconscious in his mother's pouch. He emerges from that pouch essentially adult and independent. He'll hardly remember his
mother, let alone have any affection for, or any imprinted reflex
of affection for, her. Being so, the Ruml couldn't develop a
society on the same basis as ours.''

"Well?'' said Swanson. "What's their basis?''

"Are you sure you know what ours is?'' Jase asked. "Oh,
that's right, you said you heard what I told Mele in the hospital
just now. Well, I'll say it again to make sure. Our instinct as
humans is to protect the race as individuals. The Ruml, lacking
the early formative years of human development, have instead
an impulse to protect the race as an idea—a system of Honor
which tends to insure the survival of the race.''

He looked directly at Swanson.

"That's what I was working for,'' he said. "Some way to
convince them they should live peacefully side by side with humans. But a way that could be expressed in terms of Honor as
they saw it—not in terms of our own human rights and feelings
about the matter, which are invisible to a Ruml. Literally, they
don't exist for him. To us—for example—it would be immoral
to condemn our best friend unjustly to death just to impress other
people. To someone like Kator there was no connection between
morals and such an action. What was moral to him was to succeed in Founding his Kingdom. Everything that helped him to
that end was moral because it was aimed at improving the Ruml
race—by justifying the survival and spread of his particular superior genes as Head of a Family with unlimited children,
whereas because of space limitations on the already settled
worlds most Ruml are restricted to one son.''

Jase paused and closed his eyes for a moment, to rest. He
heard the others fidgeting impatiently and opened his eyes.

"What's immoral, then?'' asked Swanson, as if he wished to
prod Jase back into talking rather than as if he was actually
interested in the answer. But Jase chuckled, a little weakly.

"I'm glad you asked that,'' he said. "I was just going to get
to it. It's immoral to fail. That's what's immoral among the
Rumls. The whole Ruml race is like a kingdom of subjects,

ready and waiting to be taken over by anyone who has the guts to put on the crown and lead them forward into the future. But if he puts on the crown, he has to present them with unvarying success—that's why only one Ruml in millions tries it. Any failure, no matter how slight, condemns him. That's why I added that section to Kator's recording."

"What do you mean?" said Swanson.

"I mean—"

"Just a minute!" interrupted one of the uniformed men by the window looking out on the spaceship. "Something's happening. There's more of them coming out. There's one in the center with a sort of a metal belt—"

"The Keysman." Jase tried to get up. "That'll be the Keysman. Someone ought to go meet him—"

"Sit down." Swanson's hand held him in the chair. "Tell us why you did that with Kator's recording."

Jason smiled sadly.

"To prove him a failure," he said. "The fact we'd known about him all this time, and the fact I claimed—that we'd been using him—made him a failure. That made everything he had done immoral instead of moral. He had been a false leader. He should have driven the Expedition ship into the nearest sun or cut his throat."

"Why didn't he? Did you know he wouldn't?" demanded Swanson.

"I knew," Jase nodded. "I'd been living in his mind and body for weeks. He was too great a man—too great a Ruml, if you like—to take the easy way out. Instead of killing himself and ending his shame, and it's a shame human beings can't even imagine, at killing fellow Ruml who might otherwise have sired sons who would be true leaders, he decided to live with it. He decided to go back and tell the Family Heads on Homeworld. He decided to ask them—you saw him ask them—to let him live long enough to make his knowledge of us useful to them in their action against us. You saw what happened."

"They killed him," said Swanson. His eyes were hollow with lack of sleep and tension. "They didn't know any better, then."

"They knew better. They promised him to think for a day before they acted. Remember?" Jase said. "But when they came down to it, and were faced with the fact he was a failure, they acted instead of thinking. As with all of us, Ruml and human, both. As with Mele, in a different way, when she was faced with a decision between her intellectual justice and her instinctive urge to protect me under any circumstances. Their instinctive reaction overrode their intellectual centers.''

"But they're here now,'' said Swanson.

"They've had plenty of time to think it over,'' said Jase. "They're intelligent, and civilized. They see they should have suffered Kator to endure the moral pain of staying alive and helping them. And they think we have a positive advantage over them because we know about them and they don't know about us.''

Swanson stared at Jase for a long moment.

"You knew they'd kill him!'' the spectacled man exploded. "You knew they'd kill Kator when you added that section to his recording.''

Jase felt the pain of memory like a blow in the body.

"Yes,'' he said. "Just as I knew Kator was great enough to go back instead of taking the way of an easy suicide. It was the only way to convince the Ruml we had an advantage over them.''

"But—'' Swanson stared at him, hollow-eyed. "Why stake everything on getting an advantage? Wouldn't it have been better to try to deal with them through Kator—''

Jase shook his head.

"Kator only wanted his Kingdom. Anything less than that would have been failure for him and made his life unbearable anyway, once he had set himself to the task of winning a Kingdom. You're thinking now like a human. There is no middle ground to a Ruml, because it's not his own life that's important—it's the improvement of his race embodied in the concept and system of what he calls Honor.''

Jase put his hands on the arms of the chair he sat in, ready to hoist himself up.

"We had to stop Kator. But by stopping him, we created a question of Honor, a question of whether in stopping him, we were not ourselves in organization behind some one individual who wanted to Found a Kingdom on the Ruml worlds. That question had to be resolved, in Honor. It didn't make any difference that the civilized, present-day Ruml Family Heads, once they thought about it, could entertain the concept of peaceful association between our two races. Their instincts told them that by stopping Kator, as we had to, since the alternative was becoming his creatures, we had posed a threat to the future of their race. They were in Honor bound to move against us—except for one thing.''

"What thing?'' asked Swanson. They were all staring at him now, he saw, even Thornybright.

"The control reflex. The governor. You said you heard what I told Mele in the hospital,'' said Jase. "The reflex that keeps nearly all the Ruml individuals from ever attempting to Found a Kingdom. The Ruml know only how to bet everything—or not to bet at all. Their culture rests on the discovery of pure talent. It's either success or failure—nothing in between.''

He looked about at them but saw they still did not understand.

"As I told Mele,'' he said, "the fear of failure is intense. Only as a last-ditch, desperate, back-to-the-wall measure will the Ruml nature undertake any attempt where failure seems likely or even possible. That's why games are unknown among them, and duels are automatically to the death. If you demonstrate an advantage, as I did in the section I added to Kator's recording, the instinctive impulse in the Ruml is to avoid the contest.''

"But you said—'' Swanson hesitated. "You said that intellectually they were capable of seeing through their instinctive impulses when they had time to think, as after they killed Kator.''

"That's right,'' said Jase. "And that's why they're here now. If the human race does anything to challenge their sense of racial survival, they'll fight, here and now. But if a challenge like that can be avoided—by us,'' he smiled tightly, "—the intellectual centers of their minds will have a chance to gingerly approach and entertain the idea of existing in the same area of interstellar space with monsters like ourselves.''

"Monsters?'' said Thornybright, speaking up now for the first time since Jase had come in. "Do they really think of us as monsters, Jase?''

"Why not?'' asked Jase, grimly. "Don't we think of them as monsters? After all, they've got no milk of human kindness. And we, in their eyes, have no sense of Honor.''

Swanson nodded. He straightened up, looking down at Jase.

"I get it, finally,'' he said. "Yes, I think if you're up to it, you'd better come along with us to meet them. We wouldn't want to get off on the wrong foot.''

He reached down and took Jase's arm. Jase swayed to a standing position and held himself steady. Now that it was all over, he felt as if a hidden source of strength had been released in him.

With Swanson on one side and one of the other men in civilian clothes supporting him on the other they went down the elevator and out on to the landing pad. A baggage truck with a low platform was waiting. They stepped up on the platform and rode out to the ship, where the lines of dark-furred Ruml stood clustered in formation, with the metal-belted Keysman before them.

The truck halted. They got down. Jase, with Swanson and the other man at his side, walked up to within a couple of paces of the Keysman. The Keysman stared at him.

"You—" The human words came out almost unrecognizably mangled by the narrow jaw and near-lipless mouth in the dark-furred face. "You are the Fisherman!"

"Yes," said Jase. He nodded, with the inclining of the head that was the Ruml gesture of respectful assent.

The Keysman stopped staring. He pulled himself erect. He was an older Ruml, wearing a harness with many Honors clipped to it, and the hair of his upper body was almost uniformly gray.

"I trust," he said formally and precisely in the Ruml tongue, "that I am among friends?"

"Yes," said Jase in Ruml, "Keysman. Here you are among friends."